Praise for *The Homecoming*

"[Anna Enquist's] best, most comprehensive, and most touching novel."

—*NRC Handelsblad* (The Netherlands)

"A surprising and touching novel about the loss of children, about a ruined union between a man and a woman, and, above all, about the inadequacy of facts in helping to understand people."

—*Haarlems Dagblad* (The Netherlands)

"Elizabeth is drawn so that she's completely understandable even though the problems she faces are not of our time. She is more than a seaman's wife left behind to care for the family. Sitting at home, she's almost as much of an explorer as her husband, and on one point she outdoes him: as a survivor, as a fighter against death. In the end, she knew more than James Cook about the nakedness of existence."

—Max Pam, *HP/De Tijd* (The Netherlands)

"Elizabeth, the wife of the seafaring explorer James Cook, had six children, and each one of them died. Three of the five boys succumbed to illness; the other two were lost at sea. And Elly, the only girl, was run over by a coach. Anna Enquist uses the difficult life of this captain's wife, who herself would live to ninety-four, as the premise for her novel *The Homecoming*. It is a heart-wrenching novel, written with much empathy and psychological ingenuity. Enquist has taken the known biographical facts and made a new story from them using her own vision and denouement. Elizabeth spends most of her long life waiting. Waiting for her husband, who will not return from his third and final journey. Waiting for her sons, too, who will meet with just as disastrous an end while following in his footsteps. Enquist paints a penetrating picture of the inner life of her heroine, who must cope with one blow on top of another and still not throw in the towel. As an eighteenth-century wife, Elizabeth had little input in the decisions of her husband, the Admiralty, and the king of England—this much is as clear as day in the novel. Although there are plenty of opportunities for melodrama, *The Homecoming* steers away from this. There is room for heavy feelings: angst, hope, loss, and anger at all the premature deaths. Apart from describing emotional pain, Enquist also writes about scurvy and exotic cultures and lives. The revelations about the way in which Cook met his end on the Polynesian island of Tahiti are gruesome."

—*OPZIJ* (The Netherlands)

THE
HOMECOMING

Other Titles by Anna Enquist

THE HOMECOMING

ANNA ENQUIST

TRANSLATED BY **EILEEN J. STEVENS**

 AMAZON **CROSSING**

Text copyright © 2005 by Anna Enquist
Translation copyright © 2022 by Eileen J. Stevens

Previously published as *De thuiskomst* by De Arbeiderspers in the Netherlands in 2005. Translated from Dutch by Eileen J. Stevens. First published in English by Amazon Crossing in 2022.

Published by Amazon Crossing, Seattle

www.apub.com

Amazon, the Amazon logo, and Amazon Crossing are trademarks of Amazon.com, Inc., or its affiliates.

ISBN-13: 9781542025447 (hardcover)
ISBN-10: 1542025443 (hardcover)

ISBN-13: 9781542025423 (paperback)
ISBN-10: 1542025427 (paperback)

Cover design and illustration by Philip Pascuzzo

Printed in the United States of America

First edition

For Wouter

I, whose ambition leads me not only farther than any other man has been before, but as far as I think it is possible for man to go, was not sorry at meeting with this interruption, as it in some measure relieved us.

James Cook (1728–1779)

Part 1

1

He'll expect an empty table when he comes home, she thought. He'll be lugging chests and sacks into the house, filled with journals, sketches, and maps. They'll need to lie flat on a clean table, waxed and polished until it gleams like a mirror. A table that invites you to put folders on it, and stack books and papers in perfect order. Not a rubbish dump. The table takes up almost all the space in the room facing the garden—well, not all the space, there's enough room, but there's no avoiding it. It's more like the room was built around the table, a tabernacle for a wooden altar. The whole room needs to be cleaned, maybe even whitewashed.

Elizabeth slowly skirted past the table to the bay window and looked at the garden through the diamond-shaped panes. The imperfections in the glass made it seem as if the flowers were hovering above the lawn. When she moved her head, the pale-blue irises bulged into monstrous shapes, and the garden bench jolted up and down every time she nodded. She pushed open the windows. The white-painted mullions surrounding the panes looked filthy. She wiped away a dead fly with her index finger.

Spring air wafted in. Elizabeth rested her hands on her hips and sniffed: hawthorn, violets, and some sickly sweet fumes from the gin distillery on the corner. Before long, the linden tree hanging over the garden bench would bloom, and nectar would drip onto the furniture and lawn. Then, dense clouds of frantically buzzing insects would jostle around the pale-green blossoms. Soon.

She turned to face the darkened room. The clutter on the table rose before her like a mountain range. He'll be back, she thought; in a month, this summer, maybe not until autumn, but he's coming. Somewhere in the world, in that stuffy, wooden hulk he proudly calls his ship, he's on his way. He's made his discoveries, charted the coasts, and described the foreign peoples, and the retreat has begun. Such a voyage can't last much more than three years. High time, then, to start clearing the table. It will be like excavating a disposal site where someone has been tossing their junk for years. I could think of it as a challenge, an archaeological pursuit.

A cool breeze blew against her back; the room's heavy door began to sway, and then slammed into the latch.

With arms like scythes, mow everything onto the floor. Sweep aside the dregs of the solitary years. Away with the children's drawings, bills, forgotten mending, the unread books and yellowed newspapers. Pile it all in the garden and, when there's no wind, set it alight. She'd use a staff to poke any escaping papers back into the fire; the boys would lend a hand with bellows and broomsticks; and everything, everything would transform into thick clouds of smoke and drift away over the rooftops toward the river.

But first, each item had to be looked at. You could only throw an object away once you knew what it was. Every scrap of paper would have to pass through her hands. She tightened the straps of her apron and stepped up to the table.

Extend your hand to pick up a letter, and then pull it back quickly. Walk around the table and examine and evaluate the objects from all sides. Devise a system of organization: a basket for everything that can go; a folder for business correspondence to save; one pile for the children's drawings, for personal letters; one stack of books to keep on hand, and another to put away for a rainy day. Make enough space on the wide-planked floor to keep the mounds well apart. She knew her plan of attack, but kept dawdling and dithering.

It was ten o'clock, a morning in early April; the boys were at school and she wasn't expecting anyone. There was time, but she squandered it. What was she waiting for? Not for help. She preferred to accomplish this task on her own. She didn't sit down on the narrow window seat, but continued pacing as if she'd lost something.

She was worn out. Every inch of her thirty-three-year-old body wanted to sink to the ground and stay there. Preferably outdoors, in the grass beneath the linden tree. The fatigue was hard to understand because she had slept well that week, had had enough to eat, and hadn't undertaken any arduous physical labor. And yet she felt like she'd been carrying a yoke weighed down with heavy buckets of milk.

Among the letters and newspapers, she picked out items that had been misplaced: a beribboned bonnet, a handkerchief, an orange so dried out that its seeds ticked against its leathery skin when she tossed it on the floor.

Stoop. In the basket. Stand up again in one motion and immediately grab some of the papers. That's the way.

There was a letter from Philip Stephens about money: *In accordance with your husband's wishes, the Admiralty has agreed to allocate you two hundred pounds a year during his voyage.* Keep. James will want to read this. It was his money: he earned it by sailing around the world. No reason to be plagued by an annoying sense of obligatory gratitude. It wasn't charity, or a tip. The amount, and more besides, was hers by right. She pictured the Lords of the Admiralty in a meeting, fired up about James's expedition—full of pride, patriotism, and self-importance. "Oh, yes, that wife of his also has to eat; it's a substantial amount. Will you see that she gets it?"

She shrugged. The next letter, in Hugh Palliser's hand, was about the boys. *I just learned, dearest Elizabeth, that your eldest, the hale and hearty James Jr., will enter the Royal Naval Academy at Portsmouth after the summer. He's no doubt looking forward to following in his father's footsteps. Or in his father's wake, should I say? Nice that you can keep young Nathaniel home for another year; otherwise it might be awfully lonely for you. Of course, we all hope that James will return safely this year, but you're well aware of the uncertainties surrounding these expeditions. Rest assured that I am here for you, whenever you need me.*

Hugh Palliser, the comptroller of the Navy, who'd encouraged and endorsed James and had put in a good word for him with the Admiralty. She smiled and set the letter to one side with her own papers. She would invite him around for tea in the garden so he could chat with Jamie and Nat.

She gathered bills and threw away newspaper clippings. The base of the pile she was working on came into view: three thick, dark volumes about explorations in the South Sea. The writer's name was inscribed in gold: John Hawkesworth. She picked up the books and gently knocked off the dust. James would be livid. Hawkesworth had appropriated James's journals and described the voyage as if he had made it himself. She had compared the text with the original logs and was peeved by the exaggerations and errors, annoyed with the writer as well as with her husband. What a blunder to hand over your story so naively. It was all well and good that James felt such boorish bitterness for the world of pompous aficionados of high culture, but by submitting his writings and refusing to take part in their editing, he was only harming himself. He said he felt ashamed—he couldn't spell and wasn't able to cobble together a decent sentence. True enough, but what he had to say was certainly worthwhile. Someone should come to his aid.

Me, she thought, me.

She found a picture of a boat beside Hawkesworth's folios, a detailed child's drawing. Jamie's. In it, he'd peeled away the hull of the ship, revealing storerooms full of barrels and bales, the hold, and various cabins. He'd depicted a seated man in the captain's quarters, writing at a table with his back to the viewer. There was a cow and a goat on the afterdeck.

Why shouldn't she help James with his next book? Before long, he'd be here at the table, griping and grumbling. Soon, as his mood soured, he'd be ruining his texts with exaggerated thanks and an insincere display of servitude. Such a pity. Let me do it. If he comes home before autumn, the days will be getting shorter, and we'll have plenty of long, dark evenings ahead. Working side by side on an important project would be a distraction, a good way of resuming conjugal life.

Upon his return, they would have been married more than twelve years, but they'd not yet spent an entire year under the same roof. Every spring, James invariably sailed away, only coming back in November. Christmas. A table full of maps and charts of coastal landscapes. He lived a double life. So did she. That set the rhythm, and the reassurance that went along with it. She'd only been frightened once, when he'd come home with a jagged, barely healed scar across his right palm. A powder horn had exploded, he said; could have been worse. The breach of his flawless skin was a reminder that he worked for the Navy, and fighting and devastation could be part of the job. After a day or so, her anxiety ebbed. It was in the past, he was walking through the house, she could hear his voice and follow his activities. His presence drew her attention away from the injury and what it signified.

Ever since, he'd worn a glove on his right hand. Was he ashamed of the mutilation, or trying not to alarm others? The wound was thick and seemed healed, the scar slithering like a pale snake to the wrist. She could feel it at night as he slid his hands from her thigh to her shoulders.

The scar rasping against her skin. She should cradle his hand in hers and slowly move her tongue over the wound, to incorporate the scar, to add it to the cartography of her husband's body.

There was a lot to do. Meals to be planned, prepared, and eaten; the boys' clothes washed, mended, and replaced. The kitchen garden sown, fertilized, and weeded. She did have help, people who assisted her with these tasks and nudged her or even pushed her to take the initiative. Nat, for instance, stumbling through the room to show how he'd outgrown his shoes. Or the maid, sitting beside her with a shopping basket on her lap, planning the day's menu. The gardener as well, who asked where the carrots and parsnips should be planted, and who could only get to work once she had made up her mind. There was so much to do. It seemed more than before, more than during the initial years of this second voyage around the world. The foreshadowing of James's return was already coloring the daily chores. He was bound to have an opinion about where to plant the vegetables, well thought out and based on sensible considerations regarding the angle of the sun and the water supply. She began to look at the house, garden, and children as if through his eyes, and observed that there was much that needed to be altered, cleaned, and discarded. As if she had let things slide the minute he walked out the door. But that wasn't the case. Her sense of order was simply different. Was it just her imagination? Did the critical captain exist only in her mind? Soon, young Nat's habit of climbing into bed with her every morning would be a thing of the past. Out of the question.

It would all be over after this voyage. A new life would begin, a summer life.

She'd been alone for twelve summers. It wasn't so bad. She knew what she was getting into before she decided to marry this seafarer. Loneliness didn't bother her, and at first she even looked forward to it.

There'd always been a reunion. Then the bed would seem too big or too small; there would be activity and variety. When Jamie was born, she'd cherished the solitude, enjoyed being alone with that tiny baby. Every autumn, the ship returned over the Atlantic. When the apples were ripening, the leaves turning color and falling from the trees, a coach would suddenly rattle through the street, and the front door would be flung open. A fresh wind would race through the house, and nothing would be the same.

But then, in the spring of 1768, James received orders for his first major voyage. He was to sail the South Sea, observe the transit of the stars and planets, and chart new continents. The role of commander fit him like a glove. There was no trace of subservience or insecurity as he voiced his demands for the ship, its equipment, and its instruments. Nothing but the best and the most expensive would do, and that's what he received. But they wouldn't promote him to captain: that title was reserved for the wellborn. He would remain a lieutenant for now. James wasn't bothered, as long as he could do things his way. He wanted to gather knowledge, to observe and describe. To see the world as it truly was.

The voyage would last a good three years. When the bark—a bluff-bowed collier with a shallow draft—sailed off, Elizabeth already had three young children and was expecting a fourth. She heaved a sigh of relief when James's second cousin Frances—a slip of a thing, seventeen, with a mop of red curls and darting eyes—moved in to keep her company. With her gangly limbs, you might expect her to be fumbling crockery and crashing into doors with a fully laden tray, but that was not the least bit true. She was practical: saw what needed to be done and rolled up her sleeves. She took the boys, then four and five, out to the garden when Elizabeth bathed baby Elly. Frances slept in the boys' room, and in no time, they adored her.

To Elizabeth, it was like finally having a sister. More women in the house: a little girl, a female sibling. That was new to her. She'd always been surrounded by men: a stepfather, an uncle, and male cousins. Her husband. Her sons. The father she had never known, he'd died when she was a baby and had been erased from her memory. What did he say to me? Did he pick me up when he came home and dance me through the rooms? Her mother didn't answer her questions. What had happened in the past didn't matter, and now, in her father's place, there was a stocky, black-haired man sitting in the kitchen, waiting for his steak and kidney pie. He taught her arithmetic and bookkeeping. No more children arrived. She was the only one, the daughter.

Her mother's brother had two boys, with whom Elizabeth grew up. She was the oldest and made up the games, until the boys went to school and grew tired of girly stuff. If she had had a sister, it would've been two against two. She became withdrawn. She liked to read and had access to the books belonging to her stepfather; she called him "father." She could embroider and knit. She'd managed.

She wasn't allowed in her stepfather's tavern, but she kept track of its income and expenditures in a long bound ledger. She had clear and legible penmanship and was her parents' pride and joy. If she'd had a sister, would she have engaged in useless, childish, frivolous things instead? Like strolling arm in arm along the river, spying on boys from behind a parasol, and when they turned to look, becoming absorbed in deep discussions or pinching each other and having an attack of the giggles?

One night, her uncle Charles saw her working on the accounts. "How can you do that?" he asked. "You should have been a lad. What I wouldn't give for such a daughter!"

She straightened her shoulders and bent over her bookkeeping. With a steady hand, she jotted down the day's takings. She didn't answer, just dabbed the ink with blotting paper and adjusted the lamp to shine on her work. If she did have a little sister, now was the time when she might have poked her head through the window and called to

Elizabeth to come outside, away from the low-ceilinged room reeking of tobacco and smoldering wood, where old folks boasted about her and made it sound like she was an old-timer, too.

Uncle Charles asked her mother if Elizabeth could work for him. He had a firm near the river dealing in ships' supplies. Business was booming, and it was too much for him to handle on his own. His pen pushers weren't anywhere near as sharp as his bright young niece. Elizabeth jumped at the chance, thrilled that her uncle trusted her and held her in higher esteem than his own employees. She was assigned a small desk in the overcrowded shop, and she enjoyed the mysterious merchandise: telescopes in leather cases, sextants, barometers, an assortment of globes in various sizes, and the terrifying chests for the ships' surgeons. There she sat, Elizabeth Batts, in the midst of it all, noting the price of incoming and outgoing merchandise. She liked to hunch over her paperwork and listen to her uncle's cordial voice. She tried to figure out the clients' backgrounds and characters by listening to their articulation. Sometimes she looked up, curious about an unfamiliar word or a lengthy silence. That's how she first noticed James.

He was looking for a quadrant, a complicated instrument made of gleaming copper with knobs and movable arms. Uncle Charles went into the storeroom and came out with a stack of boxes. He spent the entire morning looking at the instruments with the tall, earnest man standing at the counter. Charles would rub the copper with a piece of flannel before repacking the quadrants that didn't make the grade. Elizabeth observed the demanding client from behind her fringe of hair, until he left the shop empty handed. The boxes went back to the storeroom and the shop seemed unchanged. Uncle Charles whistled a tune; Elizabeth, blushing, jotted down her sums. Soon it would be time for dinner.

Elizabeth had a knack for making snap decisions. She knew instantly which dress she wanted, went to work for her uncle without any hesitation, and the minute he stepped into her life, she recognized her future husband. Was it an inability to harbor doubts, or a capacity to accurately judge what was good for her? She stood up, smoothed her dress, drummed her fingers on her protruding hip bones, and interrogated her uncle about the formidable client who had bought nothing. Two months later, they were married.

"He knows exactly what he wants," said Uncle Charles. "If the quality's not up to snuff, he won't accept it. I don't mind. I like a client who knows his business. He'll be back. I'm going to place an order on his behalf. Mark my words, child, we'll see that tall fellow here again."

Of course, when it turned out that *she* was what he wanted, she was flattered. He was fourteen years her senior. Didn't matter. She was used to the company of adults, felt more at ease with them than with people her own age. He was driven. He seemed to know how he wanted to spend his days, and while he would observe and study anything that got in his way, in the end, it couldn't stop him. That attitude appealed to her. She wasn't one to doubt: it never crossed her mind. He answered all her questions without giving the impression that he needed her, at least not the way her stepfather or uncle needed her: to take care of the things they couldn't be bothered doing themselves.

James made her a partner in his plans, which soon became *their* plans. Their connection was evident, but she couldn't quite pinpoint what had preceded it. He'd been waiting for her. When she came out of the door that evening, he was standing on the other side of the street. It was already dusk, and her back ached from sitting. He looked at her. She crossed the street and stood beside him. The tide was high—the river lapped against the quayside. Together, they looked at the grayish water. She remembered they'd started walking, but who'd taken the first step? Who had set the course? What had they said? He had followed a long detour in taking her home. Asked if she'd be in the shop the next morning, and if the quadrant he'd ordered would have arrived by then. She watched him walk away, admiring his decisive but elegant gait.

The next day, he was back. What followed was a barrage of encounters: a walk, a meeting with her mother and stepfather; she'd pointed the tavern out to him; they'd sheltered from a downpour—in a portico with pillars like beech trunks. The wind blew a carpet of dried leaves across the flagstones. It looked so much like a forest, you'd almost expect a deer to bolt past. Despite the cold, she was sweating from trying to keep up with his lengthy strides. He brushed the hair from her face and leaned toward her.

Oddly enough, she hadn't felt like she was being pursued, although looking back, that's exactly what he'd done. He'd been back only a week from a demanding season charting Newfoundland, and wanted to begin his next commission as a married man. He was thirty-four. She was twenty. But he didn't push her.

He examined. He peered. He observed from such a close proximity that she could see each individual hair in his heavy eyebrows, the fine red blood vessels on his chiseled cheeks, and the gleaming teeth behind his thin lips. She'd never before felt studied with such concentration and compassion. His fingers, warm despite the cold rain, caressed her ears. He cupped her wet face in the palms of his hands. Yes, that's what had happened. He'd kissed her eyelids. Whispered her name. She'd shifted in his arms, pressed her body against his, stepped forward. It just happened. The embrace seemed to alter him, as if he was no longer the observer and was finally able to lose himself in what was going on, in her.

The kiss. The kiss went on and on but didn't take any time at all. There was nothing but space. Without any effort, they stopped all time outside themselves. The hourglass stuck, Mr. Harrison's ingenious sea clock ground to a halt, and the earth stopped rotating.

When it was over, they were astonished to discover that they'd been standing in the porch of a church. They had been kissing in a house of God: you couldn't invent a twist of fate like that, but they hadn't made it up. It had happened, it had been unstoppable. Out of breath, laughing and aglow, they ran into the rain, hand in hand. The streets were their kingdom; the river flowed because they wanted it to, and time resumed its ticking.

She distanced herself from her friends and family even more than before, to focus her attention on this new and sensational project. Together, they'd furnished their house like the interior of a ship: sturdy, efficient, compact. When he left, she was pregnant.

The first years in that new rhythm—lonely summers, winters with James—her mother arrived to help with the annual chores: harvesting, making preserves, cleaning the house and garden. Did she pine for James? If she missed anything, it was a quality he revealed only to her: his ability to lose himself in her body. The fact that she could bring him to that state filled her with a strange pride. It kept her afloat for six months before she lapsed into despondence. But by then it was autumn, and he would come back.

He took his work seriously. She'd watched him sighing over mathematical treatises, making calculations in the margins, cursing at the end of the day or slamming the book shut in triumph. She'd marveled at the maps and drawings of the cold, unexplored coasts—what precision, love of details, such powers of concentration to fit page after page of endless trivialities into the grand scheme of things, the one he always carried in his head. He loved the world passionately; not to get caught up in it, but to observe and describe it. He did it at this table, which she now had to clear. For him.

When he talked about his work, she was all ears. He described the storms, the fog, the drunken and unruly sailors, the harsh punishments

meted out with a whip or a crop. But he also talked about one particular officer who taught him to chart the coast, someone with whom
he'd spent many an evening in the cabin, drawing maps. And about
Hugh Palliser, the captain who'd entrusted him with assignments that
exceeded his position. James may have had a lout for a father, but he
inspired paternal, supportive concern from his teachers, bosses, and
commanders. It was a gift, his capacity to find what he lacked at home.
The squalid worker's cottage in Yorkshire where James grew up was anything but promising, yet one powerful admirer after the other helped
James get ahead in life, until he ended up working at the shipyard in
Whitby. From there, he made his way to the sea. It was the path of all
coastal men, the only way. But sailing back and forth between Danzig,
Medemblik, Oslo, and Ostend had left James hungry for more. There
was an ocean on the other side of England, and another continent on
the far side of that. So he joined the Royal Navy.

The winter after his first voyage around the world, when they'd been
married nine years, they traveled north to visit James's father, sister,
and the men he called his "friends of yore." For Elizabeth the visit was
a strange horror. The journey in the cold, stinking coach was miserable,
and she felt anything but welcome in the stuffy house of James's sister
Margaret. James's father, an old man, sat in his chair by the hearth and
couldn't stop staring at her. When she spoke to him, he didn't answer
but continued glaring. She didn't know what to call him: Mr. Cook?
Father? So she said nothing.

James had borrowed a horse to ride to Whitby. Elizabeth was left
on her own, and missed the children. Frances was looking after them,
there was no one more trusted and reliable, but still, she missed them.
Margaret strode through the room, brought a glass to the old man,
slammed it down on the arm of his chair, and remained on her feet.
Why doesn't that individual sit down, Elizabeth thought. She and the

old man do nothing but stare at me. It's making me numb. I don't want this. I don't want to be here. But the heavyset woman—James in a dress, James with a pleated bonnet on his head—held her ground and didn't take her eyes off Elizabeth.

"London, innit," she said. Elizabeth had great difficulty understanding the woman's dialect. "Bairns not wi' you? That's no fun for uz. They 'ave a grandfatha, don't they? Aye, James knows wha' 'e's up to. Always 'as. Dark 'ere, innit? We don't care about light, we don't need it. Must be chilly in yer frock? And in bed? That's as it is 'ere. London village, a sea of light, they say. But will Dad ever see it? Or I? Does James 'ave a lantern in 'is house?"

Elizabeth was at her wit's end. Was she meant to invite these people for a visit? Or treat them to a description of urban life? Praise this desolate landscape? Or pose a question in return? Show some interest. Feign ignorance. She asked her sister-in-law about James's school days and received a scornful reply. Teacher's pet he'd been, given extra lessons. His tuition had been paid by a local gentleman farmer, one who took a keen interest in James and came several times a year to inquire after his progress. Margaret and her sister were hustled off to work in the kitchen the minute their heads reached above the countertop—no one paid *their* tuition. Anyway, it was all hearsay: James left home before they were born. She'd had to listen to those tales over and over. And then some!

She's younger than I am, Elizabeth realized, although she has a weathered face and rough hands; she's still young. The woman crossed her arms over her chest and planted her feet wide. Her raw voice boomed over Elizabeth and prevented her accurately picking up the content of the message. The tone was soaked in reproach and envy. But Margaret had never known James; to her, he was a fairy-tale character who happened to be a member of her family, a prince who wanted nothing to do with her and had turned his back on this muddy village. Now he and his big-city wife were spending ten days in her home. Margaret should have been pleased, but her feelings had an entirely different character.

We would have been better off staying at home, thought Elizabeth. Her feet were cold, but she didn't dare ask for a foot stove or move her chair closer to the hearth. If only James would return. The old man spat into the fire and then turned his gaze back to her, without saying a word.

She'd suddenly had enough of these surly folk who imagined all sorts of things about her and her life without showing the slightest interest in the true state of affairs. Did this embittered old man have any idea how hard his son had to compete with powerful aristocrats in that celebrated London, how he had to grovel, bow, and scrape to get his way? Did that jealous woman have any notion of how hard it was to spend years shouldering the sole responsibility for children and a home? To give birth while your husband was at sea? To say goodbye over and over, without knowing if you'd ever see each other again? What it was like when your husband returned home after three years, happy and excited, and you had the burden of telling him what had happened while he was away? She bid her in-laws good night and, back held erect, stalked up the stairs.

James returned two days later, cheeks cold and rosy from riding on horseback. He was buoyant and raved about seeing John Walker, the man with whom he'd apprenticed, the man who'd taught him how a ship was built and how to handle it, the man who'd taken him in once he'd made up his mind to go to sea.

"You must meet him! We'll go tomorrow. He and his friends were waiting for me when I arrived over the heath. Mary, the old house-keeper, was there, too. She threw her arms around my neck when I dismounted—couldn't control herself!"

"I'm not going," Elizabeth said. "Horses frighten me."

They could order a coach. It was important for his wife to be on good terms with his friends. He didn't have friends like these in London—people who had known him way back, as he truly was, who took pleasure in his success and weren't driven by self-interests or jealousy.

This wasn't like her. James had never had to talk her around. Whenever he made a request and explained his reasoning, she agreed. That's what had happened the first Sunday after their wedding, when she was getting ready to go to church. He didn't take part in that, he said, shuffling in his stocking feet toward the table where his most recent map was spread out. His time at home was too precious to waste on societal conventions and rituals whose point he did not see. He understood that they needed to get married in a church, because the records had to be accurate. But to him, that's as far as it went. Religious beliefs were a matter he didn't understand and he couldn't align with his love of the truth.

She had listened carefully, had given the matter serious consideration during her lonely walk to church, and had tried to listen to the sermon as if she were an impartial observer. Watch closely, James always said, before trying to explain what you have seen. She saw a man on a pedestal carrying out a verbal onslaught to forty-odd tired, complacent parishioners sitting on benches. At his command they knelt, stood up, and burst into song.

They listened because they wanted to hear, she thought on her way home. They needed someone to tell them what was what. And they wanted to be together, to look at each other, to engage in a collective activity. Since then, she no longer attended church in the winter. She went from time to time when James was at sea, in order to take part in goings-on with others. To be together.

However, he could not persuade her to visit Whitby. She understood his request, but didn't want to go. That night, in their musty bed, she simply said no. Could it be that she was pregnant again, was that the reason she didn't want to travel more than was strictly necessary? She was tired of being probed and judged, although she didn't want to say it.

"Not everyone can endure Yorkshire," James said once he understood how serious she was. They spent a restless night between those clammy sheets in his sister's house.

She was visibly pregnant when James left in the middle of the summer for his second voyage around the world.

Despite her reluctance to travel, she took the boys, just eight and seven then, to Sheerness, to watch the ship set sail. I should do more with the boys, she thought: involve them in their father's life work; show them the tantalizing sea; plant the seeds from which their aspirations will grow. The sight of the ships left Jamie speechless. He stood on tiptoes to touch the freshly painted crossbars of the capstan, and knelt in delight beside a coil of rope. Bursting with excitement, he then ran across the deck toward the goat, which was uneasily ticking its hooves against the planks. Little Nathaniel had eyes only for the musicians. There was one man with bagpipes, another with a drum; Royal Marines in thrilling uniforms. The drummer turned round and pulled out a violin from a wooden case behind his feet. He tightened the bow and tuned the strings. Then he started to play.

The boy listened in breathless silence. His small body swayed ever so slightly to the rhythm of the jig. Soon the penetrating sound of the bagpipes joined in, laying a solid bass beneath the cascading melody. It went on and on, and Nat listened. Elizabeth stood watching the tableau from a distance, restless and filled with an undefined sadness. Her husband was receiving important guests in the captain's cabin, her sons had become absorbed with various aspects of the world aboard ship, and she could feel a new baby moving under her skin. She approached Nathaniel, and hand in hand, they watched the violinist.

All of a sudden, it was time for the guests to disembark. There was a blast from the ship's horn, creaking ropes, loud shouting, and a drum roll. "I'll write you from the Cape of Good Hope," James promised, determined and brisk. He pulled the boys toward him, and they muttered the usual phrases: take care of your mother; be good; bring us presents—a flute, a little monkey—be careful; I'll write as long as I can, from the Cape.

There was no mail service beyond the Cape of Good Hope. In fact, beyond the Cape there wasn't much of anything. James would roam that "nothing" for years, putting it on the map, giving it a name. She looked at him. The tension in his arms betrayed his impatience. In this ship, filled with salt-cured meat, water barrels, cannonballs, vats of sauerkraut, sacks of flour, seeds, a blacksmith, a library, and a baker's oven, he'd sail into that watery oblivion. Now.

He had not said: you will be my beacon, guiding me home. It wasn't what she'd come to expect. He turned his attention to setting sail. She would make sure that a house remained standing, somehow or other, for him to return to. She'd taken his hand, the right one, and kissed the pale scar. He stood calmly beside her; then he smiled and gently caressed her belly.

They looked into each other's eyes without saying anything else. Jamie and Nat leaned against her legs. She took the boys by the hand and got ready to leave.

Before they reached the gangplank, a lanky lad with brown curls stopped her. "Oh, Isaac," she said, "I was planning to look for you, but it slipped my mind. There is too much going on." She was tongue-tied, seized by a strange embarrassment. The boy, her cousin, was nineteen and had signed on as soon as he heard the plans for a second voyage. Isaac had harbored vast admiration for James ever since his stint as a common seaman on James's first voyage around the world, when, with James's encouragement, he had been the first to set foot in New

Holland. Isaac had spent countless evenings at James and Elizabeth's, looking forward to the second voyage's adventures. It had made her smile: to her, he was just a child, and she was touched by his enthusiasm. Now he suddenly seemed bigger—a young man in seafaring garb, one of the trusted crew surrounding her husband. An intentional leave taker. He would see landscapes she never would; she'd only ever hear snippets of what he would soon experience. She couldn't understand the zeal with which he left everyone behind.

She kissed him. "Keep an eye on James if you can," she said. Isaac nodded and waved to the children.

Of course, the boys wanted to wait until the ship set sail, but the fickle wind had turned. The sailors went back to whatever work they had put aside to prepare for the impending departure. "This is taking too long," she said. "They could still be here tomorrow." All at once, she dreaded witnessing the actual departure. The laborious hoisting of the sails; the ropes being untied from the wharf, dragging through the water until a sailor pulled them aboard; that brief pause before the wind caught the rigging. No, she felt no desire to watch.

Back home, once the boys were asleep, she thought about the lack of mail. "You can keep a home logbook," James had suggested, "like my ship's log. You write so much better than I do. I could read it when I come back. You can tell me everything. You can read my logbook as well. Then we'll know exactly what's taken place, only a few years after the fact. Nothing but a little time in between."

She'd felt small, but couldn't understand why. Months later, his letter from the Cape of Good Hope arrived, the one he'd sent with a speedy merchant ship. She'd given birth to a happy baby boy. She'd called him George, as they'd agreed. When James's letter arrived, she was still in bed, and she pulled herself upright to read it.

Been writing in a rush for days. I'm posting letters to Banks, the Admiralty, Walker. I trust that all's good with you and the boys, and that the delivery went well. You know that the Admiralty has set money aside for you. If it's not enough, you have to write to Stephens. Don't be shy! The fish that Banks put on board for me seems to be rotten! I bought a thousand bunches of onions on Madeira, and here, dozens of geese. Isaac says hello. He's turning into quite an alert seaman.

She fell back against her pillows. Time was indeed what separated them.

I must try to experience everything intensely, she thought, so I will remember it all to tell him when he gets back. How the boys are growing, what they tell me during meals; about the birth of this new baby. I must live through and remember everything.

She chuckled about his mention of Banks's parting gift. That aristocratic botanist had sorely tested her husband, delaying the voyage's departure for months. He had secured a place for himself on the first voyage, with the full backing of the Royal Society. A massive entourage of scientists, servants, and greyhounds had boarded the ship with him. James had had some reservations, but saw no way to bar him from the *Endeavour*. With time, however, the resentment turned into admiration. Banks, once he got his sea legs, proved to be a fervent and tireless researcher. Whenever they landed, he was always the first to spring ashore, dragging his companion Solander, a portly Swede, along on his botanical forays. They drew and described and stored the plants and seeds they found. James liked that. Banks was game to try everything: he openly slept with native women and had brought a clever Tahitian on board to take back to England. The poor blighter had succumbed to fever in the Dutch East Indies, but that was beside the point. Although Banks's actions sometimes seemed to undermine Cook's authority, the captain turned a blind eye. It was all done in such a straightforward and disarming way.

The men also shared similar eating habits. They took pleasure in devouring the most exotic and repulsive creatures: cormorants, kangaroos, even dogs. A plan to eat a monkey had gone awry because Banks, at the last minute, had set the monkey—trussed to poles and squealing in fear—free. James saw him approaching the monkey, knife in hand, as if going in for the kill. Then Banks cut the ropes and the monkey bounded off. Banks was also an ally in James's battle against scurvy. Banks could find scurvy grass or wild celery anywhere. What's more, Banks wasn't shy about working alongside the seamen when the going got tough. By the end of the voyage, they had become friends.

When they returned to London in 1771, their lives went in different directions. Banks celebrated his triumph by displaying taxidermy animals, exotic items of clothing, and weapons to dukes and countesses. He visited the king, gave lectures, and didn't object when people referred to "the voyage of Banks." James, meanwhile, wrestled with his charts and the ship's logbook, which he had to rewrite. He wasn't involved in the celebrations.

When the second voyage was in its planning stage, Banks turned up with demands that were even more outrageous. He needed room on board for twenty or more people, including horn players and the good-natured Solander, of course. The *Resolution* was larger than the *Endeavour*, but it could not accommodate such an onslaught. Banks insisted the Naval authorities make alterations to the ship. An extra level was added, and James had to relinquish his captain's cabin to scientists and artists. However, during the sea trial, the vessel threatened to capsize, and cooler heads prevailed. The brand-new upper deck was dismantled. Banks had a fit at the shipyard in Sheerness and had all his belongings taken off the ship. A disagreeable exchange followed between Banks, Lord Sandwich, and Hugh Palliser. James set sail with Banks's parting gift: eight crates of salted fish, which, on closer inspection, turned out to be rotten, yet James nevertheless took the time to write Banks a letter of reconciliation. Once the danger has passed, Elizabeth thought, picturing the hairless head of her newborn son, James is able to manage it. As soon as he knows he doesn't have to bow to high-ranking individuals like Banks, he can recall the admiration and pleasure of their association.

Impressed by James's zeal for correspondence, she'd made a start on her home logbook. It must be somewhere on this table, beneath a stack of papers. Her cleanup efforts picked up speed, and she pitched entire piles of unread leaflets and newspapers into the basket. Here and there, the tabletop peeked through, dull and grimy.

She found her journal under a catalog for navigational instruments. She'd started writing it in one of her stepfather's unused ledgers; she thought her habit of sitting hunched over that type of book would be an incentive. The book fell open in her hands; she flipped the pages with her thumb. She hadn't stuck with it for long; the paper was pristine, except for a few entries at the beginning. She sat down and placed the book in front of her on the messy table.

The idea that he would read what she'd written drove her to make an effort. Didn't she want him to know what was happening on the home front? So he could follow his children's development, imagine the running of the home in his absence, know who came for a visit? Aye, aye. But when she sat beside the lamp after the children had gone to bed, pen and ink at hand, she froze. She was doing this under duress. It was required—she felt like a schoolgirl being punished. She'd been conscious of writing beautiful sentences, presenting events in such a way that she created a mature, responsible impression. For whom am I putting my best foot forward? What am I afraid of? Why can't I just write what I think? It's for my own benefit. I don't have to let anyone else read it, do I? Such thoughts confused her.

She opened the book. The dates were written in neat penmanship.

This morning we went to the market. Nat carried the basket, which was heavy: apples, salsify, and celery. We saw some lovely cod at the fishmongers.

Dull, boring days, by the sound of it. The handwriting changed after a few pages, becoming uneven—dashes and exclamation marks appeared. Sometimes half a page was left blank.

Sent Jamie for midwife at five o'clock. WON'T attempt to make it through the night. Pain!! Can hardly hold on. The boys mustn't hear me, they have to leave. Calm down.

A smattering of short sentences after the birth: *Exhausted, but content. Baby seems healthy, sturdy. Jamie and Nat went to the neighbor's, hand in hand. They didn't dare come too close. Was there a bad smell? Clean sheets on the bed, all the same. Can't sleep at all.*

Two blank pages followed. Then, in tiny, tight letters, a date: *October 30, 1772.*

James, you turned forty-four three days ago. This is a belated birthday message. You probably gave your crew an extra ration of rum. Maybe they sang for you, and I'm sure you had a festive day. Dancing to a fiddler and bagpipe on the afterdeck, that's how I picture it. If I close my eyes, I can almost smell the rum-soaked breath and feel the warmth of the tropical bay where you're wintering.

Fantasies can be misleading: you see what you want to see. I'm sure you thought about us, here at the kitchen table, the fire blazing in the hearth while we enjoyed a meal in your honor. True? No, not true. Things are very different here. We have no appetite and lack the energy to build a fire. Nathaniel slumps against my knee, pale as a ghost, and Jamie spends the entire day out on the street. I have no idea what he gets up to. My mother turns up every evening with a pan of food—and you know what an appalling cook she is. She takes half of whatever she's made back home with her when she leaves.

How shall I put it? I have to tell you. I must write this down: Georgie is dead.

He died on October 1. I was totally unprepared. Four years ago, when baby Joseph died, I knew what was coming. I saw it the minute he was born, how he would languish and waste away. And that's what happened. He was missing whatever it is you need to stay alive. I hated being unable to keep him warm, and that he was unable to drink my milk. But I knew what was coming.

Georgie was a different story: strong, active, with rosy cheeks. He drank with such gusto that he sometimes gagged, and then he'd furiously pound his fists on my breast.

I would put him down in front of the hearth on that sheepskin we brought back from Yorkshire. He'd watch the flames, kicking his fat little legs and babbling to the fire. As soon as the boys came home from school, they'd rush to kneel beside him on the floor. They were crazy about him. He'd crow with delight whenever he heard their voices. He sat on my lap at mealtimes. The last few weeks, I even gave him some pureed vegetables and applesauce. I thought of you.

I must write this down. The end of September, he developed a fever. I have to tell you. I'll keep it short: doctor, bloodletting, rubbed with ointment, higher fever, convulsions, death. He was in my bed. Died toward morning. Uncle Charles built a small coffin. I carried the cradle up to the attic, along with the tiny clothes. And the sheepskin.

Every time he saw me he chortled and held out his arms. He brought so much joy into our lives.

A month has passed. The women in the street wonder why I don't come outside. But I want to be here, indoors. It almost seems that as long as you don't know about it, it can't be true. You're thinking of a healthy baby, a George or a Georgina. He's still in your mind. With these words, I am killing him.

You'd tell me to be brave for the boys; they need me. I try, dearest James, but right now, I don't have any courage. It's unbearably cruel to see our children die. There's no one I can turn to with my sorrow. Resistance sinks like lead through my legs and leaves me paralyzed.

After this, I don't think I'll write in the home logbook anymore. I'm not sure I'll even show you what I wrote today.

She slammed the book shut and brought it to the basket. Best to burn it. Reading it wouldn't do anyone any good. But her fingers wouldn't let go of the book, which hovered briefly above the crumpled newspapers without falling. She gently laid the book on a pile of personal documents. To put in a box for later, she thought, and store out of the way, upstairs in a cupboard.

She surveyed the tabletop. Almost finished. Soon the boys will arrive and we'll be busy eating, talking, and listening. Be quick, work faster, so the task will be completed within the day. Then she could say: this morning, I cleared the table.

There was one pile of letters left. Some were still sealed, addressed to James but delivered after he had left. And one for her, from Frances.

Dearest Elizabeth—I heard—yes, they still sometimes write to me, those women who live on your street, when there's news—I heard that James had gone off on another voyage, with two ships this time, leaving you behind, like he did four years ago, pregnant!

Oh, Elizabeth, if only I could be near you. There are no words to describe the immensity of my longing. Don't get me wrong. I love being married and being Mrs. McAllister! Life is very different here in America. Do you remember how, on quiet mornings, we'd go outdoors? How the mist would be draped over the fields and it would seem as if the cows were hovering, their legs hidden in white. The way it smelled. That's England. Our house here is large and well constructed, surrounded by plenty of land. I have an orchard and a vegetable patch. It's often windy here. The neighbors live far away, an older couple without any children. Everyone here is constantly building and hammering. Yesterday, I helped fasten the storm shutters. We're expecting a hurricane. Everything that's not nailed down will be blown away. The wind picks everything up: animals, trees—even entire barns!

I'm blathering, dear Elizabeth. Please write to me once you've had your baby and tell me all about the boys. I've been an unfaithful friend to all of you by getting married and moving to America. But what else was I to do? We are just ships in the wind. Sometimes I feel like crying, but the next minute I'm cheerful, eager to whitewash the kitchen. Could I be expecting? I think about you all the time: wondering if you're uneasy, but of course you are. James's sister sent me a letter, did you hear? Sweet as pie! Does that make any sense to you? Oh, how I hope these years will not be as stormy and sad for you as the ones we spent together! Maybe by the time you get this letter, you'll be holding a healthy baby girl in your arms. They're the best: sons are always swallowed up by the sea. Oh, what am I saying? I can't get any hired help here and have to do everything myself. Not that I mind, idle hands and all that.

But I'm beating around the bush, Elizabeth. I'm concerned. I hope you give birth to a strong and healthy baby. If things turn out otherwise, I will wring my heart out, regretting that I'm not at your side. Write back soon! Kiss the boys for me. Sending you a big hug from your dear friend, Frances.

She tossed the letter in the basket and stooped to carry it into the kitchen. The fire was roaring in the stove. The table resembled a tranquil pool of water.

2

She opened the kitchen door and stepped barefoot into the garden. Tiny drops of dew clung to her ankles and the hem of her skirt. The grass was overgrown, and the trees and shrubs were almost proud in showing off their unpruned foliage. It was early. The pale sun was shining through the branches. There was no wind, and if she stood still with her eyes closed, she could smell the river. Yet another day. The boys would be up soon; she'd have to cook porridge, make tea. The kitchen would be aflutter with high-pitched children's voices.

Here, now, in the almost oppressive silence, she was alone with herself in the garden she considered her home. She spun slowly around. The quince with its pale-pink blossoms; hard to imagine anything more vulnerable, and yet the blooms would grow into rocklike fruit the size of fists; the gooseberries with their vicious, razor-sharp thorns; the mulberry and the medlar full of promise. Here and there, exotic plants emerged, strange guests in London's soil. A small pineapple on a stalk, the showy leaves of a banana plant, and a palm and agave in the sunny corner against the wall. In the back, in an unkempt field, there was some withered vegetation that looked like potato plants but wasn't, in between strange dark tubers in the irregular furrows.

James took seeds and rhizomes with him when he traveled. Everywhere he docked, he planted potato fields and plots with mustard seed. He brought carrots, melons, and peas to the natives. He tilled the soil, gently placed the seeds in their beds, covered them, and gave them water. He had been looking forward to revisiting those experimental gardens: had the islanders torn the fruit from its branches before it was ripe? Or had they grasped the need to harvest and sow? He brought plants from the islands back with him, preferably edible crops. Most were destined for the botanical gardens at Kew, but he'd had a few leftover specimens delivered here, and had carefully placed them in the moist earth. Sometimes a plant died, and she'd surreptitiously dispose of it, unsure why it had failed to flourish. The climate, the soil conditions, or the fumes from the gin factory next door? She couldn't say.

Apple and elder stood next to the scullery. Indestructible, year after year.

Ever since she'd cleared the table, she'd been looking at the house, the garden, and the children through two sets of eyes. James had prematurely entered into her way of looking at things. That double vision was a harbinger of change; already she was no longer completely on her own. He'd applaud the pineapple. He'd be displeased that the elder hadn't been pruned; he wouldn't say anything, so as not to break the fragile harmony of his return, but she'd notice him knitting his brow. A pair of blackbirds had been nesting behind the elder's feathery leaves. The female shot into the garden, landing on the grass with her plump, drab-brown body. The bird didn't call attention to herself, made no unnecessary movements, but quickly pulled a worm from the damp earth and flew straight back to her nest. Twittering, the rustling of leaves, some barely audible chirping—the eggs had hatched.

When the boys—then aged eleven and ten—left for school, she stayed behind with the pap-encrusted pan and the dirty bowls. No dawdling: pump the water at once, rinse and scrub. Her jaw set, she dried the crockery and put it away. The plates in the cupboard, the pan in the rack, spoons in the drawer. It doesn't have to be tidied up this instant, she thought, why am I pushing myself like this? He won't be back for ages. Her shoulders ached from the tension, and when she finally sat down at the kitchen table, she realized her eyes were filled with tears.

There was a gray area between absence and coming home. That's where she was now. The kitchen walls should be whitewashed, the chairs on which the boys rocked from side to side needed to be repaired. She should have a new dress made.

There was a knock at the door. When it opened, she was still lost in thought. A tall man in a captain's uniform appeared in the shadows beside the stove. She was startled.

"You weren't expecting me, sorry!" He extended his hand to place a few letters on the table. A sleeve with gold stitching.

"Hugh! Do you have any news?"

Hugh Palliser leaned his cane against a chair and sat down beside her. How could she have mistaken him for James? Hugh Palliser had an ease, a natural warmth that James lacked. She'd sat with him in the garden a few weeks ago; the boys had come home, and a lively discussion had ensued about life at sea. Questions and answers were bandied about—concerning the height of the waves, the size of the fish, and how disgusting the food could be.

She had listened, not to the children's questions or Hugh's answers, but to the music emerging from the throats of the captivated boys, and the counterpoint of Hugh Palliser's deep bass.

"What fine boys you have," he'd said when he left. "You're a good mother to them, but I hope their father doesn't stay away too long. They need him, too. Fine boys, Elizabeth."

He handed her an unopened envelope. Her name was on it, written in James's hand. She bowed her head.

"They're on their way home. James gave a chest full of maps, letters, and logbooks to the *Dutton*. A merchant vessel, very swift. I gather from his letter to Stephens that the *Resolution* could be here in just over a month. James has had an incredible voyage, but he'll want to tell you about it himself. A healthy crew, immaculate charts, and a riveting journal: everything true to James's style. As if it's all in a day's work."

She said nothing. A month. The house would suddenly seem too small, as if it didn't fit. A large body would lie beside her in bed, filling the night with unexpected creaking and snoring. She'd sit across from him. They'd hesitate before beginning their tales: *you first, no you*. At this table. As soon as he stepped over the threshold, he would see, smell, and feel that there was no baby. I must be happy, she thought. I must. She crumpled the letter. Hugh Palliser laid his hand over hers and gently pulled the paper from her cramped grasp. He touched her shoulder briefly.

"Dear girl," he whispered, "I'll help you. After this trip, he'll never have to go away again. I'll make sure of that."

Yes, she thought, yes. An aim to strive for, a promise. A man at the end of his brilliant career, who has circumnavigated the globe twice, who is the crown jewel of science and cartography. He's allowed to bask in his glory and remain forever contentedly at home. There's plenty to do. This time, he could adapt and publish his travel writings himself, rather than letting some hack or other ruin them. He could get to know his sons without an imminent departure hanging over their heads. He would see his wife.

He counts on me to maintain an orderly life. I must be the keeper of the home port; give the children a daily glimpse of their father so they won't be alarmed when he suddenly walks through the door. I have to preserve the gooseberries, make sure nothing withers in the garden. He can only leave provided I do all those things. He is able to return home because I am capable. The wind may whisk him along the icebergs near the South Pole, but in his mind, there's a garden in bloom somewhere in London, a place where happy children are playing and there's a wife who can be glad.

A woman who can be happy for him, with him. A spouse who supports him in his struggles with minor aristocrats, a steadfast wife who knows what she wants and acts accordingly.

She had once been such a wife, and undoubtedly remained so in his mind. He would see her in a month's time. She felt all the strength she possessed drain from her body. I must remain seated, she thought, not tip over, not fall to the floor.

The one beside her, the understanding messenger, put his arm around her shoulders. He understood what it was like, how home and ship could each go their own way and how jarring it could be when, after a while, the two paths converged. That he understood—or at least, she thought he did—melted what remained of her composure. She coalesced with the chaos inside of her. Ragged, uncontrolled breathing, tears like spring rain, her body trembling and shaking shamelessly.

The man beside her unbuttoned his cuff, pushed up the faded indigo sleeve of his jacket, and rolled up his shirtsleeve. Without thinking, she laid her cheek against his warm skin; her lips sensed the firm muscles beneath, she rubbed her face against the hairy forearm while drooling and sniveling. He caressed her hair with his free hand. He covered her head so she could lie on that comforting arm as long as she needed. A wet face. A naked arm.

It was like a breath of air. Her shoulders relaxed, her sobbing became regular, and soon she settled down. She lay motionless on his arm.

It was how she used to soothe her baby when it was upset without knowing why—she would clasp the child against her bare skin until it calmed down. You did it instinctively, without a plan. It just happened. She smiled and felt the hairs of his arm tickling her mouth. Every notion of time had evaporated, as if this giver of solace had lifted her briefly out of the morning. She dried her cheeks—with a tea towel? His handkerchief?—and heard hurried footsteps thumping through the pantry.

"Mother? You there?" Her oldest son stormed in and froze in place when he saw Captain Palliser at the table. Jamie had a stocky, compact build, with no trace of his father's lankiness. Thick hair in tight curls close to his scalp, bright eyes, and rapid staccato movements. Before long, Nat would be towering over him. She couldn't fathom how these boyish bodies could possibly be related to one another. The sons of the father, she thought. Different parts of James had ended up in his progeny. The younger one had inherited his physique, the eldest his decisiveness, his enterprising spirit.

Soon, Jamie would be leaving for the Naval Academy in Portsmouth. Elizabeth stood at the window, the unread letter in her hands, and listened to the conversation between man and boy. Excitement about the return of the *Resolution*: would Jamie still be at home when the ship arrived, or already at school; obviously, Portsmouth might be its port of call; then he'd be the first to see his father, he'd wait for the ship with the whole class, he in his new uniform, boots and all, he'd see his father even before his brother and mother did.

While Hugh Palliser flooded her son with tales of the expedition, she retreated to the garden. She'd tucked the letter into the neckline of her dress. The sun had grown stronger. I should surrender to the warmth, she thought, to what's happening now: a son who follows his father's exploits with enthusiasm, a friend who comforts me. Let me push aside everything that's difficult and arduous, and just live, now. She brushed the dirt off the garden bench, sat down and opened the letter. He's had his fill of discovering, she thought; he's on his way home.

Hugh Palliser will no doubt fill you in on where I've been and what I found there. It is strange to be here at the Cape of Good Hope, back in the civilized world. I go to banquets and dinners, swap stories with colleagues. I met a reliable Frenchman, name of Crozet, who has also sailed the South Sea. I would like to collate what we've each found out, to close any gaps. We've learned so much! There was nothing but emptiness, filled with dim-witted and inaccurate fantasies, and now there's certainty. Precise geographical coordinates, descriptions of islands and their peoples. I heard tales that would make your eyes pop out, about warfare and eating habits, and can verify them first hand. Have to dash. Be with you in a month. Rudder still being repaired.

Had been expecting a message from you and felt uneasy when there was no word from Mile End waiting for me. Perhaps your letter got lost? I am counting on you and cannot imagine anything is amiss. I will assume there was a problem on the transport end. We will have our work cut out for us this winter. I have a mountain of details to turn into a book. By the way, someone showed me a copy of Hawkesworth's book and I could hardly contain myself. Never again! Those so-called intellectuals bleed you dry, and then boast about things they didn't take part in and don't even understand! What an outrage. And when you consider the fortune he's raking in! I must rise above it, water under the bridge. But it won't happen again.

Dear Elizabeth, I will be with you shortly and then we will have time to discuss everything. Ask Palliser about my route. I will seal these letters and have them posted. Give the children a warm embrace for me!

Seepage. Her sorrow was like water welling up at the bottom of a dike, it was being forced out under high pressure. She had to stop her wondering, she had to turn around and face the brimming river. She could hear Hugh's and Jamie's voices coming from the kitchen.

"But they have plenty to eat," said her son, "they have pigs and birds. So why do they do it? It's not allowed!"

"But it's on the other side of the world, lad. There are so many things we don't understand. They speak a different language. Perhaps they're convinced it helps them take on their enemies' strength. In their

eyes, they're doing nothing wrong; it's just their way of conducting battle. Your father believes we can't judge them by our standards. Things
are so different there, it's hard to imagine. Gruesome, isn't it?"

"I would punish them," Jamie fiercely pronounced. "If I were the
captain, I'd use live ammunition. Teach them a lesson. I bet my father
sailed back and shot them all."

They need a father, she thought. The city is abuzz with rumors; of
course they hear things and their imaginations run wild; they become
frightened, ask questions, and I behave as if they're still little children—
as if I can protect them by being silent.

The sister ship on James's expedition had come back the previous
year, alone. The two ships had lost sight of one another during a gale
near Cook Strait. When the ship sailed into London, it was carrying an
extra passenger: the captain had brought along a native to show off to
English citizens. His name was Omai, and Banks adopted him straight-
away. A few people were missing as well. On a distant southern shore,
natives had devoured the entire crew of a launch. She'd read about it in
the papers and had hoped she could keep the news from the children.

"I don't think so, Jamie," she heard Palliser say. "I believe your
father does his best to understand those people. That's not cowardice;
it's common sense."

"Maybe they'll eat him, too."

She went into the kitchen and saw Palliser shaking his head reas-
suringly. "Your father has his wits about him; he wouldn't let things get
out of hand. What's more, he's almost home and all his crew are still
alive." Captain Palliser stood to say goodbye.

Frances. She would write to Frances, so that it would seem—if only
briefly—like she was talking to her dear friend. So many men—on
ships, in kitchens, with stories and opinions. Tonight, once the boys
were in bed, she would pour her heart out to her friend in America. She

would describe the rushed half sentences in James's letter; the inevitability with which Naval life had staked its claim on her sons; her conversations with Hugh—would she mention the bizarre incident with his bare arm? Maybe it hadn't even happened; it was hard to believe, even though she could draw the pattern of hairs on his arm. She could still feel his warmth against her cheek.

She would write that she had scrubbed and polished the table in the great room until, empty and bare, it stood gleaming.

Before James left, he'd told her to find someone to help around the house. For company; someone like Frances. She'd brushed aside the suggestion. Why would she want a strange woman under her roof? A new voice that might not even blend with hers? This time, she preferred to be alone. There were no more disasters on the horizon. Baby George had died two and a half years before. She'd managed to pull herself through, and she was determined to be a pillar of strength for her returning husband. Toward the end of a voyage, you had to avoid anything that would rock the ship; the challenge was to hold everything in line: the plants, the furniture, the people. No disruptions, please.

This morning, she'd briefly broken free of herself. That would no longer be possible, could not be repeated. Her blurred sense of time had to come to an end now, as well. She hadn't an inkling how much of the day was left, and still felt lost in that peculiar moment at the kitchen table. She rubbed her face and shook her head like an animal trying to shake off a pesky fly.

Jamie came outside with a bucket and began pumping water. Nat, she was going to pick up Nat. Of course, the day had a plan. A walk, a talk, a meal. A schedule to board as if it were a boat.

The garden gate slammed shut behind her. She crossed the road and turned into the path between two rows of gardens leading to the river. The water shimmered in the distance. She looked forward to it: there was no denying that she enjoyed the presence of water. Yet it was James who loved water, not she. What I love is water within limits, she thought, water in channels, in rivers with visible dikes, in ponds encircled by willows. She'd never really understood his love of the sea. When she tried to imagine the vastness and inconceivable enormity of the world's oceans, she became anxious. No landmarks, no roads, no boundaries. To James, each continent was in water, but to her, each body of water connected with land.

She leaned against the wall of the quay and watched the small waves striking the stones. The ripples lapped cheerfully, like frolicking children; then they withdrew indifferently and leapt in the opposite direction. Incomprehensible.

James couldn't swim. In fact, she'd never met a sailor who could. It's better that way, he said. You're lost once you hit the water, whether you can swim or not. Speed is preferable to a lengthy struggle with a fatal conclusion. She didn't understand that, either. If I loved the water, I would want to feel at home in it, she thought. To plunge into it and swim like a happy fish in my element. How could you organize your life in such a way that a wooden shell always stood between you and your greatest love? On the other side of the river, the cream-colored palaces of Greenwich stood nestled on the hillside. She spied tiny figures scurrying about, mooring a boat at the jetty. Those buildings housed the beating heart of the Admiralty; there, decisions were made about their lives. Her life. In just a few weeks, James would arrive in a speeding coach. He would race up the stairs, in a rush to see his commanders, to report on the voyage. Only then would he cross the river and, on foot, greet his family. Enter his house. Embrace his wife.

But an earlier reunion wormed its way in front of the present one, as if a distraught girl were standing within the walls of her rib cage. Back then, after his first voyage around the world, he'd strode into the house, hat in hand, tanned and muscular. She'd been taken aback and had leaned against the still-warm cooker. Frances had ushered the boys into the corridor. He'd come to a halt a few feet from her, his eyes searching the walls and floor—no doll, no high chair, no crumpled apron stained with porridge. The color had drained from his cheeks.

Yes, she should have rushed into his arms. Of course, he'd been away for years and had returned. There was an embrace, but she didn't dissolve. She remained aware of her skin, which encased the story she had yet to tell. That night, she lay beside him stiff as a plank. He was in anguish, heartbroken; but she'd gone beyond that stage. She'd have to present the events to him in their tragic order. She sat up in bed, staring at the faded wall in front of her, and rapidly uttered the words, her voice constricted.

The child, the little girl, her little girl, *their* little girl, was never sick. Happy with each new day, with every opportunity to flit about the kitchen and living room, to call flowers in the garden by their names, and to solemnly help choose vegetables at the market. She was crazy about her brothers, could spend hours at Jamie's side, watching what he drew. Her eyes sparkled whenever Nat taught her a song. When the neighbor turned up with a sack of boiled sweets, she divided them into three piles: one for Jamie, one for Nathaniel, and one for her.

Keep going. Don't dillydally. There'll be time for that later.

Frances had brought the hobbyhorse down from the attic, you know, the one mounted on a piece of wood with wheels; the one the boys played with, with a genuine mane, pulled along by a length of old ship's rope. She was delighted, thrilled. She pulled that animal through the garden, fed it grass and apples and bread. We weren't paying attention. My mind was elsewhere. Frances and I were washing the sheets in the scullery. All of a sudden, it was quiet in the garden. We didn't hear her voice. Over the wringed-out sheet in our hands, our eyes locked. That was just before the blow. In the silence, we heard horse's hooves.

Someone screamed. There was a crack, a thunderous rumble of wooden wheels on stone cobbles. It's my fault. I wasn't paying attention.

Outside, a horse snorted incessantly. Passersby ran into the garden and shouted, but I was already on the street. The first thing I saw was the toy horse, lying unharmed in the middle of the street, but then I looked at my feet, my bare feet; I must have kicked off my clogs, I wasn't wearing a bonnet, no—

"Just tell me," James said. He'd rolled over.

I was talking to his back. "The facts," he said. The facts.

Elly was lying on the ground. Uninjured, flawless. Elizabeth had felt briefly relieved: we've escaped unscathed, it's nothing.

But the child was pale and motionless. She'd knelt on her bare knees in the mud; had pulled the child onto her lap; had held her daughter tight. Above her, people were screaming. She recognized Frances's voice, shrill and strained among the men's. Someone unharnessed the horse. For the longest time, nothing happened. The strange thing was, the sun kept shining. It was an ordinary day, a London morning.

Frances sent a boy to fetch Hugh Palliser. He rowed furiously across the river. Luckily, Palliser had been in Greenwich and not at the wharf. He came right away. Odd how she could so clearly recall trivial details. His shoes and pant legs were wet from his frenzied rowing; dull buckles.

"The facts," said the man beside her. "Where were the boys?"

The doctor arrived. That was later, when Elly was already laid out in the room. Good that James was asking these questions: it meant he was listening. Maybe the neighbor had picked up Jamie and Nat from school. Not Frances, who'd stayed by her side, she was certain of that. Frances was shaking so much she could hardly help dress Elly in her burial clothes. Elizabeth's hand had been steady; she had washed, groomed, and dressed the little girl. It was April 9, 1771.

Hugh Palliser took care of the arrangements. He sat in her kitchen spooning Frances's soup into her mouth. He dealt with the carpenter, the gravedigger, and the pastor. He urged Elizabeth to rest, but she couldn't. The minute she laid her head on the pillow, a suffocating blanket of fear crept over her. She sat beside the child. She tried to shut out the sounds coming from the kitchen, to focus on the voice of her daughter that still had to be in her head, somewhere untraceable. She waited.

Frances crawled into bed with her that night, and the following nights. There weren't enough women in the house. In a flash, she realized that her daughter had been the woman of the future, and now that future was gone forever.

"The facts," James said.

The funeral. That was men's business. Women stayed home to prepare food for returning mourners. Captain Hugh Palliser would attend on James's behalf. But, on the morning of the funeral, when Elizabeth got out of bed—such a relief when the sky started to brighten, when she was no longer sleepless but simply awake—she knew she wanted to go herself. Frances helped her put on the black frock, and even found a veil somewhere. Hugh arrived with the pallbearers. He saw her standing beside the tiny coffin and nodded. She took his arm—yes, she thought, that selfsame arm, then as well—and they followed Elly along the footpath to the graveyard. White primroses were blooming in the grass by the sunken paving stones, their rosettes crisp and clear in the slanting sunlight, a carpet of flowers as far as she could see. That's what she'd observed. She no longer knew whose faces were in the pews when they slipped into the church. Hugh guided her to the front. He never let go of her hand. Through the transparent black veil, she stared at the coffin before her. She did not think, she observed.

"Facts," James whispered. There were no facts. The Psalms, the readings, and the prayers—she'd forgotten it all. Had she thought about the child's hair, her mouth, her youthful bones? How she wanted to crawl into the ground and embrace that delicate skeleton? No, that came later.

People knelt, closed their eyes. She didn't. She gazed up at the organ loft and saw the organist, Mr. Hartland, sitting at the double keyboard.

He rested his large, pale hands in his lap, and he bent forward to peer at the score on his music rack. He turned his head toward her, as if he could feel her staring. No, she wasn't embarrassed, she'd looked up hungrily at the old man; she'd never forget his wrinkled cheeks and the shiny scalp peeking through the sparse strands of hair. She'd looked into his face for a long time without blinking. They had not smiled.

Their eyes only unlocked once the pastor said "amen." She shifted her gaze to the stone floor. Stone, she thought: rock, wood, earth. It was time for the coffin to be carried outside. She tried to control her breathing. Although she was surrounded by a sea of black-clad mourners, she felt completely alone. Stand up. Watch the pallbearers approaching. Turn slowly and follow the unhurried procession. She was a solitary tree in a field, unapproachable. Then, Mr. Hartland began to play. She was momentarily shaken by the full resonance of the organ, because the tune was brimming with a momentum and joy that didn't seem to fit what was happening below. She noticed a worried look on the pastor's face; beside her, Hugh held his breath. Then he squeezed her hand and shot her the briefest of smiles. She suddenly realized it was Handel's *Water Music*. She recognized the melody. The elderly organist was calling to the sea, reminding her of James: that her husband was out there, far away, sailing the ocean, and he would return to her. All was not lost. The casket had been brought halfway down the central aisle. She followed on Hugh's arm, bathed in the music. The rich sonority disappeared, replaced by the pure woodwind register, sounding like oboes, flutes, and bassoons playing a fragile trio in perfect unison. It seemed at first like a cheerful tune, but she knew better, and so did Mr. Hartland. The way he kept rounding off the short, pleading phrases broke her heart. That's the way it was. A skipping girl on the road. In the sun. Beneath the heavy coach.

"Facts," James demanded. "Who was driving the carriage?"

Of course. Yes. The coachman hadn't dared show his face. Instead, he'd sent his wife with half a suckling pig as a peace offering. Frances had let her in while Elizabeth was upstairs in the bedroom, motionless at the window.

James rolled onto his back. "What did you do with the pig?"

She could still see the half carcass lying on a gunnysack beside the cooker: pink, with white fragments of bone. The size of a child.

"Frances took care of it. Gave it away. Buried it. Threw it in the river. I don't know, we never mentioned it again."

I haven't seen my husband for three years, she thought, and here we lie, talking about a pig. Our daughter died a violent death, and he wants to know what we did with the pig. Beneath this discussion lies a question we're not facing. I can't even say it aloud, I can hardly bear to think it. Yet I must.

She sank down so that her head was on the pillow, next to his. She glanced sideways and saw him crying. It's my fault. I should have protected her. I was her mother. I'd barricaded the stairs with a board, and kept the carving knives out of reach. But I hadn't closed the garden gate. I protected her until that one time. I'd almost pulled it off; you were already on your way home, almost—

James blew his nose and started to speak. At first, she didn't understand what he was talking about, and she let the sentences wash over her. A coral reef, darkness, a crashing sound. The ship had run aground and was taking on water. Driven by mortal terror, they'd all manned the pumps, even the officers and scientists. They'd thrown the cannons overboard, and the barrels of water, of meat. After twenty-four hours, they miraculously floated free, and they drifted along the reef in their damaged ship. He turned to his crew for advice. They formed a circle on deck, in the icy wind of the early half-light, while a few feet beneath them, water was flooding into the hold through a gaping hole. The brother of the ship's surgeon had an idea. Following his instructions, they hauled a sail—smeared with manure and unraveled rope—around the damaged side of the ship: a tremendous effort involving cables and pulleys. The men had followed orders silently, their faces set.

It worked. The sailcloth adhered to the hull and bought them just enough time to reach the shore. There, they were anchored for a month and a half to repair the ship.

"I took a huge risk," he said, "and I still wonder if I could have done things differently."

Elizabeth said nothing. The smell of the river wafted in through the open window. Where is she, where is she? She's in the graveyard, she's alone. Quiet—drive out those thoughts. Listen.

The ship had been repaired for the time being, but continued to leak. The rigging was in tatters, the ropes frayed. They went ashore at a port in Batavia, in the Dutch East Indies. They had no choice.

"No scurvy on my ship," James said. "I spent three years sailing under unspeakable conditions and didn't lose a single crew member to the sailor's disease. Not one. We disembarked in Batavia in perfect health. The Dutchmen had never seen anything like it. The state of the ship attested to the trials we'd faced, but it didn't chime with the men's firm bodies and plump cheeks. That was my pride. I sat in my cabin and wrote to London: *no men lost!*

"It's all down to willpower. Discipline. If they wouldn't bathe, I threatened to flog them. Not that I ever carried out such ultimatums. Bedclothes were aired, and clothing was washed as soon as the weather permitted. In seawater, the shirts stiff with salt, but still. If they soiled the hold, I withheld their spirit rations. At first, there was some resistance, because it was new to them. Seafarers wear the same shirt for three years to prove they're tough as old boots. They don't notice the stench, or perhaps they're used to it."

He's not home yet, she thought. He couldn't keep up with the speed of his ship and is racing to catch up. It's too soon for him to lie in his bed and cry about his child; he's still on the deck, shouting and handing out sailcloth buckets for baling water. He's lying beside me, but he's not yet here.

Food was of the utmost importance. If he could find a remedy for scurvy, it would mean a giant leap forward in the history of maritime navigation. Diet had to be the key. As a rule, sailors' gums began to swell after about six weeks at sea. Their teeth became loose and fell out. They developed bruises under their skin because their veins couldn't contain their blood. It seeped into joints and muscles, hindering all movement. The pain was unbearable, forcing them to lie motionless until death arrived. The gentlemen from the Navy thought this was normal, a law of nature! They left room for it when mustering a crew: always hire more men than necessary, because half of them will die. It was common sense. To James, it was absurd. Why did people become sick at sea and not on land? What was the difference? There had to be a reason. Pay attention. Think. Experiment. Don't resign yourself, but try to get to the bottom of facts you don't understand.

Elizabeth felt slightly envious as the speed of his narrative picked up and his voice grew deeper. He was concerned about something, there was a subject he was excited about, a goal he hoped to attain. And what did she want? A storm; she wanted an icy storm to bash the waves of the Thames against the quayside. Then she'd tie a bonnet tightly under her chin, grab the heavy cloak, and set out walking. Going nowhere, into the wind, stride by stride. But the river was as calm as a mirror, and the air was balmy.

The men had fresh food when they went ashore. You didn't squander supplies if there was wild game to be shot and fruit to be plucked. The solution must be in there somewhere. At sea, they ate salt-cured meat that gave off an awful stench, and rocklike hardtack, bored through by maggots. The ship had to be turned into an island on which animals and plants could survive. With chickens. Tiny gardens in crates behind the mast. But the wind blew the poultry overboard, and the rain washed away the soil. Even so, James sought his refuge in imitating the conditions on land as best he could. He started by firing the cook, a dull-witted and lazy chap who showed no interest in the subject of food. The replacement appointed by the Navy was a large fellow capable of frank and meaningful discussions. He had no objections to adding mashed peas, carrot juice, and bullion extract to his dishes, and even suggested tossing in some dried figs and raisins. Unfortunately, his left arm had been ripped off by a snapped cable, but he managed to develop an impressive agility with his right.

Was she still listening? She heard him well enough; his words cascaded through the bedroom, and she felt his rib cage and chest reverberating. It was strange not to be alone anymore; odd that someone would prick holes in her thoughts, interrupt them with images and concepts that were not relevant to her. He is your husband, she thought. Listen: focus your attention.

The garden scheme was a failure, but the need for vegetables remained the guiding principle behind alterations to the ship's menu. Whoever went ashore was required—in addition to their regular tasks, such as filling the water barrels and setting up the telescope—to search for anything that was green, and was only permitted back on board with a bunch of foliage tucked into his shirt: bishop's weed, mallow, comfrey, or whatever looked the part. The cook's mate collected the offerings and brought them to his boss, who would then mince the greens with his remaining arm. The following morning, the bitter pulp was stirred into the barley porridge. For breakfast.

And what if there was no land? Then there was sauerkraut. Everyone thought he was mad when he hauled those stinking vats on board. The finely sliced slivers of cabbage fermenting in salt. The only way they could keep the barrels from exploding was to place heavy stones on top of their lids. Could anyone get that sour rot down their gullets? The sailors gagged on their way through the storeroom. James wondered if the threat of flogging might work. "I had to think of our sons," he said. He turned toward her. The tanned skin of his neck ended abruptly where his uniform collar usually began. Whenever Jamie and Nat saw their parents eating some food they weren't allowed, they rushed over and whined until they were given a bite. He ordered the cook to serve the sauerkraut to no one but the officers, who were then instructed to help themselves to generous portions and rave about the taste. The crew protested this inequality. They demanded sauerkraut.

What's he going on about, she wondered. Her arms lay folded over her abdomen as if paralyzed. She could see the covers bulging in the distance, where her feet must be, but felt nothing. Even her thoughts seemed to have lost their spark.

The child died because I wasn't paying attention.

The words were there but had no meaning. Guilt. Disaster. Sauerkraut.

James's voice. "That's how it happened. Everyone stayed in good health. No loose teeth, no black-and-blue knee joints swollen like cannon-balls. When we arrived in Batavia, we were fighting fit. I wanted my carpenters to do the repairs themselves. Those tightfisted Dutchmen refused. They wanted their cut, as you might expect. There were arguments, delays. I won in the end, but by then it was too late. Swamp fever had struck. By that time, all my interventions—disinfecting, sulfurizing—were futile. My men were delirious with fever and couldn't keep anything down. The Dutchmen had hoped to earn some money by patching up the ship, but I didn't pay the bill! One sailor after the other perished. We even had to bury the doctor. I left without the harbormaster's permission. The deaths continued at sea. Every day, we slid crew members into the ocean. Men with whom we'd shared three years' worth of adventures. You know, it hardly sunk in. I was so furious with those Dutchmen and their foul, stinking canals. And in the meantime, my letter proclaiming my triumph was on its way to London."

She tried to imagine the ship of death, the bodies sewn into sail-cloth, weighted down with stones, and slid along a plank propped over the railing. Someone would read from the Good Book and someone else would play the "Last Post" on the bugle. The survivors, fearful or down-hearted, would gather in a semicircle on the deck. While I was washing sheets in the scullery, she thought. While I wasn't paying attention. How are we supposed to bring these two worlds together? It's hopeless, no point in trying. In the distance, near the river, the geese suddenly began honking. The alarming sound swelled and then died away. Who had read the Bible passages on board? It was the doctor's job, because James didn't want to take along some useless pastor, but the doctor had died. If there was no one left alive to play the bugle, was the ceremony then carried out in silence? Creaking ropes, the slap of the plank against the railing, the splash when the corpse cleaved the water's surface.

"Elizabeth," James said, "I lost thirty men in a matter of weeks. Thirty men. You could say it was my fault. I was the captain. I decided to call at Batavia. I gave the crew permission to go ashore. I should have looked after my men so that they could return home safely. That was my job and I failed. I took risks. Getting stuck on that reef was the result of one such risk. It turned out miraculously well, but things could have gone wrong. Batavia was also a risk. There, things did take a disastrous turn. Under my command. I've thought about it a lot, it kept me awake during the rest of the voyage home. Did I drive thirty men to their graves? Murder them? I don't know. I was eaten up by remorse—and still am—regretting that I'd put my faith in the Dutch and their stinking outpost. Remorse, guilt, but anger as well. I leapt from my bed, I was that furious. My plans had been thwarted by what had happened. I did not want to see my men waste away; I did not bring on that sickness, I—"

He paused. She heard his overexcited breathing gradually become regular and calm. The bedroom turned gray; the day was dawning.

"It happened," he continued. "Disasters happen. You can't always anticipate them. You are, to some extent, at the mercy of circumstance.

You have an obligation to be as alert as possible. You are not infallible. Your authority only extends so far. No further. There will always be a domain where you are powerless. I find it impossible to accept, although I realize it is true. Do you understand?"

The sky beyond the window was pale yellow. As if it were also growing lighter in her head. She drew up her legs to stretch her stiff muscles. She felt the warmth of the man beside her. It happens, she thought: you bargain with your fears and make a decision based on common sense. It usually works out for the best, but fatally, sometimes it doesn't. The guilt remains, because you are tied to your decision. And yet, we are at the mercy of what occurs. I am. He is.

The stiffness left her body. She moved closer to James. By the time they fell asleep, exhausted, it was morning.

How much time did she have left? A month, six weeks? She shuddered and inhaled the sweet, metallic scent of the river. This homecoming would be different. The prospect of a secure existence with a husband who was at home for good would help her feel stronger. She stepped away from the embankment and became aware of the strength in her calves. Her bonnet was loose. She pulled it off to feel the wind blowing through her hair. I am standing upright beside the river. A new life is coming, and I am going to embark on it with no misgivings. She turned her back to the water. The sun had finally evaporated the gray clouds and warmed the dark cloth of her dress. Just feel it: nothing is wrong. Even the sunlight is supporting me.

She looked along the embankment and spied a small figure in the distance with a black case in his hand.

Sometime after Elly's funeral, on a windy day, she'd run into the organist, Mr. Hartland, on the street. She didn't recognize him at first. She hardly looked up during those daily walks of despair. She just trudged on, one foot in front of the other; the minutes had to be endured, the hours filled with deeds that didn't point to an intolerable future. She had to walk; she couldn't bear to meet the eyes of passersby and imagined she was alone in the bustling city. She felt deformed, visibly damaged, humiliated. She wanted to hide, but that gloomy house was closing in on her. So she walked.

"Mrs. Cook?" said a gentle voice close by. She looked up, startled, and blinked to clear her vision. Then she saw Mr. Hartland's good-natured face. He did not smile but looked at her probingly. She remembered the curious eye contact they'd exchanged during the prayer, and how he'd tried to console her with his well-chosen music.

She was always welcome, he said, during that inclement encounter. He thought about her often; he'd be happy to invite her in whenever she was tired from walking and needed a place to rest. And, to her surprise, she took him up on his offer a couple of times. His housekeeper brought tea (or beer, if it was a warm day), and she sat with the organist in his cluttered workroom, not saying a word. He'd turn the pages of his score and speak of the music's power. Some instruments hung on the wall: flutes, an oboe, a violin.

What am I doing here? she'd asked herself. What am I hoping to find? I know nothing about music: what do I want from this man? This makes no sense. Then it slowly dawned on her. In those days he was a misfit, an outsider, like herself. He strove to give more attention to music during church services, just as she fought to preserve the memory of her little daughter.

When young Nathaniel had listened to that violinist on the deck of the *Resolution*, he'd been mesmerized. He jabbered on about it endlessly: he wanted to do that, too, to play songs; he wanted to be a violinist. He wanted a violin.

She asked Hartland for advice, and Nat got his violin lessons. In the beginning, the boy ran to the organist every time he wanted to practice, to have his instrument tuned. But before long, he could turn the pegs himself. Whenever he played, she sat at the kitchen table, listening. He told her stories without words. She felt happy that he could love a pastime he had discovered on his own with such passion.

There he was, her youngest son. His violin case swinging at the end of his long spindly arm, the wind whipping his fine blond hair into his eyes. He spotted her and waved with his free hand. He'd be leaving for the Naval Academy in a little more than a year. That's the way it went— what other option was available to the children of a captain? He didn't want to go, but he didn't know any better. But here and now, he smiled and walked toward his waiting mother, carrying his violin.

Suddenly, she knew everything would turn out all right. The boys would have a father who wouldn't go away anymore; one who would talk to them about seafaring, the constellations, and science. A father who would be satisfied with his achievements and would take an interest in his children's careers. They were a family. Everything would be fine.

Hugh Palliser's chiseled profile flashed before her eyes. An exchange she couldn't think about had occurred in her kitchen that morning. She could still feel the skin of his forearm against her lips, and she started and let out an involuntary groan. It's nothing, she thought, a weakness, unexplainable and temporary—it's nothing. With all her strength, she pushed aside the memory of the man who had bared his arm for her. There was Nathaniel. He was running toward her, and she caught him in her arms.

3

The last day of the long month of July was a Monday, making it both a beginning and an end. Elizabeth had woken up feeling decisive and had spent the morning packing Jamie's sea chest. Would he be seeing his father before he left for Portsmouth? Would she be allowed to keep him home until James returned? She'd run out of patience with such dilemmas. School was about to start, Jamie had been enrolled as a student: they had to get ready for his departure. Her sons would go to sea; anything else was out of the question. When James selected the crew for his first voyage around the world, he added the names of his sons to the list. At the time, they were just five and six, and they stayed home with her and Frances, but they were listed on the muster as "Charles Clerke's servant" and "carpenter's servant." Elizabeth had objected. It was a lie meant to elevate the boys to prospective sailors, and James was putting his entire career on the line. If someone spotted the sham and reported it, he would be thrown out of the Navy permanently. She didn't mention that she was irked by this unequivocal and premature decision about her children's careers. Such thoughts might cross her mind when James was away, but when he was sitting opposite her, notions like those were beyond her.

"They need the experience," he'd explained. "More years of service means faster promotions. I started much too late. If Hugh Palliser hadn't put my name forward and brought me to the attention of all and sundry, I would still be just an ordinary seaman. The boys' Naval careers must not be subject to that sort of happenstance. I want them to have a better start in life than I had."

She understood, and when Jamie and Nat were listed as crew on the second voyage, she held her tongue.

Her eldest, despite being so well traveled—at least on paper— still had to start his education. She had washed and ironed his white open-collared shirts. Now she folded them and packed them near the top of the chest. The shirts of a twelve-year-old boy. She didn't understand why Jamie's departure upset her so. Of course she would miss him; it would be awful not to hear his voice every day, not to sense his sturdy presence around the house, to no longer laugh at his stories. But there was another feeling lurking beneath the impending loss, a sort of restlessness, a dismay she couldn't quite pin down.

Jamie had been looking forward to this for months. He couldn't wait to meet his classmates, and he paraded through the room in his new boots. No point being sad on his behalf; he was following in his father's footsteps, fearless and filled with childlike anticipation. She tried to lower her shoulders, and slammed the chest shut.

She went outside with the garden shears in hand. She should get on her knees and weed out the runners spreading from the ineradicable bishop's weed, but instead, she snipped a pink bunch of flowers from the copiously blooming mallow. Her hand was already on the garden gate, she'd planned to nip over to the cemetery to visit her daughter, when she heard someone pounding on the front door. She opened it with the flowers still in her arms.

A young man—a year or two older than Jamie—stood on the sidewalk; he was an excited apprentice sailor with flushed cheeks, trying to catch his breath. He held his cap in his hand and looked straight at her.

"The captain!" he shouted. "The captain is back! I had to come and tell you. He's across the river. When he's finished, he will come home. So you know, ma'am. He arrived in a carriage with the other gentlemen. They had the clock with them. It was still running! Mr. Solander asked me to come and tell you. Mile End, he said. He was also waiting for the captain; everyone was pacing. I hung around, too, because I wanted to see him. My watch was over, but I didn't leave. He leapt out of the carriage and ran up the stairs. I saw him!"

She brought the boy into the kitchen and gave him a drink. He was so excited he couldn't sit still; he sprang out of the chair and circled her while she put the flowers in water. She arranged the stems in a vase and listened to his loud, piercing voice. *Is this the captain's plate, is that his chair? The captain's breeches were so white as he climbed the sunny stairs of the Admiralty. His gold epaulets sparkled; his gray wig was so distinguished!* She felt for a coin in her apron and herded the boy out the door. On the sidewalk, he stood staring at her, awestruck, the coin clutched in his fist. Then he turned and ran off down the street.

The flowers, pink with delicate greenery, had now become a welcome bouquet, and stood proudly in the center of the table. She shook her head and sat down, folded her arms over her stomach, and rocked slowly. James was sitting at a table less than a mile away, presenting his report about the voyage to Lord Sandwich, Stephens, perhaps even Hugh Palliser. A brief summary, mind you, because he would be in a rush to get home. To her. The more she thought about displacement and movement, the stronger the stillness took hold of her. The roasting pan—she'd have to prepare a roast, slice the vegetables, put clean sheets on the bed, clear up the children's clutter, change her dress; there was still time, she had an hour, maybe half an hour, a little while—

He came in through the back. A shadow fell across the kitchen window. She looked up and saw him standing in the garden. He'd pulled the wig off his head and tossed it onto the garden table. With both hands he massaged his scalp through his coarse dark-brown hair. He stood, legs wide, in the garden and inspected the quince, the agave, and the palm tree. Now, she thought, now. I've been waiting for years. He lingered in the garden, needed to feel the wind in his hair. He visits his superiors before coming to see me. Why are my legs so heavy? I should fly into his arms, light as a feather, because look: there he is! Ideas raced through her head without taking hold, she thought one thing, did another. Her hands brushed the pink flowers. How soft—soft and firm at the same time. Go ahead, walk to the door, pull it open, and step outside. The only path is the one that leads to the garden.

She smoothed her jacket and wiped her neck. Ten steps. He walked—suddenly in a hurry—toward her. She lifted her face. They both stopped in their tracks. A gap of a few feet separated their bodies. He lifted his arms. She saw the hand with the pale scar; it drifted in front of her face and, for a split second, she froze. Then she kissed his fingers and stepped closer, until she was in his arms.

He inspected the house as if it were a ship. When he stepped over the threshold, he ducked, as if he were entering the cramped captain's quarters. He looked around the kitchen and great room, and she saw the walls shrinking beneath his critical gaze.

He must have noticed the absence of toys, a child's jacket, a stained bib. He paced with just a few lengthy strides until he'd covered the paltry dimensions of the rooms. From time to time, he'd pick up an object—a small bowl, a crayon. He ran his hand around the base of a copper pan, and rested it on the uncluttered table. In the kitchen, he bent toward the bouquet and inhaled the pink flowers. After a while, they sat down, face-to-face.

She propped her feet on the rungs of her chair so she could wrap her arms around her knees. There is only one death, she thought, and all the other deaths thereafter stir up the same icy despair as the first. Was he crying over George, a baby he'd never held, a child from a story? Or about his crumbling expectations regarding her pregnant belly? Or were his tears for the sailor's wife who'd had to bury her child all on her own? She could only imagine that all the tears had a single source and that he—without being able or daring to say it aloud—was crying over the loss of the daughter who'd been lying buried for four years. She held herself tight, but could still feel the pull of that loss that left her powerless. It prevented her from moving, from drawing his head toward her breast, taking his hand, or even offering him a handkerchief. She just sat there, frozen, waiting for his sorrow to ebb. She examined the fabric of her skirt instead of the husband who had returned.

The boys broke the clammy inertia when they arrived, running, whooping, and throwing their arms around James. In the blink of an eye, the shrunken kitchen returned to its normal size, and Elizabeth was able to get up, take the plates and cups out of the cupboard, and prepare their meal while tossing hollow phrases—which soothed her with their ordinariness—at the boys: let your father rest; you'll get your presents later; there'll be plenty of time for stories.

She only dared look up once her voice came back to her. Jamie stood, feet firmly planted, in front of his father, chattering about the Naval Academy where he was to start the following week. Nathaniel, who was younger, clung at first to Elizabeth, and stared at James from the other side of the table. She felt his slim hand creep into hers, and she wrapped her arm around him. The boy looked up at her, his wispy hair in his eyes. She'd forgotten to cut it, she thought, grinning slightly. But within fifteen minutes, Nathaniel was sitting on James's lap and stammering about the violin and Mr. Hartland, the organist. Then he fired off a barrage of questions, leaving no gap for the answers. Jamie wanted to know how cold it was at the South Pole, the speed of the ship when all the sails were unfurled, how old you had to be to go to sea. Nat asked about the animals, whether they'd eaten the chickens, and who had been brave enough to slaughter the pig.

There he sat, talking with his only surviving children. He's answering their questions as earnestly as he answered the ones Stephens and Sandwich asked a few hours earlier. She noticed he'd put on weight. His cream-colored waistcoat stretched across his stomach, and he had undone two of the buttons. His cheeks were full. His face had been burned brown.

Time sped past; before she knew it, the boys had gone to bed and it was twilight in the garden. She hunched over the dishes and was annoyingly conscious of the man behind her, sitting at the table. A guest in her house, one whom she was obliged to welcome and accommodate. But that wasn't it; he lived here, and would continue to live here. She would have to retreat from her rooms to make space for him. Sweat stung her neck as she thought of her skin beneath her summer dress and the unfamiliar, salty skin of the other, covered by his uniform. She wanted to stamp her feet in rage, because she couldn't stir up any desire for him. Where was the fire from all those lonely summer nights? Why did she feel no joy, but instead such an awkward discomfort? He just sat there, his long legs stretched beneath the table; he sat and watched. Later, they would go upstairs. To bed.

"Would you like another?" he asked. She turned and nodded. He filled two glasses. "Leave those dishes; come and sit down."

She slid the flowers to one side and rested her hands on the table. With sudden clarity, she realized how impossible this was. He was carrying the entire world in his head; he'd experienced things she couldn't begin to imagine; had taken care of a hundred men in circumstances that were utterly foreign to her. How could he limit himself to this kitchen? How could he, from one minute to the next, become a father again, or a husband? In the brief span of time between dusk and darkness, there was no way to catch up on three years. They would have to take a leap of faith and trust that, in the coming weeks and months, they could fill in the gaps. That's the way it had to be—the way it had always been.

He drank. She heard him swallow and watched his Adam's apple bob. He pounded his glass on the table. He's fighting his way back into the house, she thought, putting his stamp on things, making them his own. Me, as well. But I'm already his, aren't I? Doesn't he already have access to everything I think?

She felt the color rising in her cheeks. He had no idea what she thought; didn't know she was counting on his not traveling anymore, nor that she'd sat, at this very table, crying onto a man's naked arm. Or that she was desperate to push all thought of that bed upstairs out of her mind.

He rose and, without a word, stood behind her chair. He rested his hands on her neck, slid her collar aside and rubbed his thumbs across her vertebrae: up toward her hairline, down along her spine. She heard the soles of his boots squeaking on the floorboards, felt the warmth of his massive body, saw the black of night through the window.

Stand up. Turn slowly into those warm arms. Inhale the scent of his waistcoat, the peculiar smell of clothes that have circled the globe. Lay your head against his chest and hear—feel—the pounding of his strong heart. Then look up, and gently place a hand on his cheek. Touch his face: the unruly eyebrows, the unexpectedly delicate eyelids, his thin lips.

He tenderly bit her finger, licked the palm of her hand, and turned out the lamp. They went upstairs, arm in arm.

She gingerly carried the uniform into the garden to air it out. She headed toward the garbage heap with the sum and substance of his captaincy draped over her arm. Throw it away, she thought. Burn it. Put it out of commission, forever. Instead, she hung the garment in the shadow of the quince tree, so the sun wouldn't fade the blue of its jacket. James was sitting next to the garden wall in civilian dress; he was padded out with more flesh than she could remember. He looked relaxed and well rested. She approached him; the grass felt soft against the soles of her feet.

He wouldn't sit still for long; soon he'd jump up and get busy. That was his nature. Once he'd shaken off the night's lethargy, he would want to be active, make plans, and talk to people. But not yet; they were becalmed for now, together in their garden.

She had no grasp of seafaring and trade winds, and didn't particularly want to know anything, yet the image of a tranquil calm between two storms did come to mind. Whenever the wind died down, it altered the tempo of life on board. Slack sails set the sailors to work, tackling whatever tasks they'd put off: cleaning, making repairs. Someone might tell stories, or perhaps a musical mariner would play a tune on his fiddle. Some would hang a line over the railing, hoping to catch a fish; others would wash their shirts. James would be in his cabin, updating his journal.

There wasn't much he could do. The *Resolution*, with its assembled treasures still on board, was en route from Portsmouth to London, and wouldn't arrive in Deptford for another week. The charts and logbooks were all across the river, in Greenwich, on the desks and tables in the Admiralty building. Sandwich and Stephens would be poring over them, filled with admiration as they devoured page after page. Until those men had finished reading, there was no wind and the world was cut down to the size of their garden. James bent over and caressed her bare instep. Then he stood up. What had she been about to do? Shell the broad beans before dinner. Pick blackberries. Finish packing Jamie's sea chest.

She sat on a low stool in the middle of the berry bushes and felt the weight of the heavy bunches, still warm from the sun, in the palm of her hand, before sliding them into the bowl on her lap. She heard James chatting with the boys. He'd taken the small globe from the living room and placed it on the garden table, to show the children where he'd sailed. He pointed out the places where he'd found land in the vast, empty ocean. The boys were proud and impressed; it was an amazing feat that their father knew more than what was printed on the globe.

"When you discover a country," Nat asked, "how do you know what it's called?"

"You just ask the locals," Jamie retorted, impatiently. "It's their country, they must know its name."

"But what if it's uninhabited? Or if you can't understand what they're saying? They don't talk the way we do, you know!"

"When you discover land, you give it a name," James said. "You measure its exact coordinates, draw it on the chart, and think of a name. Then you write it down."

But the boys wanted more details, so James told them about bays he'd named for what they'd found there: the Bay of Plenty and Poverty Bay; about capes and cliffs he'd named after his friends and superiors. Sometimes he named an island after whichever sailor saw it first.

The sun beat down on her shoulders. She took off her shawl and laid it on the grass. The smell of the berries rose from the bowl, so pungent it was almost overpowering, but still divine. There is no Great Southern Continent, she heard James explain. The Southern Continent did not exist. The so-called experts had claimed it had to be there: the landmasses in the north had to be balanced by corresponding masses on the opposite side of the earth. She heard him spinning the globe in his hands. But there's nothing there! Nothing but a frigid sea, filled with enormous floating islands of ice. Storms that freeze your face, water that solidifies before your eyes. The sails clatter like metal plates and the ropes become like iron bars. If there was land behind those icebergs, it was uninhabitable, and nothing could grow there. A white desert from which to flee as quickly as possible, before your ship was crushed.

She tried to picture the sailors with clumsy mittens and knitted caps skidding along the frozen deck, cables snapping and shooting out of their hands. They'd curse and swear, desperate to hear the order to change course and head northward, where they knew of warm islands covered in palm trees and flowering undergrowth, the pleasing bays ringed with hot sand. But James was not one to back down. She knew how he'd stand transfixed at the railing, hunting for subtle signs in wave patterns or changes in the water's color. Time and again he would point the prow to the frozen south, against everyone's wishes. He wanted to sail farther than anyone had sailed before; only the impossible could hold him back. He would be in good spirits, unlike his sailors; he relished the challenge of trumping those unmethodical armchair experts who drew new continents onto the map of the world without ever having seen or surveyed what they randomly inscribed with their burins.

Behind her, the conversation had run its course. She stretched and brought the bowl of berries into the kitchen.

They left the garden together. He held the gate open for her. Nothing was happening that day: no messengers, letters, or visitors. The languid calm would continue for a while. They walked in silence toward the river. She noticed she had trouble keeping pace with his lengthy strides. When they reached the riverbank, they paused. James pointed to the Admiralty on the other side. "The Lords are gathering," he said. "I'm going to be promoted. No way around it."

She nodded. Of course they would promote him to the highest rank of captain. All the crew members who'd received a favorable review from him would also be bumped up a rung in the maritime hierarchy. He no longer had to fight for his position, had become instead the Admiralty's radiant figurehead. They would go to any lengths to please him.

Say nothing for now. Let matters run their course and keep an eye open. Hugh Palliser will help. A privileged position ashore? Or perhaps an honorary discharge along with a generous annual stipend? She held her tongue. James turned to her and took her hand. Slowly, they walked along the water, this time in perfect rhythm.

Before long, the palaces of Greenwich were behind them, and they were ambling through the fields.

That morning, for the first time in years, Nat hadn't come into the bedroom. She'd lain awake beside James's large, warm body. He was breathing heavily in a deep sleep, and she heard her child's bare feet padding down the stairs. She got out of bed, careful not to wake James.

Her youngest was at the kitchen table in his nightshirt, peering up at her through the flaxen lock hanging over his eyes. She stood beside him and caressed his blond hair, cupping her palm on the curve of his skull.

"Will he stay here now?"

"I hope so," she said. "I think he's traveled enough."

"But who decides? Who's the boss?"

He wouldn't eat or drink a thing, and waited tensely for her answer. She explained that Stephens looked after the day-to-day matters, while Lord Sandwich was in charge.

"So that's why Papa named so many islands after him," the boy said. "I thought the captain who visited us here a while back was the boss. What was his name again?"

"Hugh Palliser." She felt her color rising and turned to face the worktop; there were plates she needed, spoons, a knife—but no, what she needed was to talk with her son.

"Captain Palliser is the boss of the ships, and all the things they require, and the crew. He decides who will work on which ship. I think it's up to him and Sandwich and Stephens to decide what happens next. Of course, your father has his say, too. Nothing happens without his approval."

The path between the fields was lined with flowering hedgerows: she saw daisies and cow parsley interspersed with the red dots of poppies. She wondered if he'd missed all this: the fertile, soggy landscape, the heavy scent of grass and sheep manure, the hedgerows with their artfully woven branches, and the rounded backs of the sheep in the background. They stopped by a fence. He turned her toward him, pushed her gently against the planks, and began rubbing his hands slowly from her hips up to her midriff. With intent focus and strength, he stroked her chest, those ridged walls in which her heart pounded, the fencing that enclosed her greedy lungs.

"This is me," she said, "here I am."

It was as if she forgot all the lonely summers—the desperation, the upheaval, the outrage. He whispered words in her ear she didn't understand, but no matter. They were standing in the riverlands the way they once had, and they had a life to look forward to, together. He's back, she thought. He has landed, and is truly home.

A letter arrived, written on heavy vellum, sealed with blood-red wax and stamped with a crown.

"I've been summoned by the king," James said. "Next week. You're to come, too."

He put the letter in the cupboard. She would brush his uniform. Did she have a dress that was suitable for the palace? She would accompany him, no matter what. If he was going to live ashore, she wanted to be part of that life. Without saying anything, she'd keep a close eye on what was happening when he talked with high-ranking gentlemen. Later on, at home, she'd draw her own conclusions, and they could discuss them together.

The family of four was sitting at the table. She wasn't hungry; the smell of food turned her stomach. Leaning back in her chair, arms crossed, she watched her husband and sons eat. She'd be sitting next to me now, a girl of eight, she thought. How strange that the boys who'd died—Joseph and Georgie—had simply vanished, while Elly is still here, growing with me and walking beside me. I'll keep it to myself. I know it's ungrateful. But it's how it *is*.

"I'll be gone by the time you visit the king!" Jamie bawled. His sea chest was in the hallway. In a few days, they'd say goodbye to their oldest son. They'd see his sturdy, thickset body sitting at the window of the stagecoach, unfazed and indifferent. They'd wave as the coach rattled off and disappeared, its cargo lashed to the roof.

"King George takes a keen interest in maritime navigation," James explained. "He foots the bill for our expeditions and keeps abreast of developments. I hear he's even fallen under Omai's spell. Of course, Banks and my esteemed colleague Furneaux wasted no time in showing off their prize at the palace."

His voice was monotonous and harsh with annoyance. James had a low opinion of the captain of his sister ship: the man was sloppy and displayed little patience with discovering, and he couldn't be bothered meticulously charting new lands. What's more, he turned a deaf ear to James's instructions. He was slipshod about airing the hold and didn't insist his sailors eat fresh food or bathe every day. James suspected that Furneaux was just as lax about matters of hygiene as his crew, although he apparently had no problem bringing a cheerful native back to England. Omai couldn't believe his luck and took to London like a fish to water. All and sundry wanted a glimpse of him, to hear him pronounce the inappropriate greeting the sailors had taught him on board. A wonder, such ribald language from the mouth of someone from the other side of the world! Omai was warmly welcomed at balls and banquets. Someone had tried—without success—to teach him to ride a horse, though he did learn to skate, or just about. He owned a hunting outfit and a gun, and could even walk while wearing elegant shoes. Sandwich and Solander had presented him to the king, whom he'd greeted with childlike glee.

On the homeward leg of his journey, while staying at the Cape of Good Hope, James had heard tales of that charming islander's social life. It had infuriated him. What was the point of pulling a native out of his own environment? Londoners gawped at the vain man as if he were a rhinoceros or a kangaroo, but by next season, he'd be old news. And then? James also found Omai to be dull witted and childish. If you were going to bring a fellow all the way back from the South Sea, you might as well find one who had something to say, so you could compile a dictionary of his language, for instance, and write the history of his island. Ice skating, indeed! The man would have to be returned home. Then, his envious tribesmen would no doubt rob him blind and cast him out.

"What are you going to say to the king?" Nat asked.

"I am going to suggest that Omai be sent home. He doesn't belong here, he'll just be unhappy."

The boy looked alarmed. "Will you bring him back yourself?"

James didn't reply. A tense silence fell abruptly over the table. Cutlery clattered.

"We'll discuss it first. Let's see what happens."

Both boys sat hunched over their plates. A knife scraped against the crockery. Elizabeth listened to the chewing and the swallowing. She tried to think of nothing.

The king had sent a coach to bring them to the palace. After the audience, the same coach stood waiting for them at the bottom of the stairs, to drive them home along the river. James and Elizabeth listened to the stamping hooves and gazed out over the water. James pulled off his gloves and stuffed them into his pocket. He briefly rested his right hand on her cheek.

A week had gone by. She noticed how quickly his days settled into a routine. In the morning, he read the mail and wrote letters, sitting at the pristine table. In the afternoon, he left through the garden gate to visit his usual taproom, where he was no doubt welcomed by friends and acquaintances, eager to listen to his yarns. Once he'd had his fill of that, he came back home. Elizabeth would be there, busy in the garden or kitchen. His travels hardly came up, and they didn't discuss the future. In the rooms and hallways, they gave each other a wide berth. But at night, in the cramped bed beneath the window, they rediscovered each other.

Jamie left for school the day before their meeting with the king. His smooth boyish face showed no trace of fear or insecurity. He did what had to be done: dragged his chest outside, gave his boots a final polish. James took him aside to give him the names of those to whom he wanted to send his regards. She watched father and son standing beneath the palm tree at the bottom of the garden, and all at once she pitied the boy who so doggedly followed in the footsteps of a father whose achievements he could never hope to match. Jamie stuck to the straight and narrow. But was that a problem? Perhaps he was happiest doing what was obvious. He wasn't an anxious child, and he seemed impervious to grief. She had to remind him of the anniversary of his sister's death, otherwise he'd forget. He would visit the grave with her if asked, but not of his own accord.

On the morning he left, Jamie shook James's hand and kissed his mother. Nathaniel stood transfixed by the ruckus—the coachman bustling about, shouting orders, lashing down the chest, shoving the broad hindquarters of the horses—and the only thing he got from his brother was a punch on the shoulder. Jamie laughed as he stepped into the coach. Nat moved closer to Elizabeth and reached for her hand. He's scared, she thought. He is. He's thinking about the future; how in precisely one year, he'll climb aboard that selfsame coach and be carted away. He's wondering if he wants to go, if he's up to it. He's imagining the school: its wild and whooping pupils, the lonely sleeping arrangements in the attic dormitory, the joyless meals. He does have feelings about all of that. Nat does.

James nudged her and pointed to a ship in the distance—slow and stately—drifting past on the calm waters. It made her sad, although she couldn't say why, but James's eyes lit up. She'd been surprised by his behavior at the palace. She'd expected him to stand off to one side, stiff and stern, or to be almost obsequious in the presence of such luminaries. His sister's unkempt house in Yorkshire appeared before her eyes. James's humble origins were a thorn in his side, and he often felt beholden. Tied in knots, he struggled between subservience and contempt.

He had, however, greeted Lord Sandwich with a hearty handshake and was quickly immersed in a lively conversation. She watched. What she saw wasn't a nobleman and a farmhand, but two equals. Philip Stephens joined in. She heard James chuckle aloud, relaxed and earthy. The king's entrance did nothing to dampen the mood. He had a round, pleasant face and approached James of his own accord. James bowed as if it were something he did every day of the week. How odd. Had this last voyage changed him? If so, how, and why? What had happened in the South Sea that allowed him to let go of his anger and act with such courtesy?

There were speeches, praise, and tributes. The long-awaited promotion. James accepted it all with grace, and even gave a brief reply, thanking all those present by order of rank. He closed by saluting his crew, thus calling to mind the image of a hundred ragtag sailors rubbing shoulders with these dignitaries clad in brocade and velvet.

"Did you enjoy yourself?"

He nodded. They were almost home. The observatory's dome on the green hillside had come into view.

"The king might seem like a simple fellow, but he has a good head on his shoulders. In fact, his interest in Harrison's clock really saved me. He was so fascinated by it that he set to work himself, conducting experiments in the palace. The Admiralty had washed their hands of the project; they thought it was too expensive, and Harrison too hard to handle. The king persevered, but with little success. The clock raced ahead, or ran backward, or even came to a complete standstill. But the king isn't one to give up easily; he loved those instruments, and wanted to see them live up to their potential. Then they found a powerful magnet elsewhere in the room, near to where the experiment had been carried out. Once they'd removed it, the clock kept time perfectly. The king's stubbornness did me a huge favor."

The reliable clock on board had told him the exact time in London. Wherever he was, he could calculate the difference with the time back home by comparing it with the local time, determined by the position of the celestial bodies. Once he converted the time into distance, he knew his exact location. He'd explained it to her, and sometimes she even understood it. She knew he treated the clock like a precious object. When he'd gotten back, the first thing he'd done was visit the suspicious, grumbling clockmaker. Later on, he even sent Harrison a cask of port.

James went to bed the minute they got home. She heard him dragging his feet up the stairs. Had he seemed pale, even ashen, on the way back? She'd been so relieved about how well the audience had gone, she hadn't paid much attention. Perhaps he was simply tired, and the ceremony had worn him out. She'd shaken hands with both the king and the queen—a small woman who hadn't said a word. Elizabeth held her hand up to the light and inspected it. This had to go well. If James could keep himself under control in this sort of company, and not become cross, he might have a future ashore. Up until now, he had only felt free in his role as a commander. During the first voyage, he had successfully held his ground with Banks, and during the second, he overcame all his remaining doubts, and took it for granted that people would respect and obey him. That's how he'd seemed this afternoon.

He could become an advisor to the Admiralty, a wise and experienced captain who would guide other people's voyages of discovery. He could supervise the supply plans, the shipbuilding industry, and the promotion policy. He would be home in the evenings with her and Nat, listening to the violin, talking with his second son about the future. She put it out of her mind. It wasn't up to her.

That afternoon, he'd been given command of one of the largest ships, one with seventy-four cannons on board. She wasn't sure what kind of pull that exerted on him. She could ask Hugh Palliser, but decided to hold off, afraid that actively plotting a strategy might work against her. Things had to sort themselves out, without her pulling any strings.

The Admiralty sent a message the next day: the appointment had been withdrawn, and Captain Cook was kindly requested to apply for a position as commanding officer at the Royal Hospital for Seamen in Greenwich. The command of the seventy-four cannons had been nothing more than a formality, because only captains who had been in charge of such massive ships could apply for a posting at the hospital.

"Sitting around," James said. "You do nothing but sit around all day. There are four captains, and all four have nothing to do. It's not even a hospital anymore, just a home for retired sailors. The pay is generous. It comes with an official residence. A disguised form of retirement. An honor. Costs of heating and lighting are included. All I have to do is write a letter."

She resisted the urge to race inside for a pen and paper. Was she imagining things, or was he looking poorly? It seemed as though the stuffing had gone out of him; at the garden table, he propped himself up on his arms.

"Are you all right?" She regretted the question as soon as it slipped through her lips. He straightened his back and placed his feet together. His expression remained closed.

"How could I feel anything but good here?"

Beads of sweat dotted his upper lip. But it was warm, even under the shade of the quince.

"What do you think, Elizabeth, shall we go live in Greenwich, in that palace across the river?"

Yes, she wanted to shout, yes! A rolling lawn just outside the door. Marble corridors. Peace and quiet. Time for a new child to be born, a child they could watch grow up together. One who could run up and down the observatory hill, safe in the knowledge that his father would be at the table when he was finished playing and returned home. He? If James seized this chance, they'd have a daughter. She was sure of it. She said nothing.

But there was no end to her hopeful mood. She took every opportunity to leave the house and detour along the river. She looked to the other side. An official residence with staff. The measured pace of the hospital. The certainty that he would lie beside her, night after night.

Hugh Palliser came to talk things over with James. The two orbited the large table, which was once more cluttered with stacks of letters, a chart of the South Sea, an inkpot, and scissors. Elizabeth could hear their voices from the kitchen, where she was slicing onions and celery. If she concentrated, she could pick up shards of their conversation.

"We have to take him home. Clerke should be able to do it, with the *Resolution*, once it has been patched up."

Palliser's deep bass. Silence. Then James: "Outfit a ship with ninety crew to bring back one wrongfully seized native? I understand the sense of obligation. Omai should never have been brought here, but I would add other instructions to such an expedition. The northern rim of the Pacific Ocean has hardly been explored."

"We need to put our heads together," said Palliser. "There is no question that Omai has to go home, along with all his nonsensical gifts and possessions."

"But no firearms. He has to leave those pistols and hunting rifles behind. The man is a child. He might shoot his countrymen on a whim or out of recklessness. Then they will no doubt rob him and bash in his brains. He's been here more than a year. In that time, he could have learned a trade or a skill that would be useful back there. Then the other islanders might have accepted him."

"Well," said Palliser, "he can dance the polka. He can use a claw cracker to eat a lobster. He can make an elegant bow, and he carries a walking stick when he parades through town. I'm with you, James, we should have taught him carpentry or something."

"The way they build houses is perfectly suited to the climate. Our nails rust away, at least, the ones that aren't pilfered beforehand. I was thinking more along the lines of gardening. So he would learn about soil management, sowing, weeding, and harvesting. Then he could start a plantation and train young islanders to carry on the work. Grain. Potatoes. But Omai has no patience. To him, seeds are something you roast and eat. He is ignorant and in love with himself, but also as lively and good natured as a child. We will have to orchestrate his return with utmost care. Omai cannot help it; he has fallen prey to the fashionable curiosity of the masses. When does Clerke sail?"

She heard it. Clerke's leaving, not him. Hugh Palliser will make sure of that. He can see how exhausted and travel worn James is. Hugh is in my camp. Does that mean it's a battle—have we taken sides? I only want what's best for James. So he can step back from active duty and enjoy his success. I want him to have enough peace and quiet to put the finishing touches on his charts and publish them. So he can edit and release his journals, just the way he wants them, without having to rush. I will no longer be alone. I am entitled to married life, a genuine family. But there is no justice. There is only this one chance, this possibility of crossing the river and moving into the hospital.

She poured all her pent-up energy into stirring the soup. The sound of the wooden spoon clanging against the pan drowned out the men's voices.

That evening, James withdrew to the great room. Elizabeth strolled through the garden at dusk, watering the thirsty flowers. Through the small panes of the window, she spied him bent over the table. He was writing. Later, he came into the kitchen.

"I did it," he said. The pristine white letter gleamed in his hand.

The *Resolution* had finally docked in Deptford, ready to be unloaded. But first, there was a party. Lord Sandwich, the first lord of the Admiralty, decided to celebrate the homecoming with a reception on board, including a festive meal. He stood at the railing, his mistress by his side, welcoming the guests. The Navy band was playing on the afterdeck; intense sunlight reflected off the bells of the bugles. The portly Solander wobbled gingerly up the gangplank. Clerke was there, and Stephens. Hugh Palliser charged up in a coach from the Admiralty; he'd left his wife at home. Georg Forster, the scientist, looked disdainfully on, standing silently beside his son. In the tangle of gaily attired guests,

Elizabeth recognized William Hodges, the painter, as well as William Wales, the astronomer. It was a clear, dazzling late summer day. In the distance, she could see the domes of Greenwich's Royal Hospital. Now I have time to inspect this ship at my leisure, she thought, this innocent-looking wooden shell in which he sailed the sea, was almost crushed between the ice floes, and was tossed upon the waves like a dried leaf in a storm. I can take it all in, because it's a thing of the past; something that has been.

She followed James aboard, where she was swept up in the boisterous crowd. Glasses of wine were handed round, and a woman in a yellow dress proposed a toast to their safe return, their success, and the future! Sandwich clambered onto a platform and, once the ferocious applause had died down, began to speak at length. Elizabeth leaned against the railing and observed. They looked like racehorses, these illustrious gentlemen, with their elongated equine heads and spindly legs. James was a draft horse who had somehow wandered into the wrong stable. Once, he had allowed himself to feel intimidated by the differences, but that was a thing of the past. She saw him standing next to Hugh Palliser. Those two fed from the same trough. Hugh caught her eye. She nodded and focused on the speech.

Sandwich drew a list from his jacket pocket and announced the promotions, punctuated by cheers from the crowd. First, he mentioned the officers. Then he promoted Clerke to captain of the *Resolution*, offering him the ship on which they were standing with an elegant gesture. The wineglasses were topped up, and a sailor made the rounds with a tray full of savory pies. At last, James's name was called. The crowd hushed, and Sandwich proclaimed the Admiralty's resolution to appoint Captain Cook as the fourth captain of the Royal Hospital for Seamen at Greenwich. Elizabeth looked at her husband's face; it was devoid of all expression.

Sandwich ended his speech by saying, "To give you an impression of life on this magnificent vessel, Lieutenant Richard Pickersgill will now conduct a tour."

The lieutenant, a small, muscular man with sharp features, stood waiting at the door of the great cabin. A group of guests, mostly women, jostled around him. He urged them to be careful; the floors and ladder rungs were slippery. He pointed to their satin shoes, their slick soles.

She wanted to see the entire ship, to take it all in. She was embarrassed by the giggling curiosity of the company in which she unwittingly found herself. The women wanted thrills and titillation. They shrieked when Pickersgill brandished a whip, and covered their eyes when he showed them the trough that served as the crew's latrine.

She wasn't sure what she was hoping to find. It felt like a leave-taking. The dark wooden desk—the one James took with him to write upon—was still in the captain's cabin. She resisted the temptation to open its drawers. What was she hoping to find? A lock of a child's hair wrapped in paper? In a few days, the Admiralty's lackeys would cart the desk back through their garden and into the house, returning it to its familiar place in the hall.

Separated from the group, she wandered through the cramped spaces, climbed over ladders, and squeezed through narrow passageways. The air below decks was suffocating. She took a deep breath and was hit by the stench of rot and the sharp tang of decay, camouflaged by vinegar and sulfur.

All the leftover supplies had been taken from the ship and destroyed: vats of cured meat, crates of hardtack that had been gnawed by rats and maggots, and barrels of putrid water. But a hint of stink still clung to the wood.

She stood in the storeroom, her hands dangling at her sides. The floors and tiled walls of the cooking area had been scrubbed clean. How was it possible to prepare food for more than a hundred men in such a confined space? Three times a day, every day; even during storms and heat waves.

She descended to the holds where supplies were stored. James spent days before every departure working out a storage system. He took many factors into account: perishables had to remain dry, gunpowder and spirits needed to be kept under lock and key, gifts for the islanders were stored at the back, and so forth. He was always pleased with the resulting plan, which he regarded as classified information, something he only shared with a select group of dockhands. Everyone was astonished by the amazing quantity of items he managed to cram on board.

Stuffy and cramped: that was her main impression of the ship. When people imagine a voyage at sea, they picture vast expanses and infinitude. You have to be able to withstand being overwhelmed by the boundless immensity. But that was a misconception. Whoever embarked on a voyage had to reconcile themselves with captivity, with sleeping head to toe beside stinking men, and with being cooped up in the hull of a ship. You couldn't get off. You had to surrender yourself to the noise, the foul air, and each other.

Back on deck, a group was gathered around Pickersgill. He stood amid chests and boxes, which he opened one by one to reveal what they'd brought back. He sprinkled handfuls of scarlet feathers over the delighted ladies, he draped artfully woven swatches of some unknown fabric across the shoulders of Sandwich's beloved, and he threatened the assembled party with a brightly colored, ornamentally carved spear. Elizabeth retreated to the railing and observed the women putting feathers into each other's hair, rubbing the material between their fingers, and urging the lieutenant on. James was nowhere to be seen; must be in his cabin, lord and master of his ship for the final time.

She felt his body before she saw him. Hugh Palliser had sidled up beside her and cast her a questioning glance.

"A circus," she said. "They have no idea what they're seeing, what they are touching. No notion. It doesn't interest them."

"People usually see only what they already know. That's why the ladies stick feathers in their hair. You're right, it's rare to find any genuine curiosity regarding what these objects might mean to others. James has such curiosity. But he's an exception. And that takes courage." His shoulder pressed against hers. She allowed it to happen, didn't step aside.

Lieutenant Pickersgill pulled a glass jar from one of the chests and held it aloft, sloshing the fluid within it from side to side. When the liquid settled and the sediment drifted to the bottom, the squeals of the bystanders fell silent. A strand of black hair appeared through the cloudy alcohol, and two rows of glimmering pearls turned into teeth. Only then did the spectators see two hollows for the eye sockets, a flat, fleshy nose, and shreds of skin on the severed neck.

Sandwich's sweetheart let out a yelp and rushed to the railing to vomit. Women clung to each other, and even the men turned pale.

"Cannibals!" Pickersgill cried. "Hard to believe, but we were there. We conducted a scientific experiment. At first, we thought they were just horror stories. But it's true, they do eat their enemies. We invited them on board. I had procured this head. Our cook cut off slices and fried them like steak. Then we presented the dish of human flesh to one of the natives. He ate it all up!"

On deck, there was gagging, horror, disbelief. Some stepped closer to get a better look at the desecrated head; others turned and headed toward the gangplank. Just then, Sandwich appeared in the doorway of the large stateroom, saying dinner was served.

"Eating," said Hugh Palliser beside her. "It's all about food. We think we eat to maintain our health, but there is more to it than that. Would you care to join me?"

She couldn't suppress her slight nausea and turned her gaze toward the city.

"He did it," whispered the man at her side. "He wrote the letter, his request was considered and granted; it's all been signed and sealed. Soon, you'll be living near those domes."

She nodded. It had grown quiet on deck. She rested a hand on his arm and looked him in the eye. "Thank you," she said, "I can't tell you how grateful I am."

Chests and boxes were carried into the house. Bright colors adorned every corner and niche. In the hallway, a massive cloak of feathers on a stand glowed an orangey red; painted masks and woven baskets littered the floor of the great room. James carried a crate of nuts and seeds into the scullery. He set it down gently next to the shovel and hoe, and went outside to look at the sky. He raised his chin and filled his lungs with the late summer air.

"Too dry. I'll start planting as soon as we've had some rain. It's almost too late, autumn's on its way, but I'll do it anyway. I'll cover them with mulch when the temperature drops. When these plants start coming up, you won't believe your eyes."

The large table was also filling up. The Lords across the river had finally finished looking through the journals, charts, and drawings and had sent them to their house in Mile End. Elizabeth watched the disorderly piles growing, with more letters and research reports arriving by the day. The officers' diaries, which had, as usual, been confiscated, were gradually being released. There was an immense chaos on the table, an undertaking for the coming winter; a promise of collaboration, unity, and success.

James had taken the spade to dig some shallow seedbeds along the hedge; she saw him sweeping the excess earth beneath the shrubs. She took off her apron and followed him into the garden.

He straightened up and rested his hands on his back, his face contorting briefly; then he faced her and took her hand.

"I brought back some bulbs to plant near her grave. Tiny blue flowers with an unusual scent, almost like cinnamon. I kept them aside for her; for you both."

They walked through the hallway, careful not to knock over the carved oars or the spears, tall as a man, leaning against the walls.

"We'll sort all this out: give it away, put it in storage. First, I want the boys to see everything. It'll be fine."

She didn't care; she reassured him that a full house made her happy; she was thrilled and curious to hear the stories associated with the objects that had washed ashore here. He rested his right hand on her shoulder and held the bag of bulbs in his left.

They walked silently to the church. The gate was open and she led the way to the grave. The small stone carved with Elly's name stood upright in the grass. A dark flower bed had been dug out before it, filled with snapdragons, poppies, and violets. She plucked off the dead flowers with her thumb and index finger. Then she rested her hand on the stone.

James fetched some water and poured it on the parched earth. He poked holes in the ground with a stick so she could plant the bulbs. She smoothed the earth with her bare hands; a ferrous smell pricked her nose. Keep going, she thought, this is a job that has to be done; I am completing a task on top of the abyss. It has to be done. It's the surface I must take care of, nothing more.

She pushed the last bulb into the ground and covered it. James sat down on the grass and reached for her. She nestled between his legs and leaned against his chest. The flowers floated before her eyes like hazy flecks of color. He's imagining a one-year-old child, she thought; a child who can't yet speak, who beams with pleasure when she walks toward him. One of the children.

I see something else. He doesn't know my little girl. It's between her and me. Our shattered alliance lies buried six feet beneath us.

He held her tight. She stared straight ahead: green, white, and black. It's enough to bring tears to your eyes, she thought, but she didn't cry.

4

"He's not leaving," Nat said. "I mean, he goes out in the late afternoon, but by evening, he's back. If he's not at sea, is he still a captain? Will it always be this way? Is he allowed to wear his uniform if he doesn't have a ship? Will he still be here when I'm at the Naval Academy?"

She'd sat him down on a stool in the middle of the kitchen and draped a sheet around his shoulders. His boyish blond, satiny hair drooped over his collar. She pulled the comb through it with long, gentle strokes, applying pressure with her free hand to stop the detangling from hurting him.

"Sit still, Nat, I'm going to start cutting." The boy squeezed his eyes shut in anticipation.

"You think, Oh, that's going to hurt," he said, "but you don't feel a thing. All you hear is *krrrrt, krrrrt!*"

She carefully cut his hair to just beneath his ears. From time to time she stepped back to make sure she hadn't deviated from her intended line. A wreath of shorn hair lay on the floor around them.

"He'll still be a captain," she answered, "in his uniform. He won't have a ship anymore, but he'll help find ships for other captains. He's become an advisor; he gives guidance to others. And he'll write his book. When it's finished, you'll be able to read all about his most recent voyage. Or I'll read it to you."

Nat shook his head and giggled when the clipped hairs tickled his neck. "It's making my ears itch!"

She brushed his neck and ears with the corner of the sheet. Then the boy leapt off his stool and bolted out of the kitchen. Soon she heard him tuning his violin.

He's different, she thought; he doesn't look at things the way his father and brother do. He hardly shows any interest in the earth's dimensions and has no desire to go to sea. I should keep him home. He'll be miserable at the Naval Academy. They'll tease him, hide his violin or smash it. He'll be backed into a corner by those ruffians. I should protect him, but I can't. His course is set, no way around it; a constricting tether stretches from here to Portsmouth, and then out to sea. Nothing can stop it; other boys will be jealous of his opportunities, his position. It will be the end of him.

She saved one lock of blond hair and swept the rest into the hearth. There was a flash of bluish-green sparks, and the kitchen filled with a scorched tang. She wrapped the lock of hair around her finger and listened to the violin études.

She'd known for a few weeks that she was pregnant. Everything still fit, and it didn't show, but she knew. Joy flared up in her like a reflex, but then she felt instantly ashamed and overconfident. It all came down to control. She must fulfill all her duties with serenity and composure. Looking after Nathaniel, paying regular visits to Elly's grave, poring through James's journals from cover to cover. It would be no good to withdraw secretly into an alliance with a child who did not yet exist. She couldn't allow herself any gladness; first she needed to spend the autumn settling back into this house and making peace with its new, unaccustomed order.

James had accepted the appointment at the hospital, but they still lived in their own home. He had someone row him across the river whenever he needed to be on the other side. He was gone much of the time, because the accumulations that had settled in the ship after so many years at sea had to be carefully examined and distributed. The plants and seeds were packed up and shipped to Kew; the sketches of landscapes and tattooed individuals went to the atelier of Hodges, the painter, who converted them into formidable oil paintings; and the knowledge, the residue of the experiences that James had collected in his mind, had to be shared with scientists from various disciplines. He spent his afternoons in one tavern or another, conferring first with geographers and astronomers, then with biologists and physicians. He was so full of fascinating observations and ideas—about the spread of disease and the prevention of sailor mortality; the constellations in the Southern Hemisphere; the social structure of island populations, their religious rituals, their exotic manner of shipbuilding, their clothing or lack thereof—that he felt compelled to pass along that knowledge to other learned minds as soon as he could.

He was met with respect, even admiration. He was given a permanent chair at the meetings of the fellows of the Royal Society.

"Sometimes I almost feel they're about to stand up and bow when I walk in," he said. "It's getting out of hand."

But it did him good, and he enjoyed the sharp-witted discussions. The adulation didn't bother him, but he wasn't crazy about the thrill seeking of some of his associates. He'd return home scowling, and it would be a while before he could unleash his scorn and fury.

"Not a shred of genuine interest. Naked girls, that's all they're after. Atrocities and executions. Orgies. They may be aristocrats, schooled at the best universities, but all they want are the spicy details. The trouble is, they don't know how to think. Or to look. Take Lord Monboddo, for example, a judge, no less—you know the one, with dark hair and those doleful, rheumy eyes—we got to talking this afternoon, but he wasn't listening. All he wanted to hear was that the islanders are talking apes, because he believes the apes are our forefathers. He twists everything around until it fits his theory. They are people, I said, just like you and me. He backed down, disappointed. I could tell he didn't believe me."

James's busy schedule gave her more time. When he was away, she sat at the table and read his logbooks. She dutifully absorbed the geographical positions, the astronomer's notes, the weather reports, observations of the sea, its color and surface—and promptly forgot it all. She paid careful attention to the passages in which she could hear James thinking and speaking about the behavior of the crew or the fascinating animals and people who inhabited the other side of the globe.

She was always tense. She couldn't resist trying to organize the material in the best and most attractive way possible, to give future readers a clear impression of her husband's genius and courage. But beneath all that, she was afraid, and from time to time, that fear launched its warning signals. But afraid of what?

Disruption, that came the closest. There were times, like this morning, when she stood stock still in the garden and realized that her waistband was tighter than it had been a week ago—she wrapped her arms around her belly, sucked her breath in—and it became clear how hard she had been clinging to the fiction of a joyous homecoming. Not only the idea that everything would be all right, that her loneliness and bravery would of course be lifted and rewarded, but that now, things *had to* turn out all right. A compelling urgency marked in her the image of a man who, after his wanderings, is finally fulfilled and able to settle down beside the woman who's been waiting faithfully. She'd held on to that vision for many years, and now it was time for it to become a reality.

Briefly, with her arms folded protectively around the growing infant, she realized that her line of thinking was like a ribbon stretched above reality—a shimmering guideline leading her to a place where everything would be fine. Everything. Beneath it, the day-to-day

shadows raged past. Half-formulated thoughts loomed up out of dark
nooks and crannies; she glimpsed barely recognizable phantoms of people, of children. If she stood as still as she was now, leaning against the
sturdy trunk of the quince, she could briefly sense the threat that made
her knees buckle.

Maybe the man who came home wasn't the man she'd been expecting. She'd recognized his scent that first night, had lain alongside his
body like water, like a stream in a familiar riverbed, but by then it was
morning. Then they had wrapped their nighttime bodies in the same
clothes they'd left lying on the chairs, their unity cleaved by daylight. He
had come home to a different house, she could see it in his stony face:
the way his heavy brows jolted skyward when he first heard Nat's violin.
She saw how he swallowed his questions and comments, bottling them
up, as if in an effort to overcome the hurdles and pitfalls in pursuit of a
flawless and sweet-smelling field of grass.

Delight in this new pregnancy was part of the illusion. No, she
checked herself, it wasn't an illusion, that heavenly field of grass did
exist, it had to be there. But it was nothing but an empty hull, the surface of a complexity she couldn't oversee. The ghosts of other children
were lurking behind this new baby, in a yawning ravine of discrepancy
and reproach. She'd watched Joseph and Georgie die. James hadn't. She
was the one who had let Elly die because of her carelessness. Not him.
Where was his rage, his curiosity? Why wouldn't he allow the children
he'd never known to come back to life through her stories? Why didn't
he heap blame upon her; why wasn't she punished?

They weren't together in that darkness of half-understood thoughts
and fears. No, their union, glorious and triumphant, rose above all that.
It played out in a new life, heralded by a radiant fresh start: Greenwich,
a new daughter, a well-written travel book. That was the truth that
pinched her in her tight skirt, the reality that was spread out on the
table in the form of logbooks and journals, the truth that connected

and united them. She stepped free of the tree trunk and went inside the house, their house.

"Come, let's go for a walk," he said. "Wear something warm." He was slouched at the kitchen table, his legs outstretched. Nat's violin played in the distance, a mournful tune, repeated over and over with different accents and new embellishments. She stood listening—spellbound, absorbed—until James took her arm and led her outside. He turned into the lane between the pastures. Gray October light—almost lavender— was hanging over the fields, interspersed with wisps of mist. She offered him her arm and involuntarily adjusted her step to his: right with his right foot, left with his left. He smiled and squeezed her hand.

"We need to talk. Too many distractions at home. Better outside."

Yes, she thought, a chat. Tell him what I think, about the feelings, shameful and out of balance. She remained silent.

"There was a letter from Portsmouth," he said, "Jamie's report. He's doing well; his drawings especially are a cut above average. They take the students out on a coastal vessel so they can sketch the landscape, all the cliffs and coves and rock formations. Jamie has the knack. He'll make a fine cartographer. Reliable. Precise."

That's because he has no imagination, she thought. Their oldest was a serious boy who took life as it came. She could just see him sitting on the afterdeck of the training ship, a drawing board on his knees, staring at the coast. There he'd see stratified rock and small streams plunging down ravines into the sea. No knights on galloping horses, no burning fortresses or cliff-top damsels in distress.

"I hope Nathaniel will do just as well next year," James grumbled. "I am worried about him. He is pale, and not keen on things boys his age usually take an interest in. Does he have any friends? He never plays outdoors. I only see him leave the house to visit that old organist. I do not know Nat as well as you do. Do you think he will be ready for the Naval Academy, or should we wait another year?"

Now's the time to speak up, she thought. There are people who aren't happy on a boat, and their son is one of them. But James would never understand. No, he wouldn't accept that.

"Nat's interested in music." She tried to keep her voice low and calm. "Mr. Hartland thinks he's gifted: a talented musician. Nat should be studying with a professional violinist. Mr. Hartland says the boy is a joy to teach. He picks everything up on first hearing, and it's a pleasure to listen to him play."

"And then?" James halted and turned to face her. "Become a violinist? What is that? Unthinkable! It's not even a profession. My sons will become seafarers. I have added both their names to my muster lists almost from birth. Nobody is handed such a chance. They cannot throw it away. A bugler in the Navy, if needs must, but he shall go to sea!"

"James, he doesn't want to."

His eyes grew dark. "All my sons are destined for the sea. Two— Joseph and Georgie—have died. So the other two are responsible not only for their own careers, but for those of their dead brothers, as well. What Nat wants doesn't come into it."

He turned his back and stormed off. She managed, only just, to keep up; she had to focus all her attention on matching his pace, leaving her no energy to respond to his words.

"Music is nothing but decoration," he went on. "A painter can at the very least show people things they cannot readily see in real life. A writer can tell a story, or explain something. But music? That's on the periphery, a mere frill."

She thought of Mr. Hartland playing the organ at Elly's funeral. A frill? It was the only thing of substance she could remember from that morning.

"I don't want my sons left out in the cold. They were born to play a central role. That could be a modest role, perhaps even an insignificant one, but one at the focal point of progress. On my ships even the youngest carpenter's mate takes part. My job, and theirs as well, is to investigate and describe the world. We can only make improvements based on what we know. Not moralizing, or opinions, but observation. There is only *one* reality, and it must be faced. That's how it is."

A watertight argument, she thought. It's true, the way he puts it. No one would disagree with him. Yet it made no sense. One reality? Wasn't it evident every day that the house he inhabited was different from the one in which she lived?

Take the kitchen. Try to see it through the eyes of a researcher. There's a father, a mother, and a pale son of eleven. They are eating. When they're finished, the mother clears away three plates. But that's not how it is. There's another reality hiding behind that one, one in which the kitchen is swarming with children: the seven-year-old Joseph, slumped in his chair. Although he's still sickly, he's at the table, and his eight-year-old sister, Elly, is feeding him. Georgie is in a high chair, a chubby toddler cheerfully banging his wooden spoon against his empty plate. The researcher may not see this hustle and bustle, but Elizabeth does. She often has to keep herself from setting the table for the others. Three plates, no more.

"Do you understand?" James asks. He's modified his pace. "I want to help them. They don't have to do it all on their own. I'll support them, stand behind them. It'll work out, you'll see. Nat lacks vigor because he's growing so fast. You need to feed him plenty of fresh meat and a variety of vegetables. He's a good boy. Different from Jamie, but still a good boy."

They'd completed a long circuit through the fields, and their house came into view. Fanciful notions, she thought. I'm imagining things because of all the changes and the stress. I've had to think on my own for so long that now it's hard to rely on him. Yet I must. He has to make peace with the realities of life on land, and I have to allow for that. Not by nagging and balking, but by finding out what he wants, how he sees things. Working together, listening. That will give me peace of mind, too.

The image of the happy, overcrowded kitchen, so clear she could almost touch it, evaporated.

They returned to an empty house. Elizabeth lit the lamp and peeked into Nat's room. Empty. The violin was gone, the sheet music, too. He was at his teacher's house.

James was rooting around in the scullery. She heard a dull pop, and then some liquid splashing into a glass.

"Cheers!" He raised the bottle as he came back in. "Outstanding port. Banks sent it over, to thank me for the shipment of specimens I sent to Kew. I'll pour you one."

A reddish-brown color with glints of light, the syrupy liquor clung to the inner curve of the glass. She took a sip; a sweet, comforting taste. The alcohol stung the back of her throat and her nose, making her sneeze. He topped her up.

"The transport of seeds all over the world. A shame people don't realize how important that is. Banks is an exception. The Admiralty focuses on developing trade routes, the king wants to enlarge his territory, and the Royal Society aims to expand its knowledge. The supply of food is not a priority unless it has some direct bearing, as with the sauerkraut. Such a pity."

She felt her muscles relax under the liquor's influence. James's father, the cross old man from Yorkshire, had always worked the land. James had grown up hearing about the condition of the rye, the best time to plant onions, the threat of a failed harvest. Although James had left the land behind, he continued to think in terms of sowing and reaping. Hadn't he plowed and planted his seed within her, year in, year out? Then he would leave, like a true farmer, only to return when the time was ripe. Failed crops. Rot. That must have hurt and tormented him. More than that.

"The climate on most of the South Sea Islands is so favorable, you could harvest at least twice a year. That's why there is such abundance without the inhabitants having to lift a finger. Whenever somebody is hungry, they toss a stone in the air and down comes a coconut. Tilling the soil, aerating it, creating room for worms and insects; not eating the seeds right away, but putting them in the ground, covering them, watering them, weeding. I have explained it over and over. It is rarely understood. Patience does not come easy. They pull the grapes off the vines when they're still as small as drops of water. Then they screw up their faces and spit out the bitterness. Try to explain things in a language you have yet to master.

"On this trip, I revisited a few of the plantations from the previous voyage: overgrown, neglected. Sometimes a mustard plant or a pumpkin had survived and spread its tendrils. But mostly, there was nothing left. Omai should really learn the art of gardening and remain here until the harvest. But, sad to say, he lacks character and requires immediate results."

They drank some more of the heady port. Listen, she told herself. This is important, even though I don't understand why. I can hear the passion. I can picture him, looking for a level plot of land on which to set out his plants. The sailors are swimming in the bay with the island girls, shouting and laughing: no doubt, some seeds will also be sown there. James turns his back in disgust. He fears the spread of disease but can't stop what's happening. No, he won't sit under the palms with a princess, no fear of that; instead, he'll plunge his spade, brought from England, into the ground, and turn over the foreign soil. Then he'll plant his carefully selected seeds, with a seriousness his crew can't understand.

She nodded. He looked at her kindly with his deep-set eyes, which, in the lamplight, seemed almost black. She would help him, she must, no: she *wanted* to help him make his new book a success. A book whose every page would show off his seamanship and his consideration; a book in which his ideas about nutrition and cultivation would capture every reader's imagination. Tomorrow.

Her train of thought was interrupted by a noise in the kitchen. Nat came in with the violin case slung over his back. His hair was damp from the fog.

"Did you enjoy playing?" Elizabeth asked. "You were gone a long time." Nat muttered something and avoided looking at her as his eye slid over the table on which the bottle of port and the cut-crystal goblets stood gleaming. He turned to put his violin away. Those narrow shoulders, she thought, those long, spindly legs. What will happen to that child? A few months ago he still crept into bed with me, and now he doesn't want to look at me.

"To bed, young man. It's time," James said. "Sleep well!"

Nat paused in the doorway and looked at his parents. He swallowed, seemed about to speak, but then ran up the stairs.

Just one more glass. James patted her cheek while he poured. "He'll catch up. It's a lot for him to get used to: his father's here, and his brother's gone. It'll all blow over by tomorrow. We've got to pay more attention to his meals."

She gazed up at him from her chair. He was awfully thin for a man obsessed with food. He'd lost weight since he'd been home. The fire in his belly burned more fiercely than it did in other men.

He sat down and described how difficult it was to provide his men with enough fresh meat.

"When we are becalmed, they can fish; then it's a question of too much rather than too little. Once ashore, we start trading right away: beads, knives, and fabric in exchange for pork. The problem comes with the longer stretches at sea; sometimes weeks or months go by with no chance to forage. That is the reason I take along the animals. Absurd, makes the deck crowded and disorderly, and a lot of manpower goes into feeding the animals and mucking out their pens. The chickens and geese get soaked whenever a wave crashes over, and then they develop avian fever. But if I keep them below decks, we all choke from the stench, and there's a good chance they will suffocate, as well. And that's just the poultry. I also had sheep, a goat for the milk. Cattle! People often bring animals on board with them, as well, for company, or for entertainment. I can forbid it in the sailors: monkeys, cats—chuck 'em overboard. But I have to allow more leeway for the so-called scientists, though I insist they keep their animals locked up in their cabins. Take that yapper of grumpy old Forster's! Forster never had a kind word for anyone, but he always had that little dog on his lap. I'll give him one thing: when I was sick, they slaughtered it for me. Later, the officers told me he cried like a baby. They fed me broth made from Forster's four-footed friend, dog steaks for three days running. It did me a world of good."

Sick? James was never sick. She had to finish reading his journals, and soon. He was evasive when she sounded him out.

"Colic. Must have been something I ate. I developed a terrible case of the hiccups from the miserable purgative the doctor gave me. But I perked up, thanks to that dog. It was nothing, over in no time."

In bed. There, they could bridge the ravine of unshared experiences that separated them. Her worries about Nat became just words. The anxiety about James's illness suddenly seemed ridiculous. They both sank into a deep sleep.

"Lord Sandwich wants *one* book," James announced. He'd spent the morning at a meeting with the Admiralty, across the river. Its effect on him was equivocal, but she couldn't quite put her finger on why. He seemed more energetic, that was clear; he paced with longer strides and at a faster clip. Had he enjoyed his crossing in the Admiralty's yacht? Imagined himself back at sea? But there was something else: a slight hint of hurt in his gaze. When he was among men of science and letters, he was no longer the commander: he was at best their equal, but in his own eyes, he was much less than that. She could sense that insecurity.

"Forster will write one half: observations and reflections on plants, animals, and soil conditions. His son will lend a hand. I like him. Congenial young man. Speaks better English than his father. But I am afraid I cannot avoid dealing with that old codger. Arrogant devil. He is well educated, knows a lot, and is not shy of boasting about it. Sandwich seemed rather irritable to me. Curt, almost snappish."

"What do they want from you?"

"It's about *my* journey. I will write the story. Then, science can add its commentary in the form of Forster's philosophizing. I see that as a form of illustration, similar to Hodges's engravings and the charts I will provide along with the text. I want to be at the helm. I worked hard on that journal during the voyage, here's my fifth draft!"

He stood and rested his palms on the open manuscript. It was in chaos, all muddled between the lines on the pages. Crossed-out sentences; tiny scribbles accompanied by arrows and underscores; passages jotted diagonally in the margins; hastily pasted notes with even more addenda; and running throughout, exclamation marks and heavy lines penned in red ink.

She sat beside him at the large table.

"Start over," Elizabeth said. "Now you have the time and enough peace of mind, you can prepare the final version."

No, he would not be rushed. Not by that money-grubbing Forster, who demanded a fortune for his contribution, and not by the threat of being beaten to the chase by some crew member who had managed to hide his notes from the Admiralty. It was his book; his tempo.

She said that the general public could do with fewer nautical details. Just the time, place, and weather conditions. The day-to-day entries he'd collected under the title "remarkable occurrences" were of much greater value. What the natives looked like in New Zealand, Tahiti, or on that mysterious Easter Island: their manner of dress, tattoos. How they established contact, what he gave them as gifts, and what he received in return; their festivals, ceremonies, language; the misunderstandings, the remarkable friendships—those were the crucial things, the things the public would want to read again and again.

He listened. They thumbed through the pages. Here and there, his eye was caught by a particular passage: he'd smile and reread it.

"When I left Raiatea—that is an island to the north of Tahiti," he recounted, "I bid farewell to the chief, Orio. He had given us a royal welcome, even had his daughter dance for us. He liked me, and wanted us to exchange names, so that, to some extent, I would stay behind with him when I left. My sons, he said, would always be welcome. Such a dramatic farewell, he begged me to promise I would return. I couldn't do that, and I didn't want to lie to him. Once he understood that I was in earnest, he asked the location of my 'marai.' That's what they call their burial place, but it is more than that: more like an open-air church, a place to make offerings and hold gatherings. He wanted to know where I would be buried. I was moved and had to think carefully before answering him. How can a sailor ever know for sure? I felt humbled remembering all the bodies we had slipped into the sea on our way back from Batavia, when just a month earlier I had been convinced of a safe passage for all. There are no guarantees."

Elizabeth listened quietly, her hands in her lap. She saw the tears in his eyes.

"Stepney, I said. Here, where we live, our parish. They had trouble pronouncing that strange word. Orio repeated it until it sounded almost right. Then, all the islanders who were gathered on the beach to say goodbye took up the chant: it resounded from a hundred throats. Stepney is Cook's burial place. Stepney, Step-ney!"

"Who knows, maybe you were telling the truth," Elizabeth said. "You live here now. It looks as though you'll stay. Your extraordinary friend might as well imagine the graveyard in Stepney. You certainly weren't lying."

Editing the journal gave structure to the days. In the morning, while Elizabeth went to the market or brought flowers to the child's grave, James polished the definitive version of his travel book. After lunch he went into town to talk with someone or other, to keep an appointment, or just to have a drink at the pub. Then it was Elizabeth's turn to sit at the large table and read what he'd written. Pencil in hand, she corrected the spelling and syntax. Sometimes she drew a question mark beside a passage that was unclear. At first, she was reluctant to delve into the notes that were obviously not meant for her; she felt like a spy, an undercover observer in a male domain. She allowed herself to be drawn into a world where there was no place for her.

She told herself that she had to keep him from making stupid mistakes. The negotiations with the Admiralty were complicated enough; she didn't appreciate Forster's denigrating remarks about the lack of literacy and style among certain navigators.

While that made sense and was realistic, the truth was, she could hardly put the story down. It crept under her skin; she thought about it when she was strolling along the market stalls, and couldn't let it go when she listened to Nat playing his violin. Of course, it was all about fear: the dangers of horrific snowstorms near the South Pole, waves as high as a house, or treacherous shallows. But also about the extraordinary, paradisiacal situations in which the men found themselves—the half-naked women with tattooed buttocks, the tribal leaders who freely offered their spouses, and the wild, nocturnal dance parties.

Most fascinating to her were the glimpses of James that emerged from his journals. The man she loved, who was part of her, the father of her children, became—in that book—someone unknown. Not a complete stranger, because his choice of scenes and subjects, even his way of looking and thinking, along with his detailed style of writing, all seemed familiar. And yet, running through the story was an amazingly altered James. A cruel man who flogged his sailors and withheld their rations; who left his men toiling with frozen ropes until they were ready to drop, then set course for the South Pole, even though the entire crew was pining for the tropics. A tormented man whose journal entries lamented the misery inflicted upon the islanders by the explorers' arrival. Those people, who had been happy and in possession of everything they needed to survive, became obsessed with fripperies: lined jackets covered in braiding, tin plates, and hunting rifles. His greatest remorse arose from his inability to prevent the spread of venereal diseases. Before the sailors went ashore, they had to march in front of the doctor, dropping their pants to have their genitals inspected with a spatula and magnifying glass. The seamen with a clean bill of health then ran cheering from the ship, but after two weeks, James noticed the natives sitting gingerly and walking bowlegged.

She saw the friendly, interested man who seemed unafraid of the strange and repulsive. He would have his crew row him to an unfamiliar coastline, where the natives waited, armed threateningly with rocks and spears. Alone, he'd step onto the beach, arms spread to show he carried no weapons, and walk toward the people until they raised their spears and began to shout. Then he would sit on the ground, make himself small. He'd pull objects from the pockets of his uniform and place them on the sand: a handkerchief, a few beads, some coins, maybe an onion. Then he'd wait. The launch would stay beyond the breakers, the crew watching with bated breath.

In time, usually someone would break free from the circle—the most curious, the bravest, or the youngest. James wouldn't get up but would calmly allow the fellow to approach. He'd proffer one of the objects, and withdraw it if the man showed no interest. After a while, the islander would kneel, bringing his face to James's level. Then James would move closer and rub noses with the foreign, painted, foul-smelling man.

Such passages made Elizabeth's cheeks tingle and her ears burn. Only later did she realize that they made her furious: her husband should have been here, sitting on the kitchen floor with his children. Instead, he became a father to the indigenous peoples. He cared for his crew with paternal affection: fed them sauerkraut, punished them for their offenses, took an interest in their backgrounds and ambitions. She thought of Nat, dashing up the stairs without saying a word.

Everything would be different. Everything had already changed. These journals were history; domestic life would begin now, in an undivided present time in which they would both stay put.

He was here, in this stark second half of autumn. He returned to her kitchen every day and talked about the conversations he'd had. He insisted she accompany him to receptions and dinners. She'd had a bodice made from that Tahitian fabric. The strange, inflexible fibers fit snugly across her bosom and the vivid red color was a perfect match for the black taffeta of the skirt. She didn't feel entitled to these clothes, though, and felt embarrassed when she tried on the outfit for James. She stood in the center of the room, stiff and reluctant, wanting to stamp her feet, howl, and run away, but instead, she twirled slowly until she was directly in front of him. "Good," he said. "Nice. We're having dinner with Sandwich tomorrow. Wear that!"

She did, and the entire evening, she felt self-conscious about her garish upper body. During these social events, it almost seemed as if she could only be partially present. She thought about Nat, at home with her mother, eating cold meat and soup. She listened in on conversations about shipbuilding and royal patronage, and nodded with approval when people paid careful attention to James's words. She spoke little herself, not because she was shy, but because she needed to focus on what was taking place at the table. The vastness of the world is hanging over our heads, she thought. Ships finding their way around the globe, unlimited possibilities. One can move into a newly discovered land as if it were a new house, exchanging crops and shipbuilding techniques. Nothing is too remote, or too strange. She observed it, but couldn't quite reach it, aware of her core, of the new baby growing beneath her silk taffeta gown.

Hugh Palliser slipped in beside her. He gently stroked the exotic material stretched around her upper arm, and smiled.

"You've been keeping James busy," he said. "He hardly has time for his duties as an advisor. I've been trying for weeks to get him to the wharf. I want him to take a look at the *Resolution*, and give me his verdict about the extent of the repairs. But he just goes on and on about his obligations in the city. What are you two up to?"

Her arm was still tingling from the pressure of Hugh's fingers. She hardly heard what he was saying, absorbed instead by the hubbub all around them, as if they were alone together at the heart of a whirlwind.

"I'm pregnant," she said.

He raised his glass to her. It was inappropriate to share such an intimate confidence with him. She blushed. They looked across at James, on the other side of the table. He was deep in conversation with Stephens.

"Why isn't James a fellow of the Royal Society?" she asked.

"It's only a matter of time," Hugh told her. "They'd be proud to welcome him into the fold, even though he lacks an academic degree. I hear they held a meeting to discuss him. A petition is being drawn up—a number of prominent members are planning to nominate him. Rest assured, he'll get the recognition he deserves. Don't you worry."

The topic across the table was ice. She heard James say he'd always believed that only fresh water could freeze. That the massive islands of ice he encountered around the South Pole must therefore be fragments of glaciers or rivers. That wherever there was ice, land couldn't be far off.

"Nonsense! *Quatsch!* Your reasoning is flawed," old Forster barked from his seat at the far corner of the table. James ignored the scientist and continued. He'd measured the temperature of the seawater: below freezing, yet still fluid. With severe cold, the packed ice floes appeared so fast that no land-based origin seemed possible. The only explanation was that, if it became cold enough, the sea would freeze. The ice might need to cling to something first, like a drifting tree trunk or the body of a whale, but there was no denying the existence of sea ice.

"Just as I have always asserted," Forster stated. "Though of course, no one listened."

"But the salt," James went on, "what happens to the salt? At first we thought that it was absorbed into the ice, but when we melted a lump from the sea, it dissolved into the purest, sweetest water. Did that mean the ice came from an expelled block of frozen river water after all? That was not possible, we found no evidence of a terrestrial origin—no dirt, branches, or grass—in any of the blocks of ice. Not ever."

Forster sniffed scornfully. He was slight in stature, yet he ate like a horse and never turned down an extra helping.

"We did, however, stumble on a new way of taking on fresh water," said James, who'd barely touched what was on his plate. "We would haul the floating icebergs on board, using a winch to hoist them once we managed to tie a rope around them. We would then fill up the smaller boats on deck, and whenever we needed fresh water, we would hack off a chunk and melt it in the kettle. Delicious. It could be that the salt is excreted during freezing, leaving the ice free of salt. If that is so, the sea must be growing gradually saltier. This matter has not yet been resolved to everyone's satisfaction, but at least now we know that seawater can indeed freeze, just as our learned friend Forster had asserted!"

Forster, who'd been about to rebut, snapped his mouth shut.

Hugh shook his head and adjusted the linen napkin on Elizabeth's lap. "A basket full of crabs," he said, under his breath. "If you don't watch out, those scientists will chomp each other's legs off. Sandwich is fed up; every meeting with Forster ends in a shouting match. What does James think about the partnership?"

"There is no partnership. They'll each write their own book, with no meeting of minds, no parceling out of subject matter. I think James would prefer to publish alone, but he feels insecure. Why don't you ask him yourself?"

Hugh shifted position and winced.

"Does it bother you much?" she asked. When he was young, he'd been seriously injured during an onboard accident; as a result, his left leg was almost completely paralyzed, and he was in constant pain. He tried not to let it show.

"Yes. Must be the weather. It's usually worse in the autumn. Don't pay it any mind, Elizabeth; what's the use. Shall we point a decent editor in James's direction? Would that help him with his writing? He might enjoy it more if someone could spur him on."

No, she thought, don't do it, it's our project, I want to help him, with no interference from the Admiralty.

"He's working on a new draft. I'm lending a hand. We can show it to someone when we're finished. Why don't we talk about this some other time? How's your wife, by the way; doesn't she ever feel like joining you?"

Hugh cast her a sidelong glance, and rested his fork and knife on his plate.

"Nothing but unpleasant subjects this evening. When we sit beside each other, we must attempt to talk about cheerful things. All is not well with my wife. In fact, she's mad. I have to arrange constant supervision to ensure she doesn't harm herself. But I'd rather not talk about it."

Elizabeth sought the right words to distract him, but her thoughts kept circling the subject of Hugh's wife. A profound melancholy, he'd once called it. She suspected the illness was related to childlessness.

Her cheeks reddened when she remembered she'd just told Hugh that she was pregnant. In a gesture of apology, she rested a hand on his arm—what was it about those arms? But she didn't say what she was apologizing for.

"Music! Why don't we talk about music," Hugh said with a smile, clasping her hand. He said he'd been to a concert the previous month where he'd heard a symphony written by a new, relatively unknown composer; a fellow who worked for the Hungarian court. Name of Haydn. He'd never experienced anything like it: fresh, inventive, and jovial, with an unprecedented depth. "You would have loved it, Elizabeth. Nat, too."

The party was breaking up. The women were invited to regroup in the drawing room, while the men continued talking, surrounded by glasses of port and smoking paraphernalia. Should she bring up Nat, ask Hugh for advice? Would he understand her concern? She couldn't do it. James was back now. He was the only one she should turn to. It wouldn't make any difference, anyway. To Hugh, the sea was as much a foregone conclusion as it was for James.

She gently hiked her skirt and left the dining room.

Sheets of rain pelted the windowpanes in the room that housed the big table. The lamps were lit first thing in the morning, and London was covered with dark-gray clouds. The family was obliged to eat winter vegetables: James had developed a hankering for the taste, a homesickness for carrots and brussels sprouts. Elizabeth was repulsed by the slightly sulfurous odor of cabbage and let the servant girl do all the cooking.

She set about editing the journal with renewed zest, as if to prove that she and James needed no help. And yet, after her conversation with Hugh Palliser, she wasn't so sure. She had no trouble correcting the spelling or fine-tuning a sentence here or there, snipping others in two; but when she tried to overhaul an entire chapter, or contemplate the sequence of scenes or a progression in the line of thinking, the text slipped through her fingers. She was too inhibited to move passages around, or to cross them out. She couldn't shake the feeling that a strict teacher—one wearing a velvet beret—was always standing over her shoulder, ready to poke holes in her work.

But James was satisfied with her help. He wrote more freely knowing that she would go over the text later. She decided for now to keep Hugh Palliser's offer to herself.

The garden was blanketed with brown leaves. She couldn't care less. Let the earthworms drag the leaves into the ground, one by one. Sometimes she saw a leaf poking straight up in the earth, like a vase. You had to wait, wait patiently; then most things worked out of their own accord. Except for those matters which would never be right again. She bent over the text. Pay attention. Concentrate. Slowly, like the worms, go over every word.

"I've been nominated!" James strode into the room. A sprinkling of raindrops covered his jacket; his hair was damp. "Twenty-five members! You only need three nominations, but I have twenty-five. Everyone: Banks, Solander, Stephens of course, and Maskelyne—even that old so-and-so Forster! I'm going to be a fellow of the Royal Society!"

He suddenly looked ten years younger, she thought, with his face relaxed, cheerful eyes, smiling. She stood to embrace him, holding her pen aloft behind his shoulder.

"I'll have to present an introductory lecture," he said, towering over her, "in the spring. A sort of article, like a scientific treatise."

His voice was high spirited, without any trace of insecurity or resentment.

"What are you planning to talk about?" she asked. She felt him take a deep breath; his rib cage expanded.

"Food," he said. "My topic will be nourishment."

The three of them were at the table. Elizabeth had asked the servant girl to make a large pie filled with vegetables, mushrooms, and mutton. Nat helped himself to seconds and was absorbed by talk of the Royal Society.

"Are you planning to talk about cannibals, as well? They eat people there, don't they?"

James put down his cutlery and looked his son in the eye. "Yes, they do, but I still haven't found out why. I'm not sure I'll bring it up. It would be better to talk about things of which I'm certain."

"Captain Palliser told us all about it. While you were away. They ate an entire boatful of men! Ten in all!"

"In New Zealand," James said. "That was in New Zealand. There was a clash, a misunderstanding. Fighting broke out. Their custom is to eat those they've defeated. It's hard to understand; our command of the language falls short. I didn't want to punish those people, because I don't understand them. We sailed away without taking revenge."

"And if you go back, will you give them their just deserts?"

Elizabeth straightened her back.

"I don't think so, Nat," James answered. "They don't know any better, and I can't change that. We're just passersby, we always set sail again. In any event, I won't ever go back there. I'm staying here."

She filled her lungs with air. All of a sudden, the light seemed lovelier, warmer. She inhaled the aroma of the steaming, savory pie, and felt content.

"Things were different in Tahiti," James told Nat, who was still hanging on his father's words. "There, they really do sacrifice people, intentionally. They decide in advance and plan it, like we do when criminals are punished here."

"Were you there? Did you watch?"

James sighed. "Yes, I've seen it. Afterward, I tried to talk about it, to ask if it was an execution, a way of punishing people, or something else: a sacrifice to appease their gods or some such. But it wasn't clear. I had the impression they didn't want to tell me, out of embarrassment, or perhaps because it's a secret. Hodges made a drawing; I'll show it to you."

"Do they also eat children? And babies?"

"No," James said, "I've never seen them eating children or babies."

Nat turned his attention to his plate. Elizabeth folded her hands over her belly. We. In this kitchen. A family, she thought, a damaged but happy family, having a meal together.

Part 2

5

The way things looked, there wouldn't be any snow at Christmas. The days were short, the clouds hung low, but the mild temperatures were reminiscent of September. In the garden, the robust leaves of the wild hyacinth, doomed to freeze in January, were poking up between the fresh green grass. Cover them with straw? Elizabeth shrugged. There was no point, and besides, why should she protect the garden when so many other tasks demanded her attention?

Jamie was on his way home, on Christmas leave. She had to order a goose for Christmas dinner. Select some red cabbage and Golden Reinettes, have her dress let out so she could breathe despite her growing girth. And she had to talk with James about Nathaniel.

The boy seemed to be clinging to his violin. He started playing in the morning before school, and Elizabeth had to force him to eat some breakfast. Then he would absently pick at his porridge until it was time to rush out the door, leaving behind a bowl still half-full. As soon as he came home, she heard the violin. When she asked what he was practicing for, he said it was a Christmas concert. He'd be playing with Mr. Hartland during the church service; he mentioned a composer with an Italian name—Corelli? Vivaldi? She couldn't remember.

"Would you like us to come and listen, would that please you?" she asked. He averted his eyes and stirred his grayish mush. Stupid, she thought. I shouldn't have asked. We'll just go, on Christmas Eve; James as well. We'll go to church and listen to Nat, whether he wants us there or not. Jamie will have to come, too. He has no say in the matter.

She stood, her hands supporting her back. She recognized the feeling: before anything was visible—besides the slightly expanding waist—the pregnancy announced itself with an inner slackening. Tendons and ligaments stretched to make room for the new baby. She could feel it, and although it hurt, she couldn't really call it pain.

Nat eyed her tummy. He knows, she thought. He seemed about to speak, but he said nothing and left the room. Why had it become so difficult to talk with him all of a sudden? It was her fault; before she could get a word out of her mouth, she asked herself if she was saying the right thing, or if she should say something else, or perhaps nothing at all. A peculiar awkwardness—one she couldn't quite place—had crept into her dealings with Nat. If she reached out to stroke his head, he pulled away skittishly, as if she were pursuing him. And again, he hadn't finished what was on his plate. Should she chase after him, was that what he wanted? And then?

The violin's open strings sounded from upstairs. He tuned the instrument with calm precision; it was a clear snub, a signal for her to keep her distance. He was only eleven, still a child. It was no good treating him like a man, or even a lover. She had to take care of him, lift the heavy burden from his shoulders. Don't dither, don't fret, and don't haggle.

Jamie would arrive tomorrow, with stories about the Naval Academy. She could hardly look forward to his arrival, worried as she was that Nat would find the encounter threatening. She shouldn't be such a pessimist. Christmas was coming, she was pregnant, and she would eat to help the baby grow. According to her calculations, the baby was due the end of May. When Nat left home, she and James would stay behind with a new baby. It felt like a betrayal.

She walked in the unusually balmy weather to Elly's grave. James was working on his book, and she slipped out without disturbing him. Was she ashamed of her frequent visits to her daughter? You had to let go, they said, accept the fact that children die, that you commit their bodies to the earth. It was risky to look forward to a new baby, because there was always a chance it would be taken from you. James knew that; when he was young, he'd watched three sisters and a brother die. His older brother passed away when he was twenty, shortly after James went to work for Walker in Whitby. Nothing was certain, and there was no justice. It made no sense, but deep inside, she was secretly convinced that the baby she was carrying would survive. There was no truth to the belief that every loss was rewarded, that you could keep one child alive by losing another. In fact, nothing people said was true. The idea that there was a God who prematurely called the sweetest children to his side seemed to her a malevolent fabrication, like the notion that the death of a child is meant to punish its parents.

In the week following Elly's death, the pastor had come calling to unfurl his theory about suffering. Frances offered him something to drink. Elizabeth listened to him slurping and gulping while he told her she had been chosen: God was testing her with such suffering and loss. She should consider herself fortunate to undergo such a series of tribulations: husband gone, baby dead, daughter killed in an accident. He helped himself to a slice of cake and chewed thoughtfully. Then he licked his fingers.

"Frances," Elizabeth called. "Will you show the pastor out immediately?"

For a fleeting instant she'd felt relieved to see the back of that unctuous oracle, but once he'd slunk off, she was struck with a paralyzing numbness. If there was no God who decided about life and death, if dying had no purpose, then everything was chance. She was powerless. Everyone was helpless. People invented stories about destiny and the meaning of suffering to avoid feeling such maddening helplessness.

Frances had been stunned, shocked by the rudeness toward the pastor, but she'd done what Elizabeth asked of her without hesitating.

"Where will this lead?" she asked.

Elizabeth shrugged. "It's not going any further. I will no longer listen to that man. He performs the church services; we can't change that. But we don't have to listen to him."

Speaking those words had cost her tremendous effort. Her body had never felt so heavy and unyielding. And yet, it had done her good to reject the syrupy kindness mistaken by most people for consolation. But then, but then. Frances wanted her to lie down, upstairs, a half hour in bed, some rest—but the minute she lay down, fear flared up, her head began to churn uncontrollably, until she lost all perspective, at the mercy of horrific images that took possession of her, unbidden.

Don't lie down, ever.

She briskly opened the gate and entered the cemetery. Two men were digging a grave near the wall of the church. She nodded curtly and turned her face away. I should wear a veil, she thought: a mask to protect me from the prying eyes of those who live an ordinary life, who are mindlessly in step with time. But don't I do that already? The menu for the Christmas dinner, the book, the baby! But not when I'm here, with her. Then, my face remains as it was at the hour of her death. Her loss is etched on my cheeks, and no one may see it.

"We sleep in hammocks; you can really harass someone by loosening the knots, so that when they try to climb in, they crash to the floor!"

Jamie's voice had deepened. Elizabeth marveled at her eldest son—his short, strong arms; that self-confidence; the pride with which he boasted about his training.

She beamed at James. It was so good to be reunited as a family of four. Even Nathaniel seemed to perk up, peppering his brother with questions. What are they teaching you; what time do you eat, and what do they serve; how often are you at sea; what are your friends' names; are you allowed to hang your hammock wherever you like; are you punished a lot? Have you ever been seasick; were you scared; do you get homesick?

The two boys went outside together. Elizabeth began clearing the table and glanced at a drawing of a rocky coast that Jamie had brought home for his father. The lines had been sketched with confidence, and the vegetation on the cliffs was carefully detailed. Frame it and hang it, she thought.

"I spoke with Sandwich yesterday," James said. "He's had it up to here with Forster, says there's no reasoning with the fellow. Yet he's reluctant to send him packing. The Admiralty has invested heavily in Forster. There's a wealth of information in that man's notes; you can't just throw it all away. I can't imagine how Sandwich will resolve the matter. Glad I'm not in his shoes."

"Did you bring up your book?" Elizabeth asked. Thirteen dark-blue notebooks lay on the table: the latest version of his travel journal. James had been working hard the past few weeks. He'd spent hours studying the next-to-last draft, reading between the lines, trying to extract the essence of the story from the scribbled notes and added comments. While writing, he felt inhibited by the idea of the public reading his words, and he repeatedly asked her about passages that might prove offensive. But she wasn't one to judge. She was fascinated by his description of a ceremonial deflowering in which the onlookers had offered enthusiastic comments, as well as his speculations regarding faithfulness and infidelity, and his allusions to the crew's unbridled behavior. As she read, the aroma of Tahiti seemed to fill her nostrils. He described how it was—the warm green sea, filled with naked girls shamelessly floating on their backs—and what he had found there and all the ideas it had stirred up in him. It never occurred to her to disapprove. She paid attention to the syntax and punctuation, and turned a blind eye to the subject matter.

"Sandwich offered to have the whole thing looked over by an advisor. He mentioned a name, Dr. John Douglas, a canon from Windsor. He hinted that it was the king's idea, but you know what Sandwich is like: he keeps things close to his chest when it suits him. I have the distinct impression we have no choice in the matter."

Elizabeth thought about the king's wish to have the travel book edited. She'd expected to take it hard—as an insult, or a vote of no confidence—but instead, she felt relieved. The manuscript was presentable: most of the spelling mistakes and awkward sentences had been cleared up. They'd put their heads together and paid serious attention to the story line. It was Christmas, James would stay home, and there was a baby on the way. Maybe the time for a joint project had passed. Let him consult that man of the cloth. Why not?

"You could let that fellow take a look. Send him the first five notebooks, see what he says."

"You wouldn't mind?" He took the volumes from the stack and set them to one side.

"Not at all. If it's all right with you."

He stood near her and stroked her hair. "You've helped me so much," he said. "I'm no writer. It's a huge undertaking for me, and I never know when something's finished. How should I move from one scene to the next? What am I to do with all the trivial details, the ones I don't want to leave out, the ones that bog the story down? I had another look yesterday at that horrible book by Hawkesworth. He gets everything wrong as far as the facts go, but he keeps you spellbound: he knows how to spin a yarn. I just don't have the gift."

She took the notebooks from him. "Wrap them up and send them off. Let that man help you. If he turns out to be another Hawkesworth, we'll figure something out."

She felt buoyant with relief. Christmas dinner! She'd invited Hugh Palliser and his wife. Nat and Jamie would help set the table; nuts, apples, preserves, and cheeses were brought up from the cellar. The goose in the pan, stuffed with breadcrumbs and plums, was starting to emit a mouthwatering aroma. For the first time in weeks, Nat leaned against her in the kitchen.

"You played beautifully yesterday," she said. "I forgot everything while I was listening." The boy ladled melted fat over the goose's back. Nat had stood—thin and erect, violin held high—in the organ loft. She saw how he closed his eyes after the organist's introduction, and carefully placed his bow on the strings. A hush spread through the church. Even Jamie, who'd been chattering with a school friend, stopped talking and was soon entranced by his brother's playing.

"It went well," Nat said. "I knew exactly how I wanted it to go, and it worked. As if by itself. May I turn over the pudding when it's ready? Yes?"

A rush of cold wind from the corridor heralded Hugh Palliser's arrival. James came into the kitchen, his arms wrapped around an enormous ham. Hugh followed, alone.

"It was no use," he said. "She doesn't feel well, sends her apologies. But at least I'm here. Hi, Nat. I enjoyed your playing yesterday. Very good. Almost makes it worthwhile going to church on Christmas Eve."

He looked at Elizabeth, his pale-blue eyes glittering in the warm candlelight. Maybe he's just happy to be here, she told herself. The shipyard is closed, the Admiralty offices are shut, and he'd rather spend time in this kitchen than at home with his sick, childless wife.

Jamie came in, bringing the scent of fresh air with him. He politely shook Captain Palliser's hand and led him into the great room to show him something, with Nat in tow. She could follow the conversation through the open doorway.

"But then who's the boss?" Jamie asked.

"Papa, of course," Nat chimed in.

"It's a little more complicated than that." Hugh cleared his throat. "There are a few different bosses. Lord Sandwich is the first lord of the Admiralty. He's number one; he answers directly to the king, and he's in close contact with the government. Philip Stephens is in charge of the Admiralty itself, its offices. He holds sway over everything that has to do with the shipping industry. And money."

"And you?" Jamie asked.

"Well, son, I suppose I'm also a sort of boss. You could call me the inspector of the fleet. I must ensure that there are ships ready to sail on whatever expeditions Sandwich and Stephens cook up. I purchase the ships, check to see that they're seaworthy, and have them repaired if they're not. When I'm in doubt, I ask your father's advice. That about sums it up."

The sound of the goose sizzling made it more difficult to understand what they were saying. She took the pan from the fire. Soon, the meal would begin.

She'd laid the table with a heavy damask cloth, and at the last minute, she removed Mrs. Palliser's place setting. Now they were five: James between his sons on one side, she and Hugh on the other. A fire blazed in the hearth, and the table was lit with new, pale candles.

As expected, the talk turned to seafaring. Hugh and James talked about Omai's return journey. The boys listened with bated breath, and Elizabeth leaned back and folded her arms over her belly. The goose had been roasted to perfection.

Captain Clerke would be taking Omai back home to his island. He'd sail with two ships: the patched-up *Resolution* and a new vessel, to be chosen by James.

"Will Omai be taking so much with him that he'll need two ships?" Nat asked. Jamie began listing the inventory: clothes, guns, planks for building a house, marble tiles, horses, even an ox.

"Maybe they'll do something else once they've brought Omai home. I don't know for sure; a captain's orders are always kept secret. But there aren't any instructions as yet; there isn't even an official captain." Hugh paused and locked eyes with James. When he went on, his voice was businesslike, to the point.

"Yesterday, the king offered a reward for whoever discovers a northern passage. A sizable sum."

James looked surprised, and the boys were bursting with questions. Palliser explained that the route to China and the Indonesian islands was time consuming because you had to sail around Cape Horn or the Cape of Good Hope. But if you could sail north from Scotland and set course over Sweden for the east, arriving in the Northern Pacific—what a difference that would make, a golden opportunity for transport and trade!

"That route has been tried, but I get the impression those expeditions were neither adequately equipped nor well prepared. It's cold up there, and you have to pick your way through the ice. Naturally, food supplies are a problem. A new route would first have to be charted before you could even consider trade: coasts, islands, currents, the extent of polar ice. Twenty thousand pounds."

"I knew it was coming," James said, "but not that it would involve so much money. I'd say: go west, by means of Newfoundland."

He fell silent, lost in thought. Hugh explained to the boys what you could do with twenty thousand pounds, and said the king would announce the prize officially after Christmas.

"From the South Sea," James muttered, "first Tahiti, then to the north." Elizabeth passed around the goose and gave her husband another helping. He didn't seem to notice.

"Papa!" Nat's voice sliced through the clatter of the ticking cutlery and the roaring fire. "Papa, will you be winning the prize?"

She carried the plate of leftover goose into the kitchen. I don't need to hear the answer, she thought. Christmas. Everything must stay just as it is. She paused on the threshold of the kitchen, bearing the platter on her forearms. Holding her breath.

"No, son," James said. "I will not win the prize because I'm not sailing anymore. Now it's Captain Clerke's turn, and I'll find him a fine vessel. It would be wonderful if he managed to find the passage. Not just for the money, but for our understanding of those northern waters. I won't be joining him; I've done my share of voyaging."

They are disappointed, she thought while scrubbing the greasy platter. Jamie is already dreaming about what you could buy with so much money. But for Nat, life seems more familiar when his father is away. He might even imagine that he could avoid going to sea if James weren't here to send him to that school.

She called her youngest to the kitchen to help with the Christmas pudding. They laid a wreath of holly around the dark, fragrant mound, filled with currants glistening like lead pellets. Nat bore the confection into the dining room; she followed with a pitcher of cream. She felt light on her feet, and the hem of her skirt swirled around her ankles; she hadn't felt so reassured in years. She gingerly scooped the portions onto each plate, head bowed. She avoided looking at James until she passed him his serving, which she held poised over the damask while they gazed deeply into each other's eyes. Kind eyes, she thought; he has kind eyes.

She woke up in the middle of the night, alone. She sat bolt upright and pricked up her ears. All quiet on the upper floor, but vague noises were coming from below. She slipped out of bed and went downstairs, barefoot. She felt her way into the kitchen, still redolent with the rich aroma of roasted goose. There should be a candle on the worktop. She gave her eyes time to adjust. Yes, there it is. Light it. The flame flickered. She pushed open the door to the scullery.

James was vomiting into a bucket. His hair hung in wet skeins and his nightshirt clung—soaking wet—to his back. His retching and moaning reverberated loudly off the bare walls. He was on his knees on the floor's uneven pavers; the backs of his bare, skinny legs looked pasty and lifeless.

"James, what's wrong?" she exclaimed.

No reaction. His face disappeared into the bucket he embraced. She knelt beside him and rested a hand on his neck. Clammy sweat.

"Shut the door!" he managed to gasp. "The boys!"

She stood up, closed the door, grabbed a towel, and poured some water into a mug. Don't panic, she thought, just do what needs to be done.

He raised his head, and she began wiping his face, the way she would have dabbed Jamie's when he'd fallen in the mud. An appalling stench of sour, half-digested food came from the bucket.

She gave him a sip of water. The cramps promptly recommenced coursing through his upper body. Caress him. Hold him. Be patient. He settled down and pushed the bucket aside. They knelt face-to-face like a pair of waterborne grebes. She was taken aback by his sunken, yellow-tinged face. His eyes were large, dark, and glowing.

"It's nothing," he rasped. "Indigestion. A Christmas malady."

He tried to stand up, leaning heavily on her shoulder. When she asked if he could walk, he gave a curt nod, his lips compressed. Slowly, they hauled themselves up the stairs. He clung to the railing with all his strength; it seemed as if his arms were doing all the work. She stood behind him, afraid he might fall. If that happened, there wasn't much she could do; his gangly body would drag her down, too, until they were both lying at the foot of the stairs, but she gently supported his back, anyway.

Once he had returned to bed, he grimaced in an attempt to smile. She waited until he fell asleep.

The next morning, it was as if nothing had happened. He sat merrily eating porridge with the boys. Elizabeth went into the scullery. The bucket had been scrubbed clean and was standing on the rack.

Talk about it, she thought. Ask him if he's had this before, if he'd been as sick on the voyage; she needed to know what was going on. Just ask; how hard could it be? But she said nothing.

"Look," James said, "a letter from Douglas. He has gone through the notebooks I sent him. Read it. I'm curious to hear what you think."

He handed her the letter. Dr. John Douglas had a pleasant, polite style of writing and a reserved manner. He praised James's journal and told him how fascinated he'd been by the events it described. He would be honored to help get the book into shape for publication, and he invited the author to visit him in Windsor for a leisurely chat about this and that. James didn't have to worry about any drastic alterations in the contents or style, because in Douglas's humble opinion, the direct and pragmatic writing was part of the book's appeal. Signed with the utmost esteem and admiration and warmest regards.

Elizabeth looked up and nodded. "I would do it. He sounds nice, don't you think? He won't run away with your story. When are you planning to go?"

"I will not be going," James said. "It will take too much time. I need a few days to finish the next batch of notebooks before I send them off in the mail coach. I am needed at the shipyard this week. Three vessels are anchored there, one of which might be suitable. I will have to devote my time to that. But I will write to him, this Douglas. He'll understand. Otherwise he won't."

A vision popped into her head, of him on the afterdeck of the *Resolution*: a commanding stance, determined, with lively gestures and eyes that didn't miss a trick. There was no way to reconcile that impression with the man on his knees, throwing up in the pantry. She shied away from probing into his health now that he was looking so fit, but the previous night kept gnawing at her.

"Banks has invited us to his New Year's reception," James announced. "Everyone will be there; or at least, those Banks classifies as 'everyone.' Counts and duchesses."

She'd have to air out his full-dress uniform and brush it. For a group so interested in the South Sea Islands, her Tahiti dress would be just the thing. And she could still get into it—just.

"I am sure he has also invited his friends from the Royal Society," she said. "Solander will certainly be there, and some of the other people you enjoy seeing. Omai, of course. And the Burneys."

James sniffed. "They mean well, those Burneys, but they have no idea. They think they're showing an interest, but they're all wrapped up in themselves. They're so pleased that they've had such fine educations, have read the latest books and attended all the concerts. And suddenly this fascinating new world opens up before them. They cannot believe their luck. They behave as if they're entitled to it all. When I was about to leave on my first voyage, old Burney thought it a matter of course that his son should ship out with us, simply because the boy had set his heart on it!"

"But James, at least they're interested," Elizabeth replied. "And that boy, as you call him, has since undergone a thorough training in the Navy. If he was eager to travel, why shouldn't he have reported to you?"

James sat down, still holding the notebooks he was planning to send to Douglas. He brooded for a minute and said, "You are right. Of course, there is always room for a boy like that. That's not the point; he did well enough. It's something else. The way those people assume they can lay claim to everything in the world. They never stop to wonder if they will be welcome. They expect a warm reception everywhere they go, and that's what they receive. At home, they have a library full of precious books. They have their portraits painted by celebrated artists, and they spend every evening in their private box at the opera. To them, it's all perfectly ordinary. It makes me fume, even though I know they cannot help it.

"When I was at the Burneys' for a soirée after the first voyage, I felt oafish and awkward. Like an ill-bred sailor. There was no reason for my discomfort, because they—the father, the son, and that dreadful daughter—hung on my every word. They posed intelligent questions and took the time to listen to my answers, but nevertheless, I just did not fit in. Remember how I defaced their copy of Bougainville's account of his journey? At their request, mind you. The old fellow wanted to know how I had sailed around the world, so I took a pencil from my pocket and traced my route on the map at the front of Bougainville's book. The daughter—that Fanny—was hanging over my shoulder, her mouth agape, because I was doodling in their precious heirloom. Next thing you know, she was proclaiming it a historical event, saying they should preserve the pencil line for posterity! You see what I mean: they just assume their books and atlases will take up permanent residence in the display case of some museum."

On the day of Banks's party, James donned his wig and put on his dress uniform. The carriage drew up and they left. Light poured out of every window of Banks's house. The doors stood wide open; coachmen shouted, horses' hooves clattered on the cobblestones, and visitors in brightly colored attire climbed the stairs, jabbering excitedly. Banks was in the hall, welcoming his guests. His round face lit up when he saw James and Elizabeth. The two men embraced. Banks was pleased about

James's forthcoming admission to the Royal Society—never had a new member been selected with such an overwhelming endorsement. They were all looking forward to James's first lecture, his maiden speech as it were, which was bound to touch on the remarkable social order in Tahiti, the sexual habits of the natives, the human sacrifices! Before James had a chance to reply, Banks rushed off to welcome other newly arriving guests.

James took Elizabeth by the hand and led her, under the glow of the impressive chandelier, down the hall and into the salon. There, on a raised dais, Omai was singing. He wore a white silk robe that was more like a Roman toga than the traditional garb of the islands. He sang a monotonous song in his own language, his eyes closed and his mouth wide open, keeping time with his bare feet. When he finished, he pranced off the stage and began bestowing kisses on the hands of the ladies who, with a mixture of admiration and horror, had been listening. Omai accepted their praise with boyish high spirits. Someone handed him a glass; he knocked it back in one go. A young woman led him—giggling and squealing with delight—toward an elderly gentleman sitting by the fire with a notebook on his lap. Every trace of the fierce islander with the keening voice seemed to have vanished.

James pointed to the man beside the hearth. "That's Charles Burney," he said. Omai kneeled at the musicologist's feet and whispered in his ear, beating time vigorously with his head. Burney transcribed the rhythms on hastily drawn musical staves.

Elizabeth was hoping to have a word with Burney. He could tell her all about musical life in London, about Haydn, that promising composer Hugh had mentioned, and perhaps about a violinist's chances of making a career in music.

James had reservations about Burney, because he was the one who had recommended the notorious Hawkesworth to edit his journals from the *Endeavour*. He nevertheless gave the old man a hearty handshake and praised the dedication and devotion of his seafaring son, Jem. The father glowed with pride. Omai disappeared into the throng, and in the next room, a small string orchestra began to play.

James and Elizabeth strolled and chatted with people here and there, as if the house were a park.

"So kind of you to mention his son," Elizabeth said. "The boy wasn't even on the *Resolution*, was he?"

"No. He had been assigned to me, but there were some last-minute alterations, and he ended up on the other ship. He was disappointed, of course, but he took it like a true sailor. He led the investigation into the murder of the crew on that launch in New Zealand. The day after the debacle, Jem Burney went ashore and discovered his friends' gnawed remains. He wrote an excellent report about the incident."

Lord Sandwich arrived with his mistress in tow and headed straight for James. After they said hello, Elizabeth stepped back and listened from a distance to their talk of Douglas's editorial and social abilities. She scanned the crowd and saw Fanny Burney demonstrating courtly bows and dance steps to Omai. Her eyes searched for Pa Burney, with his musical manuscript book, but she couldn't find him anywhere.

Suddenly, she realized she was also searching for Hugh Palliser. It was highly unlikely that he would turn up here; he preferred chatting with friends in a coffeehouse. Or perhaps he was at home with his sick wife? But he wasn't here, wasn't with her. He'd come to dinner just a few nights ago, and she would undoubtedly see him in the coming weeks, when he and James went to look at ships. She could see him whenever she wanted; there was no reason to look for him now. Except that, apparently, she wanted to see him. She straightened her shoulders and stepped forward to hear the conversation better.

"Clerke," Sandwich said, "Charles Clerke will be the one to lead the expedition. Now that he has the appropriate rank and experience. We are still looking for another man for the new ship, with your approval, of course. Good thing you've found someone to take that writing off your hands, so now we can call on you more often. I look forward to your evaluation of the ships next week. Time is running out, and I would like to aim for a departure in March. You know the reason why."

Miss Ray, Sandwich's flamboyant paramour, tugged at his sleeve. It was time for supper, other conversationalists required their attention, and glasses needed to be refilled.

"We are leaving," James announced. They were suddenly left a bit lost, abandoned beneath the chandelier. "You need your rest, you're expecting."

She silently followed in his wake. Once outside, he took a deep breath, and she saw the color return to his cheeks. He called for the coach and helped her in. He peered fretfully out of the small window: looking for the water, she thought, and sure enough, he pointed to the river in the distance as soon as it came into view.

After they were dropped off at their doorstep, they watched the carriage disappear into the frigid night. A new year had begun.

Elizabeth wrote:

Dear Frances,

I have been meaning to write to you for ages, but the table was littered with all the various drafts of James's journals, as well as atlases, maps, and notes written on scraps of paper, none of which I dared to move. Now we've put everything away, more or less in order. We've sent the latest version of the story of the voyage to Dr. John Douglas for corrections. He badgers James, wants to discuss ways of improving the text, but James has left everything in Douglas's hands. I believe he's happy to be rid of it, although he had sworn that this time, he wanted to do it all by himself. Of course I helped him, I'd been looking forward to that, but things didn't work out quite the way I'd hoped. James seemed ill at ease;

I suspect he could feel the readers looking over his shoulder, and that kept him from thinking and writing freely.

But where are my manners? I completely forgot to ask how you coped with the storm, how things are with your husband, and with the political unrest in your new country. We read that your commander, George Washington, sent a conciliatory letter to our king. I don't believe it did any good. Instead of your longed-for independence, you're still at war!

When I think of you, which I often do, I mostly miss you. I will always be grateful for the togetherness we shared in the house—the two of us and the children. I haven't had a genuine woman friend since you left. Of course I see the neighbors, and the spouses of James's colleagues, but those friendships—if you can even call them that—are only skin deep, circumstantial at best. I never tell them what I'm really thinking. The only one I turn to, in moments of weakness, is Hugh Palliser. But he's not a girlfriend by any stretch of the imagination!

Jamie seems to be flourishing at the Naval Academy. He was home at Christmas: bigger, stronger, flaunting his newly acquired wisdom. I have my reservations about Nat, although I don't dare share them with James. He's a vulnerable child, troubled by many things, but he keeps it all to himself. Nat has been holding me at arm's length ever since James came home. He's gone into his shell. Or else I've changed. Sometimes I wonder if he's figured out that I'm pregnant again. I haven't said anything about it yet, afraid he won't like the idea. The only thing he's ever known are babies who are born and then die. One died every other year, and that meant that, at least for a while, I couldn't really be there for him. No, I hesitate to burden him, but I notice he's been staring at my belly. Should I have a talk with him? Music is his only safe haven, but next summer, when he's due at Portsmouth, he'll lose that as well. I think back to the evenings when you sang for him, and how happy he was. So difficult to know which way to turn.

We will stay here at Mile End. James doesn't have much to do at the hospital, and we want to preserve our independence. His appointment is a sinecure: his meetings with the other directors only take place once a month, if that. But I'm worried about him, too. He had an attack of acute indigestion after our Christmas dinner—scared the wits out of me. He's become nothing but skin and bones since he's been home, and he has an anxious air about him. He won't talk about it, says he's in perfect health. But in his notebooks, I read that he was seriously ill during the voyage, and had to spend days in bed with rheumatic fevers. He couldn't eat a thing! I think our English diet has done him some good, but I'm not sure.

Yesterday he left for the shipyard in a chipper mood. Hugh Palliser was waiting for him there. They'd planned to choose a ship to sail along with the Resolution *next spring, presumably under the command of Captain Clerke. He was disappointed when he came home, even though they had purchased a seaworthy vessel—it still needed a third mast and some other alterations, I can't remember the details—but he was terribly upset about the state of the* Resolution. *Precious little has been accomplished in the six months that his cherished ship has been in the dock. He blames himself; he should have been paying more attention, overseeing the carpenters and rope makers. I asked him what Hugh thought; he's the one in charge, after all, and he should have been keeping an eye on the repairs. James didn't say much. I got the impression they'd fallen out. It's sure to blow over soon; those two have so much in common. Their only genuine difference is in—how shall I put it?—the way they deal with higher-ups. James always seems on guard, feeling as if he has to prove himself. Hugh can take it or leave it; he goes his own way and doesn't give a fig what others think. I've seen a lot of him recently; he's been a tremendous support to me.*

The weather is bleak: sleet and gale-force winds. I've had stacks of hay placed around the exotic plants, so now the garden looks like what I'd imagine an Indian village to be. Nothing is blooming at Elly's. I braided a wreath for her grave, made of pine boughs and holly. James has just come in. He sends his love. Write back soon! Hugs and kisses from your friend, Elizabeth.

Now that the table had been cleared, she could get started on that waistcoat for James. She opened the chest in the corner and cautiously lifted out the heavy fabric. The fibers were completely foreign to her. According to the seamstress who'd made her Tahitian dress, the fabric felt soft, but it was so tough, scissors could hardly cut through it. She pictured herself sewing the waistcoat, sitting by the window with the dark-red material in her lap. The color was so rich and intense that if she looked at it too long, she felt dizzy. A lining of silver-colored silk would be a good match. Then she could edge the buttonholes with silver thread. Silver buttons on shanks. She spread the fabric on the table and tried to visualize how best to cut the components of the waistcoat from the length of cloth. Don't forget the nap. Some silver embroidery on the pockets? Or would that detract from the overwhelming scarlet? The trimmings could wait; first, she'd need the correct measurements.

She fished her measuring tape out of the sewing box and went into the kitchen, where James was sitting at the window, a pencil and paper in hand.

"Repairs!" he said. "It's unbelievable how little they've accomplished. And what they've done is deplorable. A crime to neglect such a magnificent ship. I think corruption plays a part, as well. They've been allocated the best materials, but I can't find any evidence of them on the ship. Who knows, maybe they sell the stuff, smuggle it over the fence and replace it with rubbish. Scandalous. I should be there every day, but where on earth am I to find the time? Douglas is sending those books back to me at every turn, expecting me to read and correct them! Why can't the man do it himself? That's his job!"

"Stand up," Elizabeth said. "I need to take your measurements."

He did as he was told, without asking why, and stood stock still in front of her. It was as if she could feel the restrained rage radiating off him in waves. He kept his mouth shut and took shallow breaths.

The circumference of the chest at its broadest and narrowest points. Shoulder width. Length from neck to waist. From waist to armpit. She bent over—the measuring tape between her teeth—and wrote down the measurements on a slip of paper.

"Finished. I have everything I need."

He paced in front of the window, hands clasped behind his back. "That paper for the Royal Society, that's what I should be thinking about. That's what's important. I'm not getting anywhere; all these obligations, all the information that floods in and demands a response. Here, I can't navigate it; it eludes me. I'm at the mercy of what's taking place around me, and there's no point making plans or trying to steer things. Something always crops up, the direction shifts all the time. Take that Forster: he interferes and slows everything down—I can see it coming, but can do nothing to stop it. On board ship, I'd call him to order. That would put a stop to his arrogance."

She picked up the slip of paper with the measurements and headed for the door. It crossed her mind that he hadn't even asked what she was making. It's all too much for him. Looking past him, she saw the haystacks in the snow. What a ridiculous sight.

"The new ship is in good condition," he began anew, "but the whole blasted expedition will have to wait until the *Resolution* has been overhauled. And nobody lifts a finger until I explain how it should be done. What will Omai be bringing with him, and how much space will his things take up? How many scientists will be on board? What about the food supplies—how many cannons, how many Marines? Things have ground to a halt, and soon it will be too late to set sail with any hope of success. Then they will have to wait another year!"

He was about to stamp his foot, but checked himself just in time, transforming his gesture into a step.

"I am going to set aside Douglas's parcel for a while," he said. "But now I will try and track down Palliser in the coffeehouse."

He left without looking back. Still holding the measuring tape, she went into the next room, where the cloth glowed deep red. She measured the circumference of his chest onto the fabric and gently chalked the points along which her scissors would pass. She hesitated before starting to cut, and folded the cloth again. Better to think it over, wait until tomorrow, or a day with fewer obstacles. She carefully tucked the note with his measurements into the red folds.

The next day, the weather turned. Within hours, the crust of snow had melted. Elizabeth was in the mood for a walk, and stood on the curb, inspecting the condition of the road: puddles, mud, and filth. A carriage plowed through the pulpy earth and ground to a halt in front of her. With the help of a coachman, Hugh Palliser got out. When his bad leg touched the ground, a spasm of pain crossed his face; then he stepped resolutely onto the sidewalk.

"James isn't home," she said. "He's gone to the engravers to look at some illustrations."

"But you're here." He kissed her cheek, and they went indoors, side by side. She felt a wave of dizziness in the hallway and leaned against the wall for support. He made an elaborate show of taking off his coat and rubbing his cold hands.

"Port!" he exclaimed. "Or Madeira. I know there's some here. James has a stockpile from the *Resolution*."

In the kitchen, she tried to pull herself together, bustling about with glasses and bottles. Hugh installed himself at the corner of the table and asked if he could prop his leg up on a chair.

"Are you in pain?"

He gave a brief nod. "It's this weather. The damp. It's better when it freezes, or in the summer. But I'm used to it. It's nothing."

She had to sit down, too, eventually, diagonally across from him. The silence rose off the table like a column. Her stomach was in knots; she searched for topics of conversation, but only contentious matters came to mind. He drank. He said nothing.

After a while she noticed that this quiet togetherness wasn't entirely unpleasant. Nothing was required. Whatever she wanted to tell him or ask him could wait. He sat, unruffled, watching her as if he had all the time in the world. She exhaled deeply and raised her glass. With a smile, their eyes met, and they both started talking at once.

"When—" he began.

"How—" she said.

They started over. He asked about the date of the baby's expected arrival. Sometime in May, she reckoned, when the entire garden would be in bloom.

"I can't imagine that now," she said. "Everything will be different. James will be here. He's never witnessed one of his own children being baptized. Or buried."

Hugh shook his head. "Things might go well, Elizabeth. You've held on to two boys. They're both still with us."

He took her hand and began absently caressing it. She felt a strong urge to cry, and forced herself to think about the pattern of James's waistcoat, tonight's menu, and the seeds she was about to order for spring. May. Almost time for Nat to leave. Don't start blubbering now, just talk about it.

"No," Hugh said, "I don't believe the boy will be happy at sea, either. Not like Jamie; it's clear Jamie can handle it, he's flourishing.

Nat's another story. But the Navy always finds room for birds of a different plumage. Things will get better for him once he's endured the hardship of training. Not everyone has to be on a ship all the time. There are positions ashore. And they need musicians, too: horn players, drummers, buglers. It's a shame he has to leave home so young, and so soon after the birth of the new baby. No, that can't be nice."

How does he know that? she wondered. He doesn't have any children. He's not afraid of the sea, and yet he seems to understand Nat's feelings. She saw her hand trembling as she refilled his glass. She made up her mind not to mention James. Hugh knows him, knows he wouldn't hear of any other calling for the boys. He knows all about it.

"Difficult for Nat, upsetting for you." He squeezed her hand. In a rush, she began talking about the work on the journals, their organization, the revisions, Douglas's friendly interference.

"Excellent, glad to hear it." He nodded. "James will finally have time to prepare the expedition. We had a difference of opinion in Deptford; maybe he mentioned it? The workmen there have been slacking off. Hard to believe, but they've painted over worm-riddled woodwork, haven't bothered to replace the rotten sections. James was seething, and justifiably so. I should have been paying attention to the repairs; he's absolutely right. Of course, I offered my apologies, and he accepted. Our friendship's none the worse for wear. I have only myself to blame. Unforgivable negligence."

"What was the problem?" she probed. "Why couldn't you keep your mind on the job?"

Her hand was enveloped in his. He stroked its back without meeting her eye.

"It's that miserable plan to return that uncivilized creature to his home. The king wants one thing, Sandwich another, and the Royal Society something else again. Where will the money come from, who should be in command, what are the instructions going to be? It keeps running through my mind, and I can't find a way out. Nevertheless: unforgivable. I should have visited the shipyard every day. But I didn't."

He fell silent.

"There's more: other matters distract and confuse me. This autumn, I have spent a great deal of time in fruitless contemplation. I'm getting old, Elizabeth. Things I could once tolerate with little effort now seem to exhaust me. So many conflicts everywhere. And at home—"

He lifted his leg off the chair and shifted position.

"I don't want to burden you with my problems. You already have enough on your plate. This Madeira is first rate. James made a wise purchase."

"How are things at home?" she asked. "Have there been any developments?"

He shook his head. "It's the same, and will remain that way. I usually say she's sick. But she's not. She's in perfect health, but unsuited to life. The doctor pumps her full of immense quantities of laudanum, so she sleeps day and night. But I can hardly close my eyes. My leg plays up whenever I try to get some rest. It's excruciating when I lie down. So I sit in my chair all night, waiting for the sun to come up. I don't want to talk about any of this with you. I don't want to complain."

"You're not complaining. You're telling me how it is. It's what I want to hear."

He rubbed his face, massaged his forehead.

"If she doesn't take her sedatives, she wanders off. The gardener once pulled her away from the pond. I've had the windows of her sleeping quarters bolted from the outside. She is attended and looked after, but in reality, she's guarded. I make sure the nurses—who are actually jailers—never take their eyes off her. It's a blessing she sleeps so much these days. When she's awake, she cries. I can't stand it. That's one of the reasons I'm so often away. Nothing to be proud of, but there you are."

"How trying," she said. "What a hopeless state of affairs. Whatever will happen next?"

"What must be must be," he said decidedly. "The situation has been stable for years. I am able to persevere as long as I have my activities. It's just that sometimes, it strikes me that I'm sorry my life has not turned out differently: I wish I could start over. An old man's regret! I am happy I can visit you now and then, pleased that James is back, delighted to take part in your family life. No, I'm not one to grumble. I wish I could go for a walk with you, but my leg isn't up to it today."

It was getting dark. They remained at the table without lighting the lamps.

"Look at this," James said, waving a stack of notebooks. Loose slips of paper fluttered out. "He expects me to look through all this once more and offer comments. We will never see the back of it. He thinks readers will be upset about the conduct of my men. Indecent, he says. He wants me to scrap it all. I thought I had already done that. How am I to know what he thinks is immoral?"

"Write to him," she suggested. "If you really don't care, let him decide what stays and what goes."

James picked up the scattered papers and arranged them in a small pile.

"I want to describe events as faithfully as possible," he said. "The locals behave differently than we do. Here, we would label their ways brazen and promiscuous. But do the islanders see it that way? No, they do not. They have their own customs. We do not understand their way of doing things, and because we are appalled by their naked bodies and public intimacies, we cry out: immoral! Should that be a reason for crossing out descriptions of what we saw? I would prefer to keep everything as is. This is no scientific report for the Royal Society, it is meant for the general public's amusement. I think I have to adapt. In Tahiti, the natives copulate in public. I saw an old man with a young girl, still a child in our eyes. Onlookers circled the pair and cheered them on, offering tips and encouragement. What kind of impression would that make on readers here? How am I to know? The young girl did not seem to mind, quite the contrary. Will I have to stand trial for including that? And let us spare a thought for the wives of my crew members. Even if I mention no one by name, scandal and upheaval will result. I will leave it all out."

He flung the notebooks on the table and paced furiously in front of the window.

"So many sensitivities. Rules. I am not cut out for this. They have to explain everything to me, and still, I don't get it. Douglas must have the final say. I will never learn. It's upbringing, I reckon: education, money. I'll wash my hands of it."

Elizabeth realized she'd been trying to provoke him when she suggested he hand the reins over to Douglas. It was humiliating to see how insecure he'd become, how willing he was to make cuts, to violate his beliefs.

All at once, she was livid. She reared back and assumed a forthright stance. With her chin raised, she looked James in the eye.

"You're giving up. It's *your* voyage, *your* book. I see no reason why you should bow to whatever rules happen to apply here. Why don't you try to change those rules, by holding fast to your standards? Are you inferior to Douglas? Sandwich? Banks? Surely you're not a lackey of the Admiralty? You're in charge. You made the discoveries; you should set the tone. I don't understand your subservient attitude."

She saw him deflate before her eyes, as if the tension had suddenly drained from his muscles; an old man stood there, awkwardly shuffling his notebooks, back hunched, shoulders drooped. He averted his gaze.

"I'm not wild about the way your sailors drop their trousers everywhere they go. I'm mortified on behalf of their wives; ashamed you couldn't put a stop to it. It's scandalous how your men spread disease

and scabies. Sometimes I'm even afraid you'll fall prey to some wor-
shipful princess, as well. That's all true. But we had a pact, James. We
wouldn't bow to convention, would not believe in things we could not
see with our own eyes, and we'd respect the facts. Now you're prepared
to draw a line through the truth. You're violating our agreement. That's
something you may not do. I want you to take a stand for us, not for
your patrons' arbitrary decorum."

She stopped abruptly, startled by her own vehemence. The silence
that followed was leaden and uncomfortable. She wanted to flee to
the kitchen, busy herself with some mundane task or other. But she
remained rooted to the spot.

"You are right." His voice sounded hoarse and weak. "You could
not be more right. But you do not understand. On board, I make the
rules. There are no uncertainties that cannot be resolved. Here, in the
city, it's different, Elizabeth. If I want to survive here, I must play by
their rules. You don't understand how difficult that is. I may know what
type of wig to wear at a reception, but if the conversation strays from
trade winds and tides, I am at a loss.

"But you are right. I should write my book the way I want to,
without concessions to good taste or decency. If that gets even one
reader thinking, rather than becoming indignant or aroused, then I'd
be satisfied. Just one.

"I will not be eating here this evening. Sandwich and I are going
across the river to dine with Stephens. Hugh Palliser will be joining us,
as well. We have to decide about the expedition. Don't wait up."

She followed him into the hallway and watched him getting ready
to leave. Hat, coat, and boots: in the blink of an eye, the distraught
writer transformed into the self-assured captain. She shivered. It was
freezing.

He pulled her close and wrapped his lapels around her. "You're
right," he repeated. "You're sensible. I will think carefully about what
you said."

Then, the boy who had come to ferry him across the river knocked on the door. She watched them leave, saw how James bent toward the boy, heard their voices die out as they turned down the path toward the river. Icy mist lay over the city; she thought to herself, it's the ninth of January, and the city is blanketed in fog.

She closed the door.

6

The weather turned bitter the second half of January. The river froze solid, but currents beneath the ice made it too dangerous to cross. Ice flows the size of tabletops scoured one another, freezing together at the edges and then breaking apart once the support of the underlying water disappeared. The ice was firmer along the banks, where boys went fishing with lines sunk to the bottom through a hole. Hoarfrost weighted the tree branches, and the road was a wasteland of icy ridges over which carriages jolted and skidded.

It was impossible to keep the house free of frost. The hearth in the great room was ablaze all day, but it wasn't enough to prevent ice crystals forming on the windows. The water that had been left forgotten on the table froze and burst its pitcher. The cold was invisible but, in broad daylight, it destroyed everything.

In the kitchen, the temperature was bearable because the large range was kept fully stoked. Unsplit tree trunks were fed into its modest-sized fuel hatch, making the air above the stovetop tremble.

Nat's music stand stood beside the stove. James sat with his notes and atlases at the kitchen table. Elizabeth, who after much hesitation had finally dared to cut into the fabric from Tahiti, sat opposite the range, stitching together the back of James's waistcoat. An icy storm raged outside, while inside, the captive flames roared.

Nat came in, his violin case under his arm. He'd pulled one of James's old hats down over his ears; his face was blue from the cold. He was about to lay his violin case on the table, but when James glared at him, he started back and carried the case to the worktop instead. His hands were red and swollen.

"Why aren't you wearing your mittens?" Elizabeth asked. Nat tossed the ridiculous old hat in a corner.

"Left them at Mr. Hartland's. Can't feel a thing in my fingers!"

Elizabeth took a pan of water from the burner and tested the temperature. Lukewarm.

"Soak your hands in here a minute; they'll be fine before you know it." The boy rolled up his sleeves and plunged his arms elbow deep into the water. He stood there, silent.

The distance separating the three people in the kitchen was no more than a few feet. Yet they all did their best to immerse themselves in their own activities. James drew lines on a chart, Nat slowly waggled his fingers in the water, and Elizabeth pushed her needle through the unyielding material.

James had not come home from his dinner with Sandwich, Stephens, and Palliser until almost dawn. When he climbed into bed and snuggled up against her, Elizabeth was jolted out of a restless sleep. His breath, reeking of alcohol, made her feel ill, and she writhed as far away from him as she could. He slept late the next morning; she didn't see him again until she got back from her walk. She'd gone to the market after visiting Elly, and had bought much too much. She piled the parcels and packages onto the worktop, and began sorting and storing the food. I'm not going to ask how it went, she thought. Nothing to worry about. I'm going to make some soup.

James stood motionless in a corner of the kitchen, staring at her back. He cleared his throat a few times, and she expected him to say something. But he remained silent.

The days passed, filled with the struggle against the cold. James seemed busy and went out every day. He found no opportunity to tell her about his dinner with Sandwich and the reason behind his drunken state. Gradually, her curiosity ebbed and her anxiety subsided. To her, he seemed shut off and remote, although she put that down to the lecture he was mulling over for the Royal Society. The cold gave everything a dreamlike, muffled quality, which seemed to extend to her small family's interpersonal relationships. She watched Nat's pale face pass by, and couldn't find the words to reach him. She wanted to ask James a question, but he disappeared before she could put it into words. The baby inside her was undeniably growing; it moved and made its presence known. Yet she felt nothing more than the remotest interest in her swelling belly.

She went out one clear, bright morning because the stuffy kitchen was starting to close in on her. The ice on the streets and pathways was covered with a layer of sand and dirt, so she didn't have to worry about falling, and she set off at a healthy clip. The rhythm of walking freed her from her strange detachment, some feeling returned to her legs and cheeks, and between the fields and meadows, she found herself again. Solutions, she thought, problems must be solved. No matter what, he has to finish his lecture, make peace with that eccentric Forster, and complete his book. After their discussion about omitting the offending passages, she'd felt reassured that James would hold his ground and resist any pressure to alter his account.

But when he'd finally roused himself after that heavy dinner, he'd written to Douglas and given him carte blanche to delete any passages he thought might offend the sensibilities of cultivated readers.

"I have no time for this," he'd said. "Check to see I haven't made too many mistakes. Do I have to rewrite it?"

She read the note, and as usual, she felt aggravated by his exaggerated closing, *your humble servant.* She was also appalled by his surrender; she wanted to know why, why this decision, why now, what was standing in the way of him keeping control of his own writing? But something held her back. A wax seal, a mail coach; done.

Without realizing where she was going, she was heading home. She turned the corner onto her street and almost collided with Hugh Palliser. He was propped up by his walking stick, and appeared rattled to run into her. Her delighted smile died away, and there they stood, face-to-face, awkward and uncomfortable.

After a silence that seemed interminable, he said, "I owe you an explanation. Let's go somewhere we can talk; what do you say?"

He gave her his arm, and they slowly made their way to the coffee-house. She noticed how painstaking his movements were, how heavily he leaned on her. Inside, it was snug and warm. They took off their coats and scarves and sat down. Hugh ordered mulled wine.

"I could do nothing to prevent it. I'm more sorry than I can say. Let there be no mistake. We didn't have to persuade him. It was his decision."

Elizabeth looked at him blankly. It was warm in here; she pushed her cap to the back of her head and leaned against the wall. Why was he so nervous?

"We were in the tower room. Stephens had had a leg of venison braised, and he'd opened the barrel of port, the one Sandwich had been saving for the occasion. A view of the river on one side, and the observatory on the other."

Port. He must be talking about the night that James came home drunk. She warmed her hands on her glass.

"You know it's about the northern passage? It's still sub rosa, but I assume James has talked it over with you. We were at the table with the world map spread out between the plates and glasses; we discussed the various possibilities, the best time of year, the necessary supplies."

Hugh rested his bad leg across the other knee and began kneading his ankle thoughtfully.

"Go on," she said.

"Crew," he said, head bowed. "How many men. Marines. Whether or not scientists should be included. That's what we talked about."

He fell silent again. Elizabeth had straightened her back and pushed her wine to one side. Somewhere in the back of her mind, she realized she didn't want to hear whatever he was about to tell her. "And?" she asked.

He looked at her. "Who could command such an expedition? It would have to be a highly experienced individual, someone with enormous skills in the area of cartography. I believe it was Stephens who mentioned Clerke. The names of various officers made the rounds: Pickersgill, Gore. As I recall, James reacted favorably to Clerke. He's popular with the crewmen. A ladies' man, Sandwich said. There was some grumbling. Would Clerke be serious enough to successfully carry out such a tough assignment? In the northern seas, paying careful attention to the diet on board is a matter of life and death. Could we trust Clerke? What if he wanted to remain on good terms with his men, and was too generous with the provisions? We know he cannot say no to requests for more rations. Too amicable. Too magnanimous. Likes to raise a glass or two himself, as we well know."

"Just say it," Elizabeth said. She could hear the icy edge in her voice; she listened as if it belonged to someone else, a woman with perfect posture who wasn't bothered about a thing.

"We bantered a bit," Palliser said. "I came to Clerke's defense. I hear nothing but good reports from his men. He may be lenient, but that can be good for the morale on board. And he spares the whip."

He paused. The landlord arrived with a steaming pitcher to refill their glasses. Hugh waited until the man scuttled off.

"We were at a loss. Sandwich was clearly dissatisfied with Clerke. He took the floor. Said he had talked about the expedition that afternoon with the king. The palace expressed specific wishes: his majesty would like to see maritime history's most important and expensive undertaking commanded by the most illustrious and experienced captain."

"Leave that bit out," she said. "Just tell me what happened."

"James stood up. I will do it, he said. If you ask me, I am ready and willing. Those were his exact words. His face was flushed; we'd all been drinking heavily. We cheered and clinked glasses. Everyone was relieved, mind you, because James had just handed us a solution to a thorny problem. Sandwich embraced him and thanked him for his decision. Stephens poured more port. The four of us sat back down and spent hours talking about the expedition. That's how it happened. We did not pressure James, did not coax him. It's what he wanted."

In the silence, she heard a horse-drawn cart on the street outside. The coachman shouted, the hoofbeats grew still, and there was a loud thump as a barrel was unloaded. The landlord opened the door and a gust of icy wind blew in. Elizabeth sat motionless, waiting for the barrel to be rolled behind the bar, the deliveryman paid, the door closed. Palliser was leaning over his leg, massaging it with both hands. The wine was still on the table, untouched.

It wasn't a surprise; in fact, she'd known all along. Now she could acknowledge the struggle it had been to keep him home. She'd done her best this past autumn, mindful of what she did, what she said. When the temperature dropped, she had covered the tropical plants with hay. She'd held her tongue when they talked about Nat's future. She'd put on her glad rags to accompany him to dinners and receptions. She'd bent over backward to please him; tried, at any cost, to understand him, even when she couldn't figure him out. She'd had to wrestle every day with an unfamiliarity and tension that wouldn't go away. And now, relief?

She took a deep breath and felt the baby inside her kicking the wall of her belly. She smiled. She became aware of a slowly growing ice-cold rage.

"You," she said, "you made a promise to me. Not because I asked you, but of your own accord. You would make sure he never had to sail away again. We had our doubts, don't you remember? Questions about his health, his resilience; about his capacity to prepare for yet another inhumanly strenuous effort. We were of one mind: it would never happen again. I had blind faith in our agreement. I counted on you.

"You say he wants to do it. That's for sure. Without a doubt. You couldn't be more right. Of course it's what he wants. The sea is his element. He cannot keep himself from embarking. That is not the point.

"You say: we didn't ask him or coax him. No, of course not. You're too cunning for that; too diplomatic and civilized. Just imagine, having to ask for something! The Admiralty doesn't ask. It gives orders. And if that's not appropriate, it finds other means. No, persuading someone is much too commonplace, and too dangerous, because it means you have to show your hand. The Admiralty doesn't wish. It commands.

"You handled this like experts. Congratulations. You could not have devised a better plan. What a brilliant move, suggesting Clerke. You know how fond James is of him. And the qualms he has about him. Did you take into account Clerke's idiotic lecture to the Royal Society? About those so-called giants of Patagonia, the ones he had never set eyes on? You must've known about that. And you are well aware of James's high regard for the Royal Society. Hats off to you!

"And then that subtle reference to the king's wishes. A work of art! How could any self-made man disregard the king's request? A king who supported him in his fight for Harrison's clock, a king who is passionate about discoveries and who has the wherewithal to invest in them?

"No, you didn't coax him. You didn't ask anything. It happened all by itself. You must have been so surprised."

Then it was gone: her fury, her flood of words. She flung her shawl over her shoulders and straightened her cap. She stood up. Hugh moved to rise from his chair, but she indicated he should remain seated. For just a minute, an eternal instant, she looked him in the eye. Disappointment? Despair? Desire?

Then she turned on her heel and stalked out, her back straight as a reed. The door banged shut behind her.

She poked her head into the corridor and called his name. "He's not here!" Nat shouted down from his room. Elizabeth pulled the door shut and began pacing in front of the house. She felt the sweat sting her back; her cheeks were glowing. A hearthside chat, in that claustrophobic room? Perish the thought. Even the open sky above the river wasn't big enough to contain her agitation and anger. Step, turn, step; she barely realized she was waiting.

She spotted him the minute he came around the corner. He looked at her, hesitatingly, wanting to go inside, into the warm house. She shook her head, calm and resolute, took his arm, and led him around the back, into the garden. After brushing away the snow, she sat down on the bench beneath the bare quince. With an impatient wave she directed him to sit beside her. The garden table in front of them was crowned with a bulging burden of snow, on which the birds had left tracks like the penciled arrows on a nautical chart.

"You will catch your death," he rasped, "why don't we go inside?" She looked at him but remained silent. Arms crossed, feet planted in the snow. From the house, a musical scale was audible, ascending higher and higher. She waited.

"Let me explain," he finally said. "Ever since that night, I have been thinking. Why did I say it? I turn it over and over in my head. Is it the reward? Twenty thousand pounds. What a difference that would make! A house in the city with a grand foyer, chandeliers, and a stable for our private carriages. There would be a reception one night at the Banks's, a ball at the Cooks' the next. Is that what I want? Could be. But that is not the reason I go to sea. This patch of ground suits me fine, although I am no stranger to envy of those who, by birth, feel at home in more elaborate gardens."

He drew circles in the snow with his boots. Far away, the violin was playing almost static double stops; sometimes a single note would slowly shift.

"Prestige. Respect. On board a ship, I'm in command. Wherever we go ashore, I am treated like a prince. That pleases me, and that's a fact. At sea, I leave behind the awkwardness that sometimes overtakes me here. That makes it hard for me to pass that role on to someone else. I could entrust the command to Charles Clerke, although I have my doubts about his objectivity. He has a good feel for the mood on board; he's friendly and doesn't put on airs. When they bring up John Gore, however, I can hardly control myself. On the *Endeavour*, he tried my patience considerably, boasting about his experience in the tropics and undermining my authority. He is also pedantic. Yet perhaps in his own way, he would make a good captain. I realize I will one day have to let someone else take the helm. I will have to settle down on land, I know that, too. If not now, then in a few years' time. I find that difficult, and although it certainly plays a role, it was not the deciding factor."

The sound of the violin ceased. It was deathly still in the snow-covered garden, as if the trees and shrubs were holding their breath.

"After I was born, my mother had six more children. Four of them died. She went from being a lively, resourceful woman to a gray shadow, dragging herself from room to room. I tried to cheer her up, thinking it was my fault she was so sad. John, my big brother, was gone the whole day; he worked the land with my father. I stayed behind, and fought against that suffocating sorrow. I lost. I couldn't save her. When I was finally allowed to go to school, I felt liberated. Skottowe, the landlord my father worked for, recognized something in me, and he paid my tuition. I believe my mother may have had a hand in that. I can still vaguely recall them in the barn, whispering to one another fiercely, standing much too close—but maybe I'm just imagining things. I was very young at the time.

"Letters and numbers showed me the way out of that joyless house. When I was finished with my schooling, Skottowe brought me to Staithes. You cannot believe your eyes when you go there. The village lies on a narrow strip of land overshadowed by towering cliffs, the houses are wedged against the steep slope, and they all face the sea. I got a job in the store, selling sugar, beans, nails, and soap. I filled paper bags with prunes, and whenever I looked up, I saw the gray waves of the North Sea. Nothing ever happens in Staithes. Small fishing boats are anchored in the harbor. They sail out at night and come back in the morning. The fishermen sell their catch on the narrow quay. That's it.

"On one of my first days working there, something happened that I found incredible. It was getting on toward six, the day was almost at an end, and there were no more customers in the shop. Suddenly, people began rushing outside, the entire village gathered at the low wall along the water. The tide was high, one wave after the other crashed over the stone ramparts. The townsfolk stood there, getting splashed, their feet submerged in wet foam. They clapped and cheered with every breaking wave. After about a quarter of an hour, the tide went out, and people drifted back to their homes. That's Staithes. The turning of the tide is the high point of the day.

"Beyond the breakers, I could see ships laden with coal sailing from Newcastle to London. Closer to the coast, there were barges transporting piss to the alum quarries. That dreary activity sums up the total misery of the region. Barrels and barrels of painstakingly chiseled shale are stored along the cliffs, stinking and smoldering. After a year, the muck is shoveled into vats of lye and mixed with rotting seaweed and human urine. What a stench! In the end, all that's left are alum crystals, used for dying textiles. The passing barges haul barrels of piss from

London pubs, because the coast is too sparsely populated to produce enough of its own.

"Everything there struck me as utterly miserable, hopeless. By day, endless trade and the incoming tide; at night, memories of that gloomy house in the hinterland. When I thought about going home for Christmas, I broke into a cold sweat. Then a message arrived, saying that my brother, while carting manure, had fallen from a wagon and broken his neck."

Elizabeth looked straight ahead, impassive. Two magpies chased one another near the hay she'd heaped around the palm tree. Their angry, impatient cawing echoed off the garden walls and drilled into her ears.

"When I think back on that time, I still feel downhearted. I didn't go home, out of cowardice. I sent a letter saying I was too busy to get away. Busy—in Staithes! I stared endlessly at the gray sea, stood there watching and waiting, as if something was about to happen, as if someone would come and rescue me from that paralysis. In my bedroom above the shop, the window was opaque, caked with salt. I opened it as far as I could. It was raining, and the quay was deserted. Then, two boys arrived. They untied a small boat, rowed out of the little harbor, and hoisted a sail once they were beyond the breakers. I watched that little boat sail away, and knew all at once that the sea would be my destiny. I'd seen hundreds of boats go out, but this time, the departure meant something to me. The sea spread before me, representing freedom. The next day, I walked to Whitby and signed on with Walker."

She'd rested her palms on her knees and looked at her reddened skin, chapped by the cold. She could feel no pain. The magpies had flown away, and the garden was quiet, a white room in which nothing happened.

"Beyond that miserable life on land where I could not find my way, beyond the suffering I could not remedy, the poverty I could do nothing about, there lay a wide, immense world that I could reach by sea. It sounds like an escape, and that is precisely what it was. But it was more than that. Something else slowly dawned on me, at the end of my escape route. Command, control, and having an overview were also part of my longing for the sea. The world is there, its islands and continents, but our knowledge of that world and the possible routes traversing it is limited. I developed a tremendous need to discover and describe countries and nautical routes in such a way that future generations would be able to follow in my footsteps.

"I want to stretch a network of waterways around the globe so that there are no more unknown regions. I must go to sea because the world is there."

He waved vaguely in the direction of the river. It was dusk, and the cold seemed to be intensifying. A branch snapped; tiny, glittering snow crystals began falling from the leaden sky.

"That's it, Elizabeth. I cannot explain it any better than that. It has nothing to do with you. You are wonderful, the best wife I could have chosen. It's not that I want to run away from you. I'd much rather stay with you always, beside you at the table, walking side by side. But the sea is there. I must. Not because it's honorable, not because the king asked, but because it is my destiny."

The snowflakes were growing larger and heavier. They swirled down and landed on their heads, their shoulders, their thighs. It was getting dark.

"You must understand. I am not doing anything against you. You are not involved. There is something in me I cannot deny. I feel it as soon as I walk up the gangplank. When I stand on deck and look out over the sea, when I feel the ship swaying beneath my feet and hear the stays clatter against the mast, I become a different person. I become myself."

The snowflakes danced silently in the beam of a distant lantern. Her bonnet was heavy with snow. An icy clump slid along her neckerchief, down her neck. She didn't budge.

The kitchen door flew open.

"Why are you sitting there? Why don't you come inside?"

Nat's voice was sharp. He's just a child, she thought. He doesn't know what to do. The fire in the stove goes out, the kitchen cools down. He's hungry and alone. All at once, she could feel the cold, and her teeth began to chatter. She pushed herself off the garden bench with hands that had grown stiff. James's hat was covered with snow. He got up as well. They stood rigid, side by side, dusting the snow off their clothes. He slapped his hat against the garden bench and then brushed the snow off her bonnet. Dragging their feet, they walked toward the kitchen without looking at each other.

She took off her sodden shoes and shivered. James scrabbled around with some logs by the stove. She hauled herself slowly up the stairs. Take off that wet skirt. Find some dry stockings, a different dress. She carefully hung up her damp clothes and went downstairs as soon as she was ready. It was evening, an ordinary evening; they had to eat.

Nat had put out some bread, plates, a hunk of cheese, and a platter of sliced ham. It was all jumbled together: there were crumbs and crusts of cheese; she spied an earthenware pot of gherkins and thought of the garden, those tiny cucumbers, such lovely plants. What a joy to pickle them in salt and vinegar, a little dill. She'd do it again this year—where was he, by the way? There was a half-eaten slice of bread on the work-top, but Nat was nowhere to be seen. James came back from the scullery with a tankard of ale. She picked up the bread knife and began slicing.

Then they sat down opposite each other. Her jaw was still too clenched to admit any food, and so she watched him help himself to ham, cheese, and the crunchy gherkins. I must try to say something, she thought, but I'm so tired, I can't. I've never been so exhausted. Not ever. Not after giving birth, not after a departure, not after a funeral. Never felt so weary as after that talk in the garden. It's a colossal effort to sit up straight, to breathe and hold my head up. She noticed her entire body trembling but could do nothing to stop it. Then I won't stop it, she thought; I'll just shake.

She heard James chew, swallow, take a swig of ale. The snow on his wet boots melted; the moisture seeped into the tiles, leaving dark stains. The stove was ablaze. Good thing he'd been able to rekindle the fire. Where's Nat? We must first think about Nat. A child who has to forage for his own supper because his parents are sitting immobile in the snow. That's not right, it mustn't happen again. She flexed her painful, chilly hands. Cleared her throat.

"Have you given your official word?"

He shook his head. "I still need to send a letter of confirmation to Sandwich. I have not done that yet."

All is not lost, she thought. There's still a little breathing room; I don't really have to face it yet. Only once that letter's been sent. But that thought made little difference and didn't ease her mind. The burden of his decision remained just as heavy, and she felt as though she were wandering through a thick fog. She cleared the table mechanically. James lingered in the kitchen. Go away, she thought; I need to be alone, I can't think with you looking at me. Or did she want him to take the four steps toward her and wrap his arms around her? Say it was all a misunderstanding, some temporary madness—not a single hair on his head could ever dream of leaving her and breaking all the promises he'd made, aloud or otherwise. She almost lost her grip on the pot of pickles. Why doesn't he go to the other room, to look at his charts? She placed the last plate in the cupboard and wiped her hands on her skirt. As if he isn't here, she thought. Act like he's already gone. Go ahead, you know how it's done.

He didn't follow her upstairs. She carefully opened the door to Nat's room. The boy was lying on top of the covers, asleep with his clothes on. Elizabeth sat at the foot of his bed and pulled off his shoes. She clasped her son's feet, one by one, and rubbed them warm. The boy groaned, his eyes flickered briefly, but he didn't seem to see her. She inched the heavy bedspread out from underneath him and covered him up. He curled to face the wall; she remained seated with her hand resting on the bulge covering his feet. The curtains were open, and she saw snowflakes floating steadily, unstoppable.

She woke from a dreamless sleep. Lying on her back, she could feel her baby moving inside her. She pushed against her belly, and the child pushed back with its tiny foot, an arm, or its little bottom. Get up. The icy water she splashed on her face left her gasping for breath.

She made porridge for her son and inspected his clothes. His shirt was filthy and his jacket too tight. While he ate, she rummaged through chests and cupboards for some of Jamie's hand-me-downs and found a nice linen shirt and a blue jacket with hardly any signs of wear. She was appalled by how thin Nat had become. The vertebrae on his back protruded like pointy knobs, and the skin over his ribs was stretched taught. He raised his arms like a child so she could slip the shirt over his head. She dragged him to the mirror and helped him put on the jacket. When he saw himself, he laughed and tossed his hair with a stalwart flick of the head.

"We'll stop by the shoemaker's this afternoon," she said. "You're to have new boots. Now eat your pap, you have to go."

He obediently spooned his bowl clean. "Snow is rain," he said. "Cold rain that sticks to the ground. Where is Papa?"

"Working. He's trying to find men for the new expedition. He has a lot to do. Are you coming home straight after school?"

Nat nodded, grabbed his bag from the chest, and bolted for the door. "Button your jacket!" Elizabeth said. "Put on your cap and give me a kiss." She leaned over and felt the small, wet boyish lips on her cheek.

She watched him leave, bounding like a carefree deer across the street, zigzagging every few steps.

She spent the day in a gloomy haze as if everything inside her were blanketed with snow. The maidservant arrived and made a huge racket in the scullery while Elizabeth tidied the living room. In the cupboard, she chanced upon that red waistcoat she'd been planning to make for James: the scrap of paper with his measurements, a spool of silver thread. She folded everything together, wrapped it in paper, and tucked it away in the large chest. When she stood up, James was in the doorway, observing her, silent. She nodded, an idiotic gesture that made no sense, as if he were some passing acquaintance she'd run into on the street. "I have to go," he said.

The shoemaker was on his knees, meticulously outlining Nat's feet. "I'll allow some room for growth," he said, looking up with his neck kinked. "But not too much, otherwise they'll fall off his feet when he runs." The workshop smelled of oil and leather; Elizabeth was sitting on a stool by the door, studying the shelves of down-at-heel shoes waiting to be repaired, the tools spread here and there, the affable fellow's bald crown.

He showed Nat a piece of leather. "Feel this," he said, "it's soft and smooth but very strong. Take a whiff, too." Nat, standing in his stocking feet in the middle of the room, obediently did as he was told and nodded his approval.

"Two weeks," the cobbler said, "I'll deliver them in two weeks." He looked questioningly at Elizabeth.

"That will be fine," she said. "Maybe my husband needs new boots, too. You could take his measurements then."

The shoemaker patted his waistcoat pocket. "I never leave home without my trusty tape measure. At your service! I'll do my utmost. Madam, young sir, I bid you good day!" Nat squeezed his feet back into his old shoes and shook the shoemaker's hand.

"What shall we do now?" she asked, once they were back on the street. The boy looked at her, taken aback. "Aren't we going home?"

"Whatever you want. What do you fancy?"

"Grandma's," Nat said. "Let's go to Grandma's and eat some sweet patties."

Elizabeth checked her purse: there was enough for a carriage to Barking. She took her son by the hand.

Her mother couldn't believe her eyes when Elizabeth and Nathaniel walked into the tavern. She came out from behind the bar and hugged her grandson. "You just had a birthday," she said. "Turned twelve, am I right? I have a little something for you, just wait." She took a coin from the cash box and pushed it into Nat's fist. Only then did the woman turn to face Elizabeth.

"Doesn't matter," she said. "I'm happy whenever you do manage to visit; I don't hold it against you. You're married to a celebrated man; you're busy, I know. Can you feel any signs of life?"

Elizabeth nodded. Suddenly, she was acutely aware of the size of her pregnant belly. In fact, her skirt was much too tight, and her back ached. She wanted to sit down, rest her swollen ankles on a stool, and complain. The overheated room reeked of stale beer. She loosened her waistband and sank into a roomy chair. Nat slipped into the kitchen. She heard him chatting with her stepfather.

"Things here are going well, you know," her mother said. "Plenty of customers, and I have a new helper for the evenings, when it's full. My teeth are bothering me. They're falling out. The only things I can eat are soup and porridge." The old woman opened wide, and Elizabeth reluctantly peered into her mother's mouth to see the ravaged gray stumps interspersed with pale-pink craters.

"I've tried oil of cloves. And plenty of gin: that cuts the pain. What a treasure, your Nat. Does he have to go to that Naval institute so soon? Well, I suppose they do have to learn a trade, those whippersnappers.

You can't start early enough. You were just a stripling yourself when you sat down with those ledger books, weren't you?"

She should try to stanch the current of blather, she thought, but couldn't help letting it wash over her. It wasn't until her mother paused to refresh her drink that a gap appeared between the sentences.

"Mother," she said. The woman looked at her, friendly, expectant. "He's leaving once more. I haven't told Nat yet." She put a warning finger to her lips. "He promised to stay home, but he's sailing off again." She felt the tears smarting behind her eyes; so childish, so predictable, it made her furious.

The old woman crept closer, bottle in hand. She sat down beside Elizabeth and sipped thoughtfully from her glass. "Will he make a lot of money?"

Elizabeth nodded. "Most likely, plus a sizable reward on top of that, if he manages to carry out the assignment. But he already earns enough." She heard how weak and uncertain her voice sounded. She pulled a handkerchief out of her sleeve, blew her nose and wiped her eyes.

"You can't stop it," her mother said. "They're men, aren't they? They want out."

Elizabeth couldn't help but laugh at this woman, bolstered by gin, dressed in dark gray, spewing comforting words of wisdom from her mutilated mouth. Mary laughed along with her daughter and rested a hand on Elizabeth's knee.

"That's good. All you can do is laugh. What are they trying to achieve, why all the fuss, where are they hoping to go? He'll come back, he always has. Just wait, one day he'll have had enough of traveling. You can't talk him out of it. He's as stubborn as an old mule, you know that. Here, have some." She held up the bottle.

"Just a drop," said Elizabeth. The sharp smell of gin made her queasy, but she forced herself to swallow a sip. The alcohol seared her throat so that she almost started crying afresh. The smell of singed fat wafted out of the kitchen.

"When's the baby due?"

Elizabeth slid deeper in her chair. "May. He'll be gone by then, if everything goes according to plan."

"Well, that's nothing new for you, is it? I'll come help; John can manage here on his own for a while. Or do you still have that friend of yours, Fanny, Franny?"

"Frances," Elizabeth replied. "No. She emigrated to America. What was it like for you to be on your own when Daddy died? You've never talked about it."

The old woman topped up her glass and massaged her jaw.

"Uncle Charles lent a hand. And I soon ran into your stepfather. It was all such a long time ago, I never think about it anymore. You mustn't fret. Things are the way they are, child. You'll only wear yourself out if you try and change things. And you'll be disappointed, because everything goes the way it does, and you can't do anything about it. Not a thing."

I can't help it, she thought. James says it's not up to me, I'm not involved. But isn't it about me, about us? He's leaving me in the lurch, isn't he? Why does everyone think about *his* motives, and nobody puts themselves in my shoes? Have I got it all wrong, is there something I don't understand? If only I could be more like my mother. Not worrying. While my future comes crashing down around my ears!

She drained her glass. Nat came in bearing a platter of steaming patties. He was grinning from ear to ear.

It had been ages since she'd felt so at ease. All four of them eating, their elbows resting on the grimy, cluttered table. Nat was in high spirits, talking with her stepfather; she heard stories he never shared at home.

There were grease stains on his new shirt. Never mind. She leaned back and shifted her bulge toward the front. Soon they'd be in that miserable coach, going back to that dismal house; she didn't want to think about it. Nat was on his third plate of patties, talking about his violin with his mouth full. He bragged about his teacher, who could do anything: play the organ, compose, bow a violin.

"He's stopped playing the trumpet. Doesn't have the teeth for it anymore. But he can still sing; he's teaching me that, too."

"You should come and fiddle here sometime," her mother suggested. "Earn a little pocket money on a Saturday night. When you're a little older." She looked obliquely at Elizabeth, who nodded in assent. What am I doing? she asked herself. I'm not going to allow my child to play in a seedy tavern full of drunken sailors. I don't agree with that, do I? She held up her glass for more gin. The sound of a bell jingling was followed by rapid footsteps.

"Isaac!" her mother exclaimed. "A night full of surprises! Come sit down, help yourself to some sweet patties. Look who's here: your cousin Elizabeth and her little virtuoso."

Elizabeth discreetly tried to refasten her skirt, but her fingers couldn't find the clasps. Nat leapt up to shake Isaac's hand. Don't bother, she thought; what's the difference. I'm at home. Her cousin had grown more muscular and had lost his boyishness. She was struck by how much he looked like her mother, his aunt. The hair—his lush, chestnut waves and her salt-and-pepper hanks—fell around their faces in the same way.

"Aunt Mary," Isaac said, "don't get up; I'll come join you."

He pulled up a chair and sat straddle legged at the head of the table, between Elizabeth and Mary. He loosened his neckerchief and unbuttoned his waistcoat. Elizabeth's stepfather, John, brought them some beer. Isaac took a swig and wiped his full lips with the back of his hand. Nat couldn't take his eyes off him.

"Don't you remember, Nat?" she asked. "Isaac went with Papa. We saw them on the *Resolution* just before they set sail. You were listening to the bagpipes. And the violin."

"I've been around the world twice with your father," Isaac told the boy. "Thanks to him, I was the first to set foot in New Holland. That was on our voyage with the *Endeavour*. We'd sailed into a gorgeous bay and dropped anchor. Everyone was excited and happy because we'd finally sighted land. The captain lowered the launch and waved me in. We rowed toward the beach. It was hard to see if there were any people; maybe there were some a little farther along, among the trees. The captain had the scope round his neck. The launch scraped bottom, and we stood up. 'You first, Isaac,' the captain said, allowing me to step into the surf. That's how I became the first foreigner to set foot in the new country."

"Were there any people?" Nat asked.

"They acted as if they couldn't see us," Isaac answered. "That was mighty peculiar. A great big ship there, in their bay; they'd never seen anything like it, of course. But it was as if we didn't exist. They just carried on with whatever they were doing: gathering shells, tending the fire. They looked right through us. The captain offered them trinkets; he placed some nails and beads beside their hut. They left the gifts lying there. Their eyes slid over them—they must have seen everything, but it didn't sink in. We—with our ships and objects—didn't exist."

"Are you free now?" Mary asked.

"Just back. I'm on half-pay. Put my name down for the new expedition. I'm biding my time." He looked shyly at Elizabeth while he was chatting. "Nothing is more breathtaking than sailing the Pacific. The last time, I helped draw up the charts. Land that nobody knows about. And then suddenly, because of our drawings, it exists! That's something I'd like to be part of again, preferably with Captain Cook, of course. Will he be joining us on the voyage?"

"Nothing's been decided," Elizabeth said. "They're pressuring him; they would like him to go. We still have to talk it over."

She felt nothing, and spoke the treacherous words as if they were a hollow announcement. Then she realized that Nat was listening, and regretted opening her mouth. James's possible departure was between her and her husband, between her and Hugh Palliser; the children had no part in it.

Nat continued eating, unruffled. After he'd devoured his fourth helping of patties, he worked up the courage to interrogate Isaac about Naval training.

"We had two horn players in our class," Isaac said. "They took part in all the lessons and had to climb the rigging like the rest of us, but they were allowed to practice their instruments every day. At night, they played us a tune before we went to bed. That pair of intertwined voices was something beautiful; unbelievably sad and wondrous at the same time. You should become a horn player, Nat."

Elizabeth stood up and refastened her sagging skirt. She followed her mother into the kitchen, balancing a stack of dirty plates on her arm. An oil lamp flickered in the draft, so their elongated shadows fluttered eerily against the whitewashed walls.

Mary fished a vial of tincture of clove out of her apron and used a finger to rub it into her aching gums. Elizabeth sank into the stool. No dishwashing, for pity's sake. Nothing else at all, please. She pulled off her cap and rested her head on the wall.

"Spend the night here," Mary suggested. "Isaac's going back to the city; he can deliver a message to James. You and Nat can have the guest bed."

She nodded. Suddenly, scalding tears were coursing down her cheeks, sad but not unpleasant. Mary kept worrying her inflamed jaw. Men's voices could be heard in the distance. The bell rang from time to time, announcing the arrival of a new customer. No one interrupted the two women in the kitchen.

Mary pulled her finger out of her mouth.

"When you want something, you become disappointed," she said. "Things are always different than you expect. You've set your heart on something; I can see it in your eyes. It's the way you've always been, even as a little girl. You have plans; you know how you want things to turn out. That leaves you vulnerable, my child. Now you're stuck with the consequences." She picked up a grimy dishrag and handed it to her daughter; Elizabeth used it to slowly wipe her wet cheeks.

"The only thing you can do is give in. You have to be like the grass. When they trample you with their heavy clogs, you bend. Sooner or later, they'll move their feet. Then you'll rise up once more. But if you remain upright, like a reed, you'll break. This will pass, Elizabeth. One way or another, everything comes to an end. Just wait. Don't resist, because then you'll lose."

"Like the grass," Elizabeth whispered. How lovely. The grass along the riverbank: submerged, dried out, eaten, trampled. It always bounces back. I will become like the grass. Like the grass.

7

She saw him ducking somewhat sheepishly into the great room. But he
didn't shut the door behind him, so she was able to hear the treacherous
sounds: the chair legs scraping the floor, the opening of the inkpot, the
crackling of the paper, and finally, the whispering murmur of the pen.
With no interruption. He knew what he wanted to write.

They bumped into each other in the hallway; he held the sealed
letter in his hand.

"A formality," he said, "in essence, it's just a formality. I agreed to do
what I already promised, and will now turn my attention to the preparations. That means I'll be the one to select the crew, choose the cargo, the
ports of call along the way, the route. I've asked Sandwich to reinstate
me to my post at the hospital as soon as I return. Just so you know."

He held up the letter. "This is an official step in the course of events.
It means nothing. I can have myself relieved anytime, right up until the
last minute if I so wish."

She nodded. It had no more meaning than a heavy boot crushing
the grass. She'd sow cardoon this year, against the warm garden wall.
She was already looking forward to the three-foot plants that she'd tie
up with torn strips of bedsheet, the leaves bunched together to keep
the sun from burning the stems awake. She'd cut the white stalks into
pieces and steam them. By then it would be nearly autumn, and she'd
be standing there with a flat belly, one child lying in the cradle while

another had left. It doesn't mean a thing. She found it hard to imagine, just as she could not believe that anything would ever grow in the frozen garden again. One day at a time, she thought. Step by step. Who was going to eat all that cardoon?

That afternoon, two letters arrived: one for him and one for her. They sat opposite one another, reading beside the hearth in the great room. James was the first to look up. "Sandwich's answer," he said. "He didn't waste any time. I have been appointed. Tomorrow I'll go hoist my banner on the *Resolution*. And see how those miserable tinkerers at the dock are getting along with the repairs. I can go back to Greenwich whenever I want; says so right here in writing. What's your news?"

She folded her letter and tucked it inside her jacket. "Mother. How much she enjoyed it, last time, when Nat and I dropped in." To her surprise, she didn't blush, didn't even think twice about the lie.

"Not like your mother to write; I didn't know she had it in her. You must have really brightened her day. I will be out for a while. They are waiting for me at the coffeehouse."

When she heard the door slam, she retrieved the letter and reread it.

Elizabeth. Dearest Elizabeth,
Since our last, unfortunate meeting, I do not know where to turn.
I think about you day and night, about your disappointment,
your anger. I talk with you incessantly. You blame me for James's
leaving. That I understand. He shouldn't go, he's too tired, and in
any event, it's too soon after his recent return. But you must under-
stand that I cannot hold him back. I've known him longer than
you have, and as a fellow seaman, better than you have. There's
no point trying to convince him to stay home. Believe me, darling
Elizabeth. That's how it is.

I cannot bear your coldness. We must not misunderstand one another. Your friendship means more to me than I can say. Please allow me to explain myself. See me this afternoon, when I come to visit. I beg of you.

Hugh

The hand holding the letter dropped into her lap. She sat there, motionless, thinking of chores that required muscular strength: wringing out sheets, working the soil, scrubbing the floor. Time passed.

When she heard a knock at the door, she sprang up, flushed and confused. She heard the maid's footsteps in the hallway, an unfamiliar male voice, some talk, laughter. Curiosity drove her out of the room; she rushed into the corridor and saw the shoemaker holding a package.

"The boots for the young gentleman," he crowed. "Would you like to see them?" The wrapping paper rustled to the ground. The man caressed the leather and passed the child-sized boots to Elizabeth. Oh, she thought, he already has such wide feet; bigger than I'd suspected. No creases; no scuffmarks. With his modest weight, he'll make his mark on these shoes; they'll shape to his toes, his heels. She ran her hand over the unblemished shanks, her fingers along the stitching under the smooth soles; she pressed her nose between the aromatic pair.

"Was I supposed to measure the captain?" asked the shoemaker. She looked up and pressed the boots to her chest. "I completely forgot," she said. "He's at the coffeehouse; you can go and ask. I'm not sure."

The man nodded and left her standing in the hallway, surrounded by the fragrance of leather.

There was another knock on the door. She'd been warned and waited silently in the great room for Hugh Palliser to be admitted. She placed the boots on the table and looked him in the eye.

He seemed downright miserable; pale, with red-rimmed eyes and a carelessly buttoned jacket. Without waiting for her to ask, he sat down facing her, shoved the boots to one side, and leaned toward her on his forearms.

Him, she thought; him. He who was meant to help me. Who understood me. The one who wouldn't let me go. Who seemed to know what I was thinking better than I did. Who followed my daughter's coffin beside me. What is happening, what's this about? Did I honestly expect this man to make an effort to hold my family together? Why would he do that? If he does anything at all, it's on James's behalf. And I was stupid enough to equate those two things. This disappointment, this cruel unmasking, is my own fault. I let myself get carried away. I had wishes and desires.

Images spun through her head: her mother, with a mouth full of gray stumps, speaking of grass. James, with his back turned, listening to the story of Elly's death. Hugh allowing her to cry against his bare forearm.

Elizabeth laid her own arms on the table. She opened her hands. "I have nothing to offer you, nothing to tell," she said. "It would be better if you left."

In a flash, he seized her forearms. She was stunned by the strength with which he grasped her flesh. He brought his face close to hers and was just opening his mouth when the door flew open. Startled, they both looked up at James, whose tall body filled the doorframe. His gaze shifted from the intertwined arms on the table to Hugh's distraught face and Elizabeth's blazing cheeks. Then he looked over their heads, into the garden, and they finally let go of each other.

He's going to faint, she thought. Hugh's face was pale as death. He looked distractedly at his useless hands resting on the table. No salvation would come from him. Was it up to her to break the silence? But how? It had grown chilly in the room; she saw that the fire in the hearth had dwindled to a flameless smolder.

"I was waiting for you in the coffeehouse," James said. "But you're here. Are you coming? I'm ready."

His voice revealed nothing, even though he had a keen eye. During his travels he was completely reliant on his powers of observation. He read the intentions of others through their facial expressions, posture, and gestures. Peaceful? Hostile? Because there was no shared language, he had little choice. Why, then, could he not see what was taking place right here?

He'd turned impatiently to adjust his cravat in front of the mirror. Their eyes met for an instant. Nothing happened.

Hugh rose slowly and creakily. James stepped back into the room and handed Hugh his cane, just in the nick of time, by the look of things.

"Not very spry today," Hugh uttered hoarsely. He coughed elaborately into his handkerchief. "Shall we have a drink first? I'll be all right after that. Elizabeth, I look forward to talking with you in more depth sometime soon. Until then."

She was too astounded even to nod, and listened to the shuffling in the corridor. Then she stood and peered out the narrow window facing the street. James had given Hugh an arm; the men set off down the street, side by side. She saw their lips moving, their eyes lighting up, the shake of a head, a grin—she saw two friends who were delighted to have run into each other. She noticed how similar they looked from behind. Tall and thin, with narrow calves and prominent shoulders. Their faces were different, though: James, with his heavy eyebrows and piercing eyes, made a fierce impression, while the expression on Hugh's well-proportioned oval face was usually pleasantly ironic. But she couldn't see that now.

I should feel something, she thought: anger, indignation, something along those lines. Grief, or the gloom that follows abandonment. But I feel nothing. I'm waiting for a gale to rise within me, but there's no wind. She rubbed her belly until she felt the baby move. Pressure and counterpressure: a small, budding game.

Nat came home, and his eyes lit up when he saw the boots. They drank tea and talked about the finer points of caring for leather. He fetched the jar of boot grease from the scullery, and they began rubbing and polishing, holding one boot each. The leather became darker, deeper, emerged gleaming from beneath the polishing cloths. Nat sighed. He kicked his worn shoes underneath the table and slid effortlessly into the smooth, new calves of his boots. Perfect.

Dear Frances, it's almost spring, and the winter aconite and crocuses are blooming in our garden; high time I wrote to you. News of the war reaches us, of course; I read it in the papers and think of you. I hope you're not in any danger—that there's no sign of trouble in the back of beyond where you live. I have no understanding of politics; I do know, however, that I'm sick of our government's arrogance and power grabbing. What's wrong with you forming an independent nation? What's it got to do with England? All that fighting, so many boys dying for nothing—no. Pointless.

But sometimes I think I do understand. It's like letting go of a child. Then I compare America with our Jamie, who was so eager to leave home. Sometimes I would also like to send a ship full of cannons to fetch him back. But when I see how happy he is in Portsmouth, that desire dries up. Then I leave him alone.

This past winter, Nathaniel seemed reluctant about his future. He became very quiet and withdrawn. But he's been doing better of late. My cousin Isaac—surely you remember him—had a talk with Nat and put his mind at ease about life at sea. I have to

*admit I abhor the idea of letting go of Nat. He's so vulnerable, so
unsuitable for that wild gang at school—but perhaps my vision is
clouded, and he'll find his feet there, some means of doing what he
loves. As a mother, you're always trying to catch up; your child is
almost always further along and braver than you think.*

*I want to tell you about James. You know he's been appointed
to the hospital, an honorary position, a sort of pension for services
rendered. I was elated, because it meant peace at last, a family life,
without all the fear and uncertainty. I'm writing in the past tense,
Frances, because it seems that those plans have changed. The Royal
Society, the Admiralty, and yes, even the king—they're all fired
up with scientific passion and curiosity. Now that the Southern
Hemisphere has been described in detail, the northern half also
needs to be charted. James offered to lead the expedition. Of course,
they gratefully accepted his proposal on the spot. Now that I put
it on paper like this, it may seem as though I'm at peace with the
decision, but I don't mind telling you I have no idea what to think.
Will I spend the summer alone in this house? James at sea, both
boys at school, and me here rambling through these empty halls
and rooms? And the baby, although I hardly dare to think of it.*

*In fact, I don't believe it will go ahead. I think that James is
pretending, that at the last minute, he'll hand over command to
his colleague and simply remain ashore. It's a strong hunch, one I
can't set aside. I just know it.*

*Right now, he's working hard on the preparations. He says the
ships at the Deptford yard have been badly neglected, and he has to
do something about that. He makes lists of what to take. I see them
lying on the table. He conducts interviews with the officers who've
signed up. But once everything is done, once he's satisfied that the
entire venture is adequately fitted out—then he'll step aside.*

*Or am I fooling myself? I so long for him to see the birth of this
child, to watch it grow up. Frances, what am I to do?*

I visited my mother recently. She told me to let it go, not to put
up any resistance. I don't know what to think about that.
Sending you a big hug, dear Frances. Please write back soon.

As giddy as a child, she thought, when she saw him. There was a spring
in his step, and his shoulders were held back. His face lit up when he
saw her, and he waved the letter in his hand.

"Member of the Royal Society!" he called, a little too loudly, his
voice almost breaking. "They've accepted me. I'm to present my introductory lecture on March 7."

His hair stood on end, and his coat was hanging open. She had an
unbearable urge to say something, do something. She got up, took a few
steps toward him; why was she so pleased, so surprised? His acceptance
had been a foregone conclusion, she hadn't doubted it for a second—
but apparently, he had. Why? She felt embarrassed.

"How nice, James," she said, wrapping her arms around him. She
exhaled her congratulations into his waistcoat, felt his ribs, the edge of
his shoulder blades, the heavy pumping of his lungs.

He broke free; he needed to keep moving. "Every year, they award
a medal for the best lecture, did you know? If you win, it means you
really are someone; you've gone up against the sharpest minds. You're
at the forefront of science."

A bottomless pit, she thought. It will never be enough. You shovel
in heaps of recognition and praise, but it doesn't help. I must stop
thinking; I should not look at him like this, not maintain such a critical
distance, but simply take part. Rejoice with him.

"Have you finished your presentation? How long do you have to
speak? Will it be open to the public?"

"No, I don't think so," he said. "A closed meeting, members only.
My lecture has to last an hour. I've written some things down, but have
no idea if it's long enough. Or too long. Would you like to hear it?"

She nodded and led the way to the other room, where she sat at the table expectantly, arms crossed.

"Practice," she said. "Give me your watch, so I can time it."

James pulled out a stack of papers and started putting them in order. He unfastened his watch and placed it on the table in front of Elizabeth. Then he stood—legs set wide—in the vacant space between the table and the door, and began to speak.

"Slower," she said. "Imagine you're in a lecture hall, a huge room filled with people. Look at them. Say 'good evening.' Grab their attention."

He looked at her, surprised. He smiled.

"I need a lectern, like I'll have there. A place for my bits and bobs. And a glass of water."

They scurried about, like children preparing a play. He brought down Nathaniel's music stand; she carried a pitcher of water into the room.

He straightened his cuffs, placed the papers in front of him, and welcomed the imaginary audience.

"The title of my lecture is: 'The Method Taken for Preserving the Health of the Crew of His Majesty's Ship the *Resolution* during Her Late Voyage round the World.'"

He looked up and, without glancing at his notes, began speaking in a spirited manner. Telling a story, as it were. She was swept along; she didn't have to make any effort to remain captivated. When he started, she forced herself to look at his watch. She used her fingers to remember the time: eleven fifteen. Don't forget.

At first, her eyes latched onto distracting trifles: a stain on his white trousers, the pointing finger with which he marked a list in the air, his soles scraping the floor. Before long, she stopped noticing.

He colorfully described the threats to health on board: the sailors' filthy habit—especially during bad weather—of relieving themselves in the hold; the bugs, fleas, and lice making themselves at home in unwashed clothes and greasy hair. The heat in the tropics, the cold at the pole, made infinitely harder to withstand by the sailors' habit of swapping clothing with the natives in exchange for foodstuffs and love. The love itself, and the sickness with which it was associated. And finally, the provisions—maggot-filled hardtack, stinking salted meat, putrid water.

James told of the measures he'd taken, and how he'd persuaded the crew to follow his orders. When explanation and example failed, he threatened them with punishment. Winter clothes were kept under lock and key, only distributed when the temperature dropped below freezing, and then gathered up again. The hold where the sailors slept was subjected to regular inspections and swabbed every day with vinegar water. Fresh food had top priority. Failing that, sauerkraut was back on the menu.

There wasn't much to be done about the lovemaking; he couldn't lock up his men. "I permit it because I can do nothing to stop it," he said, although it clearly pained him. Of course, the doctor examined everyone who went ashore, but it seemed as if the disease could remain hidden in men who—at first glance—appeared healthy. Toward evening, it was horrifying to watch the exodus of sailors and Marines, joyfully sprinting toward the indigenous girls, laughing, dancing, and drinking the night away. As the sun set, the captain sat in his cabin and imagined how, at that very moment, a disease was being spread on the island for which there was no cure. Appalling. He sometimes saw the consequences when, years later, he happened to revisit the same island. Then he felt ashamed.

Figures! Mortality rates! He compared the loss of crewmen on the Navy's ships and in the merchant marine with his own results during the two world voyages. Scurvy was a thing of the past. He briefly sketched its hideous symptoms. Wiped off the face of the earth! If, after ten weeks of sailing along the Antarctic ice, someone exhibited the first scant signs, they were promptly treated with carrot juice. Upon landing, anywhere at all, he sent a green squad out to collect edible plants. It helped. Hygiene, diet, and discipline had driven away the disease.

She was proud of what he had thought of, what he had done, and the way he talked about it. He had reached the end of his lecture and had started summing up an endless list of names. Expressions of gratitude. Apologies for his headstrong approach to problems. Praise for the Royal Navy. Tributes to the benevolence of Lord Sandwich, hallelujahs for the king—

"Five minutes too long," she said.

He looked up in surprise, dropped his arms limply along his flanks, and stepped back.

"I was sure it would be too short," he said, sounding oddly hoarse and feeble. "Are you sure?"

She handed him the watch. Twenty minutes past twelve. He grinned and tucked the small timepiece into his waistcoat pocket. Relieved, he drained his glass of water.

"What do you think? If it's too long, I can talk faster. Or should I leave out that bit about venereal disease? That would be better, I think. It's such an unseemly topic. And one against which I am powerless. If I cross it out, everything will fit within the allotted time."

"Nonsense," Elizabeth said. "Your presentation is about illness. That is an illness, whether you can do something about it or not. It's science, James; it's about the facts, not about success. It makes no sense if you're not honest and leave things out for the sake of decency. You have to scrap all those expressions of gratitude and honorable mentions; they're utter nonsense. Why should you be grateful? They're lucky to have you; there is no reason at all to flatter Sandwich and the king. Just leave that part out."

"You mean it? Is that allowed?"

"Of course. You present your conclusions, the results of your procedures, and then you thank the audience for their attention. That's how it's done."

Where did that come from? As if she understood the rules of the game. But she knew it; she felt sure she was right, and his reassured and satisfied expression proved it. Maybe it's possible, she thought. If she gave him enough support, understood him enough—then they could face that perplexing society together; then he could also feel like a captain in the lecture hall, as well as in the palace.

All at once, she was exhausted. She leaned back in her chair and propped up her belly with her hands. Hugh's amicable face popped into her head, and she tried to banish the image; he was a traitor, wasn't he? He'd dropped her and neglected James's ship: a double betrayal, unforgivable.

But, she thought, but—

She tried to get hold of herself. She had to face this on her own; never again would she trust someone who pretended to be a friend. She'd been naive. Weak. He had comforted her, had offered her his naked arm. It were as if a black abyss had opened up inside her. To sink. To disappear. She gasped for breath and hoisted herself upright in the chair; noticed she was blushing. Stop, she thought; stop thinking. It's about James now, about us.

He'd rearranged his notes and carefully tucked them into a leather folder.

"You are a wonder," he said. "Thank you. You have helped me so much. If I am awarded that medal, it will be yours."

She stood up to embrace him. She smoothed his crumpled lapels, brushed the hair off his forehead, and pulled his cuffs down over his wrists. They stood at the window, arms entwined, and looked into the garden.

"Here," he said. "This is it. Our realm. We have to make do with it. I will have a couple of holes dug for your cardoon plot. There, at the back, against the wall. All this ground, there is no movement. We're marooned."

"Yes," she said. "A fine lecture. It will be a great success. You can do good things even when you're at anchor. Let go of that gratitude. You've gotten here on your own."

He nodded, still looking outside.

"Gardens. Another thing I would have liked to include: the world garden plan. Just imagine: on every island, a vegetable patch and an orchard, potato fields and a pasture with a few goats and pigs. Chickens. Then every visiting ship would be able to replenish its supplies. You could train some bright islanders to become gardeners. The king could pay their wages. A fence around it, and an entry gate adorned with a crown and the Union Jack. It's usually such a bother to purchase victuals; you waste days on end attending ceremonies and plotting. Sometimes there's nothing to be had. What a relief it would be if there were some sort of shop. Shall I put that in as well?"

She laughed. He looked cross at first but then joined in.

Whether he stays or goes, she thought, I'm going to have a baby, and someone has to help me. In three months, the time will come, it will just happen. The uncertainty surrounding James's departure cast everything into doubt, and the temptation to sit in a chair with her back to the future was great. The baby kicked the walls of her belly. She hauled herself up the stairs to the attic, to inspect the cradle. She lifted out the narrow mattress and blankets; she could air them out, wash them. The cradle itself was too big and heavy to lug downstairs; someone else would have to do that. It smelled of mildew and damp; light fell through a window at the end of the space, and in the gloom, the cradle stood like some dark animal. She kicked it, suddenly furious at this ominous baby pen. Two children—Georgie and Joseph—had died in that small bed. She was mad to keep it in the house; she should burn it, chop it up and toss it in the oven. The new baby deserved a new cradle, something light, made of bamboo, cane, whatever—something different. She'd cast out that sullied mattress, along with the blankets, and Elly's bedclothes.

She clutched the moldy rags to her chest and didn't know what to do next. Sit down, she thought; rest awhile on that foot stove over there. The thing is, I don't want to go on, but I have to. Soon, I'll be happy with the new baby, truly delighted. That mustn't happen, because then I'll be disloyal to *her*. I can never again be genuinely glad. But then, that's a betrayal of the new baby.

Her eyes adjusted to the darkness, and she spied, propped behind a large chest, the hobbyhorse Elly had taken into the street. Frances must have carried it upstairs, out of sight, gone.

She took it out and held the rope in her hand. It was the last thing Elly had clasped in her four-year-old fist. Her horse. The end of the rope was frayed and worn. She rubbed it over her face, her eyes; she tried to pick up the scent of her child, searching for the aroma of salty child sweat. There was nothing. A moth-eaten horse with a piece of rope tied to it. Moldering blankets, a filthy mattress.

She carefully draped the bedclothes over the horse and used the mattress to hide it from sight. It could stay that way. There was nothing else for her up in the attic, among the discarded bits of furniture and the strange artifacts James had carted home. It was a dusty museum that left her feeling more oppressed by the minute. Masks stared down at her, with black holes for eyes. Braided, feather-adorned reed mats, ornamental baskets, spears with sharp points—and scattered among all those exotic items were the miserable remains of an unhappy household: a cupboard with no door, a stack of threadbare towels, a bucket with a hole in the bottom.

Just thinking about the energy and determination it would take to have the whole wretched mess hauled away left her down at heart. She slammed the low door behind her and climbed back down the stairs.

Even though it was still freezing cold, there was a hint of spring in the air. Snowdrops and winter aconite were blooming between the grayish grass, and when the wind died down, she could feel the sun on her face.

The midwife laid her hands on Elizabeth's belly. She closed her eyes and concentrated on the baby's position and size. Two more months, she said. A lively baby; he's kicking up a storm. He? Elizabeth thought, astonished. All this time I've been carrying a daughter; how can there suddenly be a son inside of me? That woman's lost her touch, it's not possible. A baby girl can kick, too. They agreed about blankets, warm water, and a supply of diapers. She would send Nat to fetch the midwife at the first sign of labor. The woman said she wouldn't have to wait for hours on her own. I'll keep you company. We'll wait together.

James will be here after all, sitting beside the bed, she thought. He'll go downstairs during the delivery; we'll call him when the baby has arrived. Then he'll come up with a bottle of port and three glasses. He'll hold his baby daughter, glowing with pride and joy. We'll drink to her health, to her safety. I'm not alone at all. But she said nothing.

She walked along the river. The water glistened in the sun, and the moorhens—those nervous birds—were already building their nests. Two figures walked a few hundred yards ahead of her: a skinny boy and a man. She was startled to recognize her son; she'd never seen him moving with such sprightly animation. Who was that beside him? She quickened her pace until she could clearly make him out: her cousin Isaac. Now she could hear their voices, as well; Nat's excited, high-pitched tone and Isaac's clear answers. She slowed down, afraid Nat would deflate if he caught sight of her. Leave him be, she thought; he's laughing, asking questions, showing an interest in the things Isaac can tell him. Let it pass; I'll find out later what it all meant.

She ducked into a small footpath between the gardens and headed home. A half hour later, Nat turned up in the kitchen, his shoulders slumped. She was about to ask him what he'd talked about with Isaac, but before she knew it, he'd vanished, and she heard him tuning his instrument.

Soup. She fished the marrowbone out of the steaming broth and set to work slicing cabbage and winter carrots. She started when someone ticked on the windowpane; the knife slipped, and she cut her fingers. With her bloody fingertips in her mouth, she watched as Isaac closed the door gently behind him.

"Did I give you a fright? I'm sorry. Let me see. Come here; I'll pump some water for you. You have to rinse it thoroughly, otherwise it'll give you trouble."

That skittishness, she thought; I must get over that. As if I'm on the verge of being caught red handed.

"Do you have a piece of clean cloth?" He took hold of her wrist and held her hand beneath the stream of water. "The cut's not deep. Hold your hand aloft for a while. It'll be fine before you know it."

He tied a handkerchief around her fingers and pulled up a chair for her. She rested her elbow on the table and propped up her right forearm, capped with a white cloth like a flag of surrender. They both had to laugh.

"I saw you walking with Nat. The two of you seemed so happy."

"Orientation," Isaac said. "I'm familiarizing him with the rules of the Naval Academy. How you can best get along. He's lucky that Jamie's there already; it's an advantage to have an older student as a protector; then they won't be so quick to bully you. Captain's kids. That can be difficult. The others respect it, but they can also be envious. Before he goes to bed, he'll have to check the knots holding up his hammock. He'll have to take those new boots of his to bed, too, otherwise they'll snip off a piece of the leather! I've explained all that to him. And how imperative it is for him to find a friend right away, on the first day. Someone who looks trustworthy. Sleep beside each other, keep an eye out, offer to help. That sort of thing."

He's so young, she thought, so enthusiastic, so high spirited. The future is a party, one he's looking forward to.

"He must do something with his music," Isaac went on. "A violin's not much use on board. In your free time, you can fiddle a tune for dancing and drinking, but it would be better if he could play the bugle. Then he'd be a ship's musician. He's going to ask his teacher if he can start now. Then he can continue with his lessons when he goes to school. I love the bugle. That's what we talked about. Will the captain be home soon? I want to ask him if I can be on his ship, not on the other one. Do you think he'll go along with that?"

Elizabeth removed the handkerchief from her fingertips and examined the bloodied gash. This was real; she'd feel the wound for weeks to come, see the straight line. Time. Body.

"Of course he'll want you by his side," she said. "That's if he goes."

"If? It's all arranged, we've been notified! The captain will be in charge. You could sign up. I did it right away; been waiting for the chance."

Must she disappoint him? Explain that it was just a ploy, a way to maintain control of the expedition? Better to say nothing. Clerke would take good care of Isaac, too.

"I'll be sure and tell the captain. I'll pass along your compliments, and tell him you look forward to joining him at the drawing table. All right?"

Isaac gave an elated nod. He was proud of his cartographic skills. One of the charts he'd drawn would be included in the new book: was she aware of that? And now he would get to map out other, more northern, unknown coastlines and headlands, tirelessly and according to the rules, until the entire world was meticulously described. He rocked to and fro in his chair and drew imaginary coastlines in the air.

"I need to lie down," she announced. "I'm glad you spoke with Nat. He needed that, and I can't help him. Thank you."

Isaac stood up, flustered by the sudden turn in the conversation, the hurried goodbye.

"Look after your fingers, you don't want them to get infected. I'll be back soon." He kissed her cheek. She remained seated and watched him lope jauntily away.

In the first week of March 1776, James presented his introductory lecture at the Royal Society. Elizabeth had aired his uniform jacket and a new shirt, and helped him with his wig. When the carriage that had been sent to collect him rattled up, James folded his notes into his inside pocket, gave Elizabeth a quick kiss, and dashed off without bothering to close the door. She waved as the coach set off.

Hours later, James returned, satisfied, and told her about the compliments he'd received from the scholars who'd attended. Everyone had been there. Even Forster had listened attentively. The lecture had lasted exactly one hour and was followed by a lively discussion. About facts, not speculations, and led by men with practical experience: physicians and botanists, rather than the philosophers, who had remained silent. A splendid evening; James was too excited to go straight to bed. They sat together beside a fire that had gone out, and Elizabeth listened to the music of his voice, although the words didn't sink in.

Now that the presentation was behind him, he could turn his attention to meeting with the officers who'd been posted on the *Resolution*. To that end, he spent his afternoons at home. One day, the weather was unusually mild, the windows of the great room had been thrown open, and birds were scratching around in the garden. Elizabeth made herself scarce during these visits, usually withdrawing to the bedroom. But that day, it felt stuffy. She'd dozed briefly, and woke up when the garden gate creaked open below. Men's voices, the shuffling of leather soles on stone. She slipped out of bed and sat on the window seat, shielded by the curtain, and carefully inched the window open a little farther.

James sauntered through the garden, his hands behind his back. Beside him was a man of twenty-five or so, in an immaculate uniform, every bit as tall and thin as James. They inspected the tropical plants and discussed the islands those plants had come from.

"I've seen the same plants in the king's garden," the young man said. "Although there, they're considerably larger."

"An outstanding gardener works there," James said, "one who may be joining us on the voyage. David Nelson is his name. Banks has a high opinion of him as well, and rightly so."

The man nodded. "Who else will be joining us? Nelson isn't a botanist, is he? I believe it's of the utmost importance that there are sufficient people with a scientific background, scholars with a wide range of knowledge. Isn't that one of the extraordinary characteristics of your voyages?"

There was a charged silence. Then James exploded; she could barely recognize his voice, so fiercely piercing, blaring against the garden walls.

"They can drop dead, those scholars! And the rest of science along with them. A damned bunch of pretentious wretches. They disturb the order on board, that's what they do! Think they are above the rules, better than the rest. Don't get me started. I will never set sail with such scoundrels again—philosophers, professors, whatever they call themselves. If they try to board my ship, I'll toss them over the railing with no mercy. Arrogant snobs. They can go to the devil! They're deplorable, I tell you, deplorable!"

The young man stared petrified at his captain, who was whirling in a rage on the lawn. A short time later, James halted, pulled a handkerchief from his sleeve, and wiped his face. He picked up the conversation where he'd left off, as if nothing had happened; she heard him mention Webber, a young landscape painter who hoped to join the expedition. The visitor, afraid his words might be taken the wrong way, gingerly voiced his admiration for the artist. William Anderson was mentioned, the ship's surgeon who had become proficient in the language of the islanders, along with his assistant, Samwell, a musical womanizer, and Ellis, who could paint birds with amazing deftness. No scientists, nothing but ordinary crew members: gardeners, carpenters, and surgeons who—in addition to their work—cherished science as a hobby. That's how he wanted it.

She saw the young man take his leave with a timid handshake, clasping his hat in his other hand. James sat down beneath the quince and heaved an audible sigh.

Elizabeth remained seated at her window, behind the bedroom curtain. She wasn't really surprised by the vehemence she had just witnessed; it was fitting that he had lost control in front of a stranger. At home, he didn't behave that way. He was always in control of himself, just as she was.

She glanced sideways at the large bed, where she'd lain just after Elly had died, with no idea where to turn. Then she'd heard irregular footsteps on the stairs. The door slid open, and Hugh Palliser had come in and sat beside her on the edge of the bed. She couldn't see him, but she felt the mattress sag, and she recognized his scent: pipe tobacco, salt. She'd howled into the pillow, writhing in pain, slobbering in anguish. As long as he was there, she could immerse herself in her despair with no fear of drowning. He hardly did a thing; rested a hand lightly on her back, whispered a word now and then. Futile, he'd said; all for nothing. Devastated, he'd said; future destroyed, hope lost. Dear child. She slowly regained her composure, and he helped her downstairs. Odd that she'd never felt ashamed in front of him. It had just happened.

Did James feel any shame about his tantrum? There was no evidence of that at the dinner table. They were eating lamb, an early spring surprise from the butcher, and she'd prepared it with onions and winter carrots because it was still too early for spring vegetables. Nat gnawed a vertebra while James thoughtfully dissected a rib. It was a tranquil scene, brightened by the last rays of the spring sun.

"Who was that this afternoon?" she casually inquired.

James looked up. "James King. One of the fellows who trained under Palliser. Gifted lad; took a couple of years off to study in Paris. Paris! Son of a pastor. But he did study astronomy. Very useful; exactly the sort I can use. A decent, easygoing young chap. And a good officer. Draws up reliable reports."

"Was it a pleasant conversation?" She didn't dare go any further than that.

"Yes," James answered. "This lamb's delicious. First-rate meal, Elizabeth. D'you like it too, Nat?"

Nat nodded and continued chewing. Had he been at home during his father's outburst? Probably not. He'd gone back to spending every afternoon with Mr. Hartland, who—after his violin lessons—was trying to teach him to coax a sound out of the bugle.

Was James cruel on board? Would he impose harsh punishments during his outbursts? She had always regarded him as a model of calm and fairness. He didn't like to see others suffer and had a distinct aversion to public floggings and executions. She'd always been convinced—or at least, until this afternoon—that as a captain, he would use persuasion to assert his will, or the power of reason. The Royal Navy was known for its strict code of discipline; sailors were thrashed with a cat-o'-nine-tails until they bled. They were tied to the mast in the blazing sun; their ears sliced off their heads. She knew it: she'd seen the lists on which the punishments were neatly noted beside the corresponding offenses. Would James impose such penalties? Or have them carried out? Stand and watch?

She'd seen punishments mentioned in the journals once or twice: a captured deserter had been tied to the mast and a fellow who had deliberately shot a native had been whipped. It sounded reasonable. But was everything that happened noted in the journal?

He sank his teeth into the meat and tore the flesh off the spindly ribs. Maybe he left out everything that would cast him in a bad light, and raged like a rampant beast without leaving any written evidence. She knew he could become irate. The compulsive thievery of the islanders left him seething. They took everything: pulling nails out of the ship and hiding plates, buttons, and calipers under their cloaks. He didn't mind about the theft of personal belongings, but he couldn't stand them stealing Crown property. He would certainly punish local inhabitants who tried to take the astronomical instruments, or run off with the quadrant or the telescope, or who dared to try to dismantle Harrison's sacred clock. He'd use the cat-o'-nine-tails, but not to the point of drawing blood, surely not.

His fury could also be sparked by the crew's stubborn refusal to eat food he regarded as wholesome. The sailors were expected to drink salubrious beer, brewed from spruce tops, but if they declined, he'd cut off their ration of rum. Educational measures. Policy. But what she'd witnessed in the garden had been something else entirely. She'd seen a man who was briefly out of control, unfettered, wild. That memory didn't mesh with this quiet man at the table, enjoying his meal. She nudged the bowl of lingonberry compote in his direction.

"Let's take a little trip," he said. "The weather's going to be fine for a few days. We can sail to Kew tomorrow and visit the botanical gardens. The ship is more or less ready, I don't need to be at the shipyard, and I'm in the mood for a change of scene. I'll request a boat; they can row us there, so you don't have to sit in a jostling coach."

Yes, she thought, why not? Gliding over the river, the sun reflected on the water, the call of seagulls and avocets overhead—why ever not?

The boat lay moored at the jetty at the end of the path between the gardens. Six rowers in red jackets were waiting. She stepped in and was momentarily unsettled by the rocking of the boat. "Spread your feet," said James. "Move with it. Flex your knees. Sit here, on the cushion."

He helped her to the bench at the back of the boat but remained on his feet while the rowers shoved off and began to pick up speed. Then he sat beside her.

"This is how we always go ashore," he explained. "I drop anchor in a bay, then we lower the launch and row to the beach. Just like now."

The boat skimmed at breakneck speed alongside the meadows and forests, under the bridge, past the castle, on toward the domes and steeples of London.

"High tide," James said, "we're going with the flow. These are good rowers. There's hardly any wind."

How did the rowers know where they were going, Elizabeth wondered. The Marines sat facing the stern, pulling themselves across the river, back to front. Maybe they saw the riverbank from the corner of their eyes, or used subtle changes in temperature to sense when they were approaching open water or land. She didn't understand the mysteries of navigation. She lowered her eyes to avoid the feeling of being ogled by six rowers. The water was a grayish brown; the blades of the oars disappeared again and again, reemerging at the end of each stroke.

The boat slid past Westminster Abbey and left behind the hustle and bustle of the city. Then they were passing through more meadows and marshlands. James pointed to the church towers of Clapham, and there, in the distance, Richmond. She let it all wash over her; she allowed the city and the countryside to pass her by, as if she were sitting still and a giant hand was pulling the landscape along.

They moored. Shouting, dripping oars, a rope tied to a bollard. James gave a tip to the rowers, who ducked into a tavern the minute the passengers were on the embankment. One Marine stayed behind to keep an eye on the boat and to warn his mates when it was time to spring back into action.

James offered Elizabeth his arm, and they approached the gate of the royal gardens.

"Banks is the unpaid director here. He's laid claim to the gardens, because he thinks he knows the most; he's probably right about that. The king is pleased and approves of all the plans. More staff, the construction of greenhouses, diverting streams to create waterfalls and ponds—here, with the king's blessing, anything is possible. Just look at those flower beds! It's obvious that dedicated people work here. Hey, Nelson!" The thin man who had been leaning over a shrub straightened up when he heard his name. His wrinkled face broke into a grin as soon as he recognized James. Shoes scuffing along the gravel path, a handshake, a bow.

"Chests," the man said, "I have prepared boxes, chests, and reams of tissue paper. A flower press, labels, a supply of spirits for preserving specimens. All set to send to Deptford. I'm ready. I will keep an eye on things here until we leave: the frost damage, the bulbs cropping up. Please allow me to wish you a pleasant stroll."

They headed inland, up a gently sloping hill. There, the shrubbery was fuller; she noticed tall trees here and there, their buds about to burst open. It was the same every year, she thought; there was no stopping the mindless, miserable spring. The sap, congealed in winter, began its unstoppable flow, and the sun's warmth gave a command that the obedient trees obeyed. They forgot how they had lost their leaves in the scourge of autumn storms, and began anew, without memory, with childlike hope.

"Look," James said, "that tree bears a fruit that's not unlike bread. When you dip it in seawater, it's as if you're eating bread with salt. Beyond that there are some trees you can tap for a kind of gum. The giant ferns are the best, but they don't thrive here. And the palms—so many species and varieties!"

He clearly saw something different than she did. He was wandering through a tropical rainforest, dark green and filled with economic possibilities. She walked across a barren plain full of half-dead gray twigs tortured by the cold. He saw lavish shrubs with strangely shaped leaves, like hands, like tongues of fire; she saw limp, colorless branches lying on the cold earth.

They heard voices. They weren't alone in the garden. They spied a group of people at the end of an overgrown passage. When they drew near, James and Elizabeth saw a foursome of liveried servants ringing a man in a simple green cloak, bareheaded, the wind tousling his hair. Where was his wig? Elizabeth saw that one of the lackeys was holding it. The man caught sight of them as they emerged from the footpath, and his face lit up.

"Captain Cook!" he bellowed. "What a perfect surprise!" He made no effort to smooth his hair or button his cloak as he approached them with his arms outstretched.

"Good morning, Your Majesty," James said. Elizabeth lifted the hem of her skirt and made a slight curtsy.

"Captain! Madam! Let us walk!" The king shooed away his servants, who promptly withdrew into a shed.

"Our dear friend, the illustrious Banks, has done a wonderful job here. And it's becoming even better! Bigger! The orangery, the greenhouses, the ponds for aquatic plants! The entire world will be brought together here. Thanks to you, sir!" The king grabbed James and Elizabeth by the hand; they walked along the desolate flower beds like three toddlers in a row.

"This is my greatest joy. I am so looking forward to the coming shipments. The Arctic flora! Northern bilberries, lingonberries, cranberries! The dwarf birch! You won't let me down, will you?"

Elizabeth felt powerful cramps running through the royal hand. Should she caress the hand, to calm the overexcited monarch?

"They want me to take command of the entire world. British trading posts and colonies everywhere. I go along with the idea, as I must, but you know, it leaves me cold. I find England quite big enough. Of course, you do have to plant your flag here and there; that's the custom, and we have to respect that. But it's nothing more than that! A flag doesn't put down roots, am I right?" The king emitted an odd, high-pitched laugh. "Just put those rags on poles anywhere. Doesn't matter to me. But please don't tell anyone! The exchange of crops, that's the important thing. Thanks to the voyages of discovery, the rest of the world can benefit from the blessings of our fields. Potatoes. Pear trees! Spelt! My dear captain, do you know how sorry I am that we tend to forget the fauna? I have a plan. Come!"

He pulled them to a bench beneath a huge weeping willow. They sat down, hidden behind a curtain of drooping branches colored by a yellowish-green haze of near-bursting buds. The king leaned toward James and spoke in a hushed voice.

"Cattle—cows, heifers, calves, even oxen! And of course, rams and ewes, goats, rabbits, and poultry: that goes without saying. But I also had horses in mind, six in number."

The king made a grand gesture as if stroking a horse's flank. Then he clamped James's arm again and aimed his high, raspy voice into his ear.

"We'll concentrate on Tahiti; that beautiful island must become our outpost. How do people get around there?"

"They sail, Your Highness," James answered. "They use boats to travel around the island. Then they go ashore and walk wherever they need to go."

"On foot? They walk? Everyone?"

"They certainly do a lot of walking. Those who are considered holy, the local sovereign or highest priest, are sometimes carried."

"Yes, yes, in a sedan chair, certainly," the king exclaimed. "Powerless behind a canopy. And bobbing and swaying, always terrified lest one of the carriers should stumble. Now I'm sure of it: you must bring the horse to Tahiti, as a gift from the British king. Galloping through forests and over mountains! Of course, they will have to learn to ride. I had the oxen in mind for improving arable farming. And we must not forget the cows. What can the cattle do? Keep the grazing land cleared. What's more, they will bring the entire dairy industry with them. Cheese production! Milk distribution! I believe my gifts will increase the fertility of the island tenfold. What joy! Such gratitude! And you are going to help me."

"It will be a tight fit on board," James said. "The animals take up a lot of space, and the feed we will need to bring along for them, even more. Water. I will formulate a plan. Large livestock don't take to the sea. Might be an idea to purchase the animals from the Dutch, at the Cape of Good Hope."

The king looked crestfallen. "But they're a gift from me! English horses, British beef. A gesture from one island to another!"

He sprang up and continued his walk. Elizabeth saw the footmen following at a cautious distance. Why didn't James say that the plan was nonsensical? Shoveling manure, filling water troughs in raging storms, enduring the complaining bleats of those beasts? Life in Tahiti, as far as she could glean from the journals, seemed to her pretty good as it was. There wasn't much need for milk and cheese beneath the tropical sun. She tried to imagine the sound of horses' hooves against the planks of the deck, the ship turning into an immense sounding board for those terrified drum rolls. A diabolical undertaking.

James promised to come up with a plan soon. The lackeys approached and caught the monarch's attention.

"I must take my leave. You see, they're coming to get me. They keep me on a strict schedule; I have to follow it to the letter. A miracle to have run into you here, to share my plans with you. I walk here every day, you know; it calms me down, gives me a chance to reflect. And here they come again. I would much rather spend the day walking with you."

The king took his leave with a profound sadness. They watched as the lackeys grabbed him under the arm and hustled him away. He seemed to resist and managed one last look back, his wispy hair flapping in the wind.

"British cattle! Promise me! British beef!"

James nodded. Elizabeth felt the urge to wave, but held herself in check. The king disappeared between the trees.

The weeks flew past. The wood anemones bloomed, the riverbank became littered with bright constellations of celandine, and Elizabeth noticed the buds of the primrose swelling in the cemetery. April, the month of rampant, unstoppable growth.

There was no end to the preparations for the voyage; as soon as one problem was solved, another took its place. She no longer kept track and simply let the days flow past. Despite her advanced pregnancy, she accompanied James to dinners and tea parties where the upcoming expedition was talked about for hours. She sat there as if it had nothing to do with her and, with her arms resting on her belly, tried to make sure that James was getting enough to eat.

As word of the preparations for the voyage spread, more people took a mind to going along. She heard James detailing the hardships: the biting cold and meager rations. Most were put off, but the writer James Boswell was remarkably persistent. He introduced himself as a fellow traveler, and not one to shy away from challenging circumstances. Elizabeth guessed he was around thirty-five, although his face was smooth and boyish. He wore a gold-embroidered vest and a coat trimmed with fur—not what you'd call seaworthy material, she thought. He only had eyes for James and didn't exchange a single word with her.

"He thinks it's exciting," James said later. "An adventure he can boast about afterward. But he would not last long on board. He is mulling it over. We talked about how, after a visit to Tahiti, you might believe you know something, but it's all just an illusion. You don't speak the language, or you speak it poorly. Suppose you point to a tree. They say a word, you repeat it. Then you think you know the word for 'tree' in their language. But perhaps they said the name of the specific type of tree. Or maybe they said, 'wood,' or the color of the trunk. You can't know for sure. To say nothing of being able to grasp the essence of less-visible matters, such as criminal justice, love, or language itself. He believes you should station a linguist there for three years or so. He's right. If the king was to offer a grant, he'd sign up immediately, he said."

Boswell returned the same week to bring James a copy of his book about his Corsican travels. In it, he'd left a long, admiring inscription. It was a glorious morning, and the men sat in the garden, chatting. Now and then Elizabeth could pick out a few words—travel reports, language use, or the arrangement of the chapters? James was flattered by his interest, she thought; he's asking advice from a genuine writer. She heard Boswell contend that the best way to introduce a new character is with speech, to keep the story alive. James sputtered in protest: how was he supposed to recall word for word what someone had said?

"But you are the writer! You can make it up yourself!"

She expected a tantrum, but instead, James began to laugh. She brought out the tea tray and poured. James pulled her onto the garden bench beside him.

"I won't be going," Boswell said.

"No," James agreed, "I thought as much. You are needed here."

Silence. In the stillness a blackbird began to sing, tentatively at first, then with growing conviction. Boswell listened, eyes closed. James looked at Elizabeth and smiled. The bird was perched on the ridge of the roof, its mustard-yellow beak held high. He whistled a cadenza of triads, complete with trills and triumphant staccato notes. The virtuoso display evolved into a song, a melody that floated purely through the air and stretched like a dome over the tranquil garden.

She smiled back.

8

The baby dropped, giving Elizabeth more room to breathe. Just a few more weeks, she thought, then I'll see my daughter. It was May; the chestnuts were blooming and the cardoon seedlings, sheltered by the fence, had sprouted. Waiting, expectant. Patiently preparing for the birth.

It suited her, and she longed for nothing else. As soon as something important happened, reality would flood into her life like foamy water breaking through a river dam; Nat would climb into that carriage, James would untie the cables of the *Resolution*, and Elly would be deader than dead beneath the sod, while another little girl wore her frocks. Waiting meant postponing decisions, keeping possibilities open, remaining silent. Waiting with such an enormous belly meant saying no to obligations, being allowed to be absentminded and distracted, lying on the sofa in the middle of the day.

She refused to accompany James to the party at the shipyard to celebrate the completion of the repairs. She was repulsed by the thought of the claustrophobic cabins, the full-to-bursting hold, and the creaking ropes. The smell of tar—no thank you, she'd rather stay home. The entire departure and all the ceremonies surrounding it were nothing but a game. It had to happen, and everyone had to be convinced, but it was a ritual dance, signifying nothing. She was certain that once James received news of the birth of his daughter, he would leap to shore, wave the ships off, and race home. Or, would the birth be the prelude to total abandonment? As long as the baby was still in her womb, everyone gathered round: her mother, her husband, and her son. She was aware of their proximity and attention, but she didn't let any of those precious people get too close. Was it conceivable that they would turn and run as soon as the child was born? It had crossed her mind, so it was certainly imaginable, but she had so many notions, and not all of them, by a long shot, could be transformed into something tangible. Hugh Palliser's face popped into her head, in alarmingly sharp focus. She shivered. Lie down a minute. She sank onto the sofa that James had moved into the great room for her, and pulled an old quilt over her belly. She dented the pillow and took off her bonnet. The lush green of the trees and shrubs filtered the light.

She was awakened by the lacerating tones of a bugle. For a moment she was completely disoriented, and she looked around—bookcase, tablecloth, oil lamp—she'd never seen the room from this low vantage point; fear boiled in the pit of her stomach. Where was she, how far along was she, was James still here, and if so, where? And where was Elly? It was only when she sat upright that the room and its furniture returned to normal, and she could recognize the bugle by its familiar motif, slow and mournful; Nat was practicing in his room. Pain nagged her lower back. Surely it wasn't starting? Already? Should she warn the midwife, send for her mother, try to find James? She forced herself to pay close attention to her son. Nat played the simple triad perfectly in time, neither rushing nor slowing down. She listened so intently that the melody echoed within her. Her breathing became measured, and she calmed down.

And now? She'd gotten up to pee, then considered making tea but decided against it when she imagined lifting the heavy kettle. She hobbled back to the sofa. She pried off her shoes, her head bent between her spread legs, clenching her teeth to banish a shooting pain in her back. She rested her head on the pillow and exhaled as if after strenuous exercise.

"Mother?" Nat cracked open the door and poked his face in. He didn't spot her right away; she saw him peering around, slightly exasperated. He knitted his brow the same way James did, and swiveled his head from the table to the bookcase, until he saw her. He approached her with the bugle in his hand.

"You're not sick, are you? Why are you lying down? Did you hear me?"

Elizabeth patted the sofa and shoved over so he could sit beside her. Behind the fine hair curtaining his face, his youthful forehead gleamed. No longer as flawless as it had been six months ago, it was now dotted with tiny red blemishes. Pale whiskers grew on his upper lip. Soon, it would be time for James to teach him to shave.

"You played beautifully. Glad it's going so well."

Nat caressed the bell of his instrument. He said that Mr. Hartland had written to a colleague in Portsmouth to ask who Nat should take lessons with when he went there after the summer.

"Mr. Hartland takes good care of you," Elizabeth said. "I should care for you, as well. As soon as I'm back on my feet, we'll make a start on your sea chest. You already have the boots."

Nat looked at the floor. He doesn't want to see my stomach, she thought. The pain burned more violently in her back and groin. The boy has to go; how could she give birth with a frightened child in the house? Where was James? Was it too early to fetch the midwife? Who could she send? The maid could go on foot, but it was still too soon. She was starting to panic; that wasn't good. Think. Stay calm.

Strange that memory couldn't handle the unique quality of pain. The fact that childbirth is painful is recorded, she could speak of it; could honestly say it was the worst pain she'd ever experienced. But she had forgotten how it felt. That memory, hidden in the body itself, had now begun to stir. Oh yes, she thought, that's how it felt, that's the way it was back then, that's how it will be later on. She broke into a sweat.

"To Barking." She gasped. "Pack some clothes. I'll give you money. For the carriage."

Nat looked at her, puzzled.

"Go to Grandma. Tell her to come here. You're to stay there."

She felt wretched and sick to her stomach. Where was James?

"But I have to go to school," Nat said, "and to my lesson."

Elizabeth bit the inside of her cheek to overmaster the pain in her groin with something sharper.

"Just for a few days. Stay over. Go get your things. Hand me my purse."

She sank back into the cushions and closed her eyes.

Nat talked with the maid in the kitchen. The kitchen door slammed, clogs clattered along the cobbled garden path, and someone stormed up the stairs, then shifted a heavy chest and stomped back and forth over the floorboards. She could hear it all clear as a bell, but she didn't respond to any of it.

She tried to halt the process until her son had left. He thumped downstairs, lugging something heavy, as she could deduce from his irregular footsteps and slow tempo. In the hallway, his burden fell with a thud, and he came into the room, his jacket flung loosely over his shoulders, his bugle in a case on his back.

"My purse," she said. The boy looked high and low: mantelpiece, windowsill, table, darning basket.

"Try the kitchen? In the pocket of my apron? Wait, I'll give you a hand."

She slid her feet onto the floor and stood up.

"You must take twice as much as you need, so Grandma can pay for her trip, as well. Come on, time to go."

A gulf of warm water washed out of her; she was suddenly standing in a lukewarm puddle, her feet wet. Nat, on his way to the kitchen, froze in horror.

"I'll get my piggy bank." He bolted upstairs. Elizabeth sat down in her sopping skirt. All wrong, she thought. Hopeless. He thinks his mother has wet herself; he's ashamed. If I try to explain what really happened, I'll only make it worse.

Voices in the garden. The pump squealing. The midwife comes in; James is standing behind her in the hallway.

"It just happened," Elizabeth said. All at once, she couldn't control her tears. James moved toward her, but the midwife waved him off.

"First, we're going to get everything ready. Is there a tarpaulin on the bed? Towels? Water? Mrs. Cook, we're going upstairs."

"Wait a minute," Elizabeth sobbed, "it's coming back. Another pain."

Nat came back into the room, his piggy bank in the crook of his arm. "I can't get it out," he said.

"Ask your father," grunted the midwife. "Our hands are full."

"The tarp from the dinghy," James mumbled. He vanished into the scullery and returned with a dark-brown piece of sailcloth.

"Upstairs! Spread it over the bed. Towels on top. Go on up, sir, we'll follow you shortly."

The midwife helped Elizabeth to her feet. Nat stood pale and perplexed in the middle of the room.

"Give him some money. He's going to Mary's. This instant," Elizabeth urged James quietly.

"Yes, of course." He placed the tarp on the floor to reach into his pocket. Nat took the money; his eyes glanced over the bugle and the trunk, but he still didn't move.

"It'll be fine. Just go," Elizabeth said. Supported by the midwife, she shambled a few steps until she stood facing him. His downy upper lip was trembling.

"Maybe you can come home tomorrow. We'll send someone to fetch you. Say hello to Grandpa and Isaac for me." She stroked his hair and nudged him into the hallway. He gathered his things and left, looking back the whole time.

"Captain!" the midwife bellowed. "Upstairs with that tarp!"

At last she was lying in bed. The midwife slid the wet skirt into the laundry basket and bent between Elizabeth's raised legs to see how far the dilation had progressed.

"We'll have to wait," she said. "It'll be a while." She covered Elizabeth's stomach and legs and patted her cheek.

"Stay awake, mind! You'll have to get to work soon."

"Where is my husband?" Elizabeth asked. She could see the bright-blue sky through her bedroom window. Sharp-edged, brilliant-white clouds scudding along on the wind, which bent the treetops and ripped through the foliage, as if all the dust and dirt had to be swept forcefully away before the birth.

It was criminal to bring a child into such a turbulent, blustery world, she thought. She's safe now; she takes whatever she requires from me, and I keep her as warm as she needs to be. Soon the draft will rush over her wet skin, and she will cry for the first time.

"I sent him packing," the midwife said. "He'll be in the coffeehouse around the corner, that's the closest. First he'll put the boy on the coach. After that, it's just waiting. We'll send word when the time comes."

As if he has to approve of the child, she thought. I push it out and it's laid in his arms for inspection. He must acknowledge that he's the father: he'll look for something familiar in the frame, in the tiny face. Paternity remains an uncertain matter.

She thought back to the evening she'd spent drinking gin in her mother's tavern. Isaac had talked about the previous expedition, about the return voyage, an island on the way home; where was it again? St. Helena. The governor had received them; they hadn't seen him on the outward journey. Named Skottowe. The captain had known him way back, Isaac was eager to explain. What a coincidence: the governor's father was the very same landowner James's father had worked for! Hard to understand why they hadn't met the first time they'd docked there. Back then, the captain couldn't wait to set off again. He'd stocked up on onions, replenished the water supply, and immediately hoisted the sails.

However, on the return voyage, they did meet. The governor and the captain, men who had once been separated by an immense chasm of class and standing, now strolled around the island as equals. The strange thing was, Isaac went on, they were like two peas in a pod. Even their manner of walking was the same. And the set of their eyes! The eyebrows!

Both men had been brought up on the same ground, Isaac reasoned; perhaps the uncanny similarity had something to do with the amount of lime in the soil, or the quality of the air that both had breathed, or the water they had drunk. But still, it was uncanny.

Elizabeth had held her tongue, but she recalled the whispered argument between James's mother and the elder Skottowe in the barn, the one that had so upset James, who was then just a small boy. Maybe James's father, that crotchety old man sitting by the fire in Yorkshire, had good reason to feel hard done by; the sisters were right to be envious.

A stabbing pain brought her back to the matter at hand. Motherhood. How to birth a baby she'd rather keep inside herself? The midwife took another look at the progress of the dilation.

"At the next contraction," she said, "bear down."

But she didn't want to. She drew up her legs and bowed her head toward her chest; she held her breath and pushed until she was red in the face. But it was a half-hearted effort, doomed to fail.

The midwife puttered around in the bedroom, stacking baby clothes and scraps of clean cloth on a table. It was stuffy. Elizabeth asked to have the window opened, she had a sudden longing for the scent of her blossoming garden. The aroma of the blooming chestnut, lilies hidden like white pearls between erect leaves, lilac—but the midwife shook her head. No draft. Could be fatal to both mother and child. The birth had to take place in complete calm.

Time passed. Pushing. Pain. Seeing stars. Back into the pillow. Then the following contraction arrived. The sunlight became yellower, the wind died down. Someone stumbled up the stairs.

Mary came in and placed a tray with bottles and glasses on the table. She gave the midwife a clench-lipped nod. A garish shawl covered her shoulders: yellow, red, and black. Elizabeth felt lightheaded just looking at it.

"How are your teeth, mother?"

Mary grunted and began filling the glasses; beer for the midwife, a tumbler of gin for herself. She sat beside the bed, glass in hand.

"He'll spend the night in Isaac's bed. Don't worry. When I left, they were splicing rope. Nat was learning a thing or two. How long have you been at it?"

Elizabeth, absorbed by the pain, couldn't reply.

"Too long," answered the midwife. "This is your fifth, isn't it, Mrs. Cook? It shouldn't be taking so long. You must try harder."

"Sixth," huffed Elizabeth.

"Should be faster, in that case." The midwife gulped her beer and began chatting with Mary over the dome of Elizabeth's pointed stomach. It was growing dark. Elizabeth felt tears leaking from the corners of her eyes, damp tracks, gradually cooling, trickling down her temples, into her ears, onto the pillow. The two women sat on opposite sides of the bed exchanging horror stories—babies lying transverse, babies getting horribly stuck, babies too big ever to be born.

It all went over her head. The pain was so intense, her lower body would be lame forever. With every contraction, the conversation broke off and the women bent over her, holding her legs and urging her on. She smelled her mother's unwashed hair and felt the calloused hands of the midwife on her thigh.

"He's crowning," the midwife cried. "You must keep pushing; if you don't persevere, he'll pull back."

She, she wanted to say, *she*. My daughter. The daughter with whom I am imprisoned. We can go nowhere. I can't leave her to her lot, but I can't go back, either. I shall burst, snap from the conflicting movements. It's over. I can't go on. They'll have to. I'll die. It's for the best.

From a distance, she heard a man's voice. A tall figure filled the doorframe. She slipped away. Black.

When she came around, she was looking into James's pale face.

"The captain had better wait downstairs," said the midwife. "We need the space here."

Elizabeth's breathing was shallow. Yes, go away, she thought; clear off, disappear, let go. If I had the strength, I'd shake off the heavy hand resting on my forehead, yank free of the vise grip around my arm. I would kick away that massive presence. They all wish the baby would come out. I can't do this anymore.

James's back. The midwife dabbing her face with a damp cloth. The grayish stumps in Mary's mouth, foul breath filling her nostrils; what's she saying? It's starting again, but I can't.

She pushes until her eyes bulge out of her head. Her lower body becomes an ocean of flooding pain that cuts off her breath. The midwife hollers. In the calm following the contraction, she looks out the window. Already dark. She hears James pacing downstairs. She will name the baby Grace, after her mother.

"She's losing a lot of fluid," said the midwife, bent between Elizabeth's legs. "It's all blood. That's not good. She needs to put more effort into it."

"I can't," Elizabeth whispered.

"Of course you can. What goes in can also come out. Has to. Think of the baby!"

The pain welled up in a wave the size of a house. She'd drown in it. She had no choice; there was no other way. No one could save her. They only paid attention to the baby, the belly, and the legs. She saw the backs of their heads. Yes, they had to try to save the baby. She'd be left behind, split in two and devastated.

"Now!" the midwife shouted. "Keep going!" She threw herself on Elizabeth's stomach and pressed the baby down while Elizabeth pushed, hopeless, futile. Her mother's face. A glass. The smell of spirits. Gin dribbled down her chin, along her neck; she licked her lips; was given another sip, drank; it was toxic, turpentine, pure poison; but what difference did it make? Grass came to mind. Like grass. Bending under the force of the water flowing past, indifferent. The women thrust her legs so high her knees pressed against her ears. She stopped thinking. All over.

The voices sounded far away. "The shoulders," said the midwife. "I'll turn him; look, yes, that's the way, here he comes! Pass me that thread."

"Oh God! What a little imp." Mary's voice, deep and hoarse.

"Some tearing." That was the midwife again. "But not bad. She'll heal. First, the baby. He needs a smack on the bottom to make him cry. Come on! Let's go!"

The thin squeals of a baby. Elizabeth exhaled and began to cry quietly. She heard the women scrabbling around with bowls, scissors, rags, and bandages. She's here, she thought, she's alive. My baby girl. Everything will be all right.

She blacked out for an instant, but came to when James ran up the stairs. Mary showed him the baby, washed and swaddled; a scrawny bundle of cloth topped by a furious, wrinkled face.

James sat next to her with the baby in his arms. His hands are much too big, she thought. Look at that, her whole body fits in the palm of his hand.

"Our son," James said, hushed. "Here, I'll lay him beside you."

Son? What's he talking about? This is Grace, this is my daughter, my second daughter. She's a little peeved; it was a difficult birth for her, too; now she has to get used to the noise and the light, and that's why our little girl looks so vexed. He should be supporting her tiny head with those great big mitts of his. Give her here. Come on.

She folded her arms around the child and brought her nose close to the bunched-up little face. Yes, that's the smell of a newborn. Indescribable but reliable, something to recognize with joy and then forget until the next time. She inhaled the baby's pure, untainted breath.

"We must give him a name," James said. "He needs a name. Let's drink to his birth."

She heard the tinkle of glasses; Mary proffered a tray. The midwife tossed some bloodied rags into a corner and then sank back in a chair, glass in hand. She drank to Elizabeth. "Congratulations!" she said. "To your son's long and happy life. Cheers!"

No name? Baby son? She looked at James, who'd placed his scarred hand on the child's cheek and was wiping away a trace of drool with his thumb.

"Grace," she said. "Her name is Grace."

"It's a boy, Elizabeth. You've given birth to a son."

She shook her head. Broke into a cold sweat. Mary's flamboyant shawl was just visible in a distant corner of the room. She tried to get her mother into focus, but it was so dark in here, you couldn't see a thing. No wonder everyone was mistaken.

"Light," she said, "bring some more lamps; no point lying here in the dark!"

Mary brought a candle closer. "I didn't think you'd make it," she said, "but you're not a quitter. Well done. Another little feller. Now drink up. For your milk." She offered her daughter a glass of beer, but Elizabeth didn't seem to notice it and kept staring, astonished, at her mother.

"It really is a bloke, you know. He pissed all over my hands. You must've been dead to the world not to 'ave seen it."

"It can't be true," Elizabeth said. "I don't believe it."

Mary began unwrapping the cloth that covered the baby's lower body, revealing the twig-like legs. She pulled back the diaper. There was a minuscule penis on a swollen scrotum, red and wrinkly as an old pomegranate.

The wrong child. Elizabeth let go, and the child rolled over the blanket toward her feet.

"So. I'll wrap him up again. He can go into his cradle. He needs to sleep."

She felt Mary lift the scant weight off her legs. They could all get out. The wrong baby. All that misery, all that pain, all that waiting. For the wrong baby.

"You need some sleep, too. Let's first name him, and then you can rest." James's voice in her ear. Another seafarer, she thought, for him.

Did they switch babies while I was looking the other way? Impossible, there's only one baby. But then, where is my little girl? Doesn't add up. It's all wrong.

"Hugh," James decided. "His name will be Hugh. In honor of Hugh Palliser. He'll be pleased with that."

He names his children the way he names islands and bays, she realized. Hugh! If only he knew. Hugh! She'd never get that name past her lips, it was too ridiculous to be true. She burst into nervous peals of laughter, couldn't help herself; it was a farce, they'd enacted a comedy here in the bedroom, and the climax had been the arrival of the wrong baby. Named Hugh. Convulsive laughter. Applause. Curtain.

The baby sucked powerfully on her nipples with his old man's mouth.

"I don't understand," Elizabeth said. "I've always had enough milk."

"It'll come," Mary growled. "Beer's the thing. Beer, day and night. That'll prime the pump."

The baby shrieked for two days and nights. Each time Elizabeth breastfed, he began sucking hopefully, but after a few minutes he became confused and resumed screaming.

"This isn't going well," Elizabeth sighed. "Look, he's getting weaker, losing weight, becoming dehydrated."

Her mother leaned over the bed and agreed with her. "I'll give him some sugar water; then he'll sleep awhile. But he needs feeding." She placed the baby on her shoulder and walked him around the room. His tiny, exhausted face looked pale against her brightly colored shawl. A wet nurse, that was the solution. The midwife surely knew of a mother who had lost her baby and was desperate, her breasts straining. She'd look into it right away.

Elizabeth slid back onto the pillows. Was the fact she couldn't feed her child a defeat, evidence of the error of her ways? She didn't care. Six times a day, a grieving woman would come into the kitchen and sit on a low chair beside the stove. Elizabeth would bring her the baby. After fifteen minutes, the woman would go away again, and Elizabeth could change her new son and put him down for a nap. Would the child ingest the wet nurse's anger and sorrow, along with her lifesaving milk? A bad start. But the wrong milk was better than no milk at all. She closed her eyes.

"Mother?" Nat was standing next to the bed, his wet hair neatly combed. He was wearing a sailor's tunic that was too big for him. "It's from Isaac. To get ready for school. It's pretty comfortable. Isaac taught me how to use a compass. And now I can tie six knots all by myself. I played, in the evening. Twice. People sang along, and danced."

She smiled and looked at the long spindly arms hanging along her boy's body.

"Would you like to see the baby?"

Nat gave her a curious look and a curt nod. Elizabeth got up, holding on to the headboard until she found her balance, and then shuffled toward the cradle, beckoning her son.

"A boy. A little brother. I thought we were going to have a girl, but it turned out to be a boy."

Nat remained upright and examined the baby from on high. "Is he sick? He seems a little pale."

"I don't have any food for him. Grandma's going to find a woman who's going to feed him. Then he'll perk up."

"What's his name?"

Elizabeth sat on the edge of the bed and drew Nat close to her. "His name is Hugh. Your father's idea."

"After Captain Palliser?"

"Yes. Do you think that name suits him?"

Nat thought about it and shook his head.

"He doesn't look like a Hugh. I think he looks more like a Benny."

Benny, Benjamin, she thought. The youngest child. The last one.

"Would you like to hold him?"

Nat was already at the door. "No thanks. I'm going to look at boats with Isaac. Where's Papa, by the way?"

"At the painter's. He's posing. For a portrait."

Nat nodded and left.

Mary came back, having found a downcast woman who was eager to take charge of feeding the baby. She explained the agreements about time, money, and access to both the house and the cradle. It would be the wrong mother with the wrong baby. Elizabeth shrugged and went into the garden. She wanted to get her old self back as soon as she could: lean, upright, and feisty. She tried to tighten her abdominal muscles, ignoring the pain in her still-raw lower body. Now that the baby's care had been arranged, she could take stock of the current situation. What was James up to? What was happening with the publication of the book? When would she have to face Hugh Palliser, the baby's godfather? She stretched her arms out on the garden table and turned toward the sun.

It was only when a shadow fell across her face that she became aware she'd heard quiet footsteps. That's how it went in reality, she thought; she had to get used to it. First you hear someone coming, then you see the person. Not the other way around. First they go away, then they come home. First you see the baby, then you think of a name.

James sat down opposite her. He looked magnificent, decked out in the full glory of his lofty rank. Golden buttons along his crisp white breeches, his cuffs protruding from his gold-edged sleeves like pale bouquets, and a perfectly coiffed gray wig upon his head.

"How did you have to sit?"

He showed her: legs spread, his right hand resting on an open map held at the corner by his left hand. His hat was on the table next to the map. His gracious and serious gaze aimed at a point just to the side of the painter's point of view. Five of the ten golden buttons on his waistcoat had been undone at random.

"An official portrait," he said, dropping the pose and shaking his arms and legs. "I had to sit for hours. The painter didn't say a word. Nathaniel Dance. He's famous. I have to go back the day after tomorrow. It's interminable. I could not stop thinking about Forster. Did you know that Sandwich asked him to write a sample chapter? He refused. Who knows what will happen next. There's a chance that two almost identical books will end up in the same volume, because after all, he's writing about the same voyage I am. Of course, that's not what Sandwich wants. But if he gives Forster the boot, he'll lose the advance they promised him. Sandwich doesn't want that, either. In any event, Forster is furious because the Admiralty has expressed doubts about his ability to write in English. I hope he will take umbrage and back down, that would be for the best. I would like to sign a contract with the printer before I leave, but first I need to know if I'll be publishing on my own, or with him."

Before he leaves, she thought. Before his so-called departure; because he's not going away, not really. He'll go as far as Plymouth or Portsmouth, or whatever those miserable ports are called; he'll muster the crew and set up the rigging, but at the last minute he'll put Clerke in charge, and board a coach for London. And then?

In the pose the painter had asked him to assume, he looked like a competent commander. A man at the height of his powers, glowing with a quiet self-confidence that no one could call into question. A man who, shortly before his departure, might say that he's changed his mind and would like to hand over the command to his peer. But which man—exhausted from hours spent shuddering and swaying in a coach—would come back to her? That same commander? Or the writer of the journals, backed into a corner? Or the short-tempered Admiralty official? Or the sick, helpless, withdrawn man vomiting into a bucket at Christmas?

"Banks," James said. "You do realize that, until the end of time, I'll be hanging over the mantelpiece in Banks's grand drawing room. He's paying for the portrait, he commissioned it. I couldn't say no, even though the timing's bad."

What does this have to do with me, she thought; what are we going on about? What are we avoiding? Why don't I bring up the things we need to discuss? Why am I waiting meekly for those spine-chilling words: the baby, the departure, and the godfather. I let time slip away, it's filled with trivialities; the cup of time is brimming with books, paintings, and dress uniforms, and I'm in no position to do anything about it.

"I'm saving the Admiralty the cost of an astronomer by letting James King join the expedition. And, as you know, I dabble in astronomy, too. Together, we can perform all the calculations. King knows his way around the instruments as well as I do. That will save the Admiralty some two or three hundred pounds, you know? I'm going to suggest that Sandwich hand that amount, or most of it, over to you. We are entitled to it. I don't want you to have any worries. A generous allowance. Free access to all the Admiralty officials, whenever you need advice about the boys, for example. The income from the new book must go directly to you. I'm going to the lawyer, I need to draw up a will. It will give you power of attorney to make all the necessary decisions. Everything must be arranged to perfection. No matter what happens."

He'd begun talking faster and louder, and when he mentioned the will, he rose to his feet. No wonder he couldn't take an interest in the realities of domestic life, she thought, with so many other important things on his mind. Salted meat, sauerkraut, science, rotten rigging, royal cattle, timetables.

The wet nurse shuffled into the garden; Elizabeth hadn't heard the gate opening, but suddenly the figure of the woman was creeping along the walls. The woman was dressed in black, of course; still mourning her own child; how dreadful to be reduced to feeding someone else's baby. How could she?

The woman gave them a nod, face set, and went into the kitchen. "Don't you have to help her?" James wondered. "Or does she do everything herself?"

The baby howled, but in the garden, the alarming sound was muffled. "She does it all herself," Elizabeth said.

She did her best to find a connection with the life around her, but somehow it slipped through her fingers, time and again. No matter how intently she listened to James's accounts of the problems with the book—heated discussions with Sandwich, a meeting with the printer that almost led to a breach of contract, letters from Forster that were hard to decipher—it all faded from memory as soon as she was alone again. There were lists on the table on which James had meticulously written down the goods to be taken, neatly divided into categories. Floor plans for the holds, with numbers corresponding to the numbers on the list. This is real, she told herself, just look: brandy, duffel coats, barrels of vinegar. These are tangible items containing volume and weight; someone will carry them on board, put them where they belong, and wipe his hands before leaving, satisfied.

James charged in and out of the house; she hardly saw him. He bought binoculars and sextants, assembled all the books about the northern seas he could lay his hands on, and went to Banks's estate to inspect Omai's "dowry." He spent all his spare time posing for Dance, donning an air of tormented composure.

In mid-June Forster announced he'd have nothing more to do with the book. That led to meetings with Sandwich and with Hugh Palliser. The gentlemen dined on board the *Resolution*, in the partially furnished great cabin. Spirits. Strong language. Indecision. Sandwich asked James to talk with Forster one last time, to try to find a solution. Was he afraid of competition from Forster's book if both accounts of the voyage were released at the same time? Who would be granted the rights to Hodges's engravings? What would they do if Forster's account cast aspersions on the Admiralty?

James—stamping with indignation—reported on the meeting to Elizabeth. It left her cold. She had no answer to his request for reasonable advice. Then he was off once more, to his next appointment.

The departure was postponed from week to week. Omai made a farewell round of his patrons' city villas and country estates. Clerke got tangled up in some family problems and left James to look after the preparations for the voyage. There was always something that kept them waiting.

In the meantime, the pale baby grew. He was as quiet as his nursemaid, but he drank and slept. The nursemaid now changed him herself; she washed the baby and hushed him to sleep after the feedings. It was out of Elizabeth's hands. She left things as they were.

Jamie sent a letter from Portsmouth. His summer recess was approaching; he would be coming home and wondered if he'd see his father, and how far along his brother was in packing his sea chest.

Elizabeth sighed and set about writing an answer. She wrote down the first thing that came into her head. She just didn't know.

In the garden, the cardoon's leaves were lying on the ground: she'd forgotten to tie them up. A desolate jungle ran along the fence. No point trying to fix it now.

James visited the lawyer and had his will drawn up. "You'll receive a copy. Keep it safe. I wrote it exactly as we agreed." She couldn't remember anything about it but nodded in assent.

More than a week later, a final decision was reached about the book. James arrived home after an extremely frustrating talk with Forster— they'd haggled over the engravings, quibbling about who had the right to present which information, all in a tone of voice that James couldn't abide, driving him into a powerless rage until, in a fit of pique, he made up his mind. Alone. He would publish on his own. No more collaboration, no dependence on anyone else. It was for the best. He wasn't planning to change a single word anyway. Douglas had approved everything, so why should he feel insecure? He stood behind his own writing, and whoever thought otherwise could read something else. It was over and done with. He had magnanimously offered to allow Forster the use of the engravings but had instructed the printer to withhold the plates until his own book was in the shops. Everything had been settled. And how!

All at once, the time had come. It happened before her eyes. The small tropical-wood desk was carted from the house, along with the chest of books and the clothes. She saw James standing by the cradle. He leaned over the baby but seemed reluctant to wake it. He carefully rested his palm on the baby's forehead. Was he saying goodbye to his son for good, or had he whispered a barely audible "until we meet again"? His expression revealed nothing. He left to pay one last visit to the coffeehouse.

"Clerke has gotten himself into a jam," he said when he came back. "His brother's gone bankrupt and Clerke, that gullible optimist, agreed to guarantee his debts. Now the brother's run off, leaving Clerke holding the bag. He's been taken into custody! Locked up! Sandwich is livid. It's been one setback after another, as if this cursed expedition was never meant to get underway. We can't wait any longer; we're already months behind schedule. This falderal will cost us another year!"

"What are you planning to do?" she asked. The question had bearing on day-to-day life. Creditors, the power of the Admiralty, the polar winter. The reality running under the surface couldn't be expressed in words: what are you really going to do, how are we to carry on? Where are the limits of this drama? She wasn't able to pose those questions.

"I'll leave tomorrow for Chatham. Take Omai with me; the poor fellow is exhausted from crying; he's been saying goodbye for weeks, bawling his eyes out. We'll sail to Plymouth and wait there for Clerke. Sandwich and Banks are trying to have him released as quickly as possible. As soon as he arrives, we'll sail for the Cape of Good Hope."

Tomorrow. Tonight's his last night. *We'll* sail, he said. Or will Clerke be sailing alone? Will tomorrow be a farewell for two weeks, three months, or four years?

"What—" she began. She was taken aback by the raspy and hesitant sound of her voice. "What exactly are you planning to do, James?"

He halted, and she saw his shoulders sag. His arms fell limply along his body; the white scar on the palm of his right hand was visible, defenseless. Silence descended on the room. It seemed endless.

"To be honest, I haven't made up my mind," he finally admitted. "I can come back once Clerke gets to Plymouth. Or I can hand over command to him at the Cape, after I've bought the livestock the king wants—horses, oxen—you remember. Once that's done, I could sail back on a merchant vessel. It's possible. I'm thinking it over. Clerke's imprisonment certainly complicates matters. It's important he's released quickly; the conditions there are inhuman—cold and damp, you can't imagine. I'm afraid this will become a battle of prestige between the various authorities. Maybe the king himself can intervene. Incredibly stupid of Clerke; he should never have put himself in such a vulnerable position. He's endangering the entire expedition. And himself. Irresponsible."

An answer, she thought, so I know what to focus on. Will I be in bed with you tonight for the last time? Will you watch this baby grow up? Will you ever find peace among the streets and houses?

They moved in separate worlds, although they did their best to reach one another. They took an interest in each other's activities, stopping from time to time to really look at and approach one another, but they ran up against an invisible fence. Since the baby's birth, she hadn't managed truly to sail alongside James, and now that the departure was approaching, he could no longer come to a standstill beside her. He touched the baby's head again and said nothing. She listened to his tirades while her thoughts drifted elsewhere.

"What am I to say to Nat?" she asked, suddenly in tears. "We can't lie to him, can't claim you'll be back in a couple of weeks, if that's not how it stands. Or the other way around."

She sobbed the words out, couldn't control herself. James stood looking at her as she sat, wiping her eyes and nose with a handkerchief; he saw her quaking shoulders, quickly drew in a deep breath as if he was about to say something, but then he turned and left the room. The door slammed shut.

Elizabeth couldn't stop crying. The vacuum between them left room for unverifiable speculations. He was convinced, she thought, that she had been far too intimate with Hugh Palliser; he couldn't get that image of their arms intertwined on the table out of his mind. Hadn't he been staring angrily at the tabletop? Maybe he even believed that Hugh was the baby's father, and the fact that she took so poorly to motherhood confirmed that suspicion. He'd named the child after Hugh in a gesture of magnanimity, to rub his scorn under their noses. He was leaving in anger.

Oh, nonsense. He was torn between land and sea, as simple as that. Hugh Palliser had nothing to do with it. Or did he? He'd done nothing to stop James. Now he was sending him to sea in a ramshackle ship. A determined lover would do anything to get rid of his rival in order to be at his beloved's side. Hugh was taking perfidious advantage of an old friendship. Betrayal was everywhere you looked; no one could be trusted.

The sobbing died down and Elizabeth got hold of herself. No point in inventing strange scenarios; she thought everything was so phony and incredible, it could almost be an opera libretto.

When the wet nurse arrived, Elizabeth forced herself not to leave. While the baby was being breastfed, she busied herself with linens and dirty laundry. She would have preferred to sit and observe the tableau, but she didn't have the nerve. It was oddly quiet in the room; she heard the baby sucking and swallowing. The nursemaid didn't speak; Elizabeth found that peculiar. You usually prattle to a baby, saying: just wait, now we'll try the other breast, go ahead, quiet now, you're still hungry, there's more to come. But the woman said nothing, the child drank, and Elizabeth stood still in a corner.

"I'll take him from you," she said when the feeding was over. "You may go."

The woman passed her the child, carefully supporting its head. "He's growing nicely," she said, "I can feel it on him." She wrapped her black togs tightly around herself and disappeared.

Elizabeth sat on the nursemaid's chair with the baby on her knee. The tiny feet pushed against her stomach. She lifted her legs slightly, and the child rose. That's how it was back then, she thought, with her, the little girl whose eyes sparkled like stars, the one who beamed when Elizabeth sang to her, emitting peals of delight from the pure cavity deep inside her little mouth.

This baby kept his eyes shut. In his elongated face, the eyelids were silvery, delicate, like rounded shells. He grimaced, a wrinkle passed over his forehead, and he briefly raised his arms and arched his back. Then his head fell to one side; a stream of milk trickled from the corner of his mouth. He burped and fell asleep.

Then it was night. Elizabeth had had the bed made up with fresh sheets. The wet nurse arrived late in the evening; the baby was filled with milk and put away until morning. Elizabeth washed herself and brushed her hair. She laid James's uniform on a chair, placing the shoes underneath; she rolled up the stockings and hung the crisp white shirt on the back.

James smiled when he saw the two-dimensional, lifeless captain hanging over the chair. He approached her, coming closer and closer. The floorboards creaked, and the light from the lamp disappeared behind his back. His scent—fresh air, sweat, and smoke—prickled her nose. She was still detached, untouched, as if she weren't there, as if the man could walk straight through her to the window to peer into the dark garden. Then he rested his palms on her breasts, and she became flesh.

To her surprise, the blood beneath her skin tingled, and the glassy stiffness to which she'd grown accustomed vanished. The restless churning of her thoughts ceased; all that agonizing brainwork could be remembered as a fact; she could shrug it off, and set it aside.

They left the lamp burning. They needed to observe, imprint the shape of shoulders and flanks, the color of skin, of hair. Eyes. My body will recall him, she thought, even if I don't: my muscles and bones will remember what he was like. His warmth, his heaviness, and his damaged hand on my skin.

She was conscious of what was happening; she was completely present, but at the same time she made an inventory of her future losses. One could miss the strangest things. Weight. The smell of his neck. The boyish, almost gleeful edge to his voice when he spoke to her in a relaxed way, without thinking. The slope of the mattress that drove her closer to him. For the last time? She gasped suddenly in dismay.

That afternoon, he'd given her a copy of the will. She'd eyed it with bewildered astonishment. A modest yearly allowance for his father and sisters; small bequests for old friends she hardly knew. The house was for her; the assets and rights to the travel books were to be divided between her and the children. She started reading more intently: the sons would have their share once they reached the age of majority, *My daughter or daughters only if they are married with my wife's permission.* Daughter?

She didn't understand. Was he confused? Had he accidentally brought along an old will? But he'd never made one before; they'd never had that kind of money. Daughters? The baby had arrived, was born and registered as a male heir even before James had visited the lawyers.

Then it dawned on her: he wanted to leave her pregnant. He could only sail away from an island once he'd sown a garden. Then he could expand the distance between them, until it was no longer possible to reach across the tenuous space. Left behind. The back turned. Abandoned. Let go.

She thought about these things while she was still snuggled against his body, and knew with calm certainty that it was possible. For the last time.

He squeezed her hand. They were silent.

Nat ran into the garden. "He's here! Come quickly!" He pulled Elizabeth by the arm. James grabbed the baby and followed. Sandwich's coach had pulled up in front of their house; the horses were stamping impatiently, the baggage rack was overflowing with chests and boxes. Omai alighted from the folding step onto the street and fell weeping into James's arms. The baby, squeezed between his father's shoulder and Omai's glowing cheek, started to howl.

James handed Omai his handkerchief. "Come, come; pull yourself together, we'll say our goodbyes." James passed the child to Elizabeth while Omai wiped his eyes. The baby's face was disfigured by wrinkles of rage. The yowling showed no sign of letting up. Elizabeth saw James approaching Nat; he drew his son toward him, clapped him firmly on the back, and whispered something she couldn't hear. Nat nodded.

Omai seized her hand; she held the infant awkwardly on one arm while Omai made a deep bow and gave her hand a lengthy kiss. She felt lightheaded. Then James guided the sobbing Tahitian back into the coach. The coachman fastened the last pieces of luggage. Omai opened the small window to announce that he would tell everyone in his country about the wonders and benefits he had experienced here in Britain. "Farewell, exalted Mrs. Cook!" he cried. Nat had taken the baby from Elizabeth and retreated onto the sidewalk. Then she was in James's arms; the morning's cool breeze brushed her cheek, and the rim of his hat bumped into her face. "Elizabeth," he began.

"Just go," she said. "It's good. Go."

"I am running away from you," he said. "I don't want to. But there's nothing else I can do. I will come back as soon as I can. I'll write."

"Just go," she repeated. "Go on; they're waiting."

She wanted to nudge him gently toward the coach, but her muscles refused. He got in; the door slammed shut. Everything was gray: the morning light, the house's facade, the underside of the foliage on the trees. The gray horses started to move; the gray coachman waved his whip; her husband was driven into the gray street.

A few weeks later, Jamie arrived home on summer leave. Deeply tanned, he strode decidedly into the house and cast an astonished look at the cradle. "What's his name?"

"His name is Hugh," Elizabeth said, "but we call him Ben."

They drank tea in the kitchen. Outside, it was scorching in the arid garden, but indoors, it was cool.

"They're anchored at Plymouth," Jamie said. "What a waste. I would have liked to take a look on board. Did you see that wild man they're bringing back?"

Nat gave an account of the departure. "His gown dragged through the horse dung, but he didn't seem to mind! He bit mom's fingers!" The boys vanished upstairs; she heard Nat playing for his brother the clarion calls he'd been practicing. Nat had lost touch with his music—he hadn't taken his violin out of its case in weeks—and she had lost touch with Nat. Or that's how it felt. The baby's arrival had driven Nat further from her. She should be happy that he was growing stronger, more independent. That he sought the company of his big brother, and had stopped kicking and screaming about his Naval training.

She was neither happy nor sad. She put the finishing touches on Nat's gear and, except for the feedings, took as much work as she could off the nursemaid's hands. She had to get to know this baby. She was his mother. One morning, she took him with her to the cemetery. He slept on the grass while she watered the plants and deadheaded the flowers. When she was finished, she sat in such a way that a shadow fell over the baby. He slept. She sat. Nothing happened.

Back home, a letter was waiting from Plymouth. She handed the baby to the nursemaid who stood waiting, dressed in her black habit, and withdrew to the other room. She pried off the sealing wax, placed the sheets in front of her on the table, pulled up a chair, and began to read.

Omai cries the whole time and doesn't know if he should despair or be over the moon. He's constantly seasick, which, luckily, takes his mind off his inner conflict. I felt strange during the voyage. I solemnly boarded ship in Chatham, where two rows of men stood waiting, and the pipes and drums were playing. They really made a show of it. Then I was happy, for a while. They can't wait to leave. They have faith. They see me, and they think: now it's going to happen. In spite of all the uncertainty—because we still don't know where we're going, or what we'll find—they think they know where we stand. I've set the strictest of schedules for the watch. It was Jem Burney who sailed Clerke's ship to Chatham, and he didn't waste any time having a crew member flogged for some offense or other. He seemed to think he was already a captain himself. He came to my cabin last night for a drink, and described his leave-taking. His father, quivering and quaking with age, waved him off. Along with that sister of his, of course. They had to pry her off his neck, apparently. I'm glad we were able to say our goodbyes at home.

I sit here the whole day writing letters. While it's still possible. The Royal Society awarded me their annual medal for the best lecture! It's made of gold and comes in a velvet-lined box. It was waiting for me here when I arrived. I'll send it to you. Guard it with your life; it represents the victory of sauerkraut over philosophy.

Now the cook is bringing in the platters. I have received and signed my instructions. It doesn't mean anything, Elizabeth. I would have preferred to wait for Clerke here, on our own south coast, but they have ordered me to sail to the Cape of Good Hope and stay there until my comrade arrives. They know what's best. And so, I'll leave here the day after tomorrow. Hmm, smells like veal. With tender young carrots and string beans. The livestock are still on the afterdeck. Those animals howl day and night.

A dark shadow slipped past the window. She'd once again forgotten to change the baby herself. She sighed, gathered the papers, and placed them on a high shelf. She spied Nat walking through the garden. He half-heartedly kicked the trunk of the quince, picked a couple of raspberries from the bush, and sat down on the grass. His hair had grown too long again. Cut it before he leaves.

"Mother?" He came into the room, a handful of grass still poking between his fingers.

"Are you bored?"

He shrugged, looked at his hands, and turned around. She followed him, watched him toss the grass back into the garden and pause, undecided. Now just be a mother. Pour some raspberry juice into a pitcher; sit with him outdoors. A talk. Of course, he's missing Isaac. And he's not looking forward to going away.

In less than two weeks, he'd be setting off with Jamie, their chests crammed with enough to last the entire school year. If she could barely think about it, how was he to bear it? The temporary bonds—alliances with a deceptive patina of eternity—which unexpectedly disintegrated, making the world appear completely different, leaving you disoriented, confused, and disappointed, with an uninterpretable sense of shame. How could she explain it to him? She hardly understood it herself. Best to be active, to do things, something your mind could focus on, a task to be completed. This aimless sitting, staring at the pale-yellow roses climbing the fence with futile optimism, was simply dangerous. The boy was sinking. She couldn't prevent it and was in danger of becoming submerged with him.

"Upstairs," she squawked, "let's go pack your chest. See what you need to bring." He stood up and followed her. A tangle of shirts and stockings lay on the boy's bed. The chest stood next to it on the floor, open, crammed, overflowing.

"It doesn't fit," he said. "There's not enough room." He strode from one side of the narrow room to the other, awkwardly flapping his long arms.

"You'll wear your boots. Extra shoes will have to go in the chest. And trousers. A couple of books. Why is the chest so full?" Elizabeth plunged both arms into the depths, lifting out clothes and books, Isaac's sailor's tunic, the bugle, and James's old hat. Her hands brushed against a hard object; something made of wood and wrapped in rustling papers. It was the violin, lying at the bottom, buried beneath a stack of sheet music. Nat had secured his treasure with balled-up socks and handkerchiefs.

"We're only allowed to take one chest. I can wear the clothes that don't fit, in layers, with my winter coat on top. It's only for one day."

He should leave the violin at home, she thought. Sensitivity, beauty. It'll be his downfall. He'd be better off leaving that side of himself here. With me.

"He sailed off after all. I thought: he'll be back as soon as he's put that uncivilized man on board." Nat was speaking to the wall, to himself.

"It's all because of Captain Clerke. He can't get away. There have been problems. Your father has to remain at his post until they've been resolved; you can understand that."

She was on her knees beside the chest and Nat looked on, over her shoulder.

"You know what? We'll put the clothes you can't do without in Jamie's luggage. He has plenty of room."

Winter coat, shirts, and shoes. "Here, bring these to your brother." She covered the instruments with underpants. The lid closed easily.

"Thank you," Nat said.

They left. The gardener pulled a cart carrying their luggage to the coach's staging post. Elizabeth followed between her two eldest sons. The baby stayed home, in the wet nurse's arms.

"Will you visit sometime?" Nat asked. His voice was changing, and he seemed disconcerted by its fluctuating register.

"If things keep going well with the baby, I'll ask Grandma to look after him. Then I'll come to Portsmouth for a few days, to see how you're doing."

"Why don't you call him Benny?" Jamie shot back. "Ben's his name, isn't it?"

She felt Nat's cool hand slip into hers. There were people gathered around the coach. Move on, let's go. It had to happen.

One Sunday she dug up the untended cardoon. She flung the frayed leaves and insect-gnawed stems onto a heap at the back of the garden and raked the empty spaces left behind. She'd hiked up her skirt and could feel the sun stinging her calves. The nursemaid had slipped away quietly, the baby was asleep, and the church bells had finished ringing.

August. James would be steering his ships across the equator. Or was he still in St. Helena, visiting that governor who so mysteriously resembled him?

She read the newspapers. The *Resolution*'s departure had received a lot of attention. Twelfth of July, 1776, in pouring rain, with headwinds. The journalists crowed about the Copley Medal, awarded to the year's most outstanding scientific contribution; they raved about the expedition's goal and evoked the frigid waters of the Arctic seas with such horror that it made readers shudder. There was no mention of Clerke, shivering in the prison's chilly dungeon, not a single word. Should she pay a visit to Banks to ask about Clerke's release? Write to Sandwich? Were they taking sufficient steps to get Clerke, her redeemer, out of jail? Would it work against her if she insisted they make more of an effort? Perhaps Sandwich would suspect the reason behind her interest and decide to leave Clerke to rot in peace, to ensure his favorite captain would remain at the helm of the expedition.

Nat wrote; it was a single sheet of paper, solemnly signed *Nathaniel Cook*. His hammock was near the wall, which was good, he said, and he hardly saw Jamie. *His class is often at sea. We are still in school to learn. Bugle lesson tomorrow. How is Ben? I don't have a friend yet, but I will look for one.*

She laid the letter on the shelf, alongside the one from James. If James didn't return, she would take Nat out of school. The thought took her by surprise. What did she mean, didn't return? If Clerke remained in custody, James would, at worst, be forced to wait a long time. And if he came home to find his son had dropped out of school? How could she think of such a thing? And yet, she had thought it.

She should, in fact, write to James, care of the harbormaster in that southernmost tip of Africa. A hopeful, supportive letter. But she didn't. What's making me so tired? she wondered; I hardly have a house-hold to run, the child is fed by a stranger; I don't do anything but am exhausted. I should visit my mother, I should finish that waistcoat for James, I should—

She sighed and sat beneath the quince tree.

Then Hugh Palliser turned up. She'd stopped expecting him; after the baby's birth, he'd thanked James for naming the boy after him and conveyed his congratulations to the mother, who was still bedridden. Two weeks later, a silver cup arrived, engraved with the name *Hugh Cook.* Around the time of the *Resolution's* departure, she'd been anxious about running into him, unsure how to behave. Since then, she'd begun calling the baby Benny whenever she thought of Hugh Palliser, thereby wiping out any thought of the child's godfather.

But there he stood, in her sunbaked garden, leaning on a cane and peering at her. He looked terrible: old, tired, and worn out. Yet he was smiling, and his voice was surprisingly chipper.

"August. The year's turning point! Good news!"

She promptly forgot about her best intentions. She had wanted to appear standoffish, invulnerable, without expectations. But her heart leapt into her throat, and she lost her voice.

"They released Clerke yesterday. Or maybe he escaped, or out-smarted them. In any event, he raced to Plymouth without sparing the horses and hoped to set sail the minute he arrived, day or night. That's how it is, Elizabeth. Finally."

He sat on the bench without waiting for an invitation. Elizabeth flopped down beside him, short of breath, crying and laughing. He flung his arm around her shoulder and drew her toward him. Almost without noticing, they began rocking together from side to side beneath the hard, pale-green quinces.

"The trip will take him a month or two," Hugh murmured. "Then there's the return voyage. He won't be back before Christmas. Sometime in the new year would be more realistic."

These were only words. As if a warm, healing rain were falling on the parched garden, a rescue and a salvation, as if she had truly come home at last, and all was well.

She felt his lips near her ear, in her neck. What was he doing? His tongue slid along her earlobe; hot, unintelligible words whispered into the hairs on the back of her neck; she felt woozy, lightheaded and absent, but wondrously in place. He'd pulled off her cap and raked his fingers through her hair. His hands encircled her face, she looked into his eyes, and there was nothing else, this was the only path to follow, good thing she'd washed her hair. Wasn't it odd how the sunlight played through the egg-shaped leaves of the quince? Close your eyes now, close them for the kiss.

What am I doing, she asked herself; why am I letting an old man put his hands all over me in my own garden, why don't I stand up and shake him off, why am I swallowing his spittle, licking his nostrils? She thought about his arm, his bare arm. He laid his hands on her breasts. Yes.

It was the way she'd imagined swimming through high waves; each time she rose to the bright surface, she thought, no one will disturb us, that mirthless old nursemaid won't be back for hours, and there are thick bushes between here and the kitchen window—then she sank back into the depths and didn't think, just moved.

Why am I so happy, so relieved? Oh yes, James is coming home, his replacement is on his way, racing over the waves to relieve James, and then, and then—

She jolted and abruptly broke free of the embrace, smoothing her clothes. She felt her bones against the hard bench. Sit up straight. Balance.

The flowers bowed toward the earth and died. Each evening, the darkness crept in earlier and earlier. The baby began to eat solids; the nursemaid only came twice a day.

Elizabeth visited her sons. She stayed in a room above a tavern in the harbor and walked hand in hand with Nat along the cliffs. He'd left his violin at his music teacher's house, ready to be played whenever he could escape from school. He didn't complain.

Hugh Palliser dropped in from time to time. They sat at the large table and drank tea. He spoke of his sick wife, and Elizabeth listened, surprised by nothing. Had he really said he sometimes thought about suffocating her with a feather pillow? Elizabeth clipped the withered foliage away from Elly's grave; spent hours sitting beside that tiny flower bed in the cold and rain, not noticing until she returned home just how numbed she'd become. November: a goose in the oven for Mary, for the stepfather—what was keeping James? A little longer, just one more Christmas. The baby could now sit up and put a bread crust into his mouth. She made sure the table didn't become heaped up with junk; the polished wood was gleaming, waiting for James.

Then the letter arrived. Jamie and Nat were home for Christmas recess; they were in the kitchen, eating and chatting. She had just put the baby to bed and was on her way down when someone knocked on the door. Nat opened it before she arrived downstairs. He held up a heavy sealed package, and passed it to her. She recognized the handwriting.

"Read it aloud!" Jamie cried. He gave Nat's shoulder a shove. "Then we'll have something to talk about when we go back to school!"

She was in a quandary. Kitchen or great room? Alone or with the boys? She clasped the letter to her chest and stood in the doorway, unable to decide.

She glanced at the closely written pages without reading them. It resembled a diary; the dates were scribbled between the crammed lines. The familiar handwriting began in its usual way, but was gradually deformed by subtle changes. Tiny, illegible squiggles alternated with unbridled outbursts. The lines bobbed up and down like waves, capped with exclamation marks like splashing foam. She began to read.

> *August 7. I curse the Admiralty. This ship leaks like a sieve. The first squall poured straight into the storerooms. Sacks of flour— completely soaked; the floor sticky with dissolved sugar. Had to make a stopover at Tenerife to repair the worst of the damage and buy new victuals. There's no keeping up with what the livestock on board devour every day. I've stuffed every possible nook and cranny with hay and oats. The next time a big wave crashes over the bow, I'll have to throw everything overboard once more, dammit. Is there any way I can keep those miserable creatures alive?*
>
> *August 12. Can hardly sleep. I lie in that ridiculous trough made of tarpaulin, swaying on ropes suspended above my desk, and listen to the animals. You think a horse neighs or whinnies, but no, when in distress, a horse bellows! And I listen to those huge beasts night after night, ranting in mortal terror. They spit up their half-digested oats, leaving long trails of slime dangling from their muzzles. I can't bear it. The loss of sleep is doing me in; last night I almost sent the ship to its doom. It was my turn on watch, and I was chatting with Anderson, the doctor, at the railing. We were making good speed. The sea was dark blue. I asked him if he could think of some sedative to calm the horses. Saint-John's-wort mixed*

in with the feed; that's what we were talking about. Suddenly: waves breaking on a reef, not ten yards ahead! Hadn't seen a thing! I shouted at the helmsman; panic, into the wind, everyone manning the ropes. Throat's still sore today, from all that yelling. Rocks sticking up like sharp spikes. They would've ripped open the belly of the ship as if it were a goose's. We were a hair's breadth away. Anderson was as white as a sheet. I don't understand it. I never miss a thing. Boa Vista. The Cape Verde Islands. I know those land masses like the back of my hand. If only those damn horses would stop their bellowing!

September 20. It's as if we accidentally washed ashore at the Cape of Good Hope. I don't have the feeling I consciously navigated here. When we arrived the day before yesterday, I was overcome with emotion. Not something I recognize in myself, and I'm reluctant to put it in writing anywhere but here. Table Mountain, with its thick blanket of gray clouds, so plentiful they can't help rolling down the steep slope. Why did that bring tears to my eyes? It felt like a homecoming, as if someone were going to tuck me in with a down comforter and lay me to rest. Idiotic. Have brought all the animals ashore. Not sleeping on board, myself. Can't bear the sight of this rotten mess.

November 5. The Dutchmen never miss a chance to lie and cheat. That was the case in Dutch Batavia, as well. Our sheep have been bitten to death by their dogs, but they refuse to pay any compensation. I bought new sheep right away, scrawny sacks of skin and bone; nothing better here to be had. I also bought one bull and two cows with calves. Pigs. Four extra horses. Chickens, goats, and rabbits. That's on top of the livestock we already had. I shall and must keep my promise to the king. We've taken a pair of peacocks on board. The birds tolerate the journey well. Omai has moved out of his hut to make room for the horses. Now he's bunking with the petty officers; I believe he prefers that to the loneliness. It's starting to be summer here. The men go on excursions through the glorious valley near Stellenbosch. They visit wineries and stare in wonder at the mountain ranges. They drink and go whoring and fritter away their money. I mustn't let it bother me; I have my hands full with all the underhanded merchants here.

Waiting every day for Clerke's arrival. Once he relieves me, Gore will take command of the Discovery. I can't pass him over but would rather see James King in that post. Burney's too unstable for my liking. Sometimes the men get to talking about that massacre in New Zealand. Then Burney turns his head away, crumples into a heap, and is unable to raise his voice above a whisper! A high-strung family.

I'm thinking of taking William Watman back to England with me. He's too old. He desperately wanted to join us again, but he lacks the strength to take his turn at the bulkhead or capstan, and after only a few weeks at sea, his physical condition is visibly deteriorating. I wonder if this seafaring life isn't so demanding that above a certain age, it's no longer viable. The huge effort. The constant vigilance. The wind buffeting your head.

November 11. Clerke arrived yesterday. He started passing around the drink—and plenty of it—first thing. He's offered to transport a portion of the herd on the Discovery. His cheeks are rosy and his eyes glitter. Everyone is overjoyed; happy to be reunited, looking forward to new adventures and returning to old promised lands. I am going crazy with worry and have hidden away in my hut with the charts and stock lists. I must speak with Clerke, tonight or tomorrow. I'll prepare a detailed instruction manual for him. I'm all on my own, dammit; everyone else is swilling booze and singing as if we were on a pleasure cruise. The horses are kicking up a storm against the wall of Omai's hut. I must have some bags of straw nailed up.

November 30. Elizabeth, I'm sorry, there's no other way. Clerke was burning up. When I embraced him, he averted his face. That was odd, but I thought: he doesn't want me to smell his stinking, inebriated breath. He has FEVER. The rosy cheeks. He shivers and shakes. Not out of excitement, but from an illness he picked up in that dank dungeon. Last week, he started coughing, a dry hack that he can't suppress. We all know what that means. Everyone must remain at their posts. We're planning to set sail tomorrow. I cannot keep my promise to you. That pains me. But that's the way it is. I will continue to write, even though you will no longer be able to read my letters. I will remain at your side, even though I am no longer there. I have made some terrible mistakes. Unforgivable blunders. Here on board, and at home. Tomorrow, weather permitting, I'll head in the direction of that ghastly South Pole. I won't ask you to forgive me. You can't. The ice must purify me, pick me clean, exonerate me.

Part 3

9

Elizabeth woke up in the ice-cold bedroom. Behind the window, the night glistened bluish-black. Someone was crying; the plaintive sobs entered her room from a distance. She rolled onto her back and put her arms on top of the blanket.

The child. Of course, the baby. She got out of bed and lit the candle. It was as if she were swimming through the chilly air, which outlined the boundaries of her body. In the hallway, she heard him more clearly. He was calling for his wet nurse. He was now more than three years old, and the nursemaid still came. Before the baby had turned one, Elizabeth discovered that the woman had been working under false pretenses: not breast-feeding Benny, but feeding him boiled cow's milk from a spouted mug. She'd had the child on her lap; she'd been talking to him. He was laughing! Elizabeth had unexpectedly returned from a visit she'd suddenly found tiresome, and she saw it through the kitchen window. The nursemaid was called Charlotte. There'd been a confrontation. A serious discussion.

"Such a sweet, quiet little boy," the nursemaid had said. "I can't wait to see him each morning. I no longer have any milk. It dried up some two months ago. But I love him."

"He's growing," Elizabeth had said. "Even without your milk, I believe he's getting bigger."

After that talk, the atmosphere in the house shifted. Charlotte stayed longer, often helping Elizabeth with this and that; sometimes they talked while the toddler was sitting on the floor between them, silently taking wooden blocks out of an old foot stove and piling them back in. When all the blocks were put away, he'd look up at Charlotte. "Well done," she'd say, "all gone." Then the little boy would smile. Elizabeth watched. He needs to grow, she thought. Once he's bigger, I'll teach him the letters of the alphabet.

Now he was howling. She went into the small bedroom where he lay in the narrow bed that used to belong to Nat. She placed the candle on the washstand; the flame flickered and then settled down. The child looked up at her, squeezed his eyes tight, and continued crying. Comfort, she thought, I must comfort him, sit down on the bed, draw the child toward me, say something to calm him down. But what? Is he afraid of the dark? Did he have a bad dream? Why don't I just ask what's bothering him?

"Zalot, Zalot!" the child cried. He smothered the words in his pillow. Elizabeth saw a damp cheek and a shoulder sticking up sharply. She edged closer and cleared her throat.

"Charlotte will be here tomorrow. Now it's time to sleep. When you wake up, she'll be here."

She couldn't touch him. She just couldn't. She tucked the sheets and blankets tightly around the crying child. He lay on his side with his fists pressed against his drooling mouth. He sobbed it out.

She left the candle where it was, closed the door behind her, and leaned against it. Through the cracks, she could hear the child attempting to pull himself together.

"Sleep. Tomorrow. Zalot." His bellows subsided into whispers. His sobbing became a mournful, prolonged weeping that gradually died down. From time to time, he let out a shuddering sigh. She thought about how he lay there. Wide awake. Eyes squeezed shut; waiting for the release of the morning, in control and motionless.

Careful not to make a sound, she went back to her bed.

She, too, lay awake, stiff as a plank, and waited for morning. Once James is back, she thought, I'll give it another try. Then Benny will be our child, and I'll be able to face it. James has been gone three and a half years now; he'll almost certainly be back sometime this year, this mile-long year that's only just begun. I'm exhausted just thinking about it. All that fuss, all over again. This time he'll stay at home, that's for sure. Maybe we should move somewhere else, someplace where the past isn't ambushing you from all sides, farther from the water. Yes. Distance does wonders. Sometimes it's a bringer of peace, and sometimes it whips up such a whirlwind of raging thoughts you don't know where to turn.

What am I going to do today? It's best if there's some regularity. It's the only thing. Keep the fires burning. It's not freezing, but it sure is cold. January 10. Well, every month is an abomination. Charlotte's coming. I'm comforting myself, the way I comforted the child. We'll sit by the range. Carry on with our mending. Charlotte is sewing new trousers for the boy. Benny. Must use his name. His incorrect name. I'll continue embroidering the waistcoat. It was still there, bright red, wrapped in paper. I finished the buttonholes at Christmas. Next, I'll add the fine tendrils of silver thread to the waistcoat pockets.

The boy had watched from across the room; he had been fascinated but he didn't dare ask any questions. The color must have drawn his attention.

"For Papa," Charlotte said. "Mother is making a waistcoat for Papa. He'll put it on when he comes home. I'm sewing a pair of trousers for you; come and look."

He leaned on Charlotte's knees and rubbed the thick ash-gray material. Elizabeth cut the silver thread, popped the frayed end into her mouth, held the needle up to the light, and threaded it in one go. If it didn't rain, Charlotte could take the boy outdoors this afternoon, while Elizabeth was at the school.

It had all started with a chance encounter on the steps outside the Admiralty building. She'd been inside to talk about money and had left in a triumphant mood. A woman, slightly younger than herself—thirty or so?—stood hesitating at the foot of the stairs. Elizabeth, to her own surprise, had struck up a conversation with her, had introduced herself and offered to help. It turned out that the woman was married to David Nelson, that dedicated gardener from the royal botanical collection in Kew. She was there to ask for money; the Lords were dragging their heels, and she was strapped for cash. Elizabeth had immediately felt a sense of solidarity, standing up together to those gentlemen in their silk stockings and tight breeches. She suddenly realized that there must be a hundred women in her position, all waiting, keeping the household afloat until the ship sailed home. The woman's name was Jane; Elizabeth turned around and marched back inside with her.

Jane had no children. Nelson had his plants, and she ran a little school for those sailors' children who lacked the resources for a proper education. That's how it started.

Elizabeth had been helping out for two years. Reading, singing, counting, and drawing. Clearing up, dancing, and helping to wash their hands. She'd immediately assumed responsibility for paying the rent. The small building was the property of the Church, and the rent had to be brought to the minister every month. Jane felt intimidated by the man; he asked to see her lesson plans and poked his nose into their choice of reading materials and songs. But Elizabeth knew how to get around him.

She had gradually grown fond of Jane Nelson, and without any formal agreement, they'd settled into a division of tasks that was mutually agreeable. It's a miracle how that can happen, Elizabeth thought. If it's just the two of you, and you're tuned in to one another, each will automatically do the thing that suits her best. Or him. It is possible. Just because things weren't that way with James—nonsense; don't think about that now.

She'd been surprised by Jane's natural, down-to-earth concern for the children. One little girl tripped on her apron, which was much too long. So Jane hemmed it. A mother of two boys was not able to bring them to school, so Jane picked them up personally every day. Elizabeth took care of the discipline and the actual teaching, whenever they got around to it. Jane dug up the back garden so the children could plant beans and potatoes. Elizabeth dealt with the disgruntled clergyman. Now that it was winter, there wasn't much going on in the children's garden. They lit the lamps at three in the afternoon. The children huddled together on the floor, while Elizabeth read them a story. On her lap was the book about the second voyage. She'd planned to read verbatim from the journals as they'd been written by James, corrected by herself, and edited by Douglas. But before long, she scarcely glanced at the densely printed pages and spoke freely in her own words. Every child at her feet had a father on board. She left out some of the passages. Fathers weren't beaten because of disobedience. She invented other things. Papas were thinking of London, were missing their children, and wondering how life was at home. She held up the book to show them Hodges's engravings, and the children were agape at the portrait of Omai. They pointed at the amazing statues on Easter Island, and shivered at the sight of the icy South Pole.

Today, she decided, I'll tell them about the return voyage. How the mariners were sailing their worn ship back home, to us. How eager they were for roasted goose and real British ale. What they'd tucked into their sea chests to bring home with them. For us.

She must have dozed off, because the slamming of the kitchen door woke her up. She stayed in bed a little longer, dreading the steep slope of the new day. There was shuffling in the hallway, bare feet on the stairs. Benny, padding toward his savior. Elizabeth roused herself from bed. She washed, pinned up her hair, forced herself to bind her body tightly, to pick out a clean dress and matching stockings. Now go downstairs, she thought, sit at the table with the child.

She came in just as Charlotte was setting a bowl of porridge in front of Benny. The child waited, perched on his boosted chair, a kitchen towel tied carefully around his delicate neck. He didn't move a muscle, but followed Charlotte with his small, deep-set eyes. There were red blotches on the papery skin of his cheeks.

"Have a seat," Charlotte said, "the tea is almost ready."

Benny methodically spooned around the edges of his bowl, saving the small dollop of sweet syrup—placed by Charlotte in the middle— for last. When he'd finished, he sat motionless, staring intently at Charlotte. He's expecting something, Elizabeth thought; he's waiting. He can bide his time with the best of them, what a sad thing in such a young child. He should be shouting about his needs, kicking up a fuss whenever they're not met fast enough. But that patient forbearance has been etched into him, perhaps by example. I must act, and now. We're going outside, I should say, to look at the swans. Let's build a house with your blocks. I'll read to you. Come.

She looked out the window. Everything was gray. It wasn't raining, but a dense fog had left the paving stones shimmering with a greasy moisture. She crossed her arms.

The iron mounts of a carriage's wheels clattered over the cobbles; a man's voice roared a command, silencing the drumbeat of horses' hooves. In the ensuing silence, there was a pounding on the front door. If you wait long enough, Elizabeth thought, something will happen. And look, before I even have time to be bored, a carriage pulls up in front of the house. Why doesn't the child run outside to look at the horses? The waiting seems to go on and on for both of us. Is there anything worse for him than waiting?

Charlotte opened the door. "Elizabeth," she said, "two gentlemen wish to speak with you. I showed them into the great room."

She slowly got to her feet. She glanced at her son's clean bowl and paused behind his elongated head. Then she left the kitchen and straightened her dress.

Stephens and Sandwich stood shoulder to shoulder in front of the large table. In full regalia, wigs and all.

"Please, gentlemen, do sit down," she said. "Shall I have some refreshments brought in?" She thought of a disturbance, some news that would break up the tranquility of waiting. The homecoming. The umpteenth homecoming.

"Perhaps it's you who should sit down, ma'am," Stephens said in his high-pitched voice. He was smaller than Sandwich, stouter as well; his grayish-blue jacket pinched around the shoulders. No one had smiled as yet.

Sandwich pulled a chair from the table and motioned for her to sit down.

She remained on her feet. Nobody said anything. There were vague sounds coming from the kitchen: Charlotte's voice, water splashing on stone, the pump squeaking.

"There's news?" She heard an impatient edge creep into her voice. Sandwich cleared his throat but remained silent. Stephens ventured toward her, rubbing his hands in front of his stomach. "Won't you please sit down, ma'am?" he repeated. Nothing happened.

"Elizabeth," Sandwich said, "we have something to tell you." His informal tone stung her, as if when he dropped the "ma'am," she was suddenly stripped of all protection, and whatever he was about to say might genuinely affect her. The three of them circled the empty seat as if playing some bizarre game of musical chairs.

"A letter arrived from Captain Clerke. By land. We came immediately. James is no more. James is dead."

She watched the tear that leaked out of Sandwich's eye and slid down his nose. She heard his voice breaking.

"On behalf of the Admiralty, we would like to offer you our condolences." Stephens nodded in sympathy and continued indicating the chair between them.

Sit down yourself, you pettifogger, she thought. Stop commanding and intimidating me, and leave me alone, let me—but no words came out. Sandwich continued.

"I have already notified Banks. And Solander. After this, we are going straight to the king. But we wanted to come here first, that goes without saying. If you will excuse us, we must, with some urgency, convey this terrible news to the palace."

Of course, she thought, the Royal Society, the Navy, the entire royal household; everyone must be told at once so they can all lament together. My husband is, after all, a public possession, paid by the Crown. Was paid. Past tense.

It didn't sink in. All she felt was an unexplainable and embarrassing sense of relief, and an uncontrollable urge to throw the gentlemen out of the house. She must think of some questions, assemble facts.

"When did this happen?" she asked without any emotion. "And how? And where?" she added after a brief silence. The gentlemen exchanged glances. Stephens's buckled shoes shuffled over the floorboards, producing a sound like scurrying mice. Come on, she thought, spit the words out and leave. Go to that king of yours, what are you waiting for?

"The letter is dated June of last year," Sandwich said. "Clerke gave it to a trade mission in Kamchatka. The letter arrived in our hands by way of St. Petersburg. The incident"—he hesitated but persevered, as if aware of the task ahead of him—"the incident took place in February. The fourteenth of February, to be precise. Captain Cook, I'd like to say James, fell during a clash with natives on an island he'd discovered during his voyage through the Pacific Ocean. Clerke calls it Hawai'i."

Stephens took over. "We will have more details once the ships return. But for now, you can rest assured that Captain Cook perished in the most honorable fashion, while carrying out his duties. Of course, we will keep you informed of any developments."

Honorable, she thought. What are they talking about? As if that makes any difference to me. It wasn't like James to get into a fight with the natives. They're saying whatever pops into their heads. How was it honorable? What's honorable about a scuffle? How can I get these fellows out of my house? I must go to the kitchen, get Charlotte to show them out.

She wanted to turn around and walk toward the door, but her legs balked. They simply didn't work. Then she raised her voice and called for the nursemaid. Sandwich and Stephens seemed alarmed. Charlotte rushed in.

"Will you show these gentlemen the door?" Elizabeth asked quietly. "Their visit is over."

Too stunned even to try to squeeze her hand, they slunk soundlessly after Charlotte into the hallway. In passing, Sandwich bowed his long horselike head in her direction. "Can I do anything for you? Alert someone—a clergyman, perhaps, or a doctor?" It seemed best not to react. When the door shut behind them, she sank into the empty chair.

Black, she thought, I must have a new black dress. The curtains must be drawn. I must go to the boys. They have to know what's happened. Before it hits the papers. Impossible. Even if I caught the mail coach right now, I still wouldn't make it in time. Jamie is somewhere at sea. Write. Immediately.

She looked to the table. The red waistcoat was at its center, pompous and neatly folded, topped with the needle and the spool of silver thread. She could just keep going. Or throw away the whole brilliant mess.

Charlotte came back in, holding the child's hand. He looks so much like James, she thought, those eyes. That long torso. Benny waited at the door, flustered, sucking on a wooden block. Charlotte looked to Elizabeth.

"Is it what I think?"

Elizabeth nodded. "A fight. February. Almost a year ago." She realized it took an enormous effort to speak. Charlotte ran her hand along Elizabeth's arm. "How dreadful. Waiting all this time for nothing. How awful for you. What now?"

Elizabeth shrugged. She noticed that the child was knock kneed. Not a pretty sight. Charlotte was right; suddenly, the waiting was over. Then the question became—indeed—how to go on. She hoped Charlotte had some idea.

Toward evening, Mary arrived in the coach from Barking. "I sent for your mother," Charlotte said. "So you won't be alone tonight."

Mary had had all her teeth pulled, and her crumpled mouth looked peculiar. Is it really her, Elizabeth wondered, or did some strange woman walk in, pretending to be my mother? She seems to know her way around my kitchen, slinging pots and pans onto the stove, and she knows where I keep the butter.

"You must take that child to bed with you," Mary said, "that will help."

"No," Elizabeth answered. "Benny will spend the night at Charlotte's."

They sat at the table, as they had yesterday, last week, and last year. No one told her she had to eat. She sat with her arms squeezed against her stomach and watched. Benny was huddled next to Charlotte, slyly observing his grandmother from the corner of his eye. If Mary tried to talk to him, he flinched and hid his face in Charlotte's flank. When they were finished eating, the nurse and the child went upstairs to pack some clothes.

"You will surely have visitors," Mary said. "They'll come to pay their respects, mind, those gentlemen. And their ladies. I stopped off at the dressmaker's; she'll be here tomorrow morning. Satin, I said. It's winter. For now, you'll have to make do with your old frock, the one from last time. I'll go look in your cupboard. Are you cold? Of course not: you can't feel a thing. Not hungry, or cold, or tired. Isn't it port you fancy?"

She sipped and pictured herself in this same kitchen, tipsy from the same beverage. No, she felt nothing. How they'd stumbled up the stairs, in bed together again for the first time. Nothing.

"That fellow with the game leg," Mary said, "you think he knows? He'll show up at your door soon enough. Or is he dead? I can't keep up."

"No, not dead," Elizabeth answered. "Hugh Palliser had to leave the Admiralty a few years back. He'd neglected his duties. James had also quarreled with him. He was sent back to sea, to fight the Americans. But the Navy said he hadn't put enough heart into the fight. There was a court-martial, did you hear? It was in the papers. Courts-martial are held aboard a ship, in the harbor. The laws aren't the same as on land. So strange. He was acquitted, but he stopped working."

Drink, she thought; drink until I'm almost sick and I feel numb and maybe then—just maybe—I'll be able to sleep later. Hugh Palliser. Far away on his estate. Unable to sleep because of the pain in his leg. What's he thinking right now? James's death will hit him hard; a true friend, a friend from the past, falls away and your life becomes narrower. He'll also feel guilty. Rightly so.

Beneath the fatigue, she felt anger. But she was too exhausted to deal with it, and noticed that she was crying softly.

"It used to be," she explained to Mary, who was looking at her questioningly, "used to be Hugh Palliser had a sixth sense about showing up whenever there was a disaster. Like clockwork."

Mary topped up the glasses. "I'm sure he'll do that again, my child, as soon as he gets word."

Elizabeth shook her head. Nothing would ever be as it had been before.

She woke up in the middle of the night with an acute sense of agitation. Mary was beside her in the large bed, snoring. She got up carefully, and only lit the candle once she was out in the corridor. It's winter; it's cold. She scuffed along to Benny's room, pulled the blanket off his bed and wrapped it over her shoulders.

The embers were still glowing in the stove. She put the candle on the kitchen table. A widow; I am a widow. What a ridiculous word. There's usually a funeral after someone dies. Not this time. James would have been buried eleven months ago; perhaps on the beach of that newly discovered island, or maybe at sea, as befits a mariner. How could she write to the boys if she didn't know the circumstances? Sandwich and Stephens had hardly said a thing. Trite platitudes. Muddled prattle for the papers—which will be filled with the news tomorrow. For now, whatever had really happened remained a riddle.

She grabbed a pen and paper from the other room and started on a short letter to her eldest. There had to be a message waiting for him when his ship docked in Portsmouth. It wasn't difficult. She wrote what she knew. Jamie had no imagination and no fear. If he was worried about anything, he would ask her, plain and simple, without hesitating or beating around the bush.

The letter to Nat was more difficult. She began over and over, each time on a clean sheet of paper. Think first, she urged herself; slow down and make an outline on the back of an envelope, a list of what has to be included; there is still time.

Your father died, was killed, had an accident, has perished, fell— there were too many words. How could she choose the right ones? The letter had to be posted with the early mail, because the news was sure to be announced today or tomorrow at Nat's school. It had to be done.

He'd been home at Christmas. He was stronger, broader. His hair was short. He was in his final year, and was one of the big kids. He hadn't said much. They'd celebrated Christmas in Barking. Nat had visited his old violin teacher. Before she knew it, she was waving goodbye to the mail coach.

If you like, you can come home for a week or so. I'm sure the school will understand, once they know the reason. Grandma is here now. In the next few days, I'm planning to ask Lord Sandwich if he will see me. He's busy reading the journals that arrived with the letter. I hope that when he's finished, he'll be able to tell me more. Then I'll be better able to explain the events to you. If you do decide to come home, be sure to bring your violin.

She reread what she'd written. Don't tug at him, she thought; he's fifteen, about to go out into the world. Or not, of course: he could also stay home and study the violin. No, she must put that out of her head. Try to remain neutral. When it comes to his future, Nat must make up his own mind. He may want to finish his education out of loyalty to his father.

Mary stumbled down the stairs with the chamber pot in her hands. Elizabeth sprang up to open the scullery door for her.

"I'm used to it," Mary said, although it wasn't clear if she meant urinating into a bucket or emptying it herself. Elizabeth looked at the thin gray braid dangling down her mother's back. It was still dark outside.

They were drinking tea beside the blazing stove. Charlotte had dropped by with Benny; the sleepover had been extended. Now they were off to look at the ducks on the riverbank. Wave to Mama, to Grandma; see you tomorrow—

"Tomorrow," repeated the child, as the garden gate slammed behind them.

"What are you planning to do?" Mary wanted to know.

"Nothing. I've written to the boys. I will have to pay a visit to Sandwich. Find out what really happened. And how. After that, write some more letters. To those sisters of his in Yorkshire. And to Walker. What did you do when my father died?"

Mary looked the other way. Her mouth hung slightly ajar.

"A pity it's not freezing, otherwise we could have a nip of gin. It's good for the cold. I'll cook for you today; that's one thing you don't have to worry about."

"Mother, answer me."

Mary sighed and rubbed her caved-in cheeks. "Apples and oranges, my child. We had a normal funeral. Afterward, we sat in the establishment, drinking. And eating. You were on my lap; I'm sure of that. You were just a baby. Your father was an ordinary man. But your husband was a public figure. If you don't watch out, they'll take everything away from you. All his letters and who knows what else will be in the papers, and everyone will have an opinion. Where will that leave you? His portrait is hanging above that rich fellow's mantle. What do you have to look at? You'll come face-to-face with it, mind you. They all know exactly what he was like: what he wanted, what he said, and what he looked like. And they'll crow about their experiences, brag about their friendships. Lord help me, what a disaster. If you take it all too seriously, you'll lose touch with the way you see things; then, out of need, you'll start believing all those tales, and you'll lose your own memories."

Elizabeth listened thoughtfully. "They have their own memories, don't they? They'll be missing someone else. The captain."

"Exactly," Mary said. "And that captain can be stolen from you. Watch out, that's how it starts!"

Jane Nelson ticked on the kitchen window. She wasn't wearing a bonnet and she rushed in, out of breath, clutching a newspaper to her chest. There were red blotches all over her diamond-shaped face, and when she looked at Elizabeth, her eyes filled with tears.

"Banks," she said, "Banks's housekeeper let the cat out of the bag. I bought a paper right away. Here it is." She spread the *London Gazette* on the table.

"This is my mother," Elizabeth said. "Mother, this is Jane. Her husband is at sea with James."

Jane wiped her tears with her sleeve. "He's a gardener, actually. He works at Kew. He's never sailed before."

Mary cleared away the cups, making more room for the newspaper. "A gardener," she muttered, "a gardener at sea. Running away, that's all they're good for."

Elizabeth stared at the printed text, but the letters were all a blur. Jane read it aloud, a report in lofty language. Did it involve James? It was formulated in such a way that it was hard to understand. A heroic battle for the flag involving treacherous "savages" who first worshipped the captain—that benefactor of all humankind—as a god, then turned on him and attacked him in a most underhanded manner. Further reports were forthcoming. The king had wept upon hearing of Cook's demise. The Admiralty had been plunged into mourning. The Royal Society was considering a ceremony of remembrance. It was a dark day for science, for the country, for progress.

There was no end to it. Jane continued reading aloud in her shrill voice. Elizabeth grabbed her hand.

"Leave it," she said. "We know. Thank you for the newspaper; kind of you. Are you planning to tell the children?"

Jane nodded. "This afternoon. Otherwise they'll hear it at home. They'll cry and be frightened. It's also about their fathers, you see. And they'll be very upset for you!" She sobbed again.

"Port. Perfect any time of day," said Mary. "Always lifts the spirits. Put that newspaper aside, my dear; it's only getting in the way." She rattled around with a carafe and glasses while Elizabeth folded the paper and carried it into the next room. There, she stood motionless at the window.

She rested her forehead against the chilly glass. I must, she thought. First, I must know how it happened. Everything. My back is straight. This hasn't affected me at all. Someone I had nothing to do with has died. Those who come to comfort me are sadder than I am. The dressmaker will be here later, for the fitting. She's working like a fiend; the dress will be ready tomorrow. I'll wear it when I visit Sandwich. They're walking on eggshells around me, but I won't break; I don't feel anything at all.

She rhythmically pounded her head against the windowpane, but the thudding sound startled her, and she turned away. Last night, she'd shoved the waistcoat to the edge of the table. Now, she picked it up and wrapped it tightly in the newspaper. Then she surveyed the room, with the parcel under her arm. No, not at the top of the cupboard, and not behind those books. What she really wanted to do was to go into the garden, dig a hole beneath the quince, and bury both the waistcoat and the newspaper. Cover it with soil, put away the shovel, wipe her hands, and be done with it.

There was that chest in the corner by the window, the one where she'd stored the various drafts of the account of the second voyage. It was almost impossible to pry open its lid—she had to force it. She lifted the papers out of the chest and rested the parcel at the bottom. Then she covered it up with the large sheets of paper embellished with James's even handwriting, her own pencil marks, and Douglas's corrections in red ink. She slammed the chest shut.

It's nighttime, Frances. I don't display many outward signs, except for getting up in the middle of the night to write letters. By day, I sit in the great room, wearing my new black satin frock, receiving all and sundry who come to pay their respects. My mother has set up her own little tavern here, or so it would seem; she's constantly bustling about with trays and carafes. She's going back to Barking next week.

I went to the Admiralty this afternoon. I'd requested a meeting with Sandwich. He sent a coach to fetch me. Good thing I didn't have to climb into a rowboat in this dress.

James sat in that room countless times, at that very table, possibly even in the same chair. Stephens was there, too, but I fixed my eyes on Sandwich. He expresses himself succinctly and doesn't hem and haw. James thought so, too. I asked if they could tell me more about the circumstances, now that they'd read the journals. They both sat there, nodding benevolently.

Sandwich began: right from the start, the voyage had been marred by enormous delays. Clerke's detention, the setbacks at the Cape of Good Hope, the peregrinations before the ships finally arrived at Tahiti to bring Omai home—and that was only the beginning. I asked if the condition of the ship had played a role in the delays. That ruffled their feathers, and both admitted that the ship had required frequent, ever more extensive repairs. The resulting time ashore—on the island of Tonga, for instance—had led to impudent thefts on the part of the inhabitants, forcing James to implement ever stricter measures. I didn't go into that. The livestock was brought ashore, partly on Tonga and partly on Tahiti. A house was built for Omai, not on Tahiti, but on another island. Everything took more time than expected. In December of 1777, if I understand correctly, they finally set sail for the north. In those uncharted waters, they discovered a group of islands where people appeared to speak the same language as is spoken on Tahiti. A miracle. Sandwich, of course, couldn't resist mentioning that James had named them the Sandwich Islands. The inhabitants

themselves call it "Hawai'i." They didn't stay there long. James
was eager to carry out the second part of his instructions and head
for the coast of North America, to search for the northern passage
via the Bering Strait. Frances, you'll need to get hold of a map or
a globe, otherwise your head will spin with all these place names
and directions.

They found no passage; just ice, ice, and more ice. James sailed
back to Hawai'i, which seemed like a suitable place to build up
their strength after the hardships of the Arctic Ocean. Before they
dropped anchor, they sailed around the entire island to chart its
coast thoroughly. The crew wouldn't have liked that, but according
to Sandwich, it resulted in a first-rate map. Once ashore, James
was given a king's welcome and was venerated like a god. The
ships and their exhausted crew members were given all the help
they needed. They stayed for about three weeks. James was dragged
to all manner of ceremonies. Watman, the old sailor James was so
fond of, died, and they buried him on the island. The sailmakers
and carpenters were working day and night. They feasted on wild
boar and sugar cane.

I listened and nodded. Hurry up, I thought; get to the point.
And that's what he did.

The ships weighed anchor on February 4, 1779, in a new
attempt to find the northern passage. Sandwich produced a sheet
of paper. It was a letter James had written to him in 1778 and
subsequently given to the governor of the island of Unalaska, who
is Russian, I believe. James writes that he doesn't have much hope
in finding a passage, that he has enough provisions to last one more
year, and he intends to spend his time studying the geography.
Sandwich's hands trembled. The letter had arrived one week before
the news of James's death. I saw the familiar handwriting, and
suddenly it hit me: the table before us was completely empty. There
were no logbooks, letters, or charts. Indeed—you cannot share that

which you do not bring into a room. I asked about it, not caring what they might think of me.

The papers weren't available, said Stephens. They were being studied in great detail by several experts. I thought they were perhaps trying to shield me from the gory eyewitness accounts of the murder, and that's why they were keeping me well away from the logbooks of Clerke and the other officers. But James's journals? What horrors could they contain? I brought it up, and Sandwich said I was right. There wasn't anything in them. James hadn't written anything about their entire stay on Hawai'i. His notes don't go beyond January 17. I was struck dumb.

Meanwhile, they took turns relating the rest. Weighed anchor on February 4. Heavy weather. Headwinds. Continued nevertheless. Then, during a storm, the Resolution's *foremast broke. By the eleventh, they were back on Hawai'i. Mast ashore, carpentry workshop set up, trade in pork and coconuts resumed. Skirmishes this time with the inhabitants. Items pilfered and no trace of the respect the expedition had enjoyed on its first visit. The men were forced to shoot at thieves who'd threatened to damage the clock. The mood had soured.*

James had always been extremely cautious with firearms. If he did give the order to shoot, it was usually with buckshot. He had another strategy for thefts of a more serious nature: he would hold the chief or high priest hostage and wait patiently with his prisoner in the great cabin until a canoe paddled alongside the ship and returned the stolen goods. It worked every time.

Now, Frances, I'm going to tell you what happened. A fight broke out on the thirteenth of February. Tools were stolen, and stones were thrown at the heads of the sailors who were filling the water barrels. The local chief managed to calm things down. The next morning, it seemed that the Discovery's *launch had been stolen. James himself rowed ashore with a couple of Marines. He entered the settlement, intending to take the chief hostage. The man prepared to leave; he knew James and was fond of him. He wanted to bring along his two young sons. Then, they heard shots coming from the other side of the bay. There was confusion, uproar, and protest. Suddenly, islanders started shouting and surrounded James, and he decided to return to the launch. Someone attacked one of the Marines; another threatened James with a dagger. Shots were fired. James gave the order to return to the ship and motioned the launch to approach. However, the lieutenant in the boat misunderstood the signal and began rowing in the opposite direction, away from the beach. As the mob advanced, James walked slowly and steadily into the surf. Someone clubbed him on the back of the head—Sandwich excused himself, it was all so painful, so horrible, he said, his voice thin and halting—James fell, was stabbed, managed to stand up again, turned to face the launch. A gang of natives wrestled him to the ground and attacked him with knives and rocks. The boat returned to the ship, leaving James and four of the Marines behind on the beach. It was just after eight in the morning; the day was yet to begin. The entire incident had lasted less than an hour.*

The boardroom was silent. Sandwich blew his nose, and Stephens looked at the floor. I felt like I'd been watching myself, that I'd been floating in a corner the whole time, and I looked down on a woman in a black dress, sitting upright, facing two gentlemen. I couldn't feel that it was me.

Clerke didn't want to take revenge; there was no point. The damage had been done. Out of loyalty to James, he sailed as fast as he could to the north, to complete the mission. Sandwich picked up the pace of his narrative; they must've thought that the meeting had lasted long enough, but in my mind I was still on that beach in Hawai'i, and so I asked about the burial.

Stephens took over. Clerke had spent days negotiating the handing over of the dead. The broken mast was hurried on board, and the men continued their repairs on the overcrowded foredeck. The burial, I said. He cleared his throat. In the end, Captain Cook's "mortal remains" were brought to the water's edge by a procession of priests and handed to Clerke. On the late afternoon of February 21, in the bay, James was given a sailor's burial. The next day, the ships weighed anchor.

Stephens began singing James's praises. Sandwich interrupted with news about my compensation. I am to receive an allowance from the king, a widow's pension from the Navy, and much more besides. I'm a rich widow, Frances. It had hardly sunk in. I was still pondering Stephen's choice of words: "mortal remains." Something peculiar was going on, but I couldn't put my finger on it. My husband had become "mortal remains," I thought, and had been dropped into the ocean. I couldn't think of anything beyond that splash. And I still can't.

After that meeting, I felt so exhausted I was afraid I might faint. Someone brought me home. I lay down. I fell asleep.

Outside, dawn is breaking. I can't tell you how I am, because I don't even know myself. I will put down my pen and embrace you, my dear Frances.

Writing the letter had worn her out, but it had also helped her to order her thoughts so she could get some sleep. The smell of coffee woke her up. The first thing that popped into her head was: the child must come home. His place is here, no matter how difficult. I will look after him, or at least be near him, in the same room. I will read to him, tell him about his father, and his brothers. A death in the house fills you with good intentions, most of which never amount to anything because you're so unbelievably weary. When death comes, you have to simplify your life, you have to eat the same thing every day, wear the same clothes, and show the door to people who tire you out. It would be better if Charlotte took care of the child. But from now on, he'll sleep here.

Benny gave her an anxious look when she came downstairs. He was sitting on Charlotte's lap. They were poring through the engravings in the travel journal open in front of them on the kitchen table.

"I'm trying to explain it to him," Charlotte said, "but I'm not sure he understands. Benny, where is Papa?"

"Away with the boat." He put his finger on an image of the *Resolution*, anchored in a Tahitian bay. In the foreground, natives drift past in canoes and boats with high, narrow sails; there is a partially dressed mother and child, waves, and majestic mountains, but Benny was drawn to a plump rooster on a wooden dock. "Chick? Chick?"

"Where's Mary?" Elizabeth asked. Constantly asking the whereabouts of someone or something was probably also related to the arrival of death, which left you feeling insecure and anxious. Before there was time for an answer, her mother stumbled in. She shoved the door open with her backside while clutching a small wooden cask.

"Gin," she said. "From next door. You live beside a gin factory, you know. I went to get acquainted, but they say they never see you. That foreman is a decent chap. He'll be my supplier. This one's a gift, on the house. Do you have any empty bottles? Handy to have a supply of gin on hand when you're expecting visitors. Hand me a funnel so I can sort this out."

Mary began carefully pouring the spirits into bottles. Charlotte prattled quietly to Benny about coconuts and bananas. What am I doing here, Elizabeth wondered; this is my house, my kitchen. My husband has been run through by islanders, drowned and stabbed to death on the other side of the world, and we're sitting here telling stories and stockpiling liquor. It's been foggy for days; you can't even see the bottom of the garden. Does any of this exist? It doesn't seem real. Perhaps we, too, are nothing more than a story.

Mary tasted the gin and smacked her lips. "You're lucky to have neighbors like these! You should partake more often; you seem a little peaky."

She passed Elizabeth a glass. The gin had a yellowish tinge and gave off a foul smell. She accepted it and placed it on the table. It's far better to say yes to everything and do nothing than to haggle and bicker. Saves your strength.

The servant girl came in with the mail. Letters, letters, and more letters. Douglas offered his help and condolences in his eloquent, civilized prose. James's sister Margaret complained in a furious, barely legible scrawl about the loss of the famous brother she hardly knew, so soon after the death of their father. And, as coldhearted as it sounded, she and her sister were eagerly awaiting the settlement of the estate, because they were living in poverty. Elizabeth wearily set the letter to one side.

There was a note from Nat:

We were called to the assembly hall, and the master told us about Captain Cook. We sang and had a moment of silence. After that, I played the bugle. I wasn't nervous. Except during the speech. I thought everyone was looking at me, and I felt hot under the collar. Jamie's at sea, he doesn't know anything yet, and they all feel sorry for him. Mother, I don't think I'll come home, it's almost time for exams, and I'd rather stay here and visit you in the summer. That hat of Papa's—the one I wore when it snowed—do you still have it? Would you send it to me? Give my love (lots!) to Grandma, and to Benny, too. Write back soon!

The lawyer sent his formal condolences and invited her, along with her "legal representative or counselor," to discuss the disposition of James's property. Counselor, she thought, legal representative? Am I feebleminded, unable to represent myself, or incapable of understanding his language? What an arrogant impression; won't he be surprised when I show up, papers in hand, and he finds out I can read.

It was quiet and cold in the great room. She sorted through the correspondence: the letter from the lawyer accompanying the will, Douglas's letter perched on top of the stack of sympathy mail. She'd have to go through it soon, think of some reserved and adequate response. That'll come, she thought, but not now. She hesitated over the letter from James's sister in Yorkshire, and then put it on top of Douglas's. No rush. Nat's letter went straight onto the table. Look for the hat. Reply.

The cupboard where she stacked the letters also housed a mountain of James's papers. She glanced over it briefly. His correspondence with Sandwich, with Douglas, with Walker, Banks, and Forster. The lists of crew members, provisions, instruments, and animals. Huge quantities of papers belonging to a living man who had plans, thoughts, and ideas. She would have to sift through it all, page by page and line by line. She'd already put the letters addressed to her in a drawer; she pulled it open and saw the final, disturbing letter with its faltering handwriting and nonexistent date. A secret, she thought. No one else may see this. Ever. She briefly longed to destroy everything, get rid of the incriminating, confusing information, so she would have nothing but her own memory, one in which she could keep James as he had been. She closed the drawer and shut the doors of the cupboard. She had no idea what he had been like. She would have to spend months, even years studying all this evidence, devote entire nights to reflection, take long walks to find out who her husband was. Had been.

Nothing has changed, she thought; he's been away for three and a half years; everything should still be the same, and yet one message, one visit, dramatically altered the room. The cupboard now calls to mind completely new thoughts, and I no longer recognize myself. When Banks was in this room a few days ago, with Solander at his side like a faithful dog, I behaved in a way I'd never behaved before. I nodded at their hymns of praise; my agreement with their elegy poured from my lips like some holier-than-thou claptrap—their worship of my husband clearly pleased me. Benefactor of all humanity. Jewel in the crown of the kingdom. Champion of science. A good shepherd to his men. Wise, thoughtful, and unselfish. A loss like an open wound.

It was endless. Solander's sausage fingers were wrapped around a handkerchief. Elizabeth just nodded and smiled wanly at the appropriate moments. Not a tear, never a cross word. She played the part of the perfect widow of a great man. And with hardly any effort.

I'm straying from myself, she thought; playing someone else so well that I lose track of the route inside. So it must be. The more I agree with them—the worshipers—the sooner they'll leave me in peace, alone with James. I'll protect him from his devotees. Can't get around to missing him. That's out of the question. If I miss anyone, it's Elly. She'd be twelve, going on thirteen now. Jamie and Nat still remember her; they were seven and six when she died. James knew her for less than a year. Who brings her back to life every day with their thoughts? Frances? Mary? You can't ask that of others. You have to do it yourself. It's a full-time job. But who should I recall when I remember James? Not Banks's James, or Sandwich's, or the king's. But whose?

She heard another visitor arriving: voices in the hallway, shuffling near the coat rack; she was ready, had transformed herself into a public widow and was waiting. But nobody came. The fire needed attention; it was much too cold to receive guests. She sighed, straightened her posture, and went into the kitchen.

Hugh Palliser was at the table, sitting next to his godson, drawing chickens on a piece of wrapping paper. Mary sat sipping the new gin on a bench beside the stove, and Charlotte was leaning against the worktop, arms folded.

"The fire's gone out," Elizabeth said.

Hugh stood up, supporting himself on the tabletop. He reached for his cane, was about to speak.

"It's cold as ice in there. I don't know—can you deal with it, Charlotte?" The words kept flowing; Hugh couldn't break in. "I think there's still some dry firewood in the pantry. But maybe you should sweep it out first, the hearth I mean, it looks filthy."

Charlotte tied on an apron and left the kitchen carrying an ash bucket.

"Chick?" the child asked. No one answered.

"I hope you will excuse me for turning up unannounced," Hugh finally managed to say. Elizabeth didn't reply. Would she have refused to see him? She wasn't sure. She looked him over. Ashen face, teary eyes, a mouth twisted in pain. What was she to do? There was no place in the house where she could be alone with him. She couldn't send him away, either. They stood at opposite ends of the table, breathing shallowly, waiting.

"We're going out," Elizabeth said. "Mother, will you look after Benny until we're back?"

Mary shook herself out of her reverie and nodded.

"Cold and clammy," Mary said. "Be sure and bundle up. You'll be soaked through, just from the air. Here, take my shawl."

She pulled the garish cloth off her shoulders and pressed it into Elizabeth's hands. Nonplussed, she carried it with her down the hall. Hugh's cane ticked behind her along the tiles.

The fog was so thick it covered her face with an oily sheen. The tree trunks glimmered as if they'd been smeared with grease. She looked straight ahead and set off at a brisk pace through the muddy street. Hugh limped beside her, out of breath. She knew but didn't care. He better not, she thought, he better not start lionizing and idolizing. She wasn't speaking to him, but if she were to talk with him, it had to be real, not sentimental, not according to convention, not the way she talked with the others. He wheezed. Her satin dress dragged through the puddles. Mary's plaid horse blanket weighed down like a yoke on her shoulders.

"Hold on," Hugh said, "I can't keep up."

She came to an abrupt halt and turned her wet face toward him. "What of it? How do you think I'm keeping up?"

He raised his free arm as if to touch her, but let it fall to his side.

"We could go to the Prospect of Whitby. It's not busy this time of day. Let's just turn the corner here."

"On the water! With a view of those miserable docks across the river! How can you think such a thing?"

She strode on, at a more restrained pace. She took small, tight steps, charged with immense tension.

"What do you suggest?"

"I don't know. You came to visit me. I don't want anything."

"You're right," Hugh said. "I came to visit because your husband is dead, you're being hounded by gentlemen who come to pay their respects, you have a lot to organize, and you have to think of everything. I came to see how you are, how my godson is faring, if I can offer you any assistance. I came to show you that I think of you. That I sympathize. That's how it is. And I would rather do that in a well-heated pub than on this freezing street."

"What you'd rather do doesn't interest me. If you don't like it, you can turn around and walk away. You're good at that, aren't you?"

"Now calm down. We're wet. Give me an arm, that makes it easier to walk. Didn't we visit a place in this neighborhood once before? We were arguing then, too. Come along."

He clasped her arm tightly. Just as he'd done then, she thought, more than four years ago. I was pregnant. He was going to make sure James stayed home. I counted on him.

They sat in the same corner. The same innkeeper served them the same mulled wine. Elizabeth draped her mother's hideous shawl over the back of a chair and looked Hugh in the eye.

"I still can't believe it," he began. "It hasn't really sunk in that James is gone. Maybe once the ships have come in without him. I keep thinking about what it must be like for you, that emptiness you've grown accustomed to, which has suddenly become permanent. The boys who no longer have a father. All at once, everything is different. Never to work with him again. Unimaginable. Of course, I left the Admiralty years ago; I wouldn't be working with James anyway. My life had already been turned upside down after that farcical court-martial. I live alone now, for the most part in Chalfont. I enjoy the countryside; when I sit in the bay window, I have a view over the park. There's a lawn, a dark beech here and there, and if I'm patient, sometimes I spot a deer. My wife's been admitted to a rest home. She's doing better there. You weren't aware of that. I would like you to come and visit; perhaps you could get some rest at my house. You seem rather harried."

He rubbed his face and glanced at her stealthily, turning his eyes away each time.

"Sandwich and Stephens gave me the boot. From one day to the next, I was stripped of my position, my work. I wasn't allowed to show my face at the shipyard, and had to clear out my office. They put my backside on a ship and sent me to sea, just like in the old days. Well, you know how that turned out. After those legal clashes, I lost my taste for it, even though I'd been exonerated. They had to offer me an alternative. It was Greenwich. I turned it down. Then they gave me what they call an honorable discharge. It feels like an old war injury, you know? I was having problems the year James was preparing his voyage. They didn't have an ounce of pity. Dismissed. Forced out."

He shook his head.

"I'm going on and on about myself, had to get it off my chest. Not what you were expecting. Please excuse me, Elizabeth. Will you tell me how things are with you, and with the boys? What you are thinking about these days? Please? Your youngest has gotten so big. He looks a lot like James. Is that nice for you, Elizabeth, or not?"

She stretched and began talking softly. She could hear how flat and colorless her voice sounded; she saw her hands lying in her satin lap as if they belonged to someone else.

"We call him Benny. He is a quiet child. Charlotte usually looks after him; it just happened that way. I still need to get used to him. He has developed a close bond with Jamie, who's often home between voyages. I believe Benny confuses him with James, thinks they're one and the same person. He goes away on the boat, and then is suddenly back home again. He doesn't understand any of it. I hope Jamie comes home soon. He still doesn't know. Nat does, though; I wrote to him right away."

"Even about the circumstances?"

She faced him. "Broadly speaking. To some extent. I didn't want to frighten him. What I'd really like to do is safeguard him from that miserable sea, but I don't want to influence him. It has to be his decision."

"He'll come," Hugh said. "He'll come home and make music again. Do you know exactly what happened? What have they told you? Have you seen the journals?"

"No. Yes. There's James's journal, of course, about the voyage itself. They didn't have it at hand and hardly mentioned it. It didn't come up. After the murder, King took over the upkeep of the journal. He'd sent his report as well, along with a lengthy letter from Clerke, or so I understand. I don't really know what happened. Why a landing that had gone well countless times should suddenly go so horribly wrong. I know what was in the papers, that James was admired and idolized by the people there. I cannot understand why they killed him. He had ten Marines backing him up, as well. Just imagine, all those bright-red coats."

The sun, she thought, pleasant but not yet scorching. The sound of the oars in the water. A bird. James peering intently at the beach, irritated about such a tedious start to the day. His thoughts already turned to getting ready for the departure. Retrieve the stolen boat, set up the repaired mast, and then hoist the sails. She forced back her tears.

"We're looking at it all wrong." She heard Hugh's voice as if from a distance. "We are graced with civilization, which is why we think the natives are happy when we arrive. We bring them gifts that seem fantastic to us: leather shoes, order and regularity, rows of beanstalks in freshly turned soil. The sea chart. The written word. The locals help us maintain our delusion by swarming around our objects like overexcited children. They risk their lives to steal the silk stockings from under our pillows. They want to get their hands on everything—uniform buttons, iron pliers, a compass, even a crowbar. But we're blind to the other side of the coin. With our omnipotent firearms, we undermine the authority of their chiefs. We expect a daily supply of hogs, poultry, and bananas— we devour their supplies. We make love to their wives and upset their social order. Just think of what we leave behind when we sail away. Broken marriages, depleted farmlands, dethroned rulers, mixed-race children. It never crosses our minds. No wonder they become hostile. Fear of our bullets is the only thing that keeps their animosity in check. It's no surprise that things get out of hand. All in all, it's a wonder things go as well as they do."

Elizabeth swayed from side to side. She pressed her fingers against the smooth satin covering her ribs and held herself tight. Why should I listen to this? He says he's here to help me, but all he does is complain about being fired and whine about the point of the expeditions. What good is that to me? It seems as if he's sitting at a great distance from me, far away. I can hardly understand him. If he came closer, everything would be different. I know it. There'd be comfort.

She abruptly stood up.

"I'm leaving." She grabbed the shawl and strode to the door. Hugh got to his feet, tossed some coins on the table, and hobbled after her.

Outside in the drizzle, she took a breath. The cobblestones glowed in the golden rays of light peeking out from behind the gray clouds. She halted in the middle of the street and turned toward Hugh.

"You," she said, "you. My so-called friend. My guardian, to whom James, in good faith, entrusted his family. I counted on you four years ago. You dropped me without a second's thought, busy as you were, bowing and scraping to Sandwich. I tried to understand, to forgive you. But I cannot call my son by your name. Even so, I didn't want to lose you. I did my best. But now, Hugh Palliser. Now you have hood-winked me for a second time! Don't look so surprised. Yes, I can use strong language as well as any of your sailors. What happened is your fault. Because you were too slapdash to keep an eye on the shipyard, James had to go to sea in a broken-down ship. He wrote to me from the Cape of Good Hope, desperate; fresh supplies had been destroyed by leakage. The lines snapped, and the pulleys burst. And that was just the start of the voyage!

"Because of your dereliction of duty, he had to stay too long every-where he went, to repair that leaky hulk. If you had provided him with good equipment, he would still be alive. Those frail excuses for masts you put on the ship snapped like matchsticks during the first hint of a storm. That's why he had to go back! That's the reason they bludgeoned him to death! How dare you complain to me that they treated you badly, and regale me with your sorry philosophizing about displays of power. All for my benefit! How are you able to get the words out of your mouth? I will never accept help from someone who has so shamelessly abandoned me, twice. Never!"

She yelled and stamped her feet. Tears of fury streamed down her cheeks.

Hugh flung his walking stick to the ground. Its silver mount clat-tered against the cobbles. He took two steps, gripped her shoulders, and shook her. "Now you must stop and listen to me."

She looked into his hardened expression and swallowed her words, in shock.

"You are right to blame me for being lax. I did not carry out my duties in Deptford as I should have. Your disappointment that James left—despite our expectations and hopes—is completely logical and understandable. But I have done nothing to deserve such fury. And I will not tolerate it. You are forgetting one thing: James was there, too! You act as though he were a spineless pawn, at the mercy of the Admiralty's whims, or the king's. But that's not how it was, Elizabeth. He was right there the whole time. Based on his status, he could have made any demands. If he'd wanted to, he could have paid more attention to his equipment. He could have refused to go to sea in a ship that was in such poor condition. Even at the Cape, it was still within his power to say no. He didn't do that. He went on. *He* did."

The warmth of the palms of his hands sank into her shoulders. She felt his thumbs grazing her collarbone.

"Your accusations are justified. I accept that. But isn't there another reason you are so irate? How can you be angry with someone who has met such a cruel fate? It's not possible, which is why you take it out on me. You're furious with your husband. James is the one who left you, not me."

She heard the raindrops falling from the branches. She felt his hot breath on her forehead. He's right, she thought, it's not possible. She turned and—heels clattering, skirt flapping—ran home.

10

Dear Frances,
My name is Jane Nelson. Please forgive me for approaching you so
unexpectedly. I am writing on behalf of—and about—your friend
Elizabeth Cook. She is also my friend. My husband was on the
same ship as our late, lamented captain. The vessels finally sailed
into London last month, after a voyage of more than four years.
But that's not what this letter is about. Mrs. Cook—Elizabeth, I
mean—and I have become friends. For some years now, we have
been running a school for needy sailors' children. Perhaps she mentioned it to you? She reads aloud so beautifully.

   I need your advice. I'm afraid I must report a new misfortune
to you. I believe you know that Nathaniel completed his studies
at the Naval Academy this past summer, with good grades. His
heart wasn't in seafaring. He was planning to return home and
resume his study of the violin. Elizabeth was looking forward to
that. Now, however . . .

   After the summer, Nathaniel was assigned to a Royal Naval
station in the West Indies. His first real posting. Bugler and sailor.
He intended to fulfill his obligation out of respect for his father's

memory. He had planned to break the contract at Christmas, and then his sailing days would be well and truly over.

He spent a few days at his mother's before he left. He was clearly relieved about his plans for the future. But excited as well about the journey; he'd never been so far from home. Elizabeth would write to you herself if she could. It's lucky we have Charlotte's help; she's like a mother to Benny. There was a hurricane. On October 5. Thirteen ships foundered off the coast of Jamaica. Everyone drowned. He was just fifteen. I am writing to tell you. The news arrived here ten days ago. She's been upstairs in bed ever since. Not eating. She doesn't want anything. She doesn't read the letters people send her. I open them and read them to her. She doesn't seem to hear. I hope that when your letter arrives, she will listen. I am sorry this is so jumbled. We don't know where else to turn. Elizabeth's mother cannot come. She's taken to her bed in Barking, where she lives. She was very attached to Nat. It's too much for such an old woman. My question is this: could you please write an uplifting letter, telling Elizabeth to eat and get up and go outside? Shall I ask Mr. Palliser to come? Do you think that's a good idea? The officers from the returned ships paid a call: Mr. Burney and Mr. King. Of course, they wanted to talk about the captain. But I said now's not a good time. She'd been looking forward to the ships' return—Elizabeth, I mean—to find out more about Mr. Cook's death. But that's all changed. If only she would eat something! The doctor comes every day. He gives her laudanum for the grief. Then she can sleep awhile. I hope you will write soon, and please forgive me for asking this of you. I found your address on an old envelope. With deepest respect and warmest regards, your Jane Nelson.

PS: I forgot to ask if all is well with you and your husband. I can't rewrite this letter because it has to be posted right away. I still have to read it to her. I don't want to do anything behind

her back. It is awkward. I'm sorry. It's not polite. With my sincere
apologies, your Jane N.

She usually kept her eyes closed. The flickering candle and shifting
shadows annoyed her. She moved as little as possible; she had lain her
body down on the mattress, legs together, arms crossed over her chest,
and she kept her limbs that way until she could no longer feel them. Her
head rested sideways on the pillow, facing the window. She retreated
into herself, as if she wanted to take stock of what was left, now that her
command over external things had been crushed. It was like swimming
underwater, propelling yourself forcibly to the depths. Chin on chest.
Was it good that Nat couldn't swim? Had that spared him a prolonged
struggle before death? No, no, not toward the water's surface, but away
from the light. She heard herself emitting an animal-like moan, how
appalling. Then she dived under again: it was summer, and she was
sitting in the garden with her boys. Benny sat on the lap of his oldest
brother, who was at work in a sketchbook. The slender body of the child
was propped against Jamie's chest. The young sailor approached his task
seriously, drawing a selection of gallinaceous birds for the child. What
a curious fascination, Elizabeth had thought; a boy of that age usually
goes on about hay carts, mail coaches, or hunting horses on the trot.
She had the newspaper spread out in front of her and was listening to
the children talking among themselves.

"Chick," Benny said. "Moor-chick. Pheasaan!"

"Moorcock," Jamie growled.

"Quail! Grouse!"

"Benny likes the 'ick' sound," Nat pointed out. "And he's right,
it does sound nicer that way. Go ahead and say moor-chick, Benny."

"Hey! You shouldn't be teaching him things that aren't correct.
I'm drawing an animal that's called a moorcock. Not a moor-chick."

"He'll be going to school soon enough," Nat replied. "He'll learn the correct names then. Or are you afraid they'll laugh at him if he says moor-chick? You should draw a peacock for him, Jamie."

Nat's hair glistened in the afternoon sun. Elizabeth had felt fortified, for the first time since the news of James's death. I have these children, she thought; they're here, they talk to one another. I am their mother.

"Papa had peacocks on board," Nat remembered. "A pair. Maybe they're strolling along the beach right now. In Tahiti."

Jamie concentrated on the imposing peacock's tail feathers. He had taken a fresh sheet of paper, to have enough room to capture the extravagantly erect plumage in all its glory. Benny followed the pencil with his eyes.

She felt sick to her stomach with loss. She was literally ill from her memories of Nat, yet she brought them to mind again and again. It was what she wanted. And what she didn't want. When the doctor arrived with his drops, she gratefully accepted the oblivion for a few hours. In the deep of the night, the sedation wore off, and she woke to a macabre world that was no longer her own. She sank her teeth into the palm of her hand and waited for dawn, her muscles rigid. Sometimes she lost control and screamed. The sound came out, she couldn't stop it. Then Charlotte, or Jane—they seemed to take turns—appeared in a flannel nightgown, with a candle, a tumbler of water, a damp cloth to wipe her face.

Sometimes both women—or could you see them as friends?—came into the bedroom together, and Elizabeth picked up scraps of their conversation. But were they genuinely friends, or was it a pose to disguise their role as the world's accomplices, trying to drag her back on board?

"It'll be weeks before we receive an answer."

"We can't wait."

"No, she's not religious. She hates clergymen. That would be going too far."

"Take this pitcher, will you? I'll adjust the pillow."

"Good thing Jamie's coming home tomorrow. Poor boy."

Water splashed in a bowl. An oil lamp replaced the flickering candle. "Elizabeth? Elizabeth!"

She registered all the sounds but didn't respond to anything. I observe, she thought; I follow the laws of science. There was some activity in the room, the frequency and intensity of footsteps increased, the whispering crescendoed into hushed talking. The women call my name, trying to draw my attention. That is an assumption, not an observation. They touch my body: first my back, covered by a blanket, then my bare hands, and finally, my hair and my face. They make various announcements: they've made soup, it's four o'clock, the mail has arrived, my eldest son is on his way. The one with the sharp edge to her voice says it's enough now. She reads a letter that she wrote to someone. It's about me. I hear her voice quivering, about to break. The smell of cooking wafts into the room. A bowl is placed on the bedside table. It's steaming. They pull me up by my shoulders. The observer has become the object.

Charlotte feeds her the way she once fed Benny. After a few spoonfuls of soup, Elizabeth slumps weakly back. The women sigh and carry their medicinal wares back downstairs. Elizabeth descends into her tangled memories, where Elly and Nat are singing, shrieking with delight; two towheaded children, three and six years old. Everything they'd ever learned—the words, the rules, how to say hello, what to wear if it snows—all for nothing. The violin fingerings, the rules of bow division, the rigging of a man-of-war, the best way to pack a sea chest—all in vain. The chest had also perished. The thought struck her like a lightning bolt. His clothes. A notebook perhaps, in which he'd written about his experiences. The bugle. If only she could, if only she could submerge herself in the black water to look for him.

Someone was reading aloud by the lamp beside her bed. Jane's voice. Through her eyelashes she glimpsed the pinstriped skirt, the trembling hands clutching a pale sheet of paper. Her husband has come back, thought Elizabeth, and yet she's sitting here. She should go home. It's a waste, all this kindness, care, and effort.

"I hope you can find solace in the brilliant memory of our beloved captain, who was so proud that his sons had pledged their hearts to the sea." Elizabeth waved her hand in rejection. "Rest assured of my deepest condolences, yours truly, Joseph Banks," Jane read aloud, the strength ebbing from her voice. She lowered the letter. Elizabeth turned her face away.

"My dearest Elizabeth," Jane started again. "Grim destiny has struck again, and you are once more the anvil on which that terrible blacksmith has hammered. How difficult to hold faith in progress if this is the price you are forced to pay. He was such a kind, sensitive boy. I miss him with so much pain in my heart, and can't begin to imagine how it must be for you. I would so like—" Elizabeth turned abruptly and batted the letter out of Jane's hands. Jane's eyes welled up as the paper drifted to the floor, with Hugh Palliser's firm signature clearly visible. She wiped away her tears with the corner of her apron, bent to pick up the letter, and vanished down the stairs.

Elizabeth was dizzy from exhaustion. There was no difference between day and night; time had become a directionless mass. She heard Nat playing Corelli in the church, saw his profile disappear behind his raised arm as he placed the bow on the strings, felt the anxious presence of James beside her. The doctor. The drops. A new candle. Loud footsteps striding into the room.

"Mother, you must get up!" Jamie stood in a wide-gait stance at the foot of the bed. She saw Jane's unsure expression peeking out from behind Jamie's broad shoulders.

What—popped into her head—what if it had been him, instead of Nat? Would that have been easier to bear? It was out of the question. A sick idea that was gone before it could alarm her. He had chiseled cheeks, that Jamie. A mouth with narrow lips that refused to smile.

"Everybody eats. You have to eat, too. That's an order."

Charlotte brought a plate bearing a piece of meat surrounded by colorless strands of cabbage. She shook her head and dived beneath the blankets. The next time she looked, the fat had congealed and the repulsive stench had gone.

Jamie squatted beside the bed and looked her in the eye. His head was framed by a light-gray window. Day? Time?

"I have to go away again. I want to see you eat something before I leave."

She wanted to tell him something but no sound came out. The skin on her lips was cracked; she could feel the ragged flakes when she tried to speak. Jamie was about to stand up. She stretched her hand toward his knee, pointed to the glass on the bedside table. He passed her some water. She heard herself swallow, a deafening sound.

"The things, Jamie," she whispered. "Where are Nat's things?"

"Are you worrying about that? You have to put it out of your head. You must eat. Get up. Out of bed." What a loud voice he had. It filled the room; out of bed, out of bed, echoed in her mind.

"I'll ask," Jamie said, his voice a little softer, "but I'm almost sure there's nothing. You always have your sea chest with you. It holds everything."

She closed her eyes, and he left. Someone had opened the window, and she smelled the fog drifting into the room, mixed with the scent of burning wood. She wasn't cold. She wasn't anything.

"Elizabeth, look," Charlotte said, "this letter just arrived. Shall I read it to you?" Charlotte placed the envelope in her field of vision. Thin, pointed letters, as if written by a trembling hand. She remained silent. Charlotte ripped open the letter.

I hesitated before writing to you. I was overcome with grief. I have gathered together the scores of the pieces he played. They're here in front of me, and I'm reading them. Unfortunately, I can't visit you because of my poor physical condition. It's been months since I left the house. I would be very grateful if you would come to see me. I know it's a lot to ask, but your son was a beacon to me, a shining lamp. It would do me good to think back on him with you. I carry his playing with me always in my thoughts.

A bitter wind was blowing through the street. Shreds of cloud raced past. The trees were almost bare again. The few birds that had ventured to spread their wings were sent spinning by the wind.

Elizabeth walked in the middle of the road, without a hat. She'd tucked her hands under her armpits and she held her back erect. She hadn't dared to go out onto the street after Elly died, but if it couldn't be avoided, she hid her face behind a veil. She'd felt deformed, violated; tainted and weak for all to see. She'd been ashamed of her condition, unable to display her loss because it was degrading. Now she offered up her pale face, etched with deep creases, to every passerby. In the weathered mirror above her washbasin, she'd inspected the ashen circles underneath her eyes. She had tried to render her flat, lifeless hair presentable, but quickly tossed aside her comb. She didn't care what she looked like or what people thought of her. She was almost ten years older than she'd been then, and a woman nearing forty is a different animal from a woman of almost thirty—but that wasn't it, she thought, as she marched upwind; it seemed as though an indifference had crept in, one of which, as a younger woman, she'd been unaware. That you could become so detached from those around you, those who cooked and took care of you and thought about you; that you could so intensely want nothing more, until all kinds of strange impulses gained the upper hand, and you no longer recognized yourself. It was a fathomless fatigue, related to time but not really to age.

She resolutely turned one corner after the other until she was on the organist's doorstep. She knocked. When a young woman wearing a crisp headscarf opened the door, she realized she'd been expecting the old housekeeper. She was baffled. Many years had passed here, as well. She must have looked odd; the girl asked if she was sure this was the right address, because they never had any visitors.

"There was a time," Elizabeth said, "when I came here often. Mr. Hartland sent me such a kind letter. I am Elizabeth Cook."

The girl clapped her hand to her mouth and opened the door wider.

"Of course, come in. He will be so pleased! My mother used to work here; she sometimes mentioned you, again just last year, when the captain—oh, forgive me, ma'am, may I offer you my condolences. I'm the one who brought you the letter yesterday. Follow me; so nice you came right away. The gentleman is sitting by the hearth. He hardly sleeps; he will be happy to see you."

The short, broad corridor with its black and white tiles. The hooks on the wall where Nat hung his jacket when he came for his violin lessons. The unpainted oak door that swung open in an unexpected direction. The girl pulled it toward her and took a step back so Elizabeth could enter the music room.

The old man sat staring into space, a blanket draped over his knees.

"Mr. Hartland, look, you have a visitor! Mrs. Cook is here! I will make tea, ma'am; please sit down, here."

She slipped past Elizabeth, fluffed a pillow on the chair beside the hearth, laid a hand on Hartland's brittle knee, and could hardly resist the urge to drag the guest into the room.

Elizabeth stood poised and looked around. There were instruments hanging on the walls: a violin and bow next to a larger stringed instrument. That must be a viola, she thought. A recorder, the softly gleaming, coiled tube of a horn. Opposite the hearth, against the wall, as far away as possible from the flames, stood an open harpsichord, as if it had just been played.

She noticed the cupboard full of scores, stacked side by side and on top of one another. On a table in front of the cupboard, there was more sheet music, and paper and an inkstand. Her gaze slowly returned to the open fire. The girl had long since left the room, and crockery could be heard clanking in the kitchen.

The man held a score on his lap. His bony hands, with their long fingers, clung to the paper. "Corelli," she read. The pages were foxed and the edges torn. She took a step forward. Mr. Hartland lifted his face. His cheeks were shimmering with tears. He cried without making a sound, his mouth open. Yolk-gray strands of hair hung on his neck. His cap had slid down to rest on his shoulder.

Elizabeth remained silent. She felt calm, without a trace of discomfort. She looked into the elderly, crying face and felt tears pricking her eyes. She gingerly approached Hartland, briefly rested her hand on his, then sat down opposite him.

Silence. The man nodded. He did not smile. She returned the nod and leaned her head against the back of the chair.

The girl fumbled with the door and carried in the tea tray, balanced on one arm. She poured with a steady hand, placing the cups on small stools beside the chairs, chatting about the weather and where she should leave the teapot, so they could help themselves—but be careful, it's still hot—and disappeared.

A log crackled in the hearth; sparks arced onto the floor and were extinguished, one by one. Hartland grasped his fallen cap and used it to rub his cheeks. He lifted the score.

"When I read this, I hear him playing." His voice was soft yet powerful and didn't match his worn-out body. "He had such a lovely, warm tone on the violin. He sat where you're sitting now, just this past summer. He was happy because you'd agreed to his giving up sailing. He was looking forward to what was to come. But duty first, he said.

The voyage wasn't a burden, because he knew it would be his last. He felt strong. He seemed happy to me."

He rubbed his hand over the score. "I can still hear—clear as a bell—how he laughed. Clear as a bell. He had a smile that could brighten anyone's day."

The sputtering of the flames. The silence. Elizabeth closed her eyes. She pictured Elly sitting in a highchair. How old would she have been? A year, maybe a year and a half at the most. She was making a mess with the porridge in her wooden bowl. This was in the tavern in Barking. Morning, still dark, the smell of stale beer. There was one guest, although the place wasn't open yet; a traveler perhaps, one who'd taken a room for the night and was now eating breakfast. He couldn't take his eyes off the child. Elly looked at him. Her round little face broke into a radiant smile. The man groped in his waistcoat pocket and pulled out a coin, which he then polished with a napkin moistened with spit. The silver shone like moonlight. He stood up and placed the coin within the girl's reach. Elizabeth, fumbling with glasses behind the bar, looked up.

"She has a smile that can make seven years of mourning fade to nothing," the man said. He went back and sat down at his table. Suddenly, Elizabeth felt anxious. She'd been pregnant then, too, with Joseph; James had just left on a voyage. That's how it was. She lifted Elly out of the highchair and carried her to the back, to the kitchen. The child clasped the coin in her clammy little fist. No idea where that coin ended up. Her children had smiles that cheered people up. She had to remember that grin, never lose sight of the image of the laughing child, so she could always call it up, just as Mr. Hartland did, with his elderly mind. Remember everything. The way Nat sat on a stool in the kitchen so she could cut his hair. The little gully in his slender neck. She still had that lock of hair, folded in a piece of paper, hidden away somewhere.

"Surprising how a new loss stirs up an old one," Hartland said, as if he could read her thoughts. "When your daughter was buried, I looked at you. I wanted to comfort you, the way I would like to comfort you now. But consolation is reserved for intact people who have suffered nothing more than a slight dent. I don't think you can bear sympathy."

He rested briefly and caressed the sheet music on his knee. The backs of his hands were covered with thick, dark veins. Nat was always afraid that working with heavy ropes might damage his hands.

"Would you permit me to speak plainly?" Mr. Hartland asked, with an urgent edge to his voice. She nodded, sitting calmly opposite him.

"Our sorrow is of no importance. It occupies all our hours; it eats us up and wears us out. But in essence, it's beside the point. It's not about us, the ones left behind. Perhaps you wonder: why isn't Nathaniel here, with us? Why wasn't he granted more time to enjoy his talent? I wonder about that, too, with bitterness. Yet it doesn't matter. He was here, he existed. That's what we should bear in mind. Our lives have been immeasurably enriched by his presence. It may sound blasphemous, but it's the way I try to think. Thankful that he existed, that in my later years I was able to listen to his playing, and his voice. That hurts. But the thought of how he genuinely was is the only thing that matters."

He wasn't crying anymore. No more steam rose off the tea.

"So afraid," Elizabeth whispered. "I am so frightened that he was desperate, in mortal terror, abandoned by everything and everyone. That he cried out for us. When I try to think about him, the way he died gets in the way. Black waves, a squall. Splintered wood. Then I can't go any further. I cannot reach him; his death is a barrier. Whatever he felt when he died stands in the way. I can't do it."

Hartland leaned forward and took her hand. The music slid to the floor.

"Those who live with music have a good life. No matter how brief it is. Nat was never alone, never lost. He always had music in his mind. Even at the moment of his death. He was not forsaken. He was filled with the most beautiful thing he knew, lifted up by the only thing that can offer deliverance."

She'd felt thirsty, and it was as if he had given her pure water to drink. I will have to hold on to what he has just said, otherwise it will slip away, beyond reach. He says that sorrow is of no importance. Whoever dies with music is not lost, he says. She exhaled deeply and felt the exhaustion slip from her shoulders.

"I would like to play you something," Mr. Hartland said, pushing himself up from his chair. Elizabeth remained seated and watched him shuffle toward the harpsichord.

"A song. An aria." He sat down diagonally on the bench in front of the instrument and looked at her with one arm leaning on the music rack. "Bach. The greatest. He wrote thirty variations on this melody. It is a perfect work that encompasses everything. Nathaniel loved it. We studied it together when he was here for the last time."

Mr. Hartland turned to face the harpsichord and looked down at the ebony keys. "In Nat's honor. To remember him," he said, looking straight ahead.

Then he raised his head, hands poised above the keyboard. The piece had begun before a single note had been played. The melody unfolded slowly above a calmly progressing bass line that set the thick strings vibrating with an audible click. Was it a complaint, Elizabeth wondered, a lament? That's what the descending melody line seemed to suggest, but each time, the sighs were firmly embraced by the underlying chords. It was a game of questions and answers. One voice that spoke out, made a statement, simply told it as it was.

The organist repeated the first section and embellished the melody with trills and garlands of tinkling notes, between which the memory of the original melody resounded. A softly whispered chord formed a semicadence. In the second part, even the bass line was subject to despair. Above that, the melody's plaintive sobs and outcries filled the meter's tight cadence until it almost burst. Everything descended, fell, crashed down.

Then, a miracle. The melody rose up from the depths, now shaped by regular, assured tones, climbing steadily and supported by the strongly ascending bass. To Elizabeth, it was as if a window had been flung open to reveal an infinite vastness. A place she could go, without tears, her head held high, in the realization that her son had loved this music. She would miss him with every step. But because this piece existed, she would be able to endure the pain.

After the stately ending, Mr. Hartland sat quietly at his instrument. Twilight had fallen. The flames in the hearth had died down, but the wood was smoldering gently. Very slowly, at her own pace, she began to rejoin the flow of time outside the music room. Then she stood up, squeezed the organist's hand, and without saying a word, pushed open the door to the hallway.

Of all the crew members who had come back, Captain James King was the most persistent. The officers who had sailed under James's command had all sent letters of condolence to his widow, filled with carefully worded memories; some turned up in person, leaving messages behind when Charlotte or Jane showed them the door. King persevered until, on one gloomy January day, Charlotte showed him into the great room.

Elizabeth sat at the table, dressed in one of her black frocks, writing thank-you notes. She registered the lanky body with its head that seemed slightly too small; she fought back a stab of pain at the sight of the captain's uniform, and offered him her hand. She thought back on her husband's angry outburst when King had first come to present himself.

"My husband spoke highly of you," she said.

King smiled like a child hungry for compliments. He said he was sorry for the loss of her son and quickly turned the subject to James.

"We shared a love of astronomy, and we were both believers in the importance of keeping good records. I've recently spent time reading— and admiring—his journals from the second voyage. A superb work, with well-chosen illustrations. It presents a comprehensive depiction of your husband's greatness."

"Did I hear that you took over responsibility for the logbook?"

King nodded. "Of course, Captain Clerke also made some entries; after all, after your husband's demise, he became the expedition's leader. However, his physical condition severely limited the scope of his activities. Are you aware, ma'am, that he died in August of that same year? We were able to bury him on land, at Kamchatka. Then, John Gore assumed command. And I became the captain of the *Discovery*. Gore wasn't much taken with the written word, and so the task fell to me."

Gore on the *Resolution*, what would James have thought of that? she wondered. Indecisive, disloyal, and not the prettiest by a long shot. Best to keep that to myself. A book about this final voyage was sure to be published. She'd have to negotiate with this King about the royalties. Stick to small talk. She told him she could definitely see a hint of James in him. He blushed.

"Do you know, I was sometimes mistaken for the captain's son? Whenever they saw us watching the skies with our telescopes and sextants, the islanders thought we were carrying out some sort of religious ritual. And if we stayed in one place for any length of time, we brought the clock ashore and set it up in a special tent, constantly guarded by two Marines. Of course, Captain Cook and I had free access, because we had to carry out the astronomical observations. They believed he was the high priest of some curious religion, and I was his son and follower! We tried to tell them what was really going on, but it was too hard to explain in that foreign tongue. Sometimes I'd allow someone to peer through the telescope. Being able to bring distant objects so close gave them a fright. Such a marvel. I left them in the dark about the kinship. To me, it was an honor."

"The voyage," Elizabeth said. "I understand that in the end, there was no passage, but what about the expedition's other goals? Omai? The animals?"

She wasn't sure she really wanted to hear the answers to her questions; what he had to say didn't interest her, but it had to be done, they had to fill up the hours somehow, good manners had to be upheld and respected.

"Captain Cook was worried about Omai. He'd been fond of him; he liked his cheerful nature and enthusiasm, but he also had some reservations. No firearms, the captain had said. Omai might not be able to control himself if his fellow tribesmen attacked him. We decided to take Omai to a smaller island where no one knew him, because we wanted to avoid any jealous reprisals. We built him a house with a front door and a working lock. Put a garden around it, planted it and all. It was a touching farewell; Omai held himself in check until he embraced the captain. Then he wept and wouldn't let go. The captain hoped that Omai would look after the garden as well as the sheep and goats we'd left behind, but he expected the worst. Omai had bought himself a canoe, a superb vessel he christened the *Royal George*. He called his house 'Britain.' Moving, indeed."

Concern, Elizabeth thought. Fatherly consideration. Why did it make her so angry? Hadn't James also shown concern for his own children? He'd helped them with their careers, he'd thought about them. Hadn't he?

"Transporting the animals had been a huge headache. The captain believed it was crucial to distribute the livestock among the various islands. His mind was made up about that. On the island known as Tonga, we left behind a bull, a cow, a stallion, and a mare. The captain was incensed when, after this generous gift, the islanders went on to steal a goat and a few turkeys destined for one of the smaller islands near Tahiti. He was tough on those thieves. Too harsh, some believed. But they foiled his plans; that was the crux of it.

"When we arrived in Tahiti, disappointment awaited us. We had been looking forward to the islanders' astonished and disbelieving reaction when we brought our horses ashore, but it seems the Spanish had eclipsed us a year before we arrived. Large, beautiful animals they were, too. We added our team. They'd stolen our thunder, but we were all relieved that the livestock had finally disembarked, once and for all. The king's mission had been accomplished. In Tahiti, two goats were also stolen. That made the captain's blood boil."

King fell silent. Elizabeth wanted to grill him further: how furious had James been, what did he do in response to the theft, why did King break off his story? She waited. King drank his tea, which had grown cold, and stared at his shoes.

"The captain had a strong sense of duty. The islanders were generally pleasant toward us, but there were undoubtedly fantasies and perhaps even schemes of which we were unaware. They tried to draw us into their local power struggles, and they became incensed when we refused; they may also have envied us our wealth. No matter how calm the situation seemed, we always had to keep an eye out for threats and danger. From time to time, the captain thought it wise to show our muscle."

Charlotte brought in a tray and poured the Madeira. "To the memory of our captain," King said. They raised their glasses.

What am I doing? Elizabeth wondered. Toasting James. I must be crazy. I don't feel very festive. This King may be talking a lot, but there are plenty of gaps in his account. He's being very selective, just like the Lords of the Admiralty were. Am I mistrustful? Maybe it's not possible to tell the story of a four-year voyage in an hour and a half. It could be he's trying, and this is the best he can do.

The spirits seemed to give King renewed courage.

"That northern passage, as you said, came to nothing. On our way up, we charted the west coast of America, so the journey wouldn't be entirely for naught. We were held back by freezing conditions, and narrowly missed having the ships trapped in the ice. We were exhausted and disheartened, and set course for the island of Hawai'i, which we'd discovered on our way north. You know how our stay there ended."

King desperately shook his small head.

"You mentioned danger, and I can't help wondering if it was a good idea to prolong your stay on the islands for so long," Elizabeth said quietly. "For all we know, things might have turned out differently if—"

"There was good reason, ma'am, several reasons in fact." He picked up the pace. "You already know we had to carry out some lengthy repairs. But there was more. The captain wanted to collect as much information as possible to shed light on the mystery of the South Sea. How, on all those tiny dots of land separated by thousands of miles of saltwater, could the same language be spoken, the same type of canoe built, and the same cloth fashioned from bark? He wanted to go beyond the artifacts; to investigate the government, the manners, and the religion. To do that, you need a longer stay. The captain made an effort to get to know the people and observe them. He visited religious ceremonies, spent time in the company of kings and priests; he attended sacred dances and participated in secret rites. He later wrote down everything he'd observed in his journal.

"He also tried to explain our achievements to them. He showed one bright islander a map of the island he had just drawn. When the man immediately recognized his own island, the captain glowed with pride. When they saw us writing or drawing, they called it 'tattooing.' That's their word for the adornments they put on their bodies. This man realized that our 'tattoos' had meaning, referring to or summarizing something. The captain was enormously delighted with this. Which gods did they worship? How was the king's succession arranged? What was the wife's role? Why did the king's young son seem more powerful than the king himself? The captain searched for answers to all these questions. He didn't find them, not quite, but he assembled the building blocks that could be of use to him."

"Did it please him?"

King paused to reflect. "A certain satisfaction was sometimes visible, yes. But it was also a heavy burden on the captain's shoulders. The language was a huge barrier. The worst of it was, his good intentions and concerns weren't always appreciated. The way they destroyed his carefully planted gardens, or ate the livestock we'd so painstakingly transported. That was hard for him to stomach."

How do you get a horse on land, Elizabeth tried to imagine. Lower it, with a hoist, into the largest launch? There would hardly be room for the rowers next to such a terrified beast. You'd have to tie up its legs; otherwise one of its hooves might punch a hole through the bottom of the boat. The launch would no doubt get stuck on a sandbar, and they'd have to chase the horse into the surf. James would be standing on the deck of the *Resolution*, watching through his telescope and cursing, mouth set, his jaw clenched in determination.

"He walked into situations others might try to avoid. His curiosity overmastered his cautiousness. Some would call it courage. Or loyalty to progress."

King went silent. Elizabeth, suddenly gripped by total exhaustion, thanked him for his visit and said goodbye. The thin captain, his hat clasped to his chest, hastened into the hallway.

Benny stood on a stool at the kitchen counter, next to Charlotte. He carefully pushed hazelnuts into the small heaps of dough on the baking sheet in front of him. Elizabeth stood beside him and heard him counting under his breath. I should rest my hand on his head, she thought, stroke his neck, or rub his tense back. An ordinary gesture. But it would only startle him, so maybe not. The child seemed to read her mind, and huddled closer to Charlotte. Elizabeth sat down at the table without saying a word.

Someone pushed open the door of the scullery. Soles scraped the stone floor.

"Anybody home?" Isaac's voice. His tone was deeper, she noticed. How nice he's come. He's a grown man now; you can feel the strength in him, and he smells like the fresh outdoors.

After they'd embraced, they stood looking at each other. His face, which had become even ruddier, was solemn.

"Nice to see you're back downstairs," he said. "I can't get over it. Such a tragedy. The captain, that was a blow. But Nat, that's, that's—" He shook his head fiercely, flinging his tears in every direction. Elizabeth rested a hand on his cheek. He was so warm he almost glowed.

"Mary is in bed, with the covers pulled over her head. She won't eat, won't talk. Just this morning she said to me, you should go and visit Elizabeth. She does think of you. Just so you know."

"Drop in next door before you go back," Elizabeth said. "Bring her a small barrel of gin. Might do her some good. She loved Nat so much. She's getting on in years. I do understand."

Charlotte had put the cookies into the oven and was getting ready to take Benny outside. The smell of cinnamon and burnt sugar was so overpowering, it almost turned Elizabeth's stomach. She asked Isaac to open a window.

"Ever since the Arctic, I don't feel the cold," he said, "but you should be careful."

"I'm not cold. James King was here, full of high praises and success stories. I can't seem to find out what it was really like. Maybe you can fill me in."

Isaac said nothing. "Shouldn't they come out?" he asked after a while, pointing to the oven. Elizabeth opened the hatch and removed the baking tray, placing it on a shelf in the scullery. Door closed, smell gone; window closed again.

"I asked King if James had been enjoying himself. He didn't know what to say. What do you think, Isaac?"

Isaac propped his elbows on the table and rested his head in his hands.

"Huge hassle with that livestock. A nightmare. The captain, I mean James, went into a rage whenever they stole an animal. But in Tahiti, when we finally got those confounded horses ashore, he and Clerke went galloping through the sand. The bay there is rimmed by a black beach, almost a mile long. They galloped over it, faster and faster, turning quickly at each end. The horses reared on their hind legs as if they were standing upright; the sand sprayed like a fountain of grit, and James yelped with joy. Then they laughed and raced those horses back over the wet sand along the water's edge. The islanders watched, their mouths agape. So did we. We'd never seen James in such high spirits."

She could picture it, could hear the waves lapping and the dull stamping of the horses' hooves along the sand, spurred on by the two captains, both now dead.

It's that easy, she reflected, to sink into a feeling of forgiveness. Nothing is important; nothing matters. I'm clinging to my urge to investigate as if it were a raft; I could just as easily slip into the water. But I damned well won't. It's my duty to find out how James died. And why. It has to be done.

"Was he sick, Isaac?"

Isaac stood up. "You're the one who should be worried about getting sick. Let's go for a little walk. Come on, I'm taking you out, whether you like it or not. Dress warmly."

She followed obediently. A low deck of clouds hung over the river. She sucked in the damp air and held tight to Isaac's arm. Step by step. She repeated her question.

"I can't be sure," Isaac said. "Sometimes he was in pain; rheumatism, gout, that sort of thing. Then he could hardly move. Those Tahitian women had a cure, unbelievable! A canoe full of women rowed up, they climbed aboard and piled into his cabin. James had to lie on the floor; we wondered if he was finally going to succumb to temptation—it was a sight, Elizabeth, a tribe of girls and women with naked breasts and tattooed bottoms—they swarmed all over him and began to massage him roughly. You could hear his bones cracking! He screamed in agony, but the women just laughed and quietly went about their work. One sat on his spine with her full weight, another walloped him in the hip, and two women almost pulled his leg out of its socket; he moaned the whole time. When they were done, James stood up without any effort, like a young fellow. The women spent the night on board and repeated the treatment a few more times; that's how they relieved James of his pain." He looked at her out of the corner of his eye. "If they relieved him of anything else, I couldn't say. We all had girlfriends. They were so hospitable, so attentive and sweet; some of us never wanted to leave. James was against it. Even when they offered him a woman—that's just their way of being polite, you know—he'd brush them off with a joke, saying he was too old and weak."

Elizabeth put one foot in front of the other. She should feel reassured. Her husband had remained faithful, even when a dozen naked women had jumped on him. But a vague uneasiness in her chest wouldn't go away.

"How was he, Isaac? Did you talk with him much; did he seek you out; was he friendly?"

"Sometimes we worked together on a chart, then he'd invite me into the great cabin. That was nice enough. He wasn't much of a talker. We would sit measuring and sketching. But that didn't happen often. He was under a lot of pressure; his plans were constantly being undermined by a lack of time, or the way the native people behaved. Thievery. I thought he was harsh. We all thought so."

"Cruel?"

Isaac bit his tongue. They walked along the lead-gray river. How I hate the water, Elizabeth thought; why don't I go live somewhere else, among the fields and forests, out of reach from the sea's grappling arm?

"There were times when he was beside himself with rage," Isaac said quietly. "Someone stole a goat and that drove him mad. He gave the order for the thief's head to be shaved and his ears sliced off. At the last minute, King stayed the barber's hand, and the poor chap jumped overboard. Don't know if I should tell you this. We couldn't make head nor tail of it. When he was really on the rampage, he'd destroy canoes and set huts on fire. Those people would spend years working on one of those canoes. Splendid boats, covered with paintings and carvings. James held them in high esteem. And yet he ordered them to be smashed to bits. That was heartless, of course. But it was done out of anger, out of powerlessness. Not that he took any pleasure in such cruelty. You understand?"

She nodded. "Was there anything else? Other behaviors that worried you?"

I should stop, she thought. I can see that I'm making him uncomfortable. It's his captain, his mentor, and his father figure. But if he doesn't tell me, we'll soon run out of things to say, maybe forever. And I don't want that, either.

"To me, the hostage takings were even more brutal," Isaac said. "I know some viewed it as a brilliant strategy, because it always brought results without bloodshed. But I found it cruel. Those hostages hadn't done anything wrong. They were scared. The wrong people were being punished. When Omai was finally settled, we went on to Raiatea, you remember, where Orio is king. He and James are friends. Or were. They'd even exchanged names. It was the last island in the archipelago where we dropped anchor. A lot of the men were finding it hard; some didn't want to leave, and ran off. We couldn't find two of the deserters; James suspected the locals of sheltering them.

"That's when he took Orio's daughter, Poetua, hostage. The whole thing lasted five days. That ravishing princess spent all that time in the great cabin, while her father tried to find the deserters. On top of everything, she was pregnant then, too. Webber painted her; might as well, he said, since she was there. He made her put flowers behind her ears and stand against a wall. She did as she was told, without any fuss. I saw it with my own eyes, because I was working on a chart and needed to get some tables from the cabin.

"The women from the village surrounded the ship in countless canoes. They stood up in their boats, crying and shouting, and they scratched their faces with sharp shells until the blood trickled over their naked bodies. Inside the cabin, their screeching was unbearable. Outside, it was positively deafening, but Poetua remained calm and polite. Dignified, like the princess she was. The men, of course, couldn't stop staring at her breasts. I kept hoping that James would set her free, put an end to that horrifying caterwauling. He didn't do anything of the sort. He ordered the ship to sail to the end of the bay; that was the only time I saw a look of fear on Poetua's face. I think she was afraid we would take her back to England, and she'd never see her father again. Even though she hadn't done anything wrong!"

They continued walking silently, side by side.

"You're sure to be promoted now," Elizabeth said.

Isaac laughed. "Slowly climbing my way out of the fo'c'sle. By the next voyage I should be sleeping amidships; I have a feeling they're going to promote me to lieutenant. And then the way's clear to end up in the stern, as captain. But I'm dreading the war. No more voyages of discovery. With my luck, I'll end up fighting the French."

"Who were James's friends?"

Isaac thought carefully. "He got along well with Clerke. He could make him smile. But Clerke was on the other ship; they only saw one another when we went ashore. On the *Resolution*, I believe James felt most at ease with Anderson. He was the doctor, you know. He had a good command of the language, so they were able to commiserate about what they were going through, and what it all meant. He died, too, our doctor. Just like Clerke, from the same illness. They knew that about each other. And they were aware that their condition would worsen

once we sailed back into the cold. They really should have stayed behind
in Tahiti; the climate there was better for their health. But luckily for
James, they both remained at their posts. Watman, that old sailor we
buried on Hawai'i, was also a friend of James's. There was no speaking
to James when Watman died, because James blamed himself for allowing such an old salt to sail with us. The man had even turned away his
pension to sign up, after he'd retired to Greenwich!

"James organized an elaborate funeral for Watman in a sanctuary
there, with the priests' blessing. James's face was as stern and inscrutable
as granite. He read from the Bible himself.

"I think he was quite fond of King, and of me, as well. But more
like a father. Clerke and Anderson were his real friends. And they were
slowly burning up with consumption. James couldn't do anything to
stop it."

"He could have forced them to stay in the tropics. To die there."

Isaac shook his head. "They never would have agreed. Officers
have their pride. They discussed it among themselves, but there was no
chance they would ever have done such a thing. When we finally sailed
northward, those sick men were constantly in my thoughts. I kept an
eye on Anderson. You glide ever so slowly into the frigid air, almost
without noticing. There's a crisp breeze. You think, it'll soon blow over,
but after a few days, you're shivering in your shirtsleeves, and before
you know it, the boatswain is handing out duffel coats and mittens. I
kind of liked that winter weather. We could see the west coast of North
America: massive mountain ranges, white with snow. If you were on
watch, the frost would cling to your hair. Before you knew it, you
started hankering after hot soup.

"There were native tribes living along the coast; they spoke a language different from that of the islanders. We couldn't understand a
word. They wore animal hides. Hunters. Always thinking about animals. That's where I picked up that bird for Benny, in exchange for a
pipe and a handkerchief."

"You scored a bull's-eye with that bird; Benny loves it."

When Isaac had sailed back into London, Elizabeth was still lying upstairs like a limp dishrag. Isaac came to visit right away. According to Charlotte, the man had suddenly appeared on their doorstep, with wild hair and carrying a large package. The bird of prey he'd brought, carved out of a type of wood that was almost black, had been Benny's constant companion ever since. Its wings were slightly bent, its claws clamped around a branch. And it weighed a ton. Every day, the child lugged the bird up and down the stairs. Benny put it on the table while he was eating.

"It was pleasant in the inlet where we'd anchored, despite the cold. We explored the rivers to see if we could find an inner passage to the Arctic waters. I remember one day—a cloudy, almost English day— when we set off exploring in the launch. James was so relaxed, so natural. He chatted with us, asked all kinds of personal questions. We could hear the locals singing from the surrounding mountains; the sound swelled and diminished. Their singing was so artful and lovely that it brought tears to my eyes. And that while they were such filthy people, covered in greasy mud—and the smell! We rowed some thirty miles that day, and we were dead tired; but to us, it was like a cruise down the Thames. We picked bilberries somewhere along the riverbank, and our mouths were blue. James sliced some dried meat on his knee, and offered us each a piece on the tip of his knife. We sat chewing quietly, leaning on our oars. An osprey flew overhead, he soared for a while along the river. I think that everyone in the boat was happy that day."

Elizabeth and Isaac left the riverbank and walked along a country lane between fields, in the direction of a distant steeple. When I ask him about friends, he brings up two critically ill men, she thought. I ask him about satisfaction, about happiness, and he mentions two trivial episodes. Why was James so tense, what drove him to such fury? Did he

think about us at all, did he have me in mind, or the children, and did
that give him any solace? Did he speak of the future, and if so, how? I
will never know, no matter how much pressure I exert on the faithful
man beside me.

"Can you tell me about the end, Isaac? What *you* saw?"

Isaac squeezed her arm tightly against his ribs. "You're torturing
yourself. Why do you want to know everything in such detail? Isn't it
bad enough that it happened?"

"I have to know. I want to be able to think about it. I need to be
able to picture it. The facts. That's an idea I learned from James."

Isaac let go of her arm and scratched his head. "I don't know if it'll
do you any good. I'm worried, you see. You don't look well. You don't
eat. You seem to be miles away."

"Nobody can tell me how Nat met his end," she whispered, "I'm
at the mercy of my imagination. You were there when James died. You
can shield me from my worst fantasies."

Isaac wrapped his arm around her shoulder. "I didn't see anything,"
he said. "I was on board, in the cabin. We were preparing to leave, so I
was packing the charts and sketches into boxes. I heard someone come
to talk with James, and then they went upstairs together. I didn't realize
it was about that stolen cutter. James swore. I didn't pay much attention, there were always problems. I heard some reports later, gunshots,
of course. To be honest, I had a drawing of the American coast in my
hands, and I figured I'd done a pretty good job with it. The hollering
and hubbub topside didn't let up. That's when I climbed on deck. It
was already over. I didn't get the feeling a calamity had taken place. I
was still dreaming about publishing those charts. How proud I would
be. I'm ashamed of that now."

"But what happened later, surely you can tell me that?"

"Chaos. Everyone was completely devastated. They wanted revenge,
to blast the island to kingdom come; they were already aiming the
cannons. They were planning to seal off the bay and hack everyone to

bits. Set the entire settlement ablaze. Captain Clerke had a hard time keeping their thirst for vengeance in check. I can still see him coming on board, wheezing and pale, with small bright-red patches high on his cheeks. He'd suddenly become our captain. Why do we need more dead, he asked; that doesn't solve anything. He was staring death in the eye himself, of course; that's why he remained so calm. He wasn't able to stop all of it, because the crew that went to fetch the mast from the island killed at least ten locals, and most of the village went up in flames. King had himself rowed to the shore, a white flag in his hands, to negotiate on Clerke's behalf. Clerke was so upset he could barely set foot on deck. It took another week of dickering before we could bury James."

"Before they handed over his body, you mean?"

Isaac bent over to tighten the buckle of his shoe. When he stood up again, his face was flushed. "Yes, his remains. The ceremony was on the twenty-first. In the evening, around six. On the deck."

There's that idiotic term again. What possessed Isaac to use it? Wouldn't it be more natural to say "James," or even "the body"?

"They'd declared the entire bay taboo, which meant that no one was allowed in the area. It was completely calm. No wind at all. I had never before noticed how menacing those high mountains are there, the ones that loomed over us. We all came on deck, everyone in his best uniform."

Where are the clothes, I wonder, the blue jacket, and the hat? He had at least two uniforms with him. They would have buried him in one of them, but the other? A third jacket was still hanging in the cupboard upstairs, for when he came home.

"Captain Clerke called me to the front. Because I'm family. I stood next to Anderson, the doctor. The drummers had draped a cloth over their instruments, and they were playing slowly. The muffled sound was ominous, as if some terrible threat was steadily approaching. Beyond the railing is the sea, I thought, soon, he'll go in. I felt completely numb. It was hard to believe that it had really happened. Clerke was too short of breath to read the scripture, and you can't ask Gore to do that type of thing, so Lieutenant King did the reading. The coffin was on a plank, draped with a flag. The bagpipe played a tune. Then the drumrolls grew louder and sped up until, all at once, they stopped. Suddenly, the plank was tipped up and the lines holding the casket were released. We all held our breath. The splash wasn't very loud, as if the sea readily opened up to accept the casket. We stood with our heads bowed until Clerke gave the signal, dismissing us. I don't know much more about what else happened that day. I suppose we ate. We were preparing to leave. I can't remember anything more about it."

They hadn't been paying attention, had been walking at a healthy pace, and suddenly they were at the church. There was Elly's tiny grave, overgrown with brownish-gray grass. Elizabeth leaned against the wall that surrounded the graveyard. She pictured the deck of the *Resolution*, crowded with downhearted men, their hats and caps in their hands. A row of Marines in red coats standing opposite the officers in blue, with Isaac awkwardly to one side. The image came to her, complete and clear cut, like a framed painting.

"He should never have gone. Did that ever occur to any of you? You paid him last respects as if he were one of your own. The commander. The father. Obviously. You're beside yourselves when he's gone, greatly inconvenienced. And we? His wife, his children? How are we to endure his disappearances? You talk about the efforts he made on your behalf, how he worked himself to the bone. He may have sat in his cabin with a naked princess, but shouldn't he have been with me in the kitchen? He rowed past those wooded slopes with you, but not along the Thames with his sons. You say it was hard to let him go, but what was it like to wave goodbye to him, time after time? Has that ever crossed your mind?"

Isaac looked as if he didn't quite understand what she was talking about.

"We," she repeated, "his family. Living and dead."

He turned his back on her and took a few steps up the road. Then he pivoted back, stamped his foot, and slapped his forehead.

"Stupid, stupid! You're right!" He stood near her. "Never thought about it. As if all this here didn't exist. You know, I was only happy when I was allowed to go along, proud if I made a sketch he liked, excited when we dropped anchor in an unfamiliar bay. I was only thinking of myself. Foolish."

Elizabeth crossed her arms and looked at the ground. Hugh Palliser had been right, she thought; there's a smoldering volcano raging inside me, aimed at someone inaccessible. Everyone who is within reach is given the full brunt. That wretched Benny who can't do a thing about it. And those loyal friends of James's, the ones who want to offer me their support and are thrown out by Charlotte. Now I'm tormenting poor Isaac because James isn't here. Look at him, remorseful about things that are completely out of his control. I must stop this, but how? I will burst if I truly feel how things really are.

Isaac nudged her. He hooked his index fingers together and moved his hands up and down.

"That's what the islanders do to show they're sincere, that they're speaking the truth. It's an oath. I will look after you. And Benny. I swear to you, Elizabeth, I will never let you down again."

He wrapped his arms around her and held her tight. She stood motionless in that warm enclosure. She gritted her teeth.

11

"I never sit here," Hugh Palliser said. "It's too grand for me, almost a ballroom."

Elizabeth swayed her hips and danced a few steps. They paused in front of the enormous fireplace. An immense log lay smoldering in the grate, an unsplit tree trunk that appeared completely charred. She sank to her knees and began to blow, too hard at first, raising a fine, swirling cloud of ash; then slower and at a more even pace. A blue line became visible on the back of the wood and then split into countless frolicking flames. She stood and fanned the fire with her skirt until the trunk was fully ablaze. She gave Hugh a triumphant look. He smiled and rested a hand on her fiery cheek.

"Let's go to my study; I'll pour you some coffee."

Glass doors opened onto the terrace. Beyond that, as far as she could see, was the park. The trees in the early spring were adorned with various shades of green that would later, when the summer was almost at an end, dissolve into a unified, faded hue. There were pools of blue beneath the treetops; bluebells, she thought. We used to have those in the garden, but they didn't thrive. So this is where he sits staring at the deer. A pity I've never been here before. Had to wait until I was forty-two. He had to invite me twenty times. He practically had to kidnap me in that ostentatious coach he sent to pick me up.

Hugh sank into his armchair and propped his leg up on a thread-bare cushion. He didn't look half-bad, and his eyes were sparkling. He patted the chair to his right.

"I like it when you sit next to me. Better than when we're facing each other. I want to see what you see."

She slipped into the chair. Would the silence drive you crazy, or was it a good thing? He seemed to enjoy it. James's account of the second voyage was propped open on a lectern. She spotted the spines of Hawkesworth's four-volume work in the bookcase.

"When is the new book coming out? It should be finished by now. Have you heard anything?"

Hugh shook his head. "Douglas is in charge; that's all I know. It'll have three volumes: two by James and one by King. But you know that; you have a contract, if I'm not mistaken. Hasn't Douglas shown you the proofs?"

"Not yet. There's no provision for that."

"So you still don't know anything, except what Stephens and Sandwich told you."

"And King," she added. "And Isaac, of course. I know the whole story. But you're right; I don't really know anything. Not how and why it could have happened, not what took place before the burial. So yes, I could say a lot about it, but in truth, I know nothing. I don't want to pressure Isaac again. I tried, of course, but he doesn't know, either. He was just an ordinary seaman back then. I've always thought I should wait for the publication of the journals. But now I think that's just one side to the story, another version of what James wrote, but still censured by the Admiralty. And the final chapter? I don't know. In any event, they want to make the story public in their own way. But does that mean it's the truth?"

He'd taken her hand and was caressing her fingers, one by one.

"What are you hunting for?"

"Understanding," she said without hesitation. "If I could understand what possessed him, maybe I'd find peace. I hold discussions with him every night. Arguments, accusations. I want to put that behind me. I can't keep it up. I'm so tired."

He kissed her fingers. She peered into the garden without pulling her hand away.

"Isaac told me about the burial. Or whatever you call it when you tip someone into the sea. I try to picture it. Down to the last detail, but it's not enough. It doesn't put my mind at rest."

"You have to walk," Palliser said. "You must bear someone off. Bring them away. Step by step, knowing full well it's their last journey."

Elizabeth looked into his eyes. He had taken her with him when Elly was buried, as a matter of course. He'd walked by her side. He understood such things.

"The most terrible thing there is," she said. "It's unimaginable, and yet, you do it. There has to be a grave, although that's just as bad. Sometimes, at home, I hear the rain and wind racing over her resting place. Dreadful. But the next morning, I go and clear away the fallen branches. I know where she is. I could dig her up. I could hold her skull."

Don't go any further, she thought. I'm expressing ideas that belong inside my head and nowhere else. I must stop. But why? He can take it, by the look of things. He knows what I'm talking about. I'd like to crawl into the damp earth with her. To rest my cheek alongside her bones.

"We'll eat shortly. You're still just skin and bones. After lunch, I'd like to show you something, in the park. You may find it ghastly, tasteless, and overdone. But I had to do it. It involves what we were just talking about, that there's no grave, no resting place. James was my friend, no matter what happened. I miss him. I had a monument built to him. You can't see it from here; it's a short distance away. We'll walk there this afternoon; I want to show it to you. It's a square column covered in words. His life story. His deeds. How significant he was. There's writing on every side of the column. The text is from the Admiralty's memorial report. I might have put it differently, but I wanted it to be official. In my park, but as official as possible. Long after we're gone, people will still walk here and stop to read the text. They'll think of him a hundred years from now. I chose a piece of extremely durable marble."

"There are times I can hardly remember what he looked like," Elizabeth said. "Then I can only picture his back, too narrow for his height, you know? And slightly hunched. I can't call his face to mind. Whenever I try, I see that painting that Dance made. His back is all that's left."

A gardener was busy putting plants into tubs outside. A spade stuck out of a wheelbarrow on the grass.

"Do you talk about him with your youngest, my godson?"

Elizabeth pulled her hand away and rubbed the side of her face. "Just call him Benny. That's the name he answers to. He reads. He devours books about the voyage. I don't know if he comprehends that they're about his father. No, I hardly mention James to him. In fact, I never know what to say to him. He loves school, absorbs everything he hears. That worries me. But unfortunately, I'm in no position to make a fuss. Perhaps everything they tell him there falls into a bottomless pit, one I failed to fill when he was younger."

Hugh raised his eyebrows. Elizabeth talked on; her voice was too shrill, even to her own ears.

"I was in a dark place when he was born. Then I was angry. When I regained my strength, I started looking after the sailors' children. I kept hoping that Benny and I would grow closer once he was older.

Now he's reached that point, but he clings to his teachers and there's no room for me."

Hugh massaged his ankle.

"Does it pain you to see how I've neglected your godchild? Are you cross?"

In the silence that followed, she could hear the flames consuming the firewood. In truth, there was always some process underway in which one element either destroyed the other or absorbed it permanently. In order not to be incorporated, you have to put up a constant fight. No wonder she was so tired.

"What are you worried about? Isn't his passion for learning a testament to his spirit?"

"He's gotten religion. I bring him to bed, wish him good night. I stand in the hallway and peek through a crack in the door; I see him get out of bed—on his knees, hands folded, eyes closed, and for minutes on end, he mutters words I don't understand! Then he crawls back under the covers. I sneak away without making a sound."

"That's an unexpected development," Hugh said. "But not illogical, and nothing to worry about, for that matter. Sounds to me like a youthful whim. It'll pass."

Elizabeth snorted. "Don't dismiss it as a trifle. You should see his serious little face. I can't bring myself to question him about it. I am much too frightened of what I might hear. But I think James would expect me to set him straight and show him the magnificence of the scientific worldview."

"But you do that already. You read to him. You give him books. Apart from that, he seems to have—for now, anyway—other needs. That's how it is for entire tribes, as you well know. You're reluctant to take his faith away because you don't know what it means to him."

"I cannot reach him. Papa is with God, he says. No, I say, your father is dead. He's gone. No he's not, Papa is in heaven; he's singing with the angels and looking down on us. There are stars in the heavens, I say; it's a dark-blue vacuum filled with stars. I point to the polestar, Orion, and the Milky Way. God's beyond that, he says, up there. The teacher says so, because it's true. That shuts me up. He sings Psalms before he falls asleep. Perfectly in tune. He'll be singing in the church choir this coming school year. In truth, I feel left out, powerless. It's my own fault. Angels! James couldn't even carry a tune."

The irritation propelled her to her feet. Hugh slowly got up from his chair and reached for his cane. The doors were opened wide onto the terrace, into the pungent spring air. They walked down the stairs, arm in arm, toward the park. Undulating fields, hillocks interlaced with a network of stone walls, dotted here and there with clusters of deep-red beech trees. No water anywhere, no sea.

"Leave him be," Hugh said. "There's no harm in it. It comforts him. How old were you when you started having doubts?"

She laughed and rested her head on his shoulder.

"How I've missed you," he said. "I missed you so much."

A delicate, mysterious aroma of onions and garlic rose from the shrubbery. "*Allium ursinum*," he explained, pointing to a patch of small white flowers hidden in the shadows.

He led her to the monument. A pompous base with a rather small globe perched atop. She saw the Pacific South Sea dotted with tiny protrusions. It amounts to nothing, she thought; so much misery, so much consternation. The theaters of progress are nothing more than pinheads: the beach in Hawai'i, the bay in Tahiti.

Her shoulders trembled involuntarily, like an animal's, as if to shake off the thought of those places of doom. The feeling of futility paralyzed her to such an extent that she couldn't even compliment him on his memorial. They slowly walked back to the house.

She'd had too much to drink. Words and tears began to flow freely. Hugh asked after her mother, and to her surprise, Elizabeth cried. She blew her nose in his handkerchief.

"Not so good," she said. "She's slipping further and further away. They've rented out the business, and now they live upstairs. There's plenty of room. The new tenants are nice; the woman cooks for them. I hear this from Isaac; don't get there much myself. When she sees me, she can't control her sobbing. She thinks of Nat. That grief overwhelms her every time. My father—my stepfather, I should say—is bent double with age and rheumatism. I have no idea what they get up to all day, and I'd rather not think about it. Every two weeks I send them a small barrel of gin, she loves the stuff. At least that's one thing that gives her pleasure. Old age is hell. I'm a terrible daughter."

"Good enough," Hugh said, "as good as you can be."

"I've also been a bad friend to you. I was so angry I slammed the door in your face."

"Those were stormy years. For both of us."

"You must have imagined things turning out differently. I regret that."

Hugh stared wordlessly into his glass. "What I pictured," he said after a long pause, "goes beyond all limits. I don't have to tell you. Between us, we needed few words. We were soul mates, Elizabeth. I am grateful to you for that."

"But aren't we still? I'm sitting beside your hearth, I'm holding your hand!"

He pulled his hand away and topped up her glass.

"You're still young. I'm an old man," he rasped. "We would—it would be a disaster, Elizabeth. I'm not suitable. You have your whole life ahead of you. You have two sons. Why would you want to burden yourself with a lame old graybeard? I mean it. It's too late."

"That's not how I feel at all," she shot back. "Whatever gave you that idea? I never think of you as a frail old man."

"And yet it's true. It's not easy to talk about it. My injury, you know. The wound affected so many functions. Disabled, you say. Impotent. Certainly."

That shook her up. "So that's why you don't have a family, why she couldn't have children!"

Hugh straightened his posture. "It's me. I haven't been able to produce any offspring since the injury. But before that, I could. I have a son; George is his name."

She was struck dumb. "A son? With whom?"

"My mother's seamstress. I was sixteen or so. I never see him, but I paid for his education. He'll inherit all of this. So many secrets, Elizabeth. Mysteries you should know about, because they have implications for us. There's no other woman I have loved as much, as wholeheartedly, as you. That will always be so, that will never change. You belong inalienably to me."

He fell silent and began rubbing his leg again.

"But I can't go on with you. No further than this, a visit on a Sunday afternoon. I would make you miserable, of that I am certain. It is not possible. I can't."

She looked at him with incomprehension.

"All those promises," he continued, "between us. Those strange, unavoidable instances of physical contact that would never lead to— well, what they should lead to."

"That's nothing to me," she called out shrilly. "You are my friend. You must be my friend."

She heard how childish her words sounded.

"And the years," he continued quietly. "I have come to the end, and everything surrounding me is gradually slowing down; that's fitting, that's good. Then you come along and stir up my soul. I don't know if that's the right way to say it, but that's how it feels. When you look into my eyes, a storm wells up inside of me. I can't take that anymore.

It leaves me in shards. I can never give you what you need, what you are entitled to, what I would like to give you."

This doesn't make any sense, she thought. He cannot be as weak as he pretends. I will not be turned away. He's left everything behind: laid down his work, had his wife institutionalized, neglected his unknown son. And now he's getting rid of me. Dropping me like a stone in a well.

She was hit by a sharp image of her little daughter. Sitting on her lap, the small rounded back nestled in the crook of her arm, the smell of her hair, like hay. It's the high points, the iconic moments that rise up and pass by. Your sorrow and anger grow over the memory like ivy. Dark hills full of spiders and hairy branches, you want to stay as far away as you can, but they anchor your existence. The warmth of a child's thighs on your lap. A man's naked arm against your cheek. Do not push them away. Do not deny them.

"I will still be your friend," he said. "Of course I will always care about you. I will help you with everything for which you require my aid. But you are young, still in your early forties. You should have a young man at your side."

I don't want a young man, she thought; I want him. Was that so? Who was he to her? Did she want to get closer simply because he had pushed her away so selfishly? Or did she want everything to stay the same; had she always placed her secret hopes in him, and now couldn't bear to see it all come to an end?

He is ashamed, that's for sure; that's at the forefront. But his crotch isn't the only thing that's broken. There's some other wreck he wants to hide from me. He's rejecting me, and yet I sense that I am important to him. I am furious, but I keep listening to him.

"Neither of us will ever break free of James," Hugh said. "He will always come between us. We might hope to shut him out by clinging to one another, but I don't think that's possible. My conscience chastises me every day. I can see that you will have no peace until you understand why he left. It occupies your mind, day in, day out. It prevents you from loving your child. You have no idea how to cope with it, so you come to me, but I have no idea, either.

"I have never said so much to you. These things. Terrible. Shall we eat? I ordered partridge; saw them hanging in the scullery yesterday."

Later, she couldn't imagine how she'd gotten through the meal. If she looked at his tense, tortured face, she lost herself in compassion. But when she looked at the dissected bird on her plate, she was speechless with rage. Confusing thoughts raced through her mind: he had eaten and drunk of her, and now that his hunger had been sated, he had tossed her aside. The entire discussion had been about his needs, and hers didn't count. She was sure of one thing: she'd hardly touched her food.

The farewell. He was on the steps, with his cane. She was in the carriage, already pulling away. He stretched out his arm toward her, called; she saw his mouth open wide. The wheels crunched through the gravel. She brusquely turned her face away. Once they'd driven through the shelter of the drive, she thumped her head against the wall of the carriage, carefully, so as not to alarm the coachman.

In the days and weeks following her visit to Chalfont, those small phrases kept buzzing through her head.

"It would be a disaster."

"We can't break free of James."

"This keeps you from loving your child."

The words spun around in her mind, she couldn't disentangle her thoughts from them.

She looked at her son—that serious, rangy child—in a new way. How sad, she thought, that I can't feel any kinship with him. We've both been abandoned by the same man, so why does this distance come between us? It feels as if James saddled me with this child as a substitute for him—plunked him down on my kitchen table: here, make do with this—so that I can only love the child once I've reconciled with the father. The idea gave her some relief, she could clearly see the logic behind it. But in a trice, the feeling had slipped out of her grasp, and all she knew was that in her mind, she had seen a path that led somewhere, offering a way out of the draining constriction she had become accustomed to, but she could no longer find the path itself.

She made sure she was waiting when Benny came home from school. She ate with him. She allowed him to do his homework at the kitchen table, and she sat there, too, not with a book but with some embroidery, so she could answer his questions without feeling as though he'd interrupted her. It was only when he'd gone to bed that she realized how much effort this task required. Then she would withdraw to the fireside in the great room, taking along the carafe of port; she'd stretch out in the armchair, stare into the flames, and feel exhausted. Charlotte, who'd increasingly become a diligent housekeeper, was finishing up the last of the chores in the kitchen, scrubbing the pans and placing them with a soft clink upside down on the counter.

It was just such an evening—April, the window was open to the garden, the weather was mild; it had rained in the afternoon, but by evening the sky had cleared—when the knocker thundered against the front door. Elizabeth pulled herself upright and heard Charlotte rushing down the hallway. A man's voice with a strange accent rumbled through the corridor.

"Shall I take your coat? I'll just see if the missus is at home. Please wait here."

The bench in the hallway groaned under a heavy load.

"A gentleman," Charlotte said, peeping through the door. "A foreigner. Here to deliver a letter."

A broad figure loomed beyond Charlotte. A bear, Elizabeth thought, a brown bear has come to visit. She stood up. The man entered the room and pulled a large fur hat off his head. His heavy black eyebrows formed one continuous ridge above his eyes. A red scar on his left cheek; full, rosy lips beneath a drooping mustache. He offered her his immense, somewhat grimy hand. The nail of the pinky extended inches beyond the finger—a strange, frosted-glass appendage that cut into her palm and made her shudder.

"Madam! At last! A peaceful night I wish you!"

She stared at the visitor, astonished. He'd lugged an overstuffed traveling bag into the room.

"Boris Afanisovich. Is name!" bellowed the man, making a small bow. "Chlebnikov. Trader in pelts. Fur. From animals—the hide." He pointed to his case. "The wolf. The bear. The seal!"

Why would someone try to sell me a fur coat this late in the evening, she asked herself, what on earth is this man doing here?

"Circled globe to find you. Mile End, Stepney, beside gray river. You want to see my skin?"

Elizabeth declined with a firm shake of the head. "Why were you trying to find me?"

He stooped to open the bag. His trousers, made from some material that resembled velvet, stretched tightly across his thighs. He noticed her look and brushed his hand along the fabric.

"Suckling seals," he said. "You interested? Everything in bag, you shall see. But first!"

He dug a flat, square package out of the depths of his suitcase and held it aloft.

"Reason for trip! Give to Mrs. Cook. Or sons. From my hand to yours."

She accepted the package.

"Accomplished," sighed the man. He started fishing around in the bag again.

"Please do have a seat," Elizabeth said. "Would you care for a drink? Who sent this letter?"

The man sat down near the hearth, and Elizabeth gratefully sank back into her chair. The parcel was wrapped in sailcloth, carefully stitched closed with sturdy twine. The cloth was greasy and covered with dark stains. Her name was written on it in an elegant hand. Her address. Almost as if it had been painted with India ink. She let the package fall onto her lap and placed her hands on top. The man poured himself a glass of port and drank, smacking his lips.

"I tell you fairy story. You listen. I buy skins from hunters. They cannot do trade, speak no tongue. Language, I mean. I travel to Kamchatka with money, travel back with fur. On horse, in sleigh, on foot. I see ships. Sick captain does not come ashore. His men want to buy hides. For hats! For the shoes, even! They tell sick man about my traveling skills."

"Captain Clerke died more than four years ago," Elizabeth said. "His final letters arrived here in 1780."

"This is final letter," the man roared, pointing his enormous finger at her lap. "Other letters were for Admiral lords. Those he give to governor. For public. But then. At night! I hear scratching at my window. I think—is bird. Knocking. Whispering. Is sailor! He pull my arm. We sneak through snow. In tiny boat I must go! Through fog over water. I see nothing, am blind! I tell you: terror come over me. No end to white sea. Then: black mountain. Is boat. A ladder of rope I must climb, I see not where it go. Frightened I am. I am man of land. They take me to patient. Bad smell. He spit in bowl. Go, he says to servants, close door, leave me alone with celebrated fur trader! His face is white like old snow. He digs under pillow and gives me letter. Very secret, he says. Only to missus. Or sons. Otherwise throw in water of gray river. You go in autumn? I go in autumn, I say. Moscow, Warsaw, Paris. With the hides. You can trust me. I take care of!"

"Seems like you took your time."

The man's eyes bulged. "Honorable missus! Trade is unpredictable. Setbacks, but if at first you no success, again try! And always letter from sick captain close to heart!" He thumped his rib cage, which resounded like a muffled gong. He used colorful language to illustrate the dangers he'd encountered along the way: a robbery, a fight. He discreetly mentioned the price he'd paid for the voyage over the dreaded sea. Things hadn't gone as well as he'd hoped with the sale of his hides, either; he'd yet to find any inroads to the well-to-do London ladies.

He pulled a grayish fur from his bag and draped it across the floor.

"You like? Genuine female wolf! I make you sack for tired feet. And here, wonder from Siberia, for forever coat. For you!"

He heaped a mountain of fur onto her lap, a shining, silvery pelt that—in the candlelight—shimmered, first bluish gray and then golden. She slid her hand along the smooth, short hairs; she thought of the beauty of the animal that had worn this skin, and how incomprehensible it was to have such a ravishing remnant on her lap.

"Yes, you I see! You mushroom, now you in basket! You buy my beauties from sea lion. I see you like."

She shook her head and tried to fold up the heavy fur before handing it back. He gave her a crestfallen look and seemed reluctant to accept the bundle, so she placed the pelt on the floor, beside his valise.

"Admiral ladies you know. They all will buy my pelts. London is cold. You give name of famous women, I bring warmth. Everyone happy. Letter I have brought for you, and now in foreign country I am tired. Money finished. Must do deal. You will help. We help each other! But first: bed for night. By you. In big captain's house."

I rather think not, shot through Elizabeth's head. She had to pull herself together, come up with a plan to extricate herself from this force of nature. First give him something, then send him away. Not the other way around. But who in the name of God would want to buy these horrible pelts?

"Banks," she said, decidedly. "Tomorrow morning, you must go immediately to Joseph Banks. He is the most important man in London, a friend of our king. He has the greatest expertise and knowledge regarding everything to do with animals and their hides. Their skin. I will write down the address for you. He will be delighted to receive you."

The intimidating edge of their talk dissipated once she stood to fetch a piece of paper. With the pen still in her hand, she summoned Charlotte.

"This gentleman has traveled a great distance, and he deserves a good night's rest."

Charlotte seemed miffed by the animal skins scattered throughout the room.

"Hat for head?" the trader inquired hopefully. "Or maybe muff? Is rabbit from steppes, snow bunny. White!"

Elizabeth pulled her purse from her skirt. "Unfortunately, we're unable to offer you a place to stay here, but there are plenty of cozy inns nearby, close to the river. Not two minutes from here. Charlotte will show you the way. Not hard to find. May I make a small contribution to help cover your costs?"

She pressed some money into the man's palm without waiting for an answer. She remained standing.

The wolf disappeared into the traveling bag. The seal. The hare. Boris Afanisovich Chlebnikov clasped her wrist and pressed a kiss to the back of her hand. The surprisingly stiff hairs of his mustache prickled her skin, and she couldn't help smiling. Charlotte led the man and his furry treasures away.

Before going upstairs with the three-pronged candlestick, she took her scissors from the sewing basket. In her bedroom, she sat on the edge of the bed and carefully snipped open the black stitches, prying back the stiff sailcloth and finally releasing a number of closely written pages from a sealed envelope, again bearing her name. She drew the candlestick closer and began to read.

> *My dear esteemed Elizabeth,*
> *Please permit me to address you thus. I am writing to you from the* Resolution, *anchored at the Kamchatka Peninsula on the Siberian coast. Yesterday, I gave the governor—the reliable and dedicated Major Behm—our lamented captain's precious journal, along with some charts, William Bayly's astronomical observations, a report of the catastrophic events written by Lieutenant King, and a letter from myself. Behm is leaving for St. Petersburg and will make sure these documents are sent to the Admiralty in London with the utmost speed and security. Then, the terrible news will reach you and the children. It breaks my heart to imagine the sight.*
> *I have thought long and hard about sending a separate letter to you. Consumption has sunk its claws into my body, and I know that for me, there will be no homecoming from this voyage. I had so hoped to tell you in person what actually happened on that beach in Hawai'i, but it is not to be. I still have enough strength to take up a pen and make sure my letter will reach you at Mile End, skirting all official channels. You will undoubtedly have heard the Admiralty's version of the circumstances already.*

Why am I writing to you? Because you are entitled to the truth. James spoke very highly of your love of facts. That has given me the courage to write this letter.

As we both know, James dedicated his life to observing reality. In this, he spared no effort. I have always admired his perspicacity. Now, in the painful twilight of my life, I'm starting to doubt the value of perception. Those who witnessed the events on the beach have written their accounts—gripping tales full of passion. But tales, nonetheless! What the senses perceived has become hidden behind the story, and what people want to believe with all their hearts has distorted their memories.

Twisting reality no longer means anything to me. Please understand: I do not wish to condemn my colleagues, any more than I want to hamper the Admiralty. The story of the cowardly, devious assault that cost James his life is a good fit with his heroic memory. Everyone will want to honor it in that form. There is absolutely nothing wrong with that—except that it's not true. It's a brilliant shell surrounding the cruel reality, painted by men loyal to their captain, who respected him and let themselves be blinded.

I cannot let the truth die with me, and have gotten up from my berth to record what I know. The night is calm. In a few hours, my boatswain's mate will fetch a fur trader named Boris Chlebnikov. I will entrust him with this letter because he seems like an enterprising and resourceful individual. He also looks strong and intimidating. But that's beside the point.

Throughout the entire voyage, both ships were plagued by theft as soon as we landed anywhere. James found that hard to bear, especially when the pilfering involved Crown property. We both agreed that robbery must be punished, but I must admit I was finding it increasingly difficult to grasp the reasons for the severity of James's penalties. It seemed to me that he wasn't able to maintain sufficient detachment from events, and lost sight of the long-term

consequences of his actions. Of course, it's possible my disease had
affected my judgment. Terminal illness naturally makes a person
more aloof. I'll give you an example.

If we caught a thief on my ship, the Discovery, I had the barber shave off half his hair, because I believe that to the culprit, the
mockery of family and friends is a far greater punishment than the
fear we—who have no relationship with him whatsoever—could
instill in him. The half-bald pilferer would then be thrown overboard to swim to shore, where he'd be the source of much mirth.
It worked.

James didn't understand that. He had the robbers flogged as if
they were soldiers who'd deserted during battle. The cruelty was out
of all proportion to the crimes that had been committed. He had
bone-deep grooves carved into the arm of one islander. He ordered
someone's ears cut off. I have given the matter a lot of thought, but
I still cannot comprehend the motives behind his actions.

It led to a lot of bad blood, not just with the locals, but with
the crew as well, who tend to mirror the officers' behavior. There
was a general increase in brutality, at least from my point of view.

At first, our stay on Hawai'i went smoothly. The population
had developed a peculiar urge to put James on a pedestal. He could
do no wrong. It's possible we took advantage of that sentiment, and
perhaps their slavish submission concealed their growing resentment. Our farewell was a grand, formidable event. I was happy
to see the back of the place, even though I knew the polar climate
would have an unfavorable effect on my health. I felt uncomfortable with all that worship.

Within a few days, bad luck forced us to head back to the
island with a splintered mast. But now, the mood had clearly
soured; the locals' behavior was formal and dismissive, and they
demanded exorbitant prices for the same victuals they'd previously
given us as gifts. We were subjected to bullying and thefts. James

meted out harsh punishments: his patience was spent. The theft of our cutter on that fateful morning set the match to the powder keg of his fury.

He'd planned to take their chief hostage. I was out of commission and still lying in my berth, but my sense of foreboding drove me onto the deck. From there, I observed the events through a telescope.

James rowed to the beach with a squad of Marines. They were dropped off and ran splashing through the surf. The launch stayed behind, beyond the breakers, with Lieutenant Williamson in charge. A meeting took place at the edge of the forest, toward the back of the beach. After a while, James appeared with the chief and his two sons. Mobs of Hawaiians drew closer. I saw them gesturing impatiently and stamping their feet. They herded James and the Marines together on the beach.

When James gave the command to shoot, his voice blared over the water. The Marines aimed and fired, not with buckshot, as was usually the case, but with live ammunition. James fired as well. The natives fell, one after the other, bleeding in the sand. It was a massacre.

In the midst of the fighting, James turned his back on the mob and walked slowly into the surf. Someone knocked him over.

That's when it happened. He raised his arm to Williamson in the boat to order him to start firing as well. Five men threw themselves on James. There was no way to save him. The surviving Marines—four had already perished—swam to the boat in panic. They left the bodies on the beach. I lowered my spyglass, dumbfounded. The looming mountain range, which until then had always seemed pleasing, suddenly took on a dark and ominous countenance. I shivered, although by then the sun had burned relentlessly through the morning mist.

Savagery spread like a plague. The crew would have liked to wipe out all the islanders and their possessions. When I think back on those days, I feel deeply ashamed: the entire village in flames. Dozens of brutal murders in the tidal areas. Decapitations. A man who was taken prisoner on board fainted from terror when heads dripping blood were waved before his eyes. Yes, it was a sickness.

The only thing I wanted was the bodies of the deceased. To that end, I had to stop the retaliations and negotiate a truce. Two priests arrived under the cover of darkness. They brought a package, which we opened—hands trembling—in my cabin. A piece of human flesh wrapped in banana leaves: from James's hind parts. Well bled, yellowed.

After six days of fighting, we finally reached an accord. Then the islanders arrived with offerings and a parcel wrapped in that brilliant, flame-red material they make from bark. James's scalp was in it, the hair stiff with clotted blood. Bones from his arms and legs. The skull, oddly small without its jaw. The hands were wrapped in a separate piece of cloth, the flesh still on them, pierced and stuffed with salt. We recognized the scar on his right hand.

The inhabitants had eaten the Marines. They had hacked James's corpse to pieces and shared them among the chiefs of the island's various provinces. That is why it took so long to piece it all back together. I have no idea what happened to the ribs and the pelvis. And what I think happened to the flesh, the genitals, and the eyes—well, I would prefer not to put that in writing.

The following morning, the chief turned up again with the feet, shoes, jawbone—complete with healthy, perfect teeth—and the bent barrel of the gun. We buried all of James's remains the next day, weighing down the coffin with cannonballs.

There's one more appalling incident I must relate. I was not present myself. I was in bed, in James's bed that was now my bed, because I had moved aboard the Resolution when I assumed command. *The officers had gathered on the night of February 14; they shouted, drank a great deal of brandy and rum, and sat around a table heaped with James's clothes and personal effects. They then rolled the dice for his shirts, his uniform, boots, watch, handkerchiefs, cutlery, brush, and wig—they divvied up and laid claim to everything, Elizabeth, everything. I only heard of it weeks later from one of the lieutenants, when his conscience got the better of him. I will not mention his name.*

I do not know the reason for that disrespectful behavior. It was never spoken of again, and James's personal effects were hidden away, as if they had simply vanished into thin air.

Now you know everything. I feel like a weight has been lifted from my shoulders. I may have burdened you with facts you would rather not have known. I realize that now you can never stop knowing them, and if my judgment about the need for this letter was misplaced, I apologize. I hand the facts over to you. Only you can decide if you want to make them public, or simply hold them in your heart.

I consider myself lucky to have known James. On the threshold of death, I now take my leave from the woman who loved him. I salute you, Elizabeth, for all time.

Charles Clerke

Jane Nelson wasn't herself. It seemed to Elizabeth that it had been going on for months. High strung, careless, easily upset. This morning, during recess, she smacked a boy who'd accidentally spilled his milk. Then she burst into tears. Elizabeth sat her down in the vestry, in the minister's easy chair, and took charge of the school. When the children had left for the day, she sat next to Jane.

"Is everything all right?"

Jane crumpled a handkerchief in her spindly fingers. "Nervous," she said. "I don't know what's wrong with me. Can't rest. I can't sleep at all. Do you think I should stop with the school? I'm no use to the children this way. Last time David was at sea, it didn't bother me at all. Why is it so different this time?"

Waiting is poison, Elizabeth thought. It doesn't improve with the years, it gets worse. You become exhausted, and it's harder to withstand. The skin hangs off your bones, new wrinkles appear on your face. That's the way it goes.

David Nelson had left with Captain Bligh just two months ago, on the *Bounty*, to pick up breadfruit seeds and saplings from Tahiti. Jane had explained that he'd taken a thousand pots with him. They're planning to plant the seedlings in Jamaica. Cheap and nourishing food. Trade is picking up, thanks to James and his South Sea contacts. Banks is behind the mission; he's crazy about the bread tree.

"Let's go for a walk," Elizabeth said. "Here's your coat. Of course, you shouldn't stop with the school; you must forge ahead. Have you forgotten saying that to me, seven years ago, when Nat died? I couldn't face it, had no idea what I was doing in that classroom, and I couldn't even remember the names of the children. And yet I was there, every day. It helped. It was good advice."

"Whenever there's a storm, I sit bolt upright in bed. Makes no sense; David is on the other side of the world. How do you manage?"

"I get out," Elizabeth answered. "Read. Potter about in the room. Have a glass of port. Picked that tip up from my mother."

A couple of years ago, Mary had permanently disappeared into the mists of childhood, and she now lay buried beside Elly. During the final stage of her life, Elizabeth had hardly been able to visit her mother, because Mary became desperately sad as soon as she set eyes on her daughter. By then, she didn't recognize anybody else, although her tearful reaction to Elizabeth continued until the end.

"Having people in the house, the way you do, that helps," Jane said. They walked arm in arm, their heads exposed to the wind.

"They come, they go. When they leave, I'm always afraid they'll never return. Fortunately for both of them, the trips are getting shorter. Isaac's been promoted to first lieutenant, did you know? Jamie is in the reserves. He's taken up riding, as if the only thing on land that can make him happy is that swaying motion. Benny still lives at home, as you'd expect."

The child would turn twelve in the spring. She had to keep him away from the water. Sending him to the Naval Academy was out of the question. And besides, there was no one left to put their foot down.

She said goodbye to Jane and walked home. The familiar sweet fumes from the gin factory, glimpses of the river's eternal glittering between the houses. The shiny, newly painted fence surrounding her garden. In front of that, in the middle of the road, always that rearing horse and the carriage wheels on top of a motionless little girl.

Isaac had spread a map on the kitchen table. Oh no, she thought, I don't want any evidence of the sea in my house; this isn't a ship's cabin.

"Look," Isaac said. It was a map of London and environs. The Thames wound its way through the middle like a vein on an old man's hand.

"Clapham." Isaac indicated with a pencil. "At the end of High Street. You have a view of the surrounding fields, yet all the shops are within walking distance. A large house, well maintained. We could move right in."

I'm forty-six, she thought. Time to leave this waiting room. To live someplace, finally, where water doesn't play a leading role. Why should I stay here? Because James said his goodbyes here. Because Nat played his violin here, because it's where Hugh sat with me in the garden. Because Elly—

"I asked around," Isaac said. "About schools and such. There's a fine school for our little professor. Nearby. They prepare students for university."

Just then, Benny came in, as if on cue. He looked curiously at the map but said nothing.

"We're going to move, Ben," Isaac said. "Your mother's going to hire a manservant. There will be receptions every week for friends and acquaintances. With pheasant legs and chervil soup."

"Will Charlotte come with us?" the boy asked. "And Jamie?" He inspected his mother's face.

Now, Elizabeth thought, now I must show him that change is allowed. "Isaac's coming, and Jamie will live with us when he's not at sea. Charlotte will take care of the housekeeping. And you will go to school in Clapham."

Isaac pulled a piece of paper from his pocket and read aloud. "Philosophy, literature, logic, rhetoric! You'll learn it all. Latin. Geometry. You can start after the summer."

Benny nodded. His face revealed no emotion. He continued to lean against the table.

"Jamie will buy a horse," Isaac went on. "There's a stable down the road. When he's home, he'll be able to go riding. You'll have a big room with a bookcase. The dining room is massive! There's a plum orchard at the bottom of the garden. It'll be great, you'll see."

The quince, Elizabeth thought. That stays here. Isaac will have to help me. The attic. All that junk of James's. The moth-eaten cloaks covered with feathers, the baskets made of cane and bark, the spears, the oars—what are we to do with it all? Maybe we can cram everything into one room, high up in the house, and lock the door. I'll take care of the papers myself. They'll go into the chest full of secrets. The trinkets are for public display. That idiotic commemorative medal made of gold. That ridiculous family "coat of arms." I'll put those curiosities in a vitrine in the dining room, along with the travel books. Shall I open the book to the page with King's account of James's tragic death? If you want to know what really happened, you'll have to look in the chest. I keep the key hidden in my skirt. That's one secret I can never escape, even if I were to toss everything into the river. It's inside of me.

After the visit from the fur trader, Elizabeth had considered taking a carriage to Chalfont to show Clerke's letter to Hugh Palliser, as if nothing had changed between them. But she'd taken time to reflect and examine her motives. I am in shock, she thought, I want reassurance. But that's not possible; the facts are alarming in and of themselves, and no one can change that.

She'd gone for a walk along the winding path between the fields, on her own. I want his help, she'd thought. He must talk with me so I know what to do. Inform the Admiralty? Pump Isaac for more information? Put an end to all that hero-worship rigmarole? Perhaps I already know full well what I want to do, and am only looking for an excuse to be near Hugh. She shook her head and bit her lip. Sunlight reflected on the puddles along the way. She leapt from one tussock to the next to keep her shoes dry. That took all her concentration.

She put Clerke's letter away without mentioning it to anyone. The account of the third voyage had been published, a splendid three-volume edition that sold out in a matter of days. She'd read the accounts of James's death as if she were a scientist: from a distance, careful her observations were not tainted by any premature interpretation. She could catch hints of the events that Clerke had described through the gaps in the narrative. The words on the white page formed one truth; what had been omitted, another.

She couldn't imagine that the subject was her own husband. James, she thought: the way he felt, his smell, the sound of his voice. I must try to remember it all. They surround him with lies, and I join in. How often do I sit at the table with someone or other, talking about how calm, charitable, and ingenious he had been? Then someone brings up the saga of the sauerkraut, and I nod sweetly. Isaac describes how James asked him to be the first to set foot on the Great Southern Continent, and I smile, mournful but content. Banks exhausts himself with praise for the plants that James collected for him, out of a love of science, out of love! My husband had such enormous respect for everything that grows, I agree, without batting an eye.

It's all balderdash. He remains a riddle. In bursts of rage, he destroyed everything that was dear to him. Why? I have to find out, I want my damned husband back; I want to be able to think about him without sinking into an enigmatic swamp. I want to understand him.

She's spent a long time staring at the image of the princess Poetua, the one painted by Webber while she was being held hostage in the great cabin. The petite breasts pointing slightly outward. The tattoos. Her look: resigned, contemptuous? She's pregnant—her left arm is resting on her swelling belly—and that makes her stronger than all the lads in that dank cabin. What had possessed James to hold a half-naked pregnant woman prisoner for days on end, in order to recover a stolen goat?

In the end, it was Isaac who rescued her. He forced her to look at the floor plan of the new house and make decisions regarding the furniture and wallpaper. He'd been on half-pay for a couple of months and had plenty of time to help her pack. They'd never really made up their minds to live together; it just happened. He gradually moved in, leaving more belongings at her house after every leave. His coat was hanging in the corridor.

"We'll move as soon as Benny is finished with school," Isaac said. "What do you want to do with the garden, is there much you want to take? If so, we'll start digging."

"Just the mallow," Elizabeth said. "Clapham will be a new beginning. No more exotic plants. We don't have to do it for James's benefit; everything's already at Kew. And in better shape."

The garden at the new house was bright and orderly. Martin, the manservant, mowed the grass under the plum trees with a scythe. She watched from the covered wooden veranda.

Elizabeth felt unusually contented. Her bedroom, large and L-shaped, easily housed a desk, a washstand, and the large bed; there was a sea of room left over. After careful consideration, she'd given the chest full of secrets a place in this room, hidden deep within a fitted cupboard. Sometimes, during the night, she thought she could hear a distant rattling, a hostile buzzing coming from the direction of the chest, so she would sit up in bed and light a candle to reassure herself that all was well.

Every Thursday afternoon, she hosted a get-together. A woman from Clapham did the cooking; Martin welcomed the guests and served at the table.

"You have friends," Isaac said, "people who enjoy seeing you. Invite them around. Have a new frock made. Put together a menu. You can do it."

Who should she invite, for heaven's sake? Charlotte, in her double role as friend and housekeeper, was always there. Jamie pulled up a chair whenever he was on leave. Benny ate with them, huddled next to Charlotte, not saying a word unless someone aimed a question directly at him. Jane Nelson came in from Stepney. She'd recruited new troops to help with the little school. Elizabeth only went once a week to read aloud, but she continued to finance the enterprise. Douglas came once every two or three weeks from Windsor. On those occasions, Benny always perked up. Elizabeth saw the two of them whispering, the boy gesturing and nodding, the color rising in his cheeks.

"What was that all about?" she asked him once after dinner.

"The subjects one can study," her youngest son answered. "What a person can be when he grows up; a clergyman, for instance. He's going to lend me some books."

She would have liked to have the organist, Mr. Hartland, as a guest at her table, but that was out of the question. Elizabeth visited him on the days she went to the little school. Mr. Hartland was bedridden. He no longer played. Once, on the doorstep in front of his house, she met a young man carrying an instrument in a large case. He wore his brown hair tied back. He was about to close the door when he spotted Elizabeth.

"Robert Hartland," he said, extending his hand. "The old man's nephew. I just played for him. He's looking forward to your visit. May I invite you to a concert sometime? My uncle told me you're a music lover."

Robert played the cello in an orchestra in London. She went to one of the concerts with Isaac. The orchestra played some works by Haydn—a symphony and a series of slow movements for string orchestra, which ended with a huge cacophony meant to represent an earthquake.

"And?" Robert asked during the intermission. "Amazing, isn't it? The ink is hardly dry. It was originally a choral work, but he adapted it. Seven adagios. Incredibly daring! An outstanding musician, the greatest. We're trying to lure him to London, but that Hungarian prince he writes for won't let him go. Esterházy is working him to the bone, forcing him to compose a new piece of chamber music every week. Artistic incarceration. Exploitation! The violin concerto is up next, you won't believe what you're about to hear."

And so it had been. The concertmaster had stood in front of the orchestra, and he'd lifted the musicians to uncharted heights. Elizabeth forgot the odor of the surrounding people, the audible breathing, the audience members squirming on the benches. When the piece was over, she felt sad and grateful at the same time. Since then, Robert Hartland had been a welcome guest at her table.

"Shouldn't you invite Hugh Palliser?" Isaac asked. "He'll be curious to know how his godson is doing. A lonely man in a big house is always happy to have a chance to get out. Go ahead and ask him. Or shall I write to him instead?"

She tried to imagine sitting at the table in the bright and cheerful dining room. All those loyalties, the secrets, the deception. The play-acting and the anger lying beneath it. Thanks to Isaac, she now had a viable existence, one she could sustain. When she thought about how mercilessly Hugh had abandoned her, she mentally wiped out all her recent gains. He's an old man, she whispered to herself. He's ashamed, he feels like a failure, hard done by. He's embarrassed about his worn-out body. I should be understanding, compassionate. He doesn't trust me. He shoves me aside like an old chair. And then there's that other thing, that problematic issue: he said James stands between us. I refuse to think about it.

"Not a good idea," she said. "You'd be better off inviting one of your colleagues. Young people at the table; that's much better for Benny."

But whatever her youngest actually liked remained a mystery to her. He was learning Latin; he earnestly studied the theological texts Douglas had given him, and—even in his new school—he sang in the choir. Sometimes she heard him practicing in his room; his high voice had a metallic ring. "O holy Lord, to thee we pray. In this night thou us defend," he sang. It terrified her in a way she couldn't explain.

He examined the family crest that had been granted to Elizabeth in 1785. She was entitled to display it on a carriage, should she ever manage to own one. To her, it was a pointless, pompous tribute: a map of the South Sea in a network of longitude and latitude coordinates, against an azure background. A red line indicated James's journey, ending in Hawai'i. Benny copied the crest on a sheet of paper. A dis-embodied arm in a captain's uniform, adorned with a wreath of laurels, hung suspended above the South Sea.

"It says *Circa orbem*," Benny said. "That means: around the world. Do I have grandparents?"

Elizabeth sat facing him. He has Nat's hair, she thought. Why don't I ever cut it myself, why do I always send him to the barber with Isaac?

"They're dead. Your grandmother was there when you were born. She saw you."

The boy wrote down their names: Grace and James, Mary and John. He drew a cross beside each name.

"In our family, Jamie's the oldest. Who came next?"

"Nat," Elizabeth answered. "Elly. Joseph. George. And then you."

His pen formed the crosses with painful precision. Why doesn't he ask, she thought, what was George like, who Joseph was? The reason he's still alive and all the others aren't? He wouldn't be able to bear my answer. And why don't I ask any questions? Can he still remember Nat, would he like to ride with me to Stepney sometime, to Elly? How does it feel to have so many dead children hanging over your head? I wouldn't have the heart to listen to his answers.

"Jamie must have children, otherwise we'll die out," Benny said. He soldiered on with his family tree.

Every night, when he was in bed, she felt driven by willpower and a sense of duty to visit him.

"Sleep well, Benny."

"Good night, Mother."

As soon as she was gone, he crept out of bed and knelt on the hard floor. Tock, tock. She listened outside the door, not daring to breathe.

"Lord, please look after the departed. Take care of Nat, Elly, Joseph, and George. Look after Papa and all my grandparents. Amen."

A fire blazed in the hearth. The panes in the dining room windows, black from the early darkness, reflected the flames. A thirty-candle chandelier hung above the table. Martin had carried the dishes to the kitchen and set a tray of port and some glasses on the table. Elizabeth leaned back in her chair and observed the faces of her dinner companions. Isaac opposite her, with his kind and familiar pate; Charlotte; Jamie, recently promoted to lieutenant, in a brand-new uniform; Robert Hartland, chattering away. I'm almost fifty, she mused, and I'm still here. More present than ever since we moved. Isaac pushes me to live, to eat delicious food, to hold conversations, to go to concerts. Never thought I'd be able to do all that again. Where has Benny gotten to now? Must be upstairs with his books. A boy of thirteen doesn't like to sit at the table very long.

Jamie was speaking and everyone listened, rapt. Captain Bligh had arrived in Portsmouth on a Dutch East Indiaman. The Naval base was aflutter with stories.

"The mutineers had put him in a launch, just a small open boat. Bligh and his loyal followers were hardly given any supplies. It was a hell of a voyage, but they made it. They eventually arrived safely in Java. All because they had no Marines on board, so they had no way of asserting their authority. There's going to be a court-martial."

Poor Jane, Elizabeth thought. David Nelson, the agriculturalist who'd been responsible for thousands of breadfruit seedlings, had followed his captain and survived the dangerous voyage in the open boat, only to die of swamp fever once they reached land. I'll go see her tomorrow; the senselessness, the absurd coincidence, the powerlessness.

The talk centered on insurrections and revolutions. What had happened in France was sure to reach England, change was already in the air, and perhaps the mutiny on the *Bounty* was a sign of things to come. No, Isaac said, that French bloodbath couldn't happen in England; here, the relationships between the classes were different, and people were more attached to tradition. Everyone would agree: the mutineers were sure to be convicted and hung from the yardarm. Paris—people were crazy over there. The waste! The chaos!

In London, Robert Hartland had been to a French play about the death of Cook; it had apparently been a huge hit in Paris. Was that because the impoverished natives had made short shrift of their prosperous visitors? Perhaps; he couldn't be sure. But here in England, people liked a spectacle; just look at how popular the play about Omai had been a few years back. The play about James was still running in Covent Garden: it had music, ballet, and stunning costumes, complete with glitter and feathers. Three acts! The story was nonsense, Robert said, involving a love affair and a jealous suitor. James championed someone or other and was killed. It was rubbish, but the music was lovely, and very well played. During the final act there was even a volcano on stage that spewed smoke.

Across the table, Elizabeth caught Isaac's eye. They looked at each other and shook their heads imperceptibly. They'd give that play a miss.

The talk of the revolution in France kept ringing in her ears. The way the executioners clipped the hair off the necks of their victims. The way the guillotine's blade dropped. How suddenly, a body was no longer whole. She couldn't help thinking of James's death; the way he'd been hacked to pieces with a knife and an ax, like a hog bought by six different families. The butcher had been familiar with joints and had cut through the tendons and ligaments so that everyone could have their share. She felt sick to her stomach, and suddenly chilly. How had he let things get to that point? Why had he so carelessly lost everything he had built up?

She forced herself to listen to Isaac, who was talking about the joys of cartography: the pleasure of successfully drawing an uncharted coast, the satisfaction, after sailing around an island, of putting it on the map in its entirety.

"It's possible to draw the entire world, and that's sure to happen. Each voyage of discovery yields a wealth of fragments, and since the invention of the sea clock, the accurate positioning allows us to put all the pieces together. Like the small stones in a mosaic. Once we've mapped something, it exists. I was always in a terrible mood whenever we sailed too far away from the coast to distinguish any details. Even worse was when a landscape was hidden behind a bank of clouds and fog. James couldn't take that either; he sometimes sailed back once the weather had cleared. That made the crew grumble, but I understood."

"Everything has to pass through your hands," Robert said. "It's the same with music. You have to play every note. It only exists once you bow it; then it has been, even if you never hear it again. That's why I want to play all those new symphonies of Haydn's, as soon as he's written them. As if I can bring them to life."

Isaac didn't seem to hear what the musician had said. He held Elizabeth's gaze and continued talking about James.

"You should have seen him when we spotted land! He could sense it from afar, he saw it in the wave formations, the color of the water. Then he sent someone up to the crow's nest. After a while, the birds arrived, so we knew there had to be a resting place nearby. Or branches floated past, a tree trunk, a coconut. Then, the sailor would shout from up in the mast, and we'd all stand at the railing, staring until the shore appeared on the horizon. James came up with a name. He baptized the island and added it to those we already knew. That made him happy. Winnings, he'd say to me; we made a profit today, wrestled a piece of knowledge out of ignorance; grab your pencils and draw it up. He set the standard. It's the way we still do things. Or we would, if we weren't constantly fighting all these wars."

Isaac's cheeks had turned red. Elizabeth's gaze fell to her lap. James had achieved everything: fame, stature, acceptance in circles that were above his standing. A family. Seafaring children. The freedom to decide whether or not to take something on. He'd won everything, lost everything. He'd sailed with the times, curious to see what would appear over the horizon. In Hawai'i, the last island, he fell out of time and stopped writing in his logbook. Were there no more fragments of reality he felt compelled to add to his corpus of knowledge? Had the clock's importance come to nothing? But how?

I know about that, she thought. I also fell out of time when the children died; I stood outside the stream that seemed to carry all the others. I lost the hours of the day and night, couldn't tell if events had occurred recently or long ago. Time stood still within me, so I couldn't estimate it anymore. And it didn't matter.

Later, I noticed that everything had kept going, and I was lagging behind. I tried to follow the current, stumbling, on my knees, half-hearted. I kept trying to catch up, looking to the past, to the time I wanted to inhabit. I know all about that.

The conversation was a cloud of sound, providing a rippling background to her thoughts. She should pay more attention; this was her table, her guests, her time.

"He'd take a clean sheet of paper," Isaac explained, "and we'd clear the table. We'd add the longitudes and latitudes, in pencil of course. I'd start drawing the compass rose in a corner, that was splendid. Then we'd bring everything we knew together, and something new appeared before our eyes; yes, the island seemed completely fresh to us, even though we were familiar with all its parts, it grew under our pencils into a well-organized whole, as if we only really knew it once it was on paper."

"I'm always sorry that it's only the outer rim," said Jamie. "Just the coast, because most of the time, you can't look any farther. There's always a blank patch in the middle of your islands. Maybe a solitary mountain, the suspected course of a river, a volcano, you might put that in. But beyond that? You'd have to trudge through all that land. Measuring. Getting to know it."

Me too, she thought. They're telling me what I must do. Collect information, find the link between the things I know, put them together to create something new, something I can understand. Thanks to Isaac and the boys, I am again tied to the tether of time. I should be able to deal with this now. I owe it to James.

It occurred to her that Captain William Bligh, the unfortunate victim of the recent mutiny, had signed the map of Hawai'i. James had not been able to collect his observations. If he hadn't been able to do it, how was she to manage?

She leaned back in her chair and felt the fire's glow. The outline of the island faded before her eyes and her attention was drawn to the void in the middle, a heart pounding with blazing white heat.

12

She'd frittered away and wasted the passing years with insignificant trifles. Her determination to undertake an investigation into James's death had vanished unnoticed. One task or another always took precedence; there was no way of escaping it, and she didn't seem to want to.

Jane Nelson had needed a lot of her attention. Elizabeth had visited her almost every day during her early widowhood. They took long walks and visited Joseph Banks to try to pry loose a pension for Jane. There, James stared sternly down at Elizabeth from the wall.

"It's a superb portrait," Banks proclaimed. "Dance captured him perfectly. So recognizable."

Nonsense, she thought. He is depicted as he may have wished to have been, but not as he was. She remembered with a stab how James had struck the same pose for her in the garden.

Attendance at the little school dwindled because more affordable schools were being set up for the poor. Elizabeth had insisted on going forward as an after-school center for children who would otherwise go home to an empty house, but in the end, even that shut down.

Jane made a remarkable recovery. She had always been thin and wiry, but now she was, without a doubt, plump. "I don't understand it," she remarked, wide-eyed. "I've had to buy two new sets of clothes already. David would have been pleased; he always said I was nothing but skin and bones."

Keep busy, Elizabeth thought, something needs to take the place of the school, otherwise the days will lose their structure and she'll just sit around. Jane suggested organizing afternoons for young sailors' wives.

"When David left, I was all over the place," she said. "If I hadn't run into you, I don't know how things would have turned out. We need to bring those sailors' wives together so they can lend each other a hand. Babysit for one another, help each other out, keep a watchful eye. There's bound to be at least one who can sew, who can teach the rest. Or a woman who understands money. One afternoon, twice a week. Trips! We could take them on the boat to Kew."

Elizabeth had helped Jane set it all up, but she bowed out soon after. The first time the women turned up in the hall at the back of the church, she realized that the idea had appealed to her more than its execution. They were still young girls, giggling, shy, defiant, putting on a brave face, skinny, stout, or pregnant. Elly came to mind; she would be twenty-five now, she should be sitting here with us. A feeling of envy hit her so hard she had to stand up and walk outside. It was the height of summer; the girls' arms were bare. Through the open window, she could hear Jane's voice, then the blathering of the women, a splash of laughter, a whoop. I can't do this, she thought. And I shouldn't. I'll spoil it for the rest.

Jane had understood and had carried on with the project on her own. She told them all about it during the Thursday dinners, and seemed gratified.

Mr. Hartland died the same season his revered Haydn came to London. He slipped away without any fear or pain, right after his nephew Robert had played him the Sarabande from Bach's Fifth Cello Suite. Now Mr. Hartland's memories of Nat are lost, Elizabeth thought. Good thing he shared them with me, so I can continue to reflect on them. She planted hellebores on his grave.

An exciting concert season began in the autumn of 1791. Haydn had written some new symphonies to charm the English audiences, and Elizabeth went to listen to them. There was a slow, solemn introduction, and listeners were taken by surprise when the actual theme began at breakneck speed. A minuet so fast one could hardly dance to it, just sashay and fly away. The orchestra seemed fuller than usual. She not only heard horns and oboes, but clarinets, flutes, and bassoons. The timpani player sat in the middle behind his colleagues, looking straight at the conductor. The pure, penetrating sounds of the trumpets immersed her in thoughts of her musical son's innocence and seriousness.

"It's too much for you," Isaac said, "we won't come here again." But she wanted to hear everything. He took her hand when it all threatened to overwhelm her. It was a wonderful season.

The summer took everyone by surprise. It simply would not warm up. The plants only grew to half their usual size and rotted away in the mud. Icy cloudbursts lashed the land, and the livestock huddled against the stone walls surrounding the fields. Martin, who wanted to beautify the garden, was at his wit's end.

"Leave it," Elizabeth said. "Maybe we'll have a beautiful autumn. Or else we'll wait until next year. It's not the end of the world."

She kept the lamp burning in the afternoons to ward off the autumnal darkness. She read. She wrote to Frances, to Dr. Douglas, to Mr. Hartland's nephew, Robert. She thought.

One by one, the men she could have approached in her quest to get to the bottom of James's fate had died. Anderson and Clerke were long gone, followed by King, and more recently, Gore. She should have been distressed, but she didn't really care, as if her understanding of James was no longer dependent on whatever facts someone else could give her, as if everything she needed to know was already right in front of her, and all she had to do was put the fragments together in a new context. She focused her concentration, lowering her book onto her lap and closing her eyes to avoid distractions. Before she knew it, she was thinking about half-drowned anemones, Thursday's menu, and the state of the fire in the hearth. Then she went outside, walking through the wind and rain so that she could at least feel something: the chilly damp on her shoulders, the heavy mud on her feet. Time, she thought, there's still time. Not everything has to be done this minute. I can chat with Isaac, watch Jamie trotting around on his horse. Do what needs to be done. Nothing more.

Benny's offhand remark about the family dying out had stuck with her and prompted her to keep a close eye on her eldest.

"I saw Jamie walking through the main street," Charlotte said. "He was with the doctor's daughter, such a sweet child, even if she is a little on the chubby side. Her name's Susanna."

At Christmas, Susanna came to dinner. She couldn't take her eyes off Jamie, and seemed to show a genuine interest in Benny's activities. She had a word with Elizabeth in the hallway, awkward and blushing. "I think it's so horrid for you, after everything you've lost, I hardly dare bring it up. I have to tell you how special this is, ma'am, that you are able to arrange such a pleasant evening."

Elizabeth was touched and said something nice in return. Isaac proposed a toast to the new couple, and Jamie looked proud.

She thought about Hugh Palliser, maybe not every day, but often enough. Letters were exchanged from time to time between Chalfont and Clapham, superficial missives in which she kept him up to date on his godson's progress; meaningless epistles about the animals on his estate; messages with a strange undercurrent and veiled allusions that left her out of sorts. He wrote to her on the anniversary of the deaths of Nat and Elly. She appreciated that, or at least, the good intentions behind it. But the doleful remoteness hidden in his words made her angry.

There's no point in us getting together, he wrote, *my life has become severely restricted and I'd prefer to keep it that way. The memories are enough for me. Such a pity we couldn't give each other the comfort we both needed, but that's how it is. We must make our peace with that.*

It made her furious. Her anger kept her awake; she scratched out razor-sharp replies with her quill, but left them lying in a drawer.

No one has ever given me such fundamental support, she thought, and I in turn have never been as open with anyone, so uninhibited, without ulterior motives, as I was with him. That he refuses to share something while we are both still alive, that he sinks into his memories while we still exist—she growled and swore with humiliation and indignation.

Then, just as the dawn crept through the windows, she would picture his long-suffering face. Whatever he wants, she thought. I'll do whatever he wants. I won't make things harder for him than they are already. I don't quite understand what it is he's struggling with, but I love him enough to let him be.

She suspected some secret with which he didn't want to burden her, and couldn't forget his cryptic remarks about James. She wasn't capable of thinking clearly, too many lines were intertwined. She would then put away her angry jottings and make herself coffee in the chilly kitchen.

Benny turned sixteen. He was taller than she and had started to resemble the way James had looked when she'd first met him. He'd remained a quiet, impressionable boy. To her surprise, she sometimes found they'd been sitting together in the same room for hours without her having noticed. He never took part in the heated discussions between Isaac and Jamie about the gossip and injustices in the Navy. Robert Hartland's tales of exciting new music left him cold; he turned down all invitations to concerts, because he preferred to study. Going to church was the only thing he did with any pleasure and of his own accord. His eyes glowed when he told them what the pastor had talked about during his sermon. Elizabeth couldn't help but ignore Benny's contributions to the conversation, although she hated herself for it. The boy was bearing witness to what was going on inside him, and she should show some interest. What was she afraid of?

"I don't see you going to sea when you're finished with school," Isaac said. "What do you want to become, d'you think?"

Benny gave his mother a sidelong glance. "A minister. I'm going to study theology. At Cambridge."

He blushed and looked down at his empty plate.

She felt her heart racing. Was it because her own son wanted to join a guild she considered hypocritical? Or because she had failed to provide him with enough security to get by without faith?

"That's great!" Jamie exclaimed. "Going to a genuine university. That's quite a change from tying knots and dead reckoning. A scholar in the family, always a good thing."

Nat had believed in music, Benny believes in God. Why can I tolerate the one and not the other? I need to talk with him. He's slipping away from me.

That evening, she was sitting on her own when Benny came in to say goodnight. Isaac had gone out.

"Come sit down."

The boy took a hesitant step toward the hearth. "I have to go to bed. Test tomorrow at school."

"Come sit a minute."

He perched gingerly on the edge of a straight-back chair and looked at her questioningly.

"Did you mean what you said this afternoon?" What a question; he always meant what he said. Just like James.

"Cambridge is the best, the director said. For theology."

"And that's what you want most."

He nodded. Now don't lose track, don't start spouting gibberish about all the other splendid professions one could study: literature, law, philosophy—just don't.

"You're sure to feel at home there," she said. "Someone who so enjoys studying, and does it so well, belongs at a university. But why theology, Benny?"

He rocked to and fro but said nothing.

"Was it the director's suggestion? A teacher's?"

"I have a quiz tomorrow in Latin. Verb tenses. I'd like to go upstairs and look it over."

"Is it because you like being in church?"

Benny seemed to collapse and slumped in his chair. He rested his elbows on his knees and supported his head with his fists.

"You know how things should be," he said, "how you should live. What's important. What you must do. Then it's all right. I like being in church, it's nice, especially when we sing. But it's all about what the minister says. What's in the Bible. That you can be saved."

His face had turned dark red. Elizabeth did her best to show she was listening without looking directly at him. She saw her hands, clenched with tension on the armrests.

"He explains difficult things. That's something I also want to learn. Why people die. How to go on. About comfort and grace. God sees everything. That you are never alone. Ever."

Now that she was over fifty, it was as if she could finally trust in life again and enjoy her composite family, her friends, and her garden.

In the evenings she and Isaac strolled arm in arm, deep into the orchard. There, they leaned against an artfully constructed stone wall and gazed out over the rolling landscape dotted with grazing animals.

Benny sailed through his university admissions test, and Elizabeth helped him pack his books and clothes. Of course, the wooden bird that Isaac had brought back from the third voyage couldn't be left behind.

"I believe it's an osprey," Isaac said.

"No," Benny said, decidedly. "It's an eagle."

Jamie, who some time ago had been promoted to first lieutenant, was put in command of a modest ship. He'll be thirty soon, Elizabeth thought. A grown man. He should get busy with that girl of his, what's holding him back?

"She's all for it," he said. "But it's me. I wonder if I can do that to her, let her marry someone who's always away? She's frightened when I'm at sea. I didn't understand it at first. I'm not afraid of anything. Whatever happens, happens. When I finally understood, I got to thinking. You were always alone. We thought that was normal, but it was hard for you, wasn't it?"

"You can't make up her mind for her. If she loves you, she'll be able to withstand it, you'll see."

Grandchildren, she thought. Some life in the house, toys, wooden bowls caked with porridge. She was surprised to find herself enjoying that fantasy.

No engagement was forthcoming as yet. He needed to think things over; he wasn't that old. James was in his midthirties when we got married. But, in his spare time, Jamie no longer ambled through the center of town with his girlfriend. He went to the stables, dressed in his gleaming boots; he rode his horse into the hills and only came back at night, covered in sweat.

"Jamie isn't one to brood," Isaac said. "In fact, he doesn't much like mulling things over or making decisions. He waits for clarity, and then he does what needs to be done. You mustn't fret."

Benny left after the summer. He turned down Elizabeth's offer to accompany him on the journey. God must be company enough for him, she thought bitterly. She watched with mixed feelings as he climbed into the carriage with his suitcase and the eagle. At the last minute, she'd handed him a pair of mittens and a scarf. She gave him an awkward peck on the cheek, aware of her need to behave like a good mother. Isaac pulled the boy close and wasn't afraid to show how much he'd miss him. Waving, calling out, gestures of farewell. Watching the child disappear.

Letters arrived with relentless punctuality. The curriculum met all expectations, the teachers engaged his attention, and the eagle was on his bookcase. He'd be home at Christmas, say hello to Charlotte.

He didn't come home at Christmas. He'd fallen ill and taken to his bed with a raging fever. The porter sent her a brief message; he'd called for the doctor and trusted that Mrs. Cook would reimburse him for the expense. The young gentleman's condition was grave.

Elizabeth packed her bag. Without her having to ask, Isaac—who happened to be on leave—accompanied her. That night, when they arrived in Cambridge, dazed by the hubbub and jostling of the journey, when they stood forlornly in front of the dormitory, their bags at their feet, the porter opened the door, silent, his face set. That's when Elizabeth knew that her youngest had died.

Benny was laid out on the bed in his monk-like dormitory room, his chin bound and his hands folded across his chest. The porter then thumped back down the stairs to fetch the doctor. Isaac, beside himself with grief, sat down on the side of the bed and kissed Benny's waxen face. Elizabeth retreated to the window. It felt as if she weren't really there.

"Severe fever," the doctor said. "He died early this morning. The minister was by his side. I bled him again last night, but to no avail. So cruel, he was a promising chap."

He squeezed Elizabeth's hand. Isaac dried his eyes with a voluminous handkerchief and offered to take care of the arrangements. Out in the corridor, he paid the doctor, saying later that he thought it would have been unseemly to carry out such a transaction in front of Benny.

They found an inn. Isaac made plans for the burial, the service, and for clearing out Benny's room. Back at their lodgings, they sat at a table, stunned.

"I can't help it," Isaac said. "I have to eat something, otherwise I'm no good to anyone. Sorry."

Go ahead, eat, she wanted to say. But she held her tongue.

"Why don't you go upstairs, lie down for an hour or so? You look positively ashen."

She lay down on the bed and covered herself with her traveling cloak. Isaac had walked back to Benny's room to say goodbye again and keep watch over him for a while.

She had no idea how to cope with this loss. She felt an unacceptable, unbearable sense of relief, together with the dull ache that accompanies missed opportunities. She fell asleep.

One of Benny's lecturers led the service. That's what Benny would have wanted, Isaac said, and we must respect his wishes. Charlotte arrived, tearful and out of sorts. Hugh Palliser wrote to apologize for not being there, and to convey his deepest sympathy. Jamie turned up at the last minute: the harbormaster had dragged him off his ship as soon as they'd docked.

Elizabeth stood and knelt on cue. She listened to the choir and, during prayers, looked into her lap. The minister—himself still a young man—had taken the reading from the First Epistle of Peter: "For all flesh *is* as grass, and all the glory of man as the flower of grass. The grass withereth, and the flower thereof falleth away."

When he began his sermon with those words, Elizabeth looked sharply into his solemn face as if he were about to say something she could take away with her, to keep, to help her remember these absurd days. But soon, she stopped hearing what he said.

A grave had been dug in the central nave of the church. She found it odd that those left behind did not have to go outside, but as Isaac said, this was for the best. Benny had set his heart on the Church, and this was one way to honor his choices.

Jamie and Isaac gathered Benny's belongings; the eagle was sent home in the mail coach, on Charlotte's lap; she couldn't stop running her hand along the animal's neck.

You should have been there, Elizabeth wrote to Hugh Palliser. *Your godson. I know he didn't mean that much to you. But still. The sorrow seems heavier with this child who was never more than a stranger to me. That bothers me a great deal. Isaac and Charlotte weep and miss him. But I've turned to ice. Jamie, always the practical one, put the bird on the sideboard, and on the first day of the new year, he left for Portsmouth. He's to command a warship, the* Spitfire.

She put Benny's books back in his room. She sat for a while, with iron discipline, at his worktable every day. She flipped through his theological notebook, she inhaled the scent of his shirt, and she ran her hands over the tabletop. It was January; she peered through the bare, black plum trees into the void.

One night, a storm came up. She sat bolt upright in bed, certain that a disaster was about to strike, a disaster she would have to endure. The following day, Martin cleared away the branches that had fallen in the orchard. Elizabeth waited behind the window. That night, she refused to go to bed.

The next morning, at ten o'clock, the Admiralty's coach pulled up. James Cook Jr., commander of the *Spitfire*, had drowned in the port of

Portsmouth while being rowed in an open launch to his ship during a raging storm. The launch had splintered against the rocks. Jamie's body had washed up on the shore, his skull crushed. His money and watch were missing. The crew of the launch was nowhere to be found. The Admiralty was overcome with regret. The spokesman was brimming with condolences. The weather was suddenly calm, a miracle. The curtains were drawn, the door closed.

She buried him with his youngest brother. Isaac displayed remarkable resolve and organized the entire ceremony. Then he used his clout with the Navy to try to get to the bottom of what had happened to Jamie on the night of January 25. He never did find out. Word had it that it was an ordinary robbery and murder, under the guise of the rising storm. These things happen; you take your chances with those rowers. If they know your pockets are full of money, they'll clout you over the head. Or not.

Isaac broke down. He stopped eating and wouldn't get out of bed. When he did come downstairs in his bathrobe, he was in tears. His dark curls were glued with sweat to his head, and he had grimy black ridges beneath his fingernails.

In her correspondence with the Admiralty regarding Jamie's estate, Elizabeth pressed them to call up her cousin Isaac Smith for active duty as soon as they could. She was relieved when, shortly thereafter, he was assigned a ship. Responsibility did him good. He pulled himself together, had a new uniform made for his emaciated body, and left.

That's when she could finally let herself go. When she looked back years later, she understood that friends and neighbors had written in desperation to Frances in America about her sorry state. Explaining that she didn't show her face in public, never even went downstairs. That in the course of three weeks, she'd eaten nothing but one tiny morsel of fish. That for months, she'd spent an hour every morning and afternoon wailing. That nothing had helped.

It had been a battle with her body. She'd lost. Bones, muscles, and organs—damaged but intact—celebrated their victory. Elizabeth got up, dressed, and went out. She had expected everything to be gray, with drab shades of black and white like Hodges's engravings from the travel books, but the dark-green storefronts with their gold lettering splashed toward her, and the sunlight reflected brashly off the vermillion jacket of the coachman, a basket full of purple pansies, and a sky-blue facade.

She had thought she'd be furious, as she'd been after Nat's death, angry with everyone who dared to address her without mentioning her loss—as if nothing had happened, as if she were still the same as before!—but she noticed that she didn't mind if people included her in daily life. There was nothing more to discuss; what had happened to her went beyond the day-to-day conversations and the thoughts behind them. It was easier not to fish for sympathy.

She resumed her Thursday afternoon receptions, even when Isaac was at sea. She accompanied Robert Hartland to a chamber music concert, string quartets written by a young Austrian composer and dedicated to that great master, Haydn. The effect on her was more profound than with the full sonority of a symphony orchestra; she was better able to distinguish what was going on when only four musicians were interweaving their melodic lines. She made a note of the master's name: Mozart.

She kept up her regular correspondence; it had to be done, and she did it. When Isaac was at home, he looked after her faithfully. He could not bring himself to talk about the boys; as soon as he opened his mouth, he was overwhelmed with tears. Every time he looked at Benny's eagle on the sideboard, his eyes welled up. He rented a carriage once a month to take her to Elly, and they visited Cambridge twice a year to lay flowers on Benny and Jamie's double grave in the church's central nave.

Why didn't she sleep with him, she wondered as they were climbing the stairs at the inn, heading for their separate rooms. Wouldn't it be better for both of us to crawl into the same bed? How did Isaac actually perceive her? When he wished her good night, he massaged her shoulders and upper arms with his firm hands. She remained in his embrace a little too long, hoping for some hint of her desires. Everything about him radiated comfort. But it filled her heart with abhorrence. The idea of his healthy, innocent body lying beside hers turned her stomach. That warmth. That coddling. She couldn't do it.

"He's terribly ill," Isaac said. "I heard it at the Admiralty; it won't be long now. And he's getting on in years. He was never the picture of health, what with that old injury. Odd he hasn't written to you."

That night, she stayed up late to write a letter to her friend in peace.

No matter what has come between us, it shouldn't stand in the way of a goodbye. I don't ask much; I do almost everything because I have to, not because I want to. My desire to look you in the eye has remained constant. I would hate to have you slip out of your life without having been able to say farewell. Or to be near you. It's the middle of the night. Charlotte and Isaac are asleep. I watch over and think about you.

Three days later, the death announcement arrived in Clapham. *Admiral Hugh Palliser passed away heroically on March 19, 1796 after a final illness. He was seventy-three years of age.*

"His title will pass on to a distant relative," said the lawyer, a small, prickly man who reminded Elizabeth of a bird. He bent his head with rapid, jerking motions over one document, then another, as if pecking at kernels of grain. Elizabeth sat across from him, at a desk piled with papers, and watched.

"There was a considerable bequest for your son, the godson of the deceased. Unfortunately, we had to revise the will after your son's demise." The lawyer cleared his throat nervously. "Extraordinary. An extraordinary man. Donations to charities. I will not tire you with the details. The fortune as a whole, indeed the majority of it, will go to the gentleman's illegitimate son. George Palliser. That took me by surprise, I don't mind telling you. We must respect the last will and testament. That goes without saying. Can I offer you anything? No? To the point, then. The reason I requested your presence here. For which my sincerest thanks, by the way. The testator entrusted me with another task, besides the legal attention to the estate. Namely, placing a document in the hands of the widow of the famous Captain Cook."

She was suddenly all ears. The lawyer plucked a folder from his papers and placed it before her.

"I was summoned. A few days before the onset of death. The testator was confined to bed. He had difficulty speaking. But the intent was clear. Said documents were to be handed over to the lady personally. Without being perused by anyone else, whosoever. I gave him my word. As you can see: the package is sealed. I, for my part, have verified your identity. Nothing stands in the way of carrying out the wishes of the deceased. I would like to thank you again for coming. It always pleases members of our fraternity when the public cooperates in such a timely fashion with the concluding of affairs."

She took the folder and left. The lawyer hopped after her through the vestibule. All the way home in the slowly advancing carriage, she clutched what she'd been given close to her chest.

The parcel consisted of three sections. There was a file with letters in her handwriting. She glanced through them before putting them in the chest where she kept James's letters. Everything was there: neutral notes about the children, emotional letters from a later period, and the ambiguous messages from more recent years. Her final words. Everything.

There was a large envelope, with a separate seal. And there was a letter, dated March 17, 1796, addressed to her. She drew the candleholder closer and started to read.

Dearest, dearest Elizabeth,

Your note arrived this afternoon. Yes, I am dying, slipping out of life, as you say. There's no point in bidding farewell to you. I do not want you to see me in my current state. I could not bear to see you. That is not a rejection, it's the way things are. You are always here—you and your slender but sturdy body that caused me so much confusion—even when you're not physically present. I think of you, you are in the background of all my thoughts. No farewell is possible, I will carry you with me to the end.

Things should have turned out differently between us. We had here—trees, deer—or elsewhere, but together, together. Forgive my incoherence. I'm about to do something I thought I'd never do.

James. My friend. Your husband. We talked about his departure and his downfall, and we both had our own, concealed notions. Your reproach regarding my share in the disastrous outcome has never faded, and it haunts me to this day. I know you've been diligent in hunting down the facts, and you think you've reached a—perhaps tentative—conclusion, combining negligence at the shipyard with James's fatigue and old age, but the leading role is reserved for cruel happenstance. We've hardly spoken of it these last few years. I held back. I kept you at arm's length. This is the reason.

When, at the beginning of January 1780, Sandwich received Clerke's dispatch with news of the death, he was in total panic. He had to visit you, the king, Banks. His desk was heaped with logbooks, letters, and charts. And James's journal. Clerke, at death's door, had hastily assembled all the materials, without any rhyme or reason and, I believe, without having perused them. Everything had to be examined and assessed with the utmost speed. Sandwich appealed to me. He sent for me, pressed the journal into my hands, and instructed me to read it quickly, with careful attention to detail, and to make note of any criticism of the Admiralty it might contain. He needed the manuscript back within three days, complete with my summary and commentary. At that time, although they'd pushed me aside, they were aware that I knew more about the run-up to the voyage than anyone else. In fact, Sandwich didn't have much choice.

I went home and read. You know the story, you've read Douglas's version. You've noticed that James made his final journal entry on January 17, 1779, one month before he died. Then King took over. Prematurely. Peculiar, isn't it? James was passionate about keeping his journal. He'd set foot on an island no one had visited before, yet he didn't write anything down. Impossible, you must've thought. You were right. He kept up his journal until the early morning of the day he died. I have read it. It was like standing on the rim of a volcano when the clouds of smoke disperse, enabling one to peer into the terrifying depths of his soul. I was shaken, but felt certain that this document must remain private. By chance, it landed in my hands before anyone else could read it, and that was a good thing. I have failed on so many levels that I deserve this heavy burden.

I examined the book's binding, consisting of individual sections sewn together with thread. I worked the fibers loose with a dull knife, so it would be natural to assume the fraying had resulted from wear and tear. I was tempted to remove two sections, because in December's entry, I came upon a furious tirade about the inadequate equipment and the Navy's reprehensible negligence.

Sailcloth, ropework, pulleys—it was all shoddy rubbish, used by the worthless individuals who had been responsible for rigging the ship. I left that section where it was. Sandwich had to read it. I had to endure the consequences. James was right.

I was of a mind to take the other section with me to my grave. Unfortunately, when the time does come, it's out of one's hands. That's really struck me these past few weeks. If I do nothing, someone else will one day stumble across these papers, and James's reputation will be stained forever. I could have destroyed them, the hearth in my room was blazing full blast. But what about you? I spent many nights wondering what to do. If I had given you the journal while I was still alive, it would've been as if I were encouraging you to take a step beyond James—toward me. There's nothing I would have liked more, but I couldn't bring myself to that point. It would have been wrong. It's simpler if you read it once I'm gone. That way, you'll be unencumbered while completing your investigation into his death, and based on your conclusions, you can take whatever action you see fit. I will bow out and leave you alone with James. It's not up to me to conceal this information from you. You are the only person who can make that decision: you can burn the journal unopened. It's up to you.

And now I will let you go, Elizabeth, my dear friend. Our lifelines coiled around each other, and wherever they met, they always set off one of those modern electrical sparks. Now you will carry on alone.

I see I'm finding it difficult to end this letter. Let Isaac take good care of you. I hear he's been promoted to captain.

My butler gave me a shave this morning. When he was finished, he showed me the results. I looked in the mirror and saw your face. You are a part of me. That's how it is.

Hugh

She hid everything in the chest, even the sealed journal. Exhausted, she collapsed into bed, where she lay awake the entire night. Slow down, she thought, don't do anything rash, wait until things have calmed down. In the middle of the night, she got up and shoved the chest into the deep cupboard. Wood groaned against wood. She locked the cupboard's door and fell asleep with the key in her hand.

Isaac left at the end of March, saying he'd be away for at least four months. Good, she thought, now get rid of the hired help, and then there'll be some peace. Charlotte had taken it upon herself to arrange an early spring cleaning, and the house was crawling with girls: brushing the carpet with tea leaves, polishing the chandeliers, and dusting the books with goose quills.

"I can't take it," she said to Charlotte. "They can come back next month, that's early enough."

Then the house was quiet. In the orchard, the white wood anemones were in bloom. The buds on the plum trees swelled. Elizabeth locked herself in her room, pulled the journal out of the chest, and placed it on her table. She broke the seal and slid the closely written pages out of the envelope. The time had come.

She'd spent the previous days rereading the official journal. About the backbreaking voyage along the American coast, the hopeless efforts to find a passage, and finally, the decision to spend the winter in the recently christened Sandwich Islands. She'd read her husband's words and tried to feel what he felt. Disappointed and enraged when he discovered that, in the year since their first landing, the dreaded venereal disease had spread throughout the islands. The local inhabitants came groaning on board with red, swollen genitals, hoping for a cure. Although James prohibited his infected crewmen from having any contact with the island women, he knew they would ignore his orders.

He was equally let down when the sailors turned up their noses at the wholesome beer he had brewed from sugar cane. She read about the painstaking voyage around the big island of Hawai'i. The men wanted to drop anchor, go onto the beach, enter paradise. James tacked, paused to study a coastal formation, lingered to chart a coral reef, and took his time. Canoes paddled up from every inlet they passed, laden with fresh fruit and vegetables; girls leapt into the waves and performed a water ballet for the sailors, who hung so far over the railing they nearly toppled overboard. Finally, on January 17, 1779, he gave in to the crew's grumbling and brought the ships to rest in a vast bay, shaded by massive peaks.

I took King, Anderson, and Webber with me in the launch. Landed on a narrow strip of beach with a sort of sanctuary behind it, similar to the ones we'd seen in Tahiti. Koa, the priest, was awaiting us, with Palea. He is our trading partner. I kept my wits about me, because the information you gather during an initial landing is always worth its weight in gold. The priest took my hand and led the way to the altar. He ran his thumb along my scar before tightening his grip. I suddenly noticed a strange silence: the beach was deserted; you could hear the screeching of the birds nesting on the side of the mountain. Once we were farther from the surf, I began to pick up a sort of murmuring. We paused in front of a couple of wooden statues; Koa began to pray, and I had an opportunity to look around. Hundreds of natives stood concealed at the edge of the forest. When they spotted us, they bowed. No ordinary bow, no— they prostrated themselves on the ground. Quite a change from the usual reception, where they rip the buttons from your jacket and you can't see or hear for all the racket. These people were whispering the same chant I'd heard from Koa, "Lono, Lono, Lono." Anderson was bringing up the rear, so I couldn't ask him what it meant. We trudged on to the altar, and while Koa helped me climb up—it was breathtakingly high—a procession arrived, bearing hogs and palm leaves. Their leader, an old fellow with no teeth, gave Koa a length of red cloth. This they draped over my shoulders. Leading a voyage of discovery is a difficult task. The position of a captain is especially demanding, if you consider preserving the peace and the health of those on board. The navigating, the foraging, and the maintenance of the ship, and all the rest on top of that! It strikes me that the Lords of the Admiralty don't take any of that into account. The individuals we meet, with their unfamiliar language, customs, and attire! The landscapes, the vegetation, and the animals! It all demands a permanent state of curiosity and a perfect memory. Attention—an attention that never slackens. Must rewrite this passage later.

Once I'd climbed that altar, I felt a mortal exhaustion. There was a statue, draped like myself, with a red cloth over its out-stretched arms. A pig lay rotting. The priest lifted it up, and its bowels fell out, covered in juicy maggots. He gathered the stinking innards with his bare hands and shoved them back into the belly of the decomposing beast. Then they took hold of my arms; I had to assume a pose like that of the statue, like Christ on the cross. I gave in. Koa plucked some meat from another pig, chewed it into a fine pulp, and spit it into his filthy hand before offering it to me. There wasn't a sound, except for the whispered chant, although masses of people were crowded around the altar. I kept my jaw firmly clenched. I did drink the kawa, although a great deal of spit is also an essential part of its preparation. It tasted more acrid and spicier than I had grown accustomed to, and it increased my state of torpor. One not only has to observe and remember everything, but also write it all down.

Now that I'm back in my cabin, the fatigue has abated. It almost seems as if people were expecting me, and they welcomed

*me with a certain degree of reverence. Have I arrived at the place
where I belong?*

*January 18, the middle of the night. I have gotten out of bed to
write at my little desk. I suddenly realized what the coast reminds
me of. That dark rock face that seems to push the village into the
sea: Staithes! That means that my homeland lies in the hinterland
beyond. I must go there as soon as I can. Now that I am sitting here
upright, an image of the icy sea we left behind springs to mind. My
hair reeks of coconut oil. They anointed us with it this afternoon.
Ice can be formed in the open ocean, no river is required. I am
now convinced of that. We sailed north where Asia and America
almost touch. There is no passage. No triumph. No twenty thousand pounds. There is absolutely no point in sailing back there this
summer. I will again return home with empty hands. Last time
there was no Southern Continent, this time no trade route. That
pleases me to some extent: an appealing black area, everything
that's not there. No success, no wife, no daughter. These are just
working notes. My memory needs support, just as Hugh Palliser
needs his cane. I will devote the next few days to researching their
morals and customs, especially their religion. Gore can handle the
day-to-day duties. When I've finished my sleuthing, I'll include
everything in a new chapter called "Remarkable Occurrences."
That's my plan.*

*January 20. King has set up the observatory tent near the altar.
Everyone can carry out their work in peace because the priests
have waved their wands decorated with dog hair and declared the
area taboo. I only have to point to an object and they bring it to
me. Wherever I go, people fall to the ground in veneration. We no*

longer have to pay for the privilege of foraging. Everything is mine. Koa, my high priest, explained it to me. Every year, the islanders row a structure—built out of a couple of wooden poles covered in a white sheet—clockwise around the island, to honor their god Lono. They make offerings to appease this god. They await his arrival in the month of January. This time, Lono has genuinely arrived, on a massive ship covered in white sails. I did not know I am a god. The islanders possess wisdom unspoiled by ostentation and ambition. I keep up the appearance of normalcy in front of my crew—such suspicious and envious men. Will Lono be offered nothing more than swine, or is the ultimate sacrifice also on the menu? How odd that at the precise moment I am crushed by defeat, I am elevated to a god. I must turn everything a hundred and eighty degrees to understand it. I have toiled for many years to possess these islands genuinely. What I mean by possessing is: devouring.

I planted mustard seeds, pumpkin pits, and onions. I released goats and cattle; I did everything I could to pierce the dark earth and have it grazed. Yes, possession.

My despicable sailors call Koa "the bishop," and during the rare times when they are not getting drunk and gallivanting with the Hawaiian women, they make demeaning jokes about the respect he shows me. Everywhere I've been, I've climbed mountains to look out over the region. Then I am overcome by hesitation, perhaps even fear. Should I let go of the idea of dominance and possession? My thoughts go in a direction I do not wish to follow.

January 26, at any rate, according to the British system of keeping time. Today, the king appeared. James King calls him a haggard old codger, but he would be well advised to show a little respect for this ruler who spontaneously removed his royal cloak and laid it on my shoulders. I was given seven cloaks in all, in vibrant colors, tightly woven from the finest bird's feathers. Gore arrived, nagging me about the need to stock up on firewood. He said he has all the other provisions ready for our departure: water, salt pork, and coconuts. I strode to the launch between two rows of prostrated natives, preceded by my cloaks, and thought about the meaning of gifts. I directed Gore's attention to the temple's dilapidated fence. He'd have enough firewood if he loaded up on those cracked posts. King butted in and demanded: weren't there some images of their gods among the posts? But who here is the highest god? I got hold of myself and suggested they talk it over first with Koa. People feel flattered when they receive a present. Certainly, a priceless gift elevates the recipient far above the giver. If I apply my secret back-to-front way of thinking, I realize that a present is also an attack, an attempt to get the recipient under the giver's thumb. Why else did I drag those horses to Tahiti? I must give this some careful thought tonight. They want me, that much is clear. I am no longer a spectator. My thoughts return to our stay in Tonga, where, against everyone's wishes, I longed to witness the human sacrifice we'd heard so much about. The ultimate gift. I had to take off my shirt and hat and wig, and I sat, naked, with my hair hanging down, among the priests, staring at the man who was waiting, his hands and feet bound to a stake. They had struck him on the head with a club. Then they heated some stones in a large fire and used forked branches to arrange them in a pit. The sacrifice was laid there and covered with earth until the flesh was so well done it fell from the bones. They call it long pig. You have pig, and long pig. That's the tastiest. The food of the gods.

Had a long talk with Koa. Infuriated at my inability to understand everything he says. Here, when someone with royal blood dies, they cut the body in pieces and distribute it among all the provinces on the island, so that the earth can have an equal share in the royal power. The person who ends up burying the bones

is then solemnly killed off, to keep him from revealing anything
more. What happens to the flesh? Koa didn't understand me. No
answer. I do not want Anderson to act as an interpreter. I felt dizzy
with the idea that such a dead prince would be spread around
the entire island, penetrating it, as it were, from the depths of his
strength.

February 2. Those on board force me into a captain's existence.
There's haggling and whining about those sacred fence posts. As
if they weren't my due! A tragic accident brought me back to my
former duties. William Watman, my oldest sailor, collapsed while
lifting a coil of rope. He was foaming at the mouth and his limbs
were twitching fearsomely. When it was over, he could no longer
use the right side of his body, nor could he speak. We laid him in
King's bunk. Samwell kept watch over him. He died the following
morning. We buried him yesterday. On land! At the priests' request,
or so everyone believed. But the holy men only carried out an idea
I had planted in their minds. My most faithful servant is already
confined to this earth. The islanders tossed nuts and bananas into
the grave. When we were finished with our service, they began
their own mournful lament, which was considerably more alluring
than ours.

February 3. My lieutenants are restless. They're ready to leave. The
islanders heaped piles of food on the beach by way of saying goodbye; all they wanted in exchange were a few worthless scraps of
iron. This is a complex conspiracy. Koa took me aside and asked
if I would leave my "son" behind. He was referring to King. Why
King? His request applies to me, I believe. King is nothing more
than a symbol. I told him I still needed my son. Maybe next year.

Koa nodded and didn't press the issue. People on this island under-stand the importance of a meal. The sailors usually prefer to eat whatever they've brought from home, but no homecoming could compare with that feast! I've eaten penguins near the South Pole, sea lions north of Unalaska, and tortoise meat in the Coral Islands. Swallowing means: extending yourself, appropriating something new. I have decided to take no action. The plot will unfold of its own accord.

February 6. Everyone moved by the farewell. Everything is differ-ent here than on the other islands. We've been treated with more respect here than anywhere else. And yet, my men seem relieved to be back at sea. They think we're heading north. I told them that first, we'll investigate this archipelago's smaller islands. They were sick when I said it. Investigate! I now realize that investigation solves nothing. Gathering facts, observing, writing reports—all futile. It creates a semblance of knowledge, a veneer to cover the powerlessness. The time for research has passed! True understanding is beyond research. I refuse to go on deck. I'm trying to achieve the same state of exhaustion I experienced on the altar. Then, true understanding was within my grasp, but it slipped through my fingers. God, how I detest these stinking sailors. There's a strong breeze. I will not interfere.

February 9. The foremast broke yesterday with a groaning snap, resulting in complete chaos on deck. I pretended to be furious, ranted at the Marines, and tore a strip off the innocent Bligh. Made a point of angrily stomping my feet on the planks, but the storm was still raging, so the effect was lost. They wanted to set course for the nearest coast, but offshore winds made that out of the question. I had the officers make up their own minds: we had no choice but to return to Hawai'i. There, we know the lay of the land and can quickly carry out repairs without being interrupted by troublemakers or thieves. Back in my cabin, I lay down with a smile on my face. Lono's coming back!

February 12. I climbed on deck to see the temple looming in the distance. Oh, my country. It was as if the gently growling volcano bid me welcome. I had expected the bay to fill with canoes, but there appeared to be little interest in our ships. That night, the king came aboard. He was curt and aloof. I admired his acting. I managed to sleep that night.

February 13. They're putting me to the test. The locals, led by the king, object to the workshop, which we of course set up on our usual spot, next to the temple. The carpenters are working on a new mast. Tongs, saws, and planes were stolen out of their hands. The priests are on my side, but their objections are only half-hearted. I couldn't resist going ashore, and stormed the village, my pistol drawn. No bowing, no reverential rows of worshipers, nothing but deviously leaping miscreants with stones raised threateningly in their hands! Was I so mistaken? A scuffle broke out in the water near the rocks, something to do with a boat, the natives and sailors pummeling each other over the head with paddles and oars. Palea was mixed up in the fray. I ordered the men to arm themselves when going ashore. Clerke wants to speak with me, he sent his servant to fetch me. I sent him away.

It is nighttime. This afternoon, a cocky native asked me if I could fight. He wanted to see some proof of my courage. I showed him the scar on my right hand. A threatening mood was in the

*air. I withdrew to think. I have to translate everything, turn it
around. A threat means seduction, an invitation to come closer.
Just now, I almost fell asleep at my desk. Before I dropped off, I had
an important flash of insight. I must try to retrieve it. It had to do
with handing out presents. It's the giver who has supreme power. I
will give this island, my island, the greatest conceivable gift, then it
will be bound with me forever. Now I know: the ultimate sacrifice.*

*Complete calm since having that thought. Even managed
to sleep, fully dressed. Don't understand why I didn't think of it
before. On the island, they've known about it for some time; Palea
understands why I've come back, Koa is fully aware, the king
as well. All the locals are in on it. And I thought they'd turned
against me! On the contrary, everyone is going along with my plan.
Yesterday, Palea came aboard and turned down an invitation for
dinner, ostensibly because he's angry about the attack with the oars.
He strode past me as if I weren't there, and in my ignorance I felt
a fit of spleen coming on! Now I see his ingenious intention. He
was carrying a short dagger, which he pointed at me with seeming
menace. A first-rate ruse! King fell for it, and pulled Palea away
from me. The priest, grim and annoyed, turned his face away. But
before he did, his eyebrow shot up. I saw it. I got the message.*

*Dawn's pale sky through the porthole. I would write February
14, were it not that I have severed my bonds with time. I await
the signal that will be given to me in complete tranquility. Then
I will prepare for the masquerade that heralds my salvation. The
wheels have been set in motion!*

*Shaved. Donned my best uniform. The sun flickers off the
ridge of the mountain. The cook's mate asked if I wanted something to eat. Ridiculous question. Quite the contrary, I wanted
to answer, and felt an uncontrollable urge to laugh. Eating! The
wonder of reversal is wasted on these men. I hid my face behind
my handkerchief and shooed the man away.*

Now must hurry. The time has come. Clerke arrived with a worried look on his face. Someone stole the Discovery's *big launch last night. I asked for all the details, to be absolutely certain. In the end, I heard what I needed to hear: the line securing the boat had been severed. He'd gone to look at it himself: it had been chopped clean with a single blow from a sharp blade.*

That's enough for me. The Marines are ready. I've put Williamson, the surly third lieutenant who always gets everything muddled up, in charge of the rowers. I take my weapon, loaded with live ammunition. I must remain vigilant for a little longer to perfectly fulfill my role in this magnificent charade. I take my hat. I close the door of my cabin. I leave my ship.

Elizabeth stood up cautiously and opened the curtains to let in the sun. She knelt in front of the large chest and pried open the bottom drawer. There was the uniform, wrapped in yellowing paper. She carefully lifted the blue coat with gold braiding out of its hiding place. She laid it on her bed. Then she took out the white breeches with golden buttons. The waistcoat. The shirt. Before laying it down, she briefly shook it out in such a way that the sleeve's ruffles fluttered in the sun like large white butterflies. She unrolled the silk stockings, wound into a tight, shimmering ball. The hat with the golden edging had been stuffed at the back, somewhat dented. She used her clenched fist to push the stiff felt back into shape.

She stood, feet apart, beside the bed, and unbuttoned her dress. She removed the pins from her bodice, pulled the drawstring from her waist, and stepped out of her petticoat. She stood in front of the full-length mirror in the corner, dressed only in her chemise and corset. Stockings, of course, her cotton stockings had to go. She tossed them in a corner. She drew James's silk stockings one by one onto her legs and fastened them above the knee with her garters. The breeches came next; she tucked her chemise in so it lay flat. She hoisted the breeches high above her waist and tied them in place with a lanyard. She sat on the edge of the bed to fasten the buttons at the knee. The ruffled shirt was still there. Almost forgot. She pulled it on, loosened her improvised belt, and repeated the procedure to fasten the trousers again. Patience. She tied up the sleeves so the ruffles just grazed her knuckles. Cravat. Still in the drawer. She folded the white cloth tightly around her neck, and slipped on the cream waistcoat. It hung down over her hips. Now she had to put on her own shoes; James's were much too big. She paced in front of the mirror, hesitating, until she plucked up enough courage to put on the coat. She tucked the hat under her arm and stepped onto the beach. What had been going on in James's head that last morning in Hawai'i?

The king is still asleep in his hut. His two young boys are playing with coconuts near the entrance and are eager to wake up their father. That seems to take forever; the villagers come out of their huts and elbow the Marines aside. When the king finally comes outside, unwashed, carrying a whiff of his bed with him, the women begin tugging his cloak. The boys have already run to the beach; the oldest has clambered into the launch and sits waiting for his father. There's a bang: shots have been fired on the other side of the bay. The women scream, they won't let go of their king. The islanders turn into a threatening mob, moving in a jumble; you can feel the warmth radiating off their bodies. At a nod, the Marines raise their weapons. The natives snarl, pick up sticks and stones from the ground; they stick out their tongues and roll their bulging eyes. A dagger, the steel flashing in the sunlight; the jab is difficult to deflect. That's all the invitation needed to commence shooting. Fire! Now it's war, now they jump us from all sides, an inextricable tangle of Marines in red coats and islanders dressed in rattan battle gear, dancing together on the black sands. We must

*retreat to the launch, says the Marine commander; this will lead
to bloodshed, mission aborted.*

*Far from it! I signal that ninny Williamson in the launch
to shoot, go ahead, we need more cover. Cover? Yes, I order the
Marines to turn around, and we line up along the tide line, facing
the raging throng. Aim, fire! I roar at the men. They hesitate, seem
perplexed, but in the end, they obey. I join in. Not with buckshot,
but with ball. One Hawaiian after the other drops, we simply
mow them down. Once the chaos and rage have reached their
boiling point, I sense that the time has come.*

*I lower my weapon and turn around. I had felt the water
behind me all that time, how it stretched out, wave after wave;
how it was sucked up with a sigh by the volcanic sand. Now,
slowly, with languid slackness, I place my feet on the wet seabed.
Sunlight jangles off the darting wavelets, is reflected on my golden
buttons, and warms my back. The launch has sailed far from the
shoreline, that backward lieutenant has decided to misunderstand
my signal, just as I expected.*

*I almost slip on the algae-slick stones. Luckily, I am able to
regain my balance. That's crucial; it's not about me falling; that's
not how it's been preordained. I step into the sea, calm as can be.
Just a few more seconds, then the stone will hit me on the head, the
knife will rip open my back; just a little longer, and I will stumble,
released into my future, truly to come home.*

She climbed the stairs step by step. Since Isaac's death, she had rarely
returned to her old bedroom, the one with the large windows opening
out onto the orchard. She now slept downstairs, as befitted a woman
over ninety; the walls around her were hung with drawings and paintings from Isaac's collection. Nothing but icebergs and seascapes. Isaac
had never been able to explain his fascination with the cold, just said

the frost nips your cheeks and the icebergs sail silently past, until one unexpectedly tips over and causes a tidal wave.

Isaac Smith, rear admiral, her friend and housemate, died peacefully.

She hardly mourned him, as if everything was leaning toward the most austere possible finale. Creating emptiness was the only thing that occupied her.

She saw herself in the full-length mirror: a gaunt woman, ramrod straight, in black. Gold rings on sturdy fingers, gray hair rolled up and pinned at the neck, faded eyebrows. The gaze from the dark eyes still sharp, but observing everything from a distance.

She opened the built-in cupboard and pulled out the chest. The key was still on her keychain, it fit; the lock clicked open effortlessly. Think ahead—she would need something to carry the papers in. A pillowcase. She pulled a bench closer and sat beside the chest with a pillowcase on her lap. She fished out piles of documents from their hiding place: her correspondence with Hugh, the letters from James, Clerke's report, the one delivered by that fur trader, and finally, the secret journal. At first, she couldn't decide about the notes from Jamie and Nat, but then she stuffed them into the bulging pillowcase as well.

She left behind the red waistcoat with silver stitching.

There was still frost on the ground, but in the orchard, the abundant sunlight made it seem like spring. At the back, next to the wall made of flat, stacked stones, was the fire pit Martin sometimes used for burning twigs and branches. Elizabeth, bearing the three-pronged candlestick, strode through the windless garden, dragging the pillowcase by its corner. A procession, she thought, a parade of memories on their way to a solemn obliteration.

She sat on the chopping block the gardener used to split wood, and pulled the papers one by one out of the pillowcase to feed into the fire.

The burning letters swirled into the pit. Pale-gray ash drifted onto the stones below. The air above the fire trembled.

I'm stoking the fire with my life, she thought; I should feel bitter, but it's a relief. Erase everything: the strange love between me and Hugh, the remnants of the children's lives, James's scandal. Transform everything into a shimmering nothingness.

The rolling landscape began just beyond the wall. Sheep and cows grazed on diamond-shaped fields nestled against the hills. Is the landscape welcoming me, she wondered, comforting me? No. Every form of interference is foreign to this landscape. It is neither passive nor submissive. It exudes tranquility, so different from the water, which is nervous and capricious and much too malleable, almost coquettish.

This land is indifferent, but that's not the right word; what am I looking for, it's on the tip of my tongue. Does this landscape accept me? No, that's too strong. It tolerates me.

The wall's sharp stones pressed into her hip bones. The connections with loved ones are there; then they pass, and are gone. That you were part of it is all there is. They fly away on the quivering wind, they crumble like ashes on the ground, they become buried beneath the earth. You don't have to keep anything. That's the wisdom of the sheep on the hillside.

She sees James as clear as day. He pulls her through the rain, they run to their shelter, and he kisses her cold face. There's Nat, he walks toward her with the violin case in his hand, a crooked, shy smile hiding behind a lock of blond hair. A man who loves her rolls up his sleeve and she cries on his naked arm, as if she has finally come home.

The little girl stands on the kitchen floor, clasping the grimy rope of her hobbyhorse in her little fist. Her eyes sparkle with delight; the girl's joy is so palpable, it takes one's breath away, and the moment sticks forever in one's memory, so strong it hurts, a clear and welcome pain.

Elizabeth rests her arms on the wall and looks out over the patient landscape.

Portrait of Elizabeth Batts Cook, by William Henderson, 1830.
Photo via The Picture Art Collection / Alamy Stock Photo.

Afterword

Much is known about the life and the death of James Cook. In the composition of this novel, I have stayed as close to the historical facts as I could. I have respected dates of birth and death, of departure and returning home, of letters and meetings. The story is woven between the cracks of those verifiable facts. For the sake of the story line, I allowed myself three liberties that cannot be historically substantiated. First, there is no evidence of any amorous relationship between Elizabeth Cook and Hugh Palliser. Second, although Isaac Smith did not sail on the third voyage, I wanted to use him to give Elizabeth an eyewitness account of Cook's final years. And finally, the missing journal entries from Cook's last weeks have never been found. Readers who would like to examine the boundary between fact and fiction in more detail are encouraged to refer to the biographies listed in the bibliography.

All the individuals who appear in this novel actually existed, except for the organist Mr. Hartland and his nephew Robert, the nurse Charlotte, the fur trader Boris Chlebnikov, and Jane, the wife of David Nelson.

Acknowledgments

One cannot write such a book without help. I would like to acknowledge and thank the individuals and organizations who offered me their assistance.

This project began with a visit to the Captain Cook Memorial Museum in Whitby, England. I learned a great deal from numerous visits to the National Maritime Museum in Greenwich, England, as well as from the website of the Captain Cook Society (www.captain cooksociety.com), and from a guided tour on board the replica of the *Endeavour*, which called at the Netherlands in the spring of 2004. The books I used are listed in the bibliography.

In the autumn of 1991, I went walking with my friend Joan Baggerman through the region of Cook's birth to Staithes and Whitby. Ever since, she has supported and taken an interest in my research and writing process.

When I found out that the indispensable biography by Beaglehole was no longer available, I placed an ad in the newspaper, whereupon Mr. D. Greidanus kindly gave me his copy. The book became the foundation of my research.

At an early stage, Roland Fagel, who worked at the time for De Arbeiderspers, spent many afternoons talking with me about Cook and a possible novel. Those conversations opened my eyes as a writer to the possibility of penetrating history.

I only genuinely began writing in the autumn of 2003, spurred on by my acquaintance with Diederik van Vleuten, an enthusiastic Cook expert who loaned me everything I could hope for from his extensive library. We carried out an electronic correspondence that forced me to make some decisions about the form and contents of the book, and contributed to its completion.

For many years, my editor Peter Nijssen managed to maintain interest in the project without putting me under any pressure. I greatly appreciated his courteous and concerned attitude, shared as well by the publisher, Lex Jansen.

During that awful period prior to sitting down to write, I received advice from Heleen Brokmeier ("write it from the perspective of his wife"), Hugo Claus ("never more—or less—than two sheets of legal-sized paper a day"), and Marcel Möring ("don't plan, just sit down and get started"). I benefited greatly from their advice.

Over the years, the following individuals sent me crucial information, ranging from scientific papers to cardoon seeds: Marleen Chrisstoffels-Speelman, Luc Coorevits, Roelof van Gelder, Leo van der Kamp, Simon Kuper, Tjark Kruiger, Harriet Mastboom, Mrs. I. E. Sprey, Mr. P. H. Spruit, Ger van Unnik, and Manfred Wolf.

I am grateful to all the individuals mentioned above for their support, interest, and invaluable contributions in helping this book reach its fruition. Special thanks goes to my family. Bengt gave me, both literally and figuratively, the room to write this book. Wouter asked about its progress almost every day. They both read the manuscript when the first two parts were finished, and managed to give me the feeling they thought it worthwhile to continue.

Margit, whom I can no longer thank, phoned me shortly before her death to tell me about a news item regarding Cook she'd seen in the paper. The realization that she knew of my plans and was curious about them helped me to persevere.

Anna Enquist, January 2005

Translator's Note

In translating this book, I was greatly aided by the assistance of the author, Anna Enquist, who was immensely helpful in answering questions and commenting on drafts. In addition, Gabriella Page-Fort, Cheryl Weisman, Jason Kirk, Valerie P., and Patty Ann E. each played an essential role in honing the text. Readers familiar with the Dutch original, first published in 2005, may notice that a few minor details have been altered. This has been done with the utmost care and the author's permission to reflect recent discoveries made by the Captain Cook Society, among others.

Bibliography

Alexander, Caroline. *The Bounty: The True Story of the Mutiny on the Bounty*. London: Penguin Books, 2004.

Beaglehole, J. C. *The Death of Captain Cook*. Wellington: Alexander Turnbull Library, 1979.

Beaglehole, J. C. *The Life of Captain James Cook*. London: Adam and Charles Black, 1974.

Boswell, James, and John Wain. *The Journals of James Boswell: 1762-1795*. London: Mandarin, 1992.

Collingridge, Vanessa. *Captain Cook: A Legacy under Fire*. Guilford, CT: Lyons Press, 2002.

Cordingly, David, ed. *Capt. James Cook, Navigator: The Achievements of Captain James Cook as a Seaman, Navigator and Surveyor*. Sydney: Campbell Publishing for National Maritime Museum, 1988.

Dash, Mike. *Batavia's Graveyard: The True Story of the Mad Heretic Who Led History's Bloodiest Mutiny*. New York: Crown, 2002.

Dugard, Martin. *Farther Than Any Man: The Rise and Fall of Captain James Cook*. New York: Washington Square Press, 2002.

Gelder, Roelof van. *Naporra's omweg: Het leven van een VOC-matroos (1731-1793)*. Amsterdam: Atlas, 2003.

Gelder, Roelof van. *Het Oost-Indisch avontuur: Duitsers in dienst van de VOC (1600-1800)*. Nijmegen: SUN, 1997.

Horwitz, Tony. *Blue Latitudes: Boldly Going Where Captain Cook Has Gone Before*. New York: Henry Holt, 2002.

Hough, Richard. *Captain James Cook: A Biography*. London: Hodder and Stoughton, 1994.

Hough, Richard. *The Murder of Captain James Cook*. London: Macmillan, 1979.

Leuftink, Arnold Edmund. *Chirurgijns zee-compas: De medische verzorging aan boord van Nederlandse zeeschepen gedurende de Gouden Eeuw*. Baarn: Het Wereldvenster, 1963.

Macintyre, Donald G. F. W., Julian Henry Hall, Timothy Chilvers, and Uffa Fox. *The Adventure of Sail, 1520-1914*. London: Elek, 1970.

Moorehead, Alan. *The Fatal Impact: The Invasion of the South Pacific, 1767-1840*. New York: Harper and Row, 1966.

Obeyesekere, Gananath. *The Apotheosis of Captain Cook: European Mythmaking in the Pacific*. Princeton, NJ: Princeton University Press, 1992.

Quilley, Geoff, and John Bonehill, eds. *William Hodges, 1744-1797: The Art of Exploration*. New Haven: Yale University Press, 2004.

Smith, Bernard. *European Vision and the South Pacific*. New Haven: Yale University Press, 1985.

Sobel, Dava. *Longitude: The True Story of a Lone Genius Who Solved the Greatest Scientific Problem of His Time*. New York: Walker, 1995.

Thomas, Nicholas. *Discoveries: the Voyages of Captain Cook*. London: Allen Lane, 2003.

Whatman, Susanna and Christina Hardyment. *The Housekeeping Book of Susanna Whatman*. London: National Trust Enterprises, 2000.

White, T. H. *The Age of Scandal: An Excursion through a Minor Period*. London: Penguin Books, 1962.

Wilford, John Noble. *The Mapmakers*. New York: Vintage Books, 2001.

Williams, Glyndwr. *Captain Cook's Voyages: 1768-1779*. London: The Folio Society, 1997.

Chronological Overview

1728
Birth of James Cook
1742
Birth of Elizabeth Batts
1746
JC apprentices with J. Walker in Whitby
1755
JC enlists in the Navy
1762
Marriage of James and Elizabeth
1763
Birth of son James ("Jamie")
1764
Birth of son Nathaniel ("Nat")
1767
Birth of daughter, Elizabeth ("Elly")
1768
Start of first voyage around the world (*Endeavour*)
Birth and death of son Joseph
1771
Death of daughter, Elly
End of first voyage
JC promoted to commander

1772
Start of second voyage (*Resolution* and *Adventure*)
Birth and death of son George
1775
End of second voyage
1776
JC admitted to the Royal Society (Academy of Sciences)
Birth of son Hugh ("Benny")
Start of third voyage (*Resolution* and *Discovery*)
1779
Dismissal of Hugh Palliser
Death of JC in Hawai'i
1780
Conclusion of third voyage
Death of Nathaniel
1784
Publication of the account of the third voyage
1788
Elizabeth moves to Clapham, with Isaac Smith
1793
Death of son Hugh
1794
Death of son James
1796
Death of Hugh Palliser
1831
Death of Isaac Smith
1835
Death of Elizabeth

About the Author

Photo © Bert Nienhuis

Anna Enquist studied piano at the academy of music in The Hague and psychology at Leiden University. She is the author of the novels *The Masterpiece*; *The Secret*, winner of the 1997 Dutch Book of the Year awarded by the public; *The Ice Carriers*; *Counterpoint*; *Quartet*; and the international bestseller *The Homecoming*, which received the Prix du Livre Corderie Royale-Hermione for its French translation. Anna is also the author of *A Leap*, a collection of dramatic monologues, as well as numerous poetry collections, including *Soldiers' Songs*, for which she was awarded the C. Buddingh' Prize; *A New Goodbye*; and *Hunting Scenes*, winner of the Lucy B. and C.W. van der Hoogt Prize.

About the Translator

Eileen J. Stevens earned her MA in linguistics with a specialization in translation from the University of Amsterdam. Her many Dutch-to-English translation credits include Connie Palmen's *Your Story, My Story*; Karin Schacknat's *In and Out of Fashion*; Vera Mertens's *The Concentration Camp*; and Ineke van Doorn's *Singing from the Inside Out*. She has also translated numerous essays on classical music and the arts. In 2020, Eileen attended an intensive two-month master class on the translation of literary nonfiction hosted by the Dutch Centre of Expertise for Literary Translation (ELV). A New Jersey native, Eileen spent twenty-five years working as a professional violinist in a Dutch orchestra and has lived in Amsterdam since 1990. For more information, visit www.keyboardtranslations.com.